A
Capital
ARRANGEMENT

BOOK SIX
THE ELLSWORTH ASSORTMENT

CHRISTINA DUDLEY

WILLIAM ELLSWORTH = (1) HENRIETTA BALDRIC   CHARLES ELLSWORTH = JEANNE MARTINEAU
               = (2) CATHERINE CATCHWAY
               = (3) ANNE FIELDING
               = (4) MIRANDA GREGORY
                     = (2) COLIN WOLFE   BENJAMIN   AUSTIN

(1) FLORENCE = ROBERT FAIRCHILD

(1) LILY = SIMON KENNER

(2) TYRONE = AGATHA WEEKS

(2) ARAMINTA = NICHOLAS CARLISLE

(3) BEATRICE

(4) WILLIAM

THE
Ellsworth Assortment

PROLOGUE

1811

**He that promiseth, hath no right
in the thing promised.**
—Thomas Hobbes, *Leviathan* (1651)

J ohn."

The voice which once boomed over the din of work yard and council room now reached John Clayton as no more than a rasp.

"I'm here, Mr. Brand."

Longing to throw wide the windows of the stifling sick room, Clayton glanced again at the stern nurse, but she must have guessed his thoughts, for her brow lowered in a challenging glare. Honestly, what harm could fresh air do Donald Brand now? The formerly robust man lay weary with pain, a stone lighter than only a fortnight earlier.

But he put these thoughts aside as coughs racked Brand. "You've been my right hand, John," gasped the older man, "since you were fourteen. Best of—best of—better than—any—could have wished." He paused for another fit, and Clayton ran a distressed hand through his own dark locks. He would have urged Brand not to tax himself, but after so many years he recognized when the man intended on saying something, come weal, come woe.

"Thank you, sir," he murmured nonetheless, hoping to relieve him. Tears filled his eyes. He knew, without Brand putting it in words, the bond they came to share over the years. Master and apprentice had become more like father and son, partner and partner, the trust between them obvious to all who employed or worked for Donald Brand. And it was because of this bond that Brand's projects had not fallen to the ground with the sudden onset of his illness.

As if he read the young man's thoughts, his mentor rallied, Clayton bending closer to catch the words: "...Came on so fast. So much to set to rights—"

"Sir, I understand. But rest easy—with the Worcester and Birmingham project well under way, and the drawings done for the Cumberland Arm proposal..." He trailed off because Brand was already frowning and weakly shaking his head.

"Not—work," Brand insisted. "Don't mean work. Trust you—work."

"What then, sir?" Indeed, was there any area of life in which Brand did *not* trust him? If there was, he had never before hinted at it.

A lengthy pause followed, in which Clayton feared the man would die before he could make himself understood, so labored did his breathing become. The nurse even put down her needlework to bustle over and find his pulse. When she was satisfied her patient was not going to give up the ghost that very instant, she contented herself with another glare at John before stalking back to her seat.

Contrarily reassured by this show of temper, Clayton almost grinned, and an answering light of amusement flickered even in Brand's eyes. They had always been able to laugh together—even when facing mechanical failures, funding delays, drunken workers, opposition from other interested parties, Parliamentary disputes—and it relieved the terrible squeeze on his heart to remember this.

Brand made another effort, this one hardly above a whisper: "Priscilla."

"Priscilla?" Clayton repeated, puzzled. "Your daughter Priscilla, sir?"

"Yes. John—take care of Priscilla."

"I?" The young man straightened, having not expected this. "Of course I will. But—what do you mean, take care of her? I had thought your cousin Miss Croy…That is, when Miss Brand has not been at school, she has always stayed with Miss Croy."

A feeble movement of Brand's hand on the coverlet, but John understood it to be dismissive. "Cissy—no head for money. Told—lawyer—Braham—executor. But—fortune.

Wished—wanted—when Priscilla older..." Though coughs overtook him again, Brand pointed at Clayton and then at his own wedding band, which he still wore a decade after Mrs. Brand's death.

Clayton. Wedding ring. Clayton again.

Clayton was speechless. While many young apprentices might dream of marrying strategically into the master's family, when John had first been articled to Donald Brand, Priscilla had been but six years old. And as her mother's death followed shortly after, the child had been shipped off to live with Brand's cousin Cecelia Croy. In the entire decade which followed, Clayton did not think he had seen the girl more than once or twice.

On a point such as this, nothing could be assumed or left to unspoken rapport. Therefore he steeled himself to ask, "Sir, are you saying you wished I might one day marry your daughter Priscilla?"

One deliberate, unmistakable nod. The bleary eyes blinked slowly, and when they opened again, they were uncharacteristically supplicating.

"But, sir," he gulped, his pulse beginning to rush, "I—I confess I could not vouch for knowing Miss Brand if I passed her on the street." Indeed, beyond a memory of reddish-blond hair and bright blue eyes, he could scarcely call up any notion of her.

"Please," whispered Brand. "Consider. Lovely. Braham—will explain. Unless—already—sweetheart?"

Clayton shook his head. That much was certain, at least. He had no sweetheart. As if, in all the hours of constant companionship the men shared, he could possibly have hidden the existence of one!

Still bewildered, the young man patted the coverlet. "Mr. Brand, I cannot suppose your daughter cares for me one way or another, given the paltriness of our acquaintance."

"No—no matter." Sweat beaded on the dying man's brow. Shaking with the effort, his hand reached for Clayton's, and the young man quickly took it between his own. "She will. She cannot do better. Braham—will explain. John—promise me."

What could he do? He owed the man everything. *Everything.* And if he, John Clayton, was zealous for Donald Brand's professional legacy, why would he not equally concern himself with the fate of the man's human one?

Clayton had thought of marriage, when he thought of it at all, as something for much later, when he was established. In his thirties, perhaps. But if Donald Brand had always guided him so well and with such wise affection, could he not be right in this as well?

There was no alternative, in any case. Not when the man lay dying and this would give him peace.

Of course he promised.

"Yes, sir. Rest easy. No harm will come to her. If she will have me, I will marry Miss Brand."

His word given, he stumbled from the room shortly afterward. Though he hardly comprehended what he had done, Clayton was not yet aware of any regrets. The relief in Brand's eyes and the tranquil sleep which then overtook him repaid the young man in full.

CHAPTER ONE

OCTOBER 1814

No spot on the coast of England is perhaps better cal-
culated for the two-fold purpose of sea-bathing and
retirement than Bognor...The smoothness of the sand,
reminds the valetudinarian of a velvet carpet, and invit-
ingly draws him to the sea side...to enjoy his ride or
walk, even at the reflux of the tide, without the least
risk, surprise, or interruption from the waves.
— John Feltham, *A Guide to All the Watering and
Seabathing Places, etc.* (1815)

On a crisp day in early October, Miss Beatrice Ellsworth stood on the sandy beach at Bognor. As the sunlight faintly penetrated her closed eyelids and the fine sea air whipped loose strands of her light-brown hair, she had no idea her being there was the result of her family's well-meaning machinations.

For Beatrice, the youngest of the Ellsworth Assortment of Winchester, had not the least notion a secret family conference had been held to discuss her, at which the decision was reached that, clearly, Something Must Be Done.

Something must be done, for, at the still-fresh young age of one and twenty, Beatrice showed premature signs of settling into contented spinster-aunthood.

"She has always been indifferent to balls and assemblies," her stepmother Mrs. Colin Wolfe sighed to her other stepdaughters and her daughter-in-law, "but now that her friend Emmy Wright has married, Bea says, hurrah, and how she 'needn't bother about all that now.'"

"It cannot be that none of the gentlemen showed interest in her," murmured Mrs. Robert Fairchild, Beatrice's oldest sister. "With her prettiness and connections and generous portion."

"Certainly they showed interest, Flossie," returned Mrs. Wolfe, who had chaperoned both Beatrice and the former Miss Wright to the dances. "But Colin says a man can only do so much when given no encouragement whatsoever, and once he has been firmly refused, he can do nothing at all."

"Exactly," Mrs. Simon Kenner, *née* Lily Ellsworth, agreed. "And after two years of Bea's indifference and rejections, not only are the good gentlemen already taken, but she is unlikely to change her mind about the ones which remain. Therefore she must see a new crop altogether."

"But where would such a crop be found?" asked her older sister.

"Isn't it obvious, Flossie? If Aggie and Tyrone are going to Bognor for a month, clearly they must take Beatrice with them."

"That would be lovely!" Aggie clapped her hands. "My little Joan and Margaret would be so glad to have their aunt along. There would be room enough for her in the house we have rented, and Bognor has the usual assembly room and such." A nostalgic smile curved her lips. "Tyrone and I cannot wait to see the sea again because it was at the seaside where he and I...came to our understanding."

"But Bea herself has no sentimental attachment to draw her and will see no reason to go along with you, Aggie," the third sister Araminta observed with her usual practicality. "She'll just stay at Beaumond and continue to cling to Mama like a barnacle." (With a nod at Mrs. Wolfe.)

"True," conceded Lily, tapping her chin thoughtfully. "Too true. Then, Aggie, you must *insist* that you require both her company and her assistance. Heaven knows Tyrone's head is always buried in a book, and little Joan and Margaret might toddle straight into the waves before he noticed. And—and Mama, cannot you and Mr. Wolfe go on a little trip as well, so that Beatrice cannot stay behind at Beaumond? You might go and see his estate and his relations in Kent."

"But if Mama goes to Kent, Bea will certainly prefer to go with her," Araminta argued impatiently. "And we don't want Bea marrying someone in Canterbury, or we will never see her again."

"I could say Mr. Wolfe and I were going on a belated honeymoon," suggested Mrs. Wolfe, blushing. "We never had one at the time because Willsie and Edmund were sick that Christmas. If it were a honeymoon, Bea would understand if we did not ask her to join us."

The others regarded her admiringly.

"Why, what a clever scheme, Mama," Lily pronounced. "It will certainly do the trick. If you are out of the picture, Beatrice would have to choose between accompanying Tyrone and Aggie, or paying a long visit to Minta or me. And we can say it would be too great a squeeze in our homes, couldn't we, Minta?"

"But then she will suggest coming to Robert and me at Hollowgate," Florence pointed out. "In fact, I am certain it will be her first solution because she knows she might have her old bedroom back, and she would be more than welcome."

"Then you must be ruthless, Floss!" Lily exhorted her. "You must say that you *so* long to make Hollowgate your own at last, now that the renovations are complete, and that you're ashamed to say it, but you're even glad Tyrone and Aggie won't be there to trouble you for a while, and that, when they do return, it's a mercy they will live in the refashioned wing, so they aren't underfoot, and you may be left to queen it to your heart's content."

"Well, that's just silly," interposed Araminta before Florence could muster a reply. "Beatrice wouldn't believe for a moment that

Flossie would say or think such a thing. Whereas if *you* were inheriting Hollowgate, Lily, I daresay she would swallow the whole story without question."

Not in the least offended by this slight to her character, Lily frowned in thought. "Hm. You may be right. Very well. Flossie need not say so much, but *I* will say it. I will say Flossie secretly thinks it, and you must back me, Minta. It's a little lie but all for the good. When Bea is safely married, we will confess all, and she will be the first to laugh and thank us."

With fewer hitches than any of them would have hoped, the plan was executed. Mr. and Mrs. Wolfe departed for Kent the day before the Tyrone Ellsworths left for Bognor, and if Beatrice's feelings were at all hurt by the thought that the Fairchilds wanted all of Hollowgate to themselves for an entire month, she could not dwell on it overlong in the face of her sister-in-law Aggie's indefatigable excitement.

"I first saw the sea at Worthing when I was heartbroken over Tyrone," Aggie explained, "but even heartbroken I still loved it! And now that I am *not* heartbroken, I intend to enjoy myself thoroughly. My mother, who spent a couple months in Bognor, says the town itself is charming but without the great crowds of other resorts. Everything one would want for accommodation and amusements—a subscription room for assemblies and such, a library beneath it, charming shops in the High Street, a coffee house for Tyrone, and so forth. But it's the sea most of all, Beatrice, which you will learn is like nothing else in the world. I cannot do it justice."

And as Beatrice opened her eyes again that brisk autumn day, she had to agree. Nothing had prepared her for the vastness. The restless, shifting colors. The salt aroma and rhythmic crash and hiss of the waves. The beach itself extended several miles east to west, with a full mile of it dedicated to bathing. No, one did not have to be heartbroken, as Aggie had been at her first encounter, to fall in love with the sea.

Aggie appeared at her elbow now, a wriggling daughter Joan in her arms. "We will bathe first thing tomorrow morning," she declared. "But today we will purchase our own bathing dresses. That was *one* thing I would rather not repeat—wearing a hired bathing dress."

The Ellsworths' home for the next month lay in Spencer Terrace, along the main road into town and not far from the Dome House where both Lady Jersey and Princess Charlotte once stayed. Number Four blended with its neighbors, sharing the same red-brick frontage over a painted-brick plinth, its discrete state only revealed by a pair of thin Doric columns flanking a fanlight-crowned door. Within were three storeys and a semi-basement, with Beatrice being assigned a neat back bedchamber overlooking the garden. In addition to the shared services of a cook in a nearby home, the lease included an ancient man and maidservant, the man Pidgeley so creaking that Tyrone felt guilty asking him to do anything even mildly strenuous, and the maid Fussell, who moved as little as possible but whose tongue ran on wheels.

"Eight of you altogether," marveled Fussell from where she sat on a stool, unpacking Beatrice's trunk, humming and clicking her tongue and murmuring to herself as she worked. "The last tenant was but one elderly lady and her half-blind niece and their maid. We'll be lively now, to be sure, with the two little girls and all of you stuffed in one place or t'other. And you a young, unmarried lady! Which will mean assemblies and dancing and I dunno what all! Well, that's how it happens. Sometimes Pidgeley and I must work ourselves to the bone, fetching and carrying for a dozen people, and sometimes there will be just one sad little fellow and his valet."

Apart from apologizing for being so many, Beatrice could think of no reply to this, but fortunately Fussell did not require one. "It's my cousin who works next door in Five," she went on, "and that's all she and Barnstable have just now—one sad fellow and his valet—though Molly says at least it's not some crabbed old man with the gout who must be heaved up every time he sits down and who is as like to throw something at you as he is to speak to you. No, this one is always writing, writing, writing—he hasn't even had a bathe yet!—and how the letters fly back and forth!"

"Perhaps he's a spy for the French," suggested Beatrice playfully, turning from the window. "Or a smuggler."

Fussell's round eyes grew rounder. "Oh, miss, I didn't think of that! I'll tell Molly straight off and see what she says."

Gasping half in dismay and half in amusement, Beatrice said, "Dear me—please don't. I was just being naughty. We have only arrived, and I would not want our new neighbor hearing I started idle rumors about him."

"Bless me, miss!" cried Fussell. "How would he ever know, when he never comes out of there? I'm no chatterbox, and neither is Molly."

At this juncture Tyrone was heard calling up the staircase, and Beatrice was obliged to leave the matter. The newcomers spent the remainder of the afternoon investigating the High Street shops and admiring the view, and so charming did she find it all that she entirely forgot her careless remark.

It was only on the third afternoon following their arrival that she had cause to remember. Aggie and Beatrice were pulling the twins Joan and Margaret in a clever little cart, having taken the girls to see the sandy beach, and they were nearly home before they got into difficulties. For after they turned into the upper road from the High Street, they found their little passengers more eager to "help pull" than to be pulled. Margaret soon succeeded in tangling her sister's trailing blanket in the cart wheel, halting progress altogether and sending Joanie into wails of protest because it was her favorite blanket, and now it would be dirty.

"Come, dear, don't put your fingers in there," Aggie coaxed. "Let Auntie Bea unwind it."

"Self do!" insisted Margaret, tugging with all her toddler might on a corner of the wool coverlet and tightening it further. Vexed, she poked a plump finger in its creases, just as Joanie gave a bounce in the cart. The wheel turned a fraction of an inch, pinching Margaret in the process and setting off her own wails.

In all the fuss of the girls crying and their mother hushing them and their aunt muttering under her breath at the stubborn twisting of the fibers, no one heard the door of Number Five, Spencer Terrace, open and shut, nor the firm footfalls approach.

"Might I be of assistance?"

The startled Ellsworth ladies looked up to see a lithely built young man, sober of dress and features, with dark hair and eyes. So surprised were the twins that they left off crying and scrambled for their mother, peeping at the interloper from the shelter of her skirts.

"Thank you, sir," said Aggie simply, bending to pick up Joanie, who was clinging like a particularly dogged limpet. At this, Margaret hopped and held up her own arms, and Aggie was obliged to reach for her as well, biting her lip to stifle a groan at the added weight.

"The blanket is wound all through the spokes," Beatrice said, stepping back to let the young man see. "Miraculous in itself, for I daresay it happened in an instant. I fear we may have to c-u-t it free."

A gleam of something which might have been humor came and went in his eye. "Dear me. We can't have that," he murmured, before quickly removing his gloves and lowering himself to one knee to inspect the damage.

"Oh, sir! Your trousers," objected Aggie. When Beatrice raised eyebrows at her, she hastily added, "I mean, your inexpressibles."

"Better they than the young lady's skirts," he replied, his fingers working nimbly.

"If it can't be untangled, we will just carry the whole kit home, blanket and all," Beatrice said. "It isn't far to Number Four."

His movements stilled briefly, and he threw her a glance. "Number Four, you say? No, that isn't far." Setting to his task again, in another eyeblink he worked the blanket free. "Ah. No need for any cart-carrying or c-u-t-t-i-n-g after all." He rose to his feet again, holding the precious item out to the twins, and Joanie released her mother long enough to snatch it from him before burying her face in Aggie's shoulder.

"Thank the gentleman, Joan," prodded her mother.

"Mraff oo," mumbled Joanie without lifting her head. Margaret, sucking on her fingers, stared enough for both girls, however.

"Amazing," observed Beatrice. "However did you do that so quickly, sir?"

He fluttered his fingers at her as he replaced his gloves. "Plenty of experience fixing things. No—wait. It might have been all the smuggling and spying I've done. Hard to say. Now, if you will excuse me..." With a touch of his hat, he made them a half-bow and walked away down Bognor Street.

"Smuggling and spying?" echoed Aggie, when he was out of earshot. She loaded the girls back in the pull-cart, and this time they went without protest. "Whatever can he mean?"

But Beatrice had gone crimson. "Oh! That Fussell! What a loose tongue she has! That man must be our neighbor in Number Five." She recounted her discussion with the maid, spelling a few of the words she would rather the twins not repeat, while Aggie collapsed in laughter.

"Dear me!" Aggie gasped. "And you dared to give *me* a look for saying 'trousers'! Well, let us be thankful he does keep so much to himself, if we are always going to show ourselves at such a disadvantage. Too bad, though, for he's a rather pleasant-looking fellow." With another chuckle she tugged the cart into motion. "Come along, girls. Let's see if we can lay hold of any sandwiches. How is it that sunshine and play can be so tiring?"

Later Beatrice would think of her time at Bognor as Before and After. Before the Accident, that is, and After it. But it was not the accident so much as the consequence of the accident which made the difference so stark. In truth, it would be more accurate to call it Before Mr. Clayton and After Mr. Clayton.

Some days after the Episode of the Blanket, the Ellsworths made an early start as they had all the previous days. Again Aggie shooed Tyrone away, flapping the end of her capacious shawl at him, for he had learned to swim at Oxford along the banks of the river Cherwell and had no need for bathing machines. Unlike at the larger, more popular resorts, no separation was made at Bognor between men's and women's bathing areas, but still he removed some distance, laughing, "I have no desire to have my foot crushed by a hoof or one of those six-foot wheels."

In retrospect, his words would prove not exactly prophetic, but certainly singular.

Shyly Beatrice stepped forward when it was her turn, glad her dipper this morning was not the commanding, red-faced, burly creature of the previous few days, but someone much slighter who didn't appear older than Bea herself. This one avoided her eyes and gestured mutely for her to enter.

After Beatrice climbed the two steps to the little dressing chamber, her dipper led the horse around to yoke it to the seagoing end.

Then, without warning, just as Beatrice had removed her shawl and was hanging it on a peg, the machine lurched forward, sending her tumbling to the sodden and sandy floor.

"Ooh," she frowned, inspecting her scraped palms. The flannel of her bathing shift protected her knees from similar injury, but the same could not be said for the dress itself, which now had a tear along one side at knee height, from which the fabric hung down. With a sigh she shrugged. It would have to be mended later but made no difference at present, for no one would see her but her dipper. Waiting upon the bench, she tucked her knees up and blew on her palms to soothe them, listening as the horse was switched around again. "What a dull life for the creature," she observed aloud. "All morning spent going a few yards up the beach and a few yards down, over and over, back and forth. I hope the reward at the end is a warm blanket and a bucket of oats."

More thumps and jolts followed, which Beatrice recognized as the bathing-machine steps being moved from the front to the back, until at long last the rear doors of the machine opened to reveal the rail-thin dipper standing under the umbrella of canvas, hands held up to receive her customer.

"Do you like your work?" Beatrice asked, taking hold of her. "The fresh air, and always to be by the sea?" She thought it must be rather tedious herself, but one must say something, and she had been too intimidated by her previous dipper to utter more than quiet thanks when it was ended.

"'Tisn't my work," replied the girl unexpectedly. "'Tis my pa's. But he's in a barley-hood."

Beatrice hadn't the least idea what a barley-hood was but understood it to mean the girl's father was indisposed. She put it from her mind, in any case, too eager to plunge in and experience the shock of the cold water and the delight of being carried hither and yon in the waves.

Between the waiting for the use of the machine, the hitching and unhitching of the horse, the drawing of the carriage back and forth, and such rigmarole, the actual time spent bathing was always sadly brief, but that morning Beatrice had not been longer than a minute in the water before some unseen and barely overheard to-do took place around the front of the machine. In alarm, the horse whinnied and tried to kick out, shifting the chamber hitched to it so that the machine tilted toward one side, before landing with a jerk and sliding down, further into the sea. All this took place in an instant, and neither Beatrice nor her dipper was aware of the danger until the stairs caught Beatrice in the back of the knees. She crumpled into the water to her neck, only to be pulled all the way under the waves when the six-foot wheel of the machine rolled over the dragging hem of her torn bathing dress.

Beatrice's undersized dipper stared in horror. She was more usually a seamstress, and crises of the sewing room were confined to crooked seams and snapped thread. Oh, she would be in for it with her pa, if something bad happened! With a frightened moan, she made a scrambling effort to catch at some part of her customer and tug her free, not an easy task for one of her size, especially as she could not swim herself and was too afraid to poke her head underwater. But she could scream with the best of them, and this she did at last when her exertions failed, in a voice both powerful and piercing. Tearing back the canvas umbrella which enclosed them she cried, "Help! Help! Anyone! She's caught! My lady's caught! Something's got her and keeps her down! Help!"

The nearest at hand was the young man in the next machine, being dipped himself by the commanding, red-faced, burly conductor Beatrice had been grateful to be spared. Before his meaty dipper could respond to the seamstress's cries, John Clayton flung off her grip, ducking under his own canvas to begin fighting his way through the surf. Though he was head and shoulders above the water, when he reached the panic-stricken girl sounding the alarm there was no sign of her charge, and, after a hesitation, he took a deep breath and dived beneath the surge.

Beatrice, in full panic and having inhaled a lungful of sea water, was in no condition to understand what was happening. Blindly, she clawed at her shift, trying to rip it loose, only to find herself the next moment gathered in iron arms and wrenched upward, the torn section of her bathing dress shearing loose and her face once more breaking the surface to be touched by the blessed air.

"You there," Clayton ordered the recent seamstress, "draw this thing back up the beach." Without waiting for an answer (and indeed, she offered none), he climbed the two steps of the bathing machine and gently deposited his burden within.

No sooner had he laid her upon the bench than another burst up the stairs into the cramped chamber.

"Dear God!" cried the interloper, rushing to the victim's side. "Beatrice! Are you all right?"

In answer, the young lady rolled on her side and promptly disgorged that portion of the English Channel she had unwillingly imbibed. She could not speak, but she could cough and groan and cough some more, and the young man spoke enough for both of them, thanking God repeatedly, if not with any fluency. He even kissed her dripping head as she coughed and gagged. Only when he had convinced himself that she was not lying dead, full fathom five, and that she would in fact recover, did he have attention to spare her rescuer.

"Sir, we are ever more in your debt," he swore, his voice shaking as he rose to his feet. "I was perhaps fifty yards distant—thank God I had my head up and was treading water, so I heard the screaming—but it took me some time to realize it was Beatrice's dipper raising the alarm. Heaven knows what might have happened if you had not reached her when you did."

Clayton nodded, still breathless himself, his mind beginning to catch up with what he had done by instinct. Anyone with experience in building, mining, and channeling, as he had, was familiar with the ever-present threat of danger or injury to the workers. This poor trapped young lady was not the first person he had dragged free from machinery, though she had been the lightest and the daintiest, despite being wet to the skin.

His color rose with the last thought because just then he glimpsed the lower half of the young lady's leg, bare and glistening where her bathing dress had rent away. Though he removed his gaze the next moment, somehow he still saw her limb in his mind's eye, slender and shapely.

Her face half hidden, she clung to the other young man now. He had knelt again, and silent tears ran down her cheeks while he fumbled at her streaming hair. A twinge of something surprised Clayton, which took him several beats to recognize as *envy*. Why, he *envied* the young man. Envied him having so cherished a sweetheart, who cleaved to him in return. But that was as far as John got in his analysis before the front door of the bathing machine crashed open and an entirely unexpected second young lady flew in, shrieking, "Bea!"

A sister to the victim? There was something familiar about her, but John only just managed to shrink out of the way as she threw herself at the embracing pair, flinging her arms about them both and bursting into tears.

CHAPTER TWO

I am from humble, he from honored name.
—Shakespeare, *All's Well That Ends Well*,
I.iii.152 (c.1602)

All was confusion for a minute until the half-drowned young lady pushed the other away. "I'm all right, Aggie. I'm all right. If you don't choke me now."

"I can't help it!" wailed the one called Aggie, "*What* would Mrs. Wolfe and your sisters have said, if I took you away to Bognor to *murder* you?"

"Doubtless they would have had a word or two for me as well," put in their young man with a mirthless smile.

"Well, whatever they might have said to *either* of you," said the victim hoarsely, "you needn't fear it now, because this gentleman saved me."

"What?" Dashing an arm over her eyes, the one called Aggie turned to regard Clayton, only to have mutual recognition shortly dawn upon them both.

"Why—it's you! That is, the man from Bognor Street who unwound Joanie's blanket, is it not?"

Though momentarily nonplussed, he managed a bow. Great heavens! If this was the young mother of the twin girls, then the young lady he had saved must be—

All at once he remembered his own condition and thought he was not, perhaps, setting his best foot forward. Not only was water still streaming from him, but he was hardly more clothed than the other young man. While many men at Bognor bathed entirely nude, thankfully Clayton had been unaware of this custom and had left his trousers on, as uncomfortable as they were when wet. The other young man was himself appareled in linen drawers alone, though without the least sign of embarrassment, and John could not guess at the trio's relationship.

"It—is," he admitted. "That is—I am. What a—er—pleasure to meet you again."

"Pleasure? What a word for it!" she said ruefully. "If it is so, you must enjoy playing the white knight." Turning back to the other young man, she lay a hand on his shoulder. "Tyrone, it is the gentleman we told you about. Our neighbor in Spencer Terrace." With a smile, she shook out her sodden bathing dress where it clung to her and curtseyed in response to his bow. "Sir, we are now twice in your debt. Nay—a hundred times! For what is Joanie's blanket compared to our Beatrice? How can we thank you enough for your quick thinking and your courage today?"

"I am relieved the young lady is unhurt," he replied. He ventured another glance at the one in question. "At least—I hope you are unhurt, miss."

She returned an unsteady smile, tugging on what remained of her flannel shift to cover herself more adequately. "Yes. That is—no. I mean—I am unhurt. Thank you. A little scared, but unhurt."

"It would be unnatural if you were not scared," he said.

"Unnatural and downright amphibious," declared the young man Tyrone, now recovered enough to give the young lady's hair a teasing rub. He then sprang up to make his own bow, for all the world as if they met in a drawing room, rather than half-clothed in a confined bathing machine. "Under the circumstances, sir, when you have saved not only a beloved blanket but also the very life of one of our party, it seems ridiculous to stand on ceremony. Therefore, I will play master of ceremonies and introduce myself as Tyrone Ellsworth of Hollowgate, Winchester. This is my wife Mrs. Ellsworth and my sister Miss Ellsworth. To whom do we owe everything, if we might ask?"

So this Ellsworth and the lady he had saved were brother and sister? That is, not man and wife or man and betrothed? A glow filled Clayton's chest which he did not care to examine, but his answering smile was genuine. "I am John Clayton of—well, I suppose you might say of London, though in truth I seem to have spent my time almost equally in various other places in the kingdom."

"Are you a soldier, then?" asked Mrs. Ellsworth.

Before he could reply, the shivering Miss Ellsworth blurted in a rasp, "We did not really think you a smuggler or a spy, Mr. Clayton. It was a little joke I made with our maid Fussell, I'm afraid, because she said you were always at home and always writing letters. It served me right that she then repeated it to her cousin, *your* maid." The speech nearly finished her and brought on another round of coughing, but she was relieved to see the remembered gleam in his eye, and when he answered, there was no resentment in his voice.

"Well, if I *were* a smuggler or a spy, Miss Ellsworth, you would understand why I should deny it outright, even when accused. You would understand why I might declare, in fact, that I am neither soldier nor smuggler nor spy, but rather an engineer."

"An engineer?" chorused his auditors.

"Yes." His mouth twitched. "Or so I say. But it is too long a tale to tell here, when everyone is wet and beginning to shiver." Mrs. Tyrone Ellsworth was indeed bundling her sister-in-law in a shawl, and Clayton did not suppose it could be a very agreeable process when one still wore wet clothing.

"A good point," agreed Tyrone Ellsworth. "Your tale must wait a little longer, sir. But what would you say to joining us for supper? This very night?"

The briefest pause followed, but then Clayton gave a nod and began to retreat toward the door. "Thank you. I would like that."

"It is done, then. Come at seven. You will find us at Number Four, Spencer Terrace." Laughing, he gave his forehead a damp smack. "But I forgot. You already knew that."

After returning to his own bathing machine to change into dry clothing, Clayton made his thoughtful way past the subscription room and library to the High Street, whose winding ascent skirted the Chapel House built by Bognor's founder Sir Richard Hotham, before ending in the princely Crescent. He was pleased to note that he was no longer short of breath, as he had been when he arrived a fortnight earlier, plagued by a lingering autumn cough. However, it had not been ill health alone which confined him to Number Five, Spencer Terrace, the previous two weeks. The Cumberland Arm project had been in a delicate place, with one of the landowners threatening defection over an eleventh-hour adjustment to the route. Hunched at his desk, Clayton wrote letter after letter, evaluating candidates to be his undersecretary and resident engineer, calling in favors, wheedling or remonstrating or reasoning as the situation demanded. If his health improved simultaneously, it was merely the work of time and silence, for there had been no occasion for other means to be tried.

Still less had there been time for loneliness.

As an engaged man, it would not have been unseemly if many of the letters flying to and fro passed between Clayton and his intended bride, yet there had been only one interchange. One reproachful note, written out by Miss Croy but in truth dictated by Miss Brand, had wrung from him a brief but courteous response. The couple had been too much apart the last two years of Miss Brand's schooling for Clayton to have acquired the habit of seeing her or even communicating with her regularly. Which explained why he did not miss her. Why he rarely missed her. Even when he felt a pang, as when he supposed Tyrone Ellsworth and his sister Miss Ellsworth to be sweethearts, it was more a vague awareness of vacancy in his life than a yearning for Priscilla Brand in particular.

And yet he must have been lonely without realizing it, for inexplicable eagerness filled him as he anticipated the evening's supper. While meeting and assisting the pretty Mrs. and Miss Ellsworth the previous afternoon had provided a fillip of novelty to his day, this was something else altogether. What a morning! As if his first cold sea bath would not have been memorable enough—to have screams pierce the air—to feel his heart race and his breath halt—to struggle over and plunge beneath the foaming waters with no clear idea of whom he might find or how he might help. To seize upon the victim and feel panic animating the slender form, hands clutching at his arm, his hands, his chest, his neck, for purchase. And then, to wrench the poor creature to the surface again and find—to find he had fetched up—Clayton flushed in remembrance. It had been like thrusting his hands blindly into dark waters, only to emerge with a sea nymph in one's arms. A mermaid. Water streaming from her flawless skin and darkened hair, her torn shift clinging. He had not recognized her as the same tidy, proper young lady of the day before. Again, the handful of others he had saved from calamity as Donald Brand's resident engineer came to mind—those victims of carelessness, drunkenness, faulty equipment, faulty construction, or countless unpredictable perils of chance or nature—no other rescue had affected him as hers did.

It was to be expected therefore that he should look forward to the evening.

When the housemaid Molly's head popped up in the stairwell some hours later, she was astonished to find the tenant standing at the window, gazing out into Upper Bognor Street, instead of in his usual place, seated at his desk as if he and the chair had been carved from one block.

"Oh, sir," she panted, more and more of her becoming visible as she climbed up with his dinner tray. "Have you been waiting? I'm sure it's the usual time. And if you aren't wanting to stay at your desk, I can set you a place in the dining room."

"What? No, Molly. Set it down there. I'll get back to work shortly, but before I do, I have a few questions for you. Tell me—it was your cousin Fussell who works next door, was it not? I confess I did not attend as closely as I might have, but she was the one who said her new tenants thought me a smuggler or a spy?"

Molly's round cheeks blushed even rosier than exertion had made them, and John thought she looked like an especially ruddy apple. Everything about her was round and fresh, perhaps because her hair was snowy white in contrast. "Now, sir, there was no harm meant, you know. Annie—Fussell—and I like a good chat, and I'm sure the young lady in Number Four meant no mischief. It's only that you *do* spend a great deal of time working and writing, writing and working, and people will talk."

This drew a grin from him that quite transformed his sober features. "Why, Molly, you speak as if these 'people' talking were nothing at all to do with you. But, come. I'm not cross. It happens

I met the neighbors by chance yesterday and again while out this morning, and they have invited me to supper, and I figure I may as well be hung for a sheep as a lamb. Meaning, I may as well spy on them in truth and learn what I can before I go."

"Oh! You met them, did you? Well then, sir," the maid rejoined eagerly, "my cousin tells me it's a husband and wife and the gentleman's younger sister. They're all from Winchester and rich enough. The gentleman manages an estate there for his older sister, but Annie says it must be more to keep him occupied or to help his sister, for they—the Tyrone Ellsworths—could easily afford a place of their own. He was rich to begin with, and his wife was a great heiress."

Instead of appearing pleased to discover he had fallen among wealthy gentlefolk, as Molly would expect any young man to be, Mr. Clayton's brow knit.

"As grand as all that, you say? And does—the younger sister—live with the Tyrone Ellsworths in Winchester?"

"She has been living nearby with her stepmother. Stepmother of her and the brother, that is. But her stepmother and stepfather have gone on their own trip—a belated wedding journey—so Miss Ellsworth chose to come to Bognor instead of staying with other family members. It seems she's the only one still unmarried, so maybe they thought to find her a husband at the seaside, but anyone could have told them it would have been better to take her somewhere more fashionable. Apart from you, sir, there aren't terribly many young or eligible gentlemen to be found in Bognor after the summer months. Yes, indeed. I warrant those Ellsworths will gladly latch on to you!"

Despite the maid's confidence, Clayton grimaced at such a prediction.

No doubt some would have deemed this an appropriate moment for him to mention that it made no difference whether the Ellsworths latched on to him or not, for he was already engaged, but the fact remained unspoken. Not because he intended to masquerade as a single man, to be sure, but because he thought it unlikely that people like the Ellsworths would consider him an eligible *parti* in the first place. What, an educated, wealthy, landed family from Winchester to ally itself with a self-taught man who must work for his living? And not always "clean" work at that, done in a spotless office in spotless attire. Not at all! While he might spend hours in meetings and answering correspondence, it was not the least bit unusual for Clayton's work to take him down into the excavations as well, to ensure the puddling rendered the channel watertight, or to replace the crank of the steam engine's fly-wheel shaft when the engine-man was too drunk or too absent to do so himself.

No.

There was no need to "warn" the Ellsworths off. The very idea was presumptuous. After the supper, if they had not already recovered their equanimity, they would probably deem him amply repaid for his services and content themselves thereafter with a nodding acquaintance. The thought of him needing to burst in at Number Four, declaring with might and main that, no no no, they must not "get ideas" about him, was more than presumptuous—it bordered on ridiculous.

Therefore, in answer he only said lightly, "I think not, Molly. Winchester is a lively enough place. Miss Ellsworth must have her choice of suitors there."

Wagging her apple head, Molly lowered her voice conspiratorially. "You would think, sir. Especially since Annie says she's a pretty thing. Pretty and rich! A girl like that should only have to snap her fingers. Which is why there must be *something we don't know*. Illness, mayhap? Or a secret sweetheart? Or unracketed love?"

That brought a chuckle. "Poor Miss Ellsworth. I hope it is merely youth and disinclination which prolongs her inexplicable singleness, and not the dreaded 'unracketed' love. But remind me never to tell you or Annie Fussell anything. If this is how you speak of her, what have you two been saying of me—unmarried at eight and twenty as I am?"

But Molly was not abashed by this, and she waved a casual hand. "You've been married to your work, sir. That's plain. But it's a shame, I say, and if you and Miss Ellsworth happened to take a liking to each other, why that would be two birds with one stone."

"So enterprising of you, Molly," he declared, seating himself on the sofa and pulling the tray nearer. "Not only do you build fires and make beds and sandwiches, but you matchmake into the bargain. But suppose I were to come to fancy *you*—you wouldn't wish that 'unracketed' love on me, would you?"

"Oh, go along with you, sir," Molly returned with an elderly giggle. With a bob she retreated, treading heavily down the stairs to share Mr. Clayton's joke with the footman.

Promptly at seven Clayton descended the few steps of Number Five, Spencer Terrace, to climb the corresponding set at Number Four. He was admitted by an ancient manservant whom he knew to be called Pidgeley and led to the drawing room where the three Ellsworths awaited him.

"Clayton!" cried a smiling Tyrone Ellsworth, coming forward to grasp his hand after bows and curtseys had been exchanged. "You are very welcome here. We have spoken of little but you since you last saw us, and it was all my wife could do, to persuade me to leave you in peace until the appointed time."

"I am glad to be here," he replied, unable to prevent a start of surprise. If they had indeed spoken of him all day, had it not at all tempered their enthusiasm for him? Perhaps he ought to mention his lack of formal education and the puddling in the ditches after all, and straight off, before they all found themselves in an awkward position.

Before he could make up his mind to do so, however, Ellsworth's wife came forward and tucked a hand in her husband's arm. "You must pardon our effusiveness, sir, but what would have become of our beloved Beatrice, if not for you? Such a service you rendered! How, *how* can we ever thank you enough?"

"Please!" He held up his hands against this deluge of gratitude. "Again, I rejoice that I was on hand, Mrs. Ellsworth. Let us say no more of it."

"Or the next time he might just let me drown," spoke up Miss Ellsworth playfully from her place beside the fire.

The wringing wet, shivering nymph of the morning was vanished, and before him stood again the neat young lady of the blanket-and-cart episode, as tidy as the gossiping Fussell and Molly had judged her. Her brown tresses, dry once more and neatly wound up, were shot through with gold and held in place by a silk bandeau which shaded from sea green to greenish-grey, a hue taken up again in her hazel-and-brown eyes. With her regular features, smooth complexion and light figure, she was altogether pleasing to Clayton's eye, and he found himself remembering the maids' conjectures. *Was* there some secret sorrow which had prevented her marrying? He could hardly credit so lovely a creature suffering unrequited love.

In the directness of his gaze her own faltered, and she addressed her next remark to his neckcloth. "If you would endure just one more word about the matter, Mr. Clayton. I promise you it will be the last. From me, at least. But I was—so discomposed this morning that I could not speak plainly. I do thank you for coming so quickly to my aid. I'm afraid I had quite lost my head."

"Anyone would have, under the circumstances," he answered gravely.

"That may be, but—I hope you will forgive me if I—choked you or scratched you in my panic. No—please—do let me say it all! I was very frightened. So frightened that I think I will be content the rest of our visit to admire the sea from the shore. But—thank you for your quick actions, sir."

He bowed again, even as Mrs. Ellsworth moved to put an arm about her sister-in-law. "Indeed, Mr. Clayton, to keep her safe, we might just wrap Beatrice in cotton wool for the remainder of our stay."

"I hope you will not, Mrs. Ellsworth," he answered, making a deprecating gesture with his hands. "Not that I wish Miss Ellsworth any harm, of course, but I have been thinking myself today about the incident and have arrived at conclusions of my own." He waited until they had all taken their seats again before continuing. "In fact, Ellsworth, I wonder if I might prevail upon you to do me a favor."

"Anything," said Tyrone at once. "Anything at all. At least, anything in my power to do." He made a dramatic sweeping motion with his arm. "'Whatsoever thou shalt ask of me, I will give it thee, unto the half of my kingdom.'"

"Gracious," chuckled Aggie. "Let us hope Mr. Clayton's request will not be as bloodthirsty as Salome's, then."

"It is nothing like that, madam," he assured her, sitting forward. "In fact, if Ellsworth does grant this favor, it would not cost lives but rather save them. Which is to say, Ellsworth, I wonder if you might teach your sister to swim."

CHAPTER THREE

These [actions] were told to his honour.
— editor H. Mackenzie et al., *The Mirror*,
No.23 (1779)

Whatever they had been expecting, this was not it, and Clayton found himself facing three amazed faces, eyes and mouths round. Miss Ellsworth had taken up some sewing, but now she sat frozen, needle in midair.

"But—but—we were going to wrap Beatrice in cotton wool," Aggie reminded him, as if she had not just said so a minute earlier.

"Yes," her husband seconded after a moment. "We thank you for the suggestion, however. Quite...original. But I will point out—teaching Bea to swim hardly qualifies as a favor for yourself, Clayton."

"Of course it would be," he answered, striving for lightness. "Because I'm a busy man. I cannot be hauling your womenfolk out of the Channel every morning." Polite smiles met this joke, but he could tell they were still recovering.

The young lady in question found her tongue at last, though she gripped her needle so tightly it pressed a groove in her skin. "Wait a moment," she said, with a flash at her brother and sister-in-law. "All of you. I beg you wouldn't talk about me or make decisions for me as if I weren't in the room."

Though surprised by this show of spirit, they began to beg her pardon, but she had already turned on the originator of the idea. "And sir, I think...the decision of whether or not I learn to swim lies solely with me."

Even on so short an acquaintance, Clayton suspected her sternness was not characteristic. There was her family's dismay, to begin with, but also the telltale tremble of her voice and chin. She was not in the habit of open defiance, then. Which meant she felt herself driven to it.

In response, his color rose. It probably had been an indecorous suggestion and none of his business, however he himself had his habits, chief among them being finding efficient solutions to difficulties. On the other hand, he reminded himself, this was a drawing room, for pity's sake, not the side of a leaky ditch!

"Of course," he said quietly. Still, conviction prodded him, and he could not suppress a restless movement.

"Perhaps you mean, Clayton, that you would like to learn to swim yourself?" Tyrone asked in an effort to smooth over the awkwardness.

Confound it, thought Clayton impatiently. *She might resent me for it, but in for a penny, in for a pound.*

"Yes," he said aloud. "That is, though I too would love to learn to swim one day, I think the need more pressing for *you,* Miss Ellsworth, and I urge you to consider it." She had resumed her stitching, but he could see how quick and jerking her movements were. "You see, Miss Ellsworth," he continued, "while your brother and sister might deem wrapping you in cotton wool for the remainder of your stay a comfortable solution, I have always thought it advisable to face a fear, if one hopes to overcome it."

"True," agreed Aggie, in spite of herself. She cast Beatrice her own uncertain look. "Why, I would absolutely agree with you, Mr. Clayton, if it came to *me.* I love sea-bathing so much, I would hate to be deprived of it, but..."

"But Aggie and I have fears of our own," rejoined Tyrone swiftly. "Fears of our family's wrath, in particular, if we were to return to Winchester without my dear little sister, or even with an injured one. Therefore the cotton-wool proposal. Isn't that right, Bea? Besides—" he gave a droll wink "—I hope she will not mind me mentioning it—and I truly wish she were *not* actually in the room, that I might say this with impunity—but Beatrice is sadly the most lily-livered of my sisters."

At this Beatrice straightened again, abandoning any pretense of sewing. In fact, she secured her needle carefully in the fabric, lest she give in to the urge to jab her brother with it. "Mr. Clayton," she began, "I pray you will ignore a little family squabbling, but, actually, Tyrone, I *do* mind you mentioning it. I may not have, say, Minta's reputation for bravery—though it might be more accurate to call it recklessness—nor Lily's, whose boldness stems more from indifference than lion-heartedness—but I think I'm at least as brave as Florence."

While neither Tyrone nor Aggie contradicted her, nor did they hasten to agree, and when Beatrice saw them exchange a quick glance, that sealed it. For that little shared look contained years of memories: little Beatrice who cried too much; little Beatrice who didn't want to go to school even as a day pupil because she wanted to follow her oldest sister and stepmother around; and even the grown Beatrice who had tried to prevent Mr. Wolfe from wooing her mama, out of dread for the changes which would follow.

Digging her fingernails into her palms she declared, "It so happens, Tyrone, I have decided I *would* like to learn to swim, thank you very much. And as you have already promised Mr. Clayton you would grant his favor, whatever it might be, that means you have bound yourself to teach me."

In response her brother spluttered, half amazed and half amused, but Aggie laughed outright. "Hoist with your own petard, Tyrone! Oh, my. Now you know how Herod felt when Salome made her request. I suspect, though, if you drown Bea, it will be your own head on the platter." With a playful nudge she added, "Come, come. You had better teach me at the same time, then. That way, if disaster strikes, perhaps between the two of us we can fish her out."

"But who will fish *me* out while the both of you are hanging like millstones about my neck? I saw how Bea nearly strangled Clayton this morning." He turned, still chuckling, to shake his head at their guest. "Good gracious—look what you've got me into. The least you could do is join us tomorrow."

Much as he would have liked to leap at the offer, and pleased as he was with Miss Ellsworth's decision, Clayton was obligated to remind himself of his earlier resolves. Clearly the family meant to befriend him, but encouraging such an intimacy without revealing his station in life would be disingenuous. In honor he must make a clean breast, that they might then beat a decorous retreat.

"I'm afraid that will be impossible," he said therefore. "Because my work keeps me very busy. Too busy."

"Oh," breathed Mrs. Ellsworth, disappointed. "Then you haven't time for us?"

"What? I—no—that isn't it," he hemmed, though it was true enough. If he were suddenly to play the Seaside Man of Leisure, a great deal would be left undone. "That is—I do have many things I am responsible for, but that is not what I meant, Mrs. Ellsworth."

"What is it, then?" demanded Tyrone. "For I confess I have already thought of several more things to invite you to."

"Beware, Mr. Clayton, or my husband will drag you to poetry readings and such," teased Aggie. "Though, if you enjoy such activities, or if you ever want poetry composed for you or read to you or the latest novel described, there is no better man for the job."

Clayton's smile was stiff. "Certainly I would call upon those talents of yours, Ellsworth, if I were able to indulge my love of reading more. But I'm afraid, in my line of work, it has been impossible."

"Indulge it here, then!" cried Aggie, thoroughly missing the point. "The library below the subscription room is capital, is it not, Tyrone? When my mother visited Bognor some years ago, she found its collection lacking, but I wrote to her that it is much improved since then."

"Absolutely," agreed her husband. "A very respectable, more than adequate selection of material. What do you say we go tomorrow, Clayton? After the morning bathe, that is. A little holiday for you, and then we will try to leave you in peace."

Clayton sighed inwardly at their persistence. "Ellsworth, you would likely find me an unsatisfactory companion in that regard. Because—because as I said this morning, I am an engineer."

"That's right!" Tyrone snapped his fingers. "And we have been wanting to ask you more about that, for where we live we rarely meet with any. Do you improve the roads? Build bridges?"

"Neither. My work is on the canals, which I have been involved in building these ten years. You see, while you have been reading and writing poetry, I have lived the life of a comparatively unlettered mechanic." This was an exaggeration, but he felt he must exaggerate, if they were not going to listen to him.

"That's a peculiar choice of words," murmured Miss Ellsworth with a tiny smile. She was sewing again, eyes on her work, but they flicked up to him briefly. "Considering how you have, in the course of a fortnight, acquired the reputation among the servants of a man chained to his desk, writing letter after letter. But perhaps those countless epistles are all of them ill-spelt and ungrammatical?"

"I said 'comparatively unlettered,'" he amended, unable to prevent a chuckle. He had the passing thought that she wanted to repay him tit for tat for the discomfiture he had caused her. "I suppose my business letters will do, to say what I want said. But what I mean is, I have neither a public school nor university education."

"And that must be dreadfully inconvenient!" was her reply. "Especially when your correspondents beg you to express yourself in rhymed couplets or to translate a contract into Latin."

Another look passed between Tyrone Ellsworth and his wife, this one unseen by Beatrice. Tyrone lifted one brow a fraction, which in married-couple language clearly indicated, *Is this truly our Beatrice speaking this way?* And Aggie responded with widened eyes: *In anyone else, I would call it flirting!*

For his part, Clayton found himself pleasantly riled. "Are you *mocking* me, Miss Ellsworth?"

Sadly for both witnesses and participants, Beatrice's response was forestalled by the entrance of Pidgeley, the servant choosing this moment to shuffle in and summon them to supper, and the interchange must be put aside while the gentlemen escorted the ladies to the dining room.

Pidgeley then creaked about, serving a succession of dishes, several of which Clayton recognized from the nearby inn (having himself sampled their offerings over the past fortnight). But while the servant's shoes and knee joints played a symphony of squeaks and pops throughout the meal, the man himself of course said nothing, leaving the conversation to begin again.

Clayton was mulling over how to reintroduce the subject of his profession, when Tyrone spared him the trouble.

"You say you've been an engineer on the canals for ten years?" he asked. "I plead ignorance about what that entails, Clayton, and hope you will explain all."

"If you like. Though I admit I am more used to answering questions than delivering monologues on my work."

The Ellsworths took him at his word, and myriad questions followed, all of which he patiently answered. But far from seeming disdainful of his manual labors or bored by his responses, the more they learned, the more curious they became. Even Miss Ellsworth, who left the questioning to her relations, attended with unfeigned interest. (At least he thought it was unfeigned. All he could be certain of was that, unlike his betrothed Miss Brand, Miss Ellsworth neither patted back yawns nor complained that, this was all very well, but it was "like listening to Papa prose on and on, all over again.") Tyrone Ellsworth went so far as to solicit his advice on a drainage problem at Hollowgate, which he answered as best he could, conjecturing how puddling techniques could be applied to farmland.

Privately, each thought how well Mr. Clayton expressed himself, despite his earlier modesty. The truth was, from the age of fourteen he had spent most of his time in company with those either directly or indirectly involved with canal-building: the engineers and the workmen, the investors and landowners, and the politicians—always the politicians. While the landowners and politicians generally hailed from the more exalted social classes, Clayton had rarely been cowed because, when he was among them, it was only the project—the work—which was discussed. And of the work he was fully master.

"I don't mind," he assured them again, when Aggie begged his pardon at last for their interrogation. "Few people in the south of England have ever seen a canal, therefore it would be extraordinary if you *did* know anything about them. And we are all of us too young to remember the mania which gripped the kingdom in the nineties, when my late mentor tells me one only had to whisper the word 'canal' to be at once besieged with would-be investors."

"Is it not so now?" asked Tyrone. "Aggie, think of my cousin Benjamin. He is always on the lookout for new ventures."

"Benjamin's new wife Maria might not thank you for encouraging him in another money-making scheme," Aggie chuckled.

"On the contrary," he returned. "Maria has me to thank for her present happiness."

"We had better explain to Mr. Clayton," put in Beatrice. "Because he so kindly explained his own mysteries to our satisfaction." She smiled at their guest around the candelabra and flower bowl in the center of the table. "You see, our dear cousins Benjamin and Austin once published a book of Tyrone's letters—"

"With my full permission and cooperation," interjected her brother.

"With his full permission and cooperation," she agreed, "and made a pretty sum upon it. Enough so that he—Benjamin—was able to marry, and Austin now has hopes of doing so. But Tyrone himself did not make a penny."

"Only because Tyrone did not need a penny," Aggie dismissed this. "Whereas poor Benjamin and Austin needed as many as they could find."

"Precisely," concurred her husband. "Which brings us back to my earlier question: Clayton, would you recommend investment in your latest project? How much are the shares?"

John put a hand to his chest and made a half-bow of acknowledgement. "Frankly, new investors are always welcome, and shares may be had at present for perhaps ten pounds apiece. But construction will take at least two years, in which time I daresay you might buoy your cousin's financial situation more easily and with less risk by writing him another book of letters."

But Tyrone laughed at this. "You say that because you are only considering one kind of risk. If I were to author another set of letters for my cousins, my father-in-law might gladly see me ride in a cart about Winchester, and he would be the first to hurl something at my head."

"My father was upset about the letters," Aggie explained with a nostalgic smile.

"No, Mr. Weeks was upset about our *elopement*," corrected her husband.

"*No*—well, yes, of course he was—but there would have been no need for an elopement, had you not needed to jilt the girl you were previously engaged to."

"And there would have been no need to jilt any girl, had she not mistakenly *manufactured* the engagement in the first place," he retorted, but Clayton could see there was no heat in the argument. Rather, they trod well-worn paths which offered more amusement than controversy.

It was Miss Ellsworth who observed, "It's quite discourteous of you two to go on and on with your private jokes and scandals, while Mr. Clayton must sit there nodding politely. Besides, suppose he were to shun us in consequence of your misconduct?"

"We can't have that!" declared Tyrone, thumping the board. (Pidgeley understood it as a demand for more wine and creaked forward to refill his glass.) "We're really quite dull and respectable, Clayton, I promise. And to show you bear us no ill will, you must tear yourself away from your precious canals and join us for tomorrow's swim lesson. Suppose Aggie and Beatrice were to pin me to the sea floor in their flapping and kicking? That would be upon your conscience."

And Clayton heard himself say, though he had not had any intention of saying it, "Very well. Why not? I might as well hang about your neck, too, Ellsworth, that we might all go down together."

When the young man bid them farewell for the evening, the Ellsworths did not at first speak of him, each perhaps waiting for another to begin the subject. Tyrone read them some more *Waverley,* but despite his excellent delivery and her usual interest in Flora

Mac-Ivor, Beatrice's mind wandered, returning again and again to her rescuer.

She had never met anyone like him. It was not his looks—though she liked his looks very much. Nor did he have wealth or rank or connection to boast of, it seemed. What was it, then? Of course there was the fact that he had saved her from injury, if not from death itself. Her heart sped to recall the terror of the moment, her bathing dress pinned beneath the wheel, her lungs filled and choking, the dim and cold deep. And then, suddenly, the powerful arms grasping her, the only solid things in a murky world—

With a shudder, Beatrice pushed the memory away again. No, it was not his rescue of her which rendered him fascinating. If anything, the episode—marked by her vulnerability and loss of control and heedless clinging to him—mortified her. No, no. It was something else altogether.

Perhaps that he hailed from a completely separate world? He had no ties to anything she knew or had known. They had no acquaintance in common; he had never even been to Winchester. On the contrary, he had lived and traveled throughout England and won the regard (he did not say so, but Beatrice gathered as much from the responsibilities he touched upon) of a wide swath of people, from ditch-diggers to members of Parliament! The fact that he worked with both his mind and his hands did not repulse her, she having one brother-in-law who practiced law and another in medicine, but neither of those professions carried the same hint of *otherness*. Mr. Clayton's work was...new. It hinted at progress and change and an unfamiliar landscape, both literally and figuratively, and Beatrice did not know how she felt about it.

Why, Mr. Clayton's profession was so new that he himself joked it was changing faster than he could predict. "Mark my words," he had said at one point. "Those steam engines which cause me so many headaches when they break down between sections of the work have already improved in the last ten years. I would not be at all surprised if one day we dispensed with canals altogether and merely carried everything we wished along tram-rails."

"Wouldn't you fear being put out of work, then?" Aggie had asked, but he had shaken his head.

"Not in the least. Canals are a means to an end, and if the investors decided it was all to be rails and steam engines tomorrow, I would be ready with a long list of improvements to help them."

That's it, Beatrice thought to herself as she remembered the exchange. *He isn't afraid of change. In fact, he welcomes it.*

Unknown to her, her ruminations were accompanied by changes in color which were not lost upon Aggie. Springing from her own chair, she joined Beatrice on the sofa. "You're shivering, goosy," she chided, putting an arm about her. "I hope you haven't caught a chill. What a day it has been for you! Are you still thinking about this morning?"

"Not if I can help it."

"How fortunate Mr. Clayton was at hand," Aggie said for the thousandth time, to which her husband nodded heartfelt agreement, also for the thousandth time. "But now that he is gone..." Aggie continued after a pause, "I did want to ask you, Bea—do you truly want to learn to swim? Or did we leave you with no choice in the matter? If you don't want to, I will make some excuse for you."

"No—I want to," answered Beatrice, although she wasn't positive it was the whole truth. "Because I *do* want to enjoy the sea and love the sea and not fear it. And I wasn't thinking about this morning just now. That is—I was, but I stopped." She clasped her hands together, her chin lifting. "I was—thinking about Mr. Clayton. What an—unusual person he is."

"Yes!" and "Exactly!" cried her family, though she was too preoccupied to be suspicious at their eagerness.

"I like him very much," declared Aggie. "And not just for saving you, Bea. He is well-mannered and knowledgeable and—and—"

"And well-spoken," Tyrone supplied. "He will greatly enliven our stay here. What fresh perspectives he will have to offer!"

"You mustn't frighten him away, however, Tyrone," warned Aggie.

"Frighten him away? What on earth are you talking about? I am the least frightening person in all England."

"Because I see it in your eye. You plan to urge him to spend afternoons in the coffee house or the library—after he has already been with us in the mornings to swim—and we must not weary him with our company before the first assembly, or he might not ask Bea—and me, of course—to dance."

"Unless I make a positive nuisance of myself, of course he will ask the both of you to dance!" protested her husband. "If he's the assembly-going sort, that is, which I would not lay bets on." But Tyrone knew his wife well enough not to miss the infinitesimal press of her lips, which said as clearly as if she had spoken, *We had better hush now, or we will give the game away! I have already said too much.* Indeed, every Ellsworth knew how easily Beatrice found reasons to resist matchmaking efforts. For her even to mention this John Clayton of her own free will was too miraculous and delicate a sign to handle roughly.

Therefore, though for once Beatrice might have been glad to have the subject prolonged, her relations abruptly dropped it.

"We had probably better go to bed," Aggie declared. "Especially if we are to have our first swim lesson tomorrow."

CHAPTER FOUR

**People in such Circumstances, where one
Thing leads to another, are unavoidably driven
far beyond their first Intentions.**
**— Anonymous, *An Inquiry into the Fitness of Attend-
ing Parliament* (1739)**

It would be a lie to say she was not scared.

Once again, Beatrice stood on the shore, this time wrapped in a thick woolen shawl beside Aggie while her brother and Mr. Clayton debated the best place to hold the lesson. While most bathers congregated east of the hotel, Tyrone pressed for a different site.

"If we were to go below the rocks," he suggested, pointing, "we would be assured greater privacy, and the waves there are somewhat dampened. It's a little ways, but surely we can convince one of the dippers to tow his bathing machine over there, that we might have somewhere to change afterward."

"Capital idea," agreed Clayton, and the next instant Tyrone was off to secure one.

Beatrice saw Mr. Clayton's head turn in her direction, and she hastened to smooth her brow. Her sleep had not been very sound the night before—she had even once dreamed herself back in the water, tugging to free her gown, only to wake panting with relief. But when the morning light crept through the gaps in the shutters, she arose determined to conquer her fear. It rather helped knowing that Mr. Clayton would be present, for while Beatrice might give way to tears or reluctance with only family about her, the presence of a stranger would spur her to courage—or at least the appearance of it.

"Capital," she echoed with assumed heartiness. Too hearty, perhaps, for Aggie threw her a skeptical look which Beatrice pretended not to see. Pulling her shawl tighter, she followed the men down the beach, the horse and bathing machine Tyrone had appropriated creaking and bumping after them. Mr. Clayton was not quite so tall as her brother, but his leaner person added to his appearance of height. And though she could not see the lines of his upper body clearly, for he wore a loose shirt over his breeches this morning to bathe, it seemed her imagination had no need for specifics. She remembered all too vividly the firmness of his chest pressing against her own and the strength of his arms, sweeping her to the surface—

"What first?" asked Aggie, when they reached the designated rocks, and the party had stowed their hats, bonnets and other accoutrements out of harm's way. She danced a little in the light breeze to keep warm.

"We'll be methodical about this," Tyrone said, his brow stern. (Beatrice was not the only one who had slept fitfully. Her brother had devoted considerable thought to how the "lessons" he received in the Cherwell at Oxford might be adapted to both ladies and the sea.) Waving them toward the water, he led them to where it lapped icily at their ankles. "The first step this morning will be to overcome any uneasiness about putting our faces in the water. Too many people try to swim whilst keeping their heads dry and entirely above the surface, which, besides making things more difficult, is nearly impossible in the waves. Swimming requires getting wet, so the sooner we accept that, the better off we will be." When his pupils nodded dutifully, he gave a satisfied clap. "Good. So what do you say we go out a little farther and take hands four, as if we were at an assembly? Then we will just dip our faces in for a count of five."

"Is this how you learned at New College?" his wife laughed, snatching up Bea's hand at once.

"No," he conceded, taking Bea's other. "At New College they tossed me in without warning. But *there* one was more likely to be clubbed with a punt pole or tangled in the reeds than to drown, so I have made some adjustments. With your permission, Clayton…"

The foursome did as instructed, forming a ring, as if in a ballroom intending to turn in circle. Slowly, Tyrone led them out until they were immersed to their hips. Feeling the strength of the surf pushing her about, Beatrice gritted her teeth. *Courage.*

Even as she exhorted herself, her eyes lifted to Mr. Clayton's across from her, and the reassuring nod and half-smile he gave her warmed her. Yes. *Courage.*

"All right," commanded Tyrone. "I'll give a squeeze when it's time to come back up, and Bea, you pass it along to Aggie. Are we ready? Yes? Then—stand firm to the scratch—and *now!*"

Screwing her eyes shut, Beatrice took a breath and thrust her face beneath the waves. Almost before she could do more than register the cold shock, Tyrone was pressing her hand, and she was pressing Aggie's and raising her head again, sputtering at the rivulets streaming down and declaring through coughs, "Why, that wasn't so bad!"

Better still were the second and third and fourth and fifth duckings, each lasting a little longer than the one before.

"What next? What next?" cried Bea after the last assay, when she succeeded in cracking open her eyelids underwater after a few seconds.

"This time when we go under, try to expel some air through your nose. *Don't* breathe in, for obvious reasons. Just try to breathe *out.*"

This was harder. All three of the learners managed to get water up their noses and had to cough and sputter and snort it out, which made them laugh in discomfort, leading to more snorting.

"Out!" insisted Tyrone. "Blow out, don't inhale. Pretend you're blowing your nose into a handkerchief."

At last it was accomplished, more or less, and their laughter changed from embarrassment to enjoyment, so they soon clamored to try more.

"All right, all right," Tyrone said, chuckling himself. "If that is not enough, next you will hold your breath just like that, but you will lift your feet up at the same time and let me support you. Don't do a thing otherwise. Don't kick or thrash. Just hold your breath and you'll find you might float. I'll take you one at a time, of course, lest the whole lot of us go drifting off to Le Havre. You first, Clayton?"

It was the most thrilling morning Beatrice could recall. She thought she might be shy of her bathing gown clinging to her while the others looked on (certainly Mr. Clayton's shirt stuck to him like a transparent second skin), but the triumph of floating conquered even her innate modesty. At first she gripped her brother's arm where it held up her midsection till he gave a mock yelp, but clutching him made it harder to balance, and she gradually loosened her hold as she grew to trust the sensation, until she released him altogether.

"Brava! Brava, Beatrice!" crowed her sister-in-law, when Beatrice stood up again, pushing her dripping hair from her brow. "Isn't this marvelous?"

"Floating is halfway to swimming," Tyrone assured them. But when Aggie begged, "Can't we go the rest of the way, then, and start to swim?" he shook his head. "Tomorrow. And the day after and the day after. Not that you have to join us, if you don't like, Clayton, but the repetition will do the trick."

"I wouldn't miss it," the young man replied, wringing out the hem of his shirt and giving his dark hair a dog-like shake. "I don't know when I've enjoyed myself more and suspect I'll be good for nothing the rest of the day, despite the mountain of correspondence I must deal with."

"Then come with me to the coffee house this afternoon," suggested Tyrone, "if you've made a respectable amount of progress. I'll knock on Number Five when I go."

"I'd like that. Thank you."

When they donned dry clothing again, the group trudged up the beach, laughing and chattering, damp clothing bundled beneath their arms. At the subscription room they parted, Clayton heading back up to Spencer Terrace while the Ellsworths chose to visit the hotel for a cup of chocolate.

"What if we were to go to the warm sea-water baths now?" Beatrice asked, cradling her cup in her hands to warm them. "I might practice putting my face in again."

"Better not," said Aggie. "I suspect they replace the water only once per day in those warm baths."

"Don't want to overdo it," agreed Tyrone.

Beatrice sighed happily. "Tyrone, you were too, too wonderful! I cannot wait for tomorrow. And how very glad I am Mr. Clayton did not approve of the cotton-wool strategy. I confess I was afraid before we began this morning, but now I feel I could climb a mountain!"

"Indeed," Aggie seconded her. "The cotton-wool idea was too cautious of us by half, Tyrone. I only hope we are not being too demanding of Mr. Clayton's time. He seemed to delight in the lesson as much as we did, but perhaps when he returns to his piles of work, he will regret promising to come tomorrow. It is too easy,

I suppose, to go from expressing our gratitude to making nuisances of ourselves."

"I will sound him this afternoon," her husband assured her. "If he refuses to come out or shows other signs of reluctance, then we will by all means desist. Or, at least, we will mitigate our zeal somewhat."

Beatrice bit her lip. And it must have been the morning's triumphs which drew the next words from her, for as Tyrone and Aggie discussed later in private, they were not at all in her nature.

"I should be very sorry if we were forced to draw back," she admitted. "Not only because he saved my life but because—he is good company and—and I like him very well."

As Clayton made his slow way up the High Street, a frown marred his features, one which had nothing to do with fatigue or the quickening breeze in his damp hair. It was not that he had not enjoyed himself as much as the Ellsworths supposed. On the contrary, it was precisely because he had enjoyed himself so thoroughly that he was troubled.

While the Ellsworths' gratitude justified their initial invitation to supper, and while his own suggestion that Miss Ellsworth learn to swim might have obligated them to include him in the lesson, anything and everything beyond that could only stem from their sincere desire to foster a friendship. A desire he found he shared, heaven help him. Indeed, he could think of nothing he would like better than to spend more time with the agreeable family.

Come, man, be honest.

He paused to let a carriage rattle by before crossing Upper Bognor Street.

Be honest.

Very well—the question he asked himself was, would he have any lingering misgivings about the budding connection, if Miss Ellsworth were not involved? He had thought they would disdain his work—they did not. And if the Ellsworths had no qualms about his profession, he had no further objections to raise, except—except that the existence of Miss Ellsworth complicated matters.

The existence of Miss Ellsworth—ay, there was the rub.

Confident as John Clayton was in his work, that assurance was confined to work sites and board rooms, machinery and parliamentary machinations. There had never been any call to judge himself as a man in relation to young ladies. He had been constantly occupied from the age of fourteen, and then before he had the leisure to turn his thoughts to the fair sex, the whole matter of attraction, love, and marriage was arranged for him. He gave his word to Donald Brand and within the week had plighted his troth to Brand's daughter Priscilla. That done, he returned to his work with a sigh, just as Priscilla returned to school and the care of Miss Croy. Over two years passed in which, if he thought of his intended, he did so as if she were a task to be completed, the time set for its accomplishment drawing ever nearer. To be sure, he had seen her briefly at holidays, but the recent completion of the Worcester and Birmingham Canal had kept him far away. Indeed, when he returned to London to begin work on the Cumberland Arm, it would be the first time in their engagement that he and Miss Brand lived near enough to each other for regular visits, she and Miss Croy having removed to town after Miss Brand finished school.

What sort of time was this, then, for doubts?

If he thought to himself that Miss Ellsworth was a charming young lady whom he would like to know better, what difference could that possibly make? And how much of that opinion could be attributed to the extraordinary circumstances which threw them together?

He was overthinking this.

Clearly his own personal desire could never come to anything, so did it therefore require him to drop the Ellsworths' acquaintance altogether? Could he not instead secretly, quietly, indulge himself, just this once? Explore what it meant, to find a young lady winsome and her company stimulating? Who knew but that, once these interests were awakened in him, he might meet Miss Brand again and see her with new eyes?

Clayton did not suppose Miss Ellsworth's heart would be in any danger. She, who had borne the attentions of however many far more eligible and appropriate Winchester men, would not be threatened by a mere engineer of no family or fortune, encountered at a seaside resort.

Having thus convinced himself and temporarily quashed his uneasiness, he climbed the steps of Number Five with a lighter heart, his mind already turning to the correspondence he would deal with once he was clean, dry, and dressed.

Precisely at three o'clock a knock was heard, and Tyrone Ellsworth was admitted by Molly. Before she could lead him up the stairs, however, Clayton was already descending.

"This is a good sign," declared Tyrone with a bow, "unless you were hoping to make your escape before I saw you."

"Nothing of the kind. I have answered the most pressing letters, and the rest can wait a few hours. I am at your disposal, Ellsworth. Let us see this library you boast of."

Amicably they set off down Upper Bognor Street, falling into easy conversation.

"I rejoice to see the morning's lessons did not weary you over-much, Clayton."

"Then you should have seen me clinging to my desk to stay up-right," he joked. "For that was more exertion than I have experienced in a fortnight."

"Gracious," returned Tyrone. "Then let us pray this little jaunt does not finish you. From your talk at supper I would have classified you as the active sort."

"So I am, ordinarily. But I am here in Bognor as a respite for my health, and it has answered well."

"Your health!" Tyrone glanced at his companion's lithe but sturdy frame. "What ailed you? Were you buried under a barrow-load of earth, or did some scaffolding collapse on you?"

"Neither, though a half-hour would fix the former and a half-year might not mend the latter," Clayton answered. Having reached the Crescent, they paused to admire the view before turning down the High Street. "It was a lingering cough from my work up in

Worcester. The doctor months ago counseled rest and sea-bathing, but there simply wasn't time for it until the project was complete. And then it turns out rest alone was enough, for I found myself fully recovered in body, mind and spirit before I even set foot in the sea. I am recovered and ready to throw myself into the next thing."

"Which is...?"

"Which is the Cumberland Arm of the Regent's Canal. We aim to break ground as soon as I return to town." John held up crossed fingers as he said so. "Though I should know by now never to count my chickens."

"Optimism, my good man!" urged Tyrone, clapping him by the shoulder. "Though now that you are indeed hale and hearty, must we lose your company so soon?"

"I have set no fixed date as yet for my return, and now..."

"And now, how can you?" supplied his companion, grinning. "For today you will subscribe to the circulating library, if I have anything to say about it. Nor could you depart before you have learned to swim. And thirdly, I freely confess my wife has hopes you will stay for an assembly or two, so that she and Beatrice will not be reduced to fighting over me as their sole partner."

A carriage emerged from the square behind the East-row houses, and Clayton glanced past it to the obelisk beyond, apprehension pricking him again. "I daresay if I left Bognor, *somebody* could be prevailed upon to dance with Mrs. and Miss Ellsworth besides you."

"I should have been more specific," said Tyrone. "I mean to say I might be their sole partner below the age of fifty. For, I do not know how you selected Bognor as your medicinal bathing place of choice—we are here because Aggie's mother praised it *relentless-ly*—but in this season it could hardly be called over-peopled with the young and fashionable. Consider the hotel," he continued, gesturing at the commodious building they approached. "In season this place is crowded to bursting, but it's sedate enough now."

He no sooner spoke than a pair of bent and balding gentlemen emerged, one leaning upon the other's arm, to shuffle across the gravel path.

"You see?" murmured Tyrone, lips twitching.

But Clayton did not respond to the jest. He frowned, and he felt again that awkwardness, that awareness that he did not hail from the same world as the Ellsworths, despite their friendly overtures. Stopping abruptly, he forced Tyrone to halt in turn and retrace his steps.

"What?"

"Look here, Ellsworth," he said, his throat tightening. "I had better say this now: I have no intention of attending any assemblies."

Tyrone blinked at him, aware of his own secret dismay. Had he been too pushing? Heavens, he had. Now Clayton thought they were trying to ensnare him on Bea's behalf, which, if not *true* was not altogether *un*true. But how could they be blamed for making the attempt, when Beatrice never showed the slightest interest in anyone marriageable? One thing was certain, however—Aggie would be disgusted with him for botching the work before it had well begun.

"All right, then," Tyrone replied, striving for nonchalance. "You're a busy man. Of course we don't mean to claim all of your time."

"It's not that." Clayton scowled past his shoulder at the glittering surf. "It's that...well...I don't really know much about it. Dancing, that is. I'm no proficient, I mean to say. I've had a lesson here or there, but I've never had a dancing master or any such thing."

"Oh! Is that all?"

Tyrone's relief was obvious, and his companion's mouth twisted grimly. "Yes. I suppose it doesn't sound like much to you, but I fear I would be uncomfortable and not any better service to the young ladies than those codgers who just shuffled past. I'd be worse, in fact, for at least they would know where to stand and in which direction to go, even if they couldn't get there in time."

"But—but—Clayton, hear me out." Tyrone looped an arm through his and dragged him in the direction of the hotel garden, which was still green at this time of year if no longer flowering. "It's a pretty dangerous admission to make, you know, to say you can't dance. Because we Ellsworths live to dance. And if Aggie and Bea heard you chose to deprive yourself of such a pleasure, they would grieve for your loss." He hesitated, debating whether he should "push" again.

"Oh, Lord," groaned Clayton, almost chuckling in spite of himself. "You're about to offer to teach me, aren't you?"

"It crossed my mind," confessed Tyrone, and then he did laugh. "We've already seen each other dripping and draggled—why not neat and tripping across the floor of Number Four, Spencer Terrace? If I don't ask you, my wife will demand to know why I didn't. And look—you will thank us, one day. If you're having to associate with lords and MPs, as well as lowly diggers and puddlers, you had better learn how to comport yourself in a ballroom. Come tonight. After supper, say, to kill an hour before bedtime. It's nothing, man! We haven't been able to dance since we arrived, there being only three of us. It would be such a treat for us all because otherwise my dear family will have to listen to another chapter of whichever book I have to hand, and last night I could already see I was losing their attention."

CHAPTER FIVE

**Our young Englishman swam willingly
down the stream of pleasure.**
— Henry Brooke, *The fool of quality* (1776)

To the outward eye, Miss Beatrice Ellsworth appeared perfectly serene. She sat in what had become her favorite armchair, a blue brocade with wide arms, near enough to the fireplace that she could prop her feet on the fender as she sewed, and it was needlework which occupied her now. The Ellsworth ladies had spent the afternoon on a walk in the direction of Yapton, pulling little Joan and Margaret in their cart and pleasantly exhausting the entire party. Afterward the nursemaid took the girls away, leaving Beatrice to her work and Aggie to loll at the desk, talking of what she would write to her dear friend and sister-in-law Araminta Carlisle rather than actually writing anything.

"...Wouldn't you say?" chuckled Aggie.

Beatrice blinked, having not been attending. "To be sure," she ventured in reply. But she bowed her head to hide a blush. In truth, she had been thinking again of Mr. Clayton and wondering if he had been free to join Tyrone or if he still sat in the next house, working away.

Aggie ran the feather of her pen through her fingers. She had noted Beatrice's abstraction but had not the least idea if it stemmed from her terrible bathing accident or something altogether more pleasant. Not for the first time did she wish her mother-in-law Mrs. Wolfe were present. Beatrice had never been the sort of young lady who shared confidences freely, but the few times she did, it was invariably with Mrs. Wolfe.

To the mutual relief of the ladies, the door opened to admit Tyrone. Beatrice straightened and resumed her stitching, but Aggie tossed her pen aside.

"Well?" she asked, when he had kissed her cheek in salute, asked after their daughters, and heard her account of the day. "So much for our afternoon. How was yours? Did Mr. Clayton join you?"

"He did. A most agreeable fellow. And though he called himself 'unlettered,' he had read a number of the offerings at the circulating library and had sensible things to say about them."

"I can't think when he would have managed it," Aggie replied, "if he's always working."

Tyrone shrugged. "One can't work 'round the clock, and I suspect that, when he has not been toiling away, he has been somewhat solitary."

"That makes sense. Who would he know in Worcester, after all, if that was where his most recent project took him?"

Throwing himself on the sofa and peeling off his gloves, Tyrone said with elaborate nonchalance, "I hope you don't mind, but I invited him to come this evening after supper."

Neither he nor Aggie missed Beatrice's head snapping up, though both were careful not to look at her.

"Because," he continued, "I mentioned the assemblies in the Subscription Room, and Clayton said no, thank you, he had no intention of doing any dancing while in Bognor."

"No dancing!" cried Aggie, as if Mr. Clayton had politely declined breathing.

Beatrice had removed her feet from the fender and turned fully to face her brother, though still she said nothing.

"Exactly," resumed Tyrone. "You understand my astonishment. Of course I pressed him on the matter, and he explained it was because he lacked the proper training. Ah ah ah—" He held up a playful hand to forestall his wife's interruption. "So I said that was all nonsense, of course, and we would gladly practice with him until he felt comfortable."

"Well, to be sure we will!"

"Moreover, I added that he would be doing us a favor to accept our tutelage, or you two would be begging for partners. The offer was made purely from self-interest, I told him."

"And has he agreed to come?"

"He has. At eight o'clock."

Daringly, Aggie said, "I like that. I mean, I like a person who isn't ashamed to admit his shortcomings and...seek to remedy them."

Tyrone made no response, thinking his wife in danger of overshooting the mark, so a silence followed, broken eventually by Beatrice herself.

"There will be no one to accompany us," she observed.

"Pooh," said Aggie, "you or I can play the tune once or twice through, and then we will hum it."

Punctual as before, Mr. Clayton was shown in by Pidgeley before the clock sounded its last chime. Beatrice's pulse quickened as she made her curtsey, and she kept two fingers on the back of the blue chair to prevent any obvious trembling. She could hardly account for herself. She had met dozens of gentlemen before—young, old, rich, poor, handsome, plain, intelligent, doltish—why should this particular one be different? And he *was* different. It must be because of the circumstances under which they met. Though if it had been, say, Pidgeley who pulled her from the Channel, would she have felt this same fluttering in her midsection whenever the footman appeared?

Surely I would, she told herself, not altogether convincingly.

Very well, then, she conceded. It was not the rescue alone which made Mr. Clayton interesting. But the rescue *must* be a part of it! It had not even been two days since the incident, after all. The further passage of time would undoubtedly conquer any lingering effects.

And then Mr. Clayton will be no different to me than any other young, handsome, intelligent, agreeable man.

For the present he embodied all those qualities, however, and she could only hope no one guessed her inward tumult.

Clapping her hands, Aggie took charge. "Mr. Clayton, I must apologize for the way we seem to be claiming your every minute of rest and recreation. You are kind to indulge us, even to the point of taking up activities you have dispensed with in the past."

He bowed. "No, Mrs. Ellsworth, it is not all altruism on my part. As your husband observed, dancing is a skill I ought not to neglect, however few opportunities I have had before now to participate. I pray you will be patient with me, for it has been quite some time since I made the attempt."

"And we pray you won't mind that we have no accompanist," returned Aggie, seating herself at the instrument and running her fingers lightly over the keys. "I gave this some thought, sir, when Tyrone told us you were coming, for I learned to dance at school, where there were at least a score of us on hand at any time, and Beatrice and Tyrone first learned at home, where there were also plenty of family members to form sets. Therefore I have settled on Rufty Tufty, for it works perfectly well with only two couples, and it includes many of the steps found in other dances. This is what it sounds like, for I'm afraid after this you will simply have to listen to us try to sing it."

While Aggie played, the rest of them moved the furniture and rolled up the carpet, Tyrone already beginning to hum the tune, and then the foursome took their places.

"Will you do me the honor, Mr. Clayton?" Aggie laughed. "Though you will dance almost as much with Beatrice as with me in this one, you do the steps first with your partner, and that will make it easier to order you about."

She was right about the pairs dancing as much with the other couple as together. Indeed, while Aggie stood to Mr. Clayton's right, it was Beatrice opposite him, and when he took Aggie's hand to accompany her forward two steps, it was to Beatrice he made his bow. The same was true for nearly every step and pattern. After siding right with Aggie, he then immediately sided left with Beatrice. For each chorus, he first took Aggie by the hand to lead her outward before turning in place and doing the same with Beatrice.

The difference lay in each lady's response to their shared partner. While Aggie could call the steps and hum and smile and encourage as she danced, Beatrice was not quite mistress of herself. To her mortification she stepped in the wrong direction once, nearly colliding with Mr. Clayton, after which she made matters worse in the next sequence by thrusting her arm forward too vigorously to catch his. As a result, they jostled each other, and Mr. Clayton was obliged to do the polite thing and beg her pardon.

"No, no," she mumbled. "That was my mistake."

Nor had she ever given thought to what a difference wearing gloves made. Of course when the Ellsworths danced at home she wore none, which meant this evening she was barehanded, as was he. But with each light grasp of his, though he neither clutched nor pressed her fingers, she too soon realized that—that she would not mind if he did. Clutch or press her fingers, that was. Each quiet touch only reminded her how firmly he had held her in contrast, when he wrenched her to the surface of the water, her person pressed full length to his.

Heavens. Let me not change color. Let me not change color. Let me not change color. (Sadly, chanting this in her mind had no effect, apart from causing her to change color.)

"You're a perfect genius at it, Clayton," Tyrone declared before long. "You absolutely *must* attend Thursday's assembly with us, or all this talent will be wasted."

"If we were the only four people there and nothing played but Rufty Tufty over and over, world without end, I would do so without hesitation," he answered mildly.

The foursome paused here in their exertions when Fussell rattled in with the tea tray. Seizing upon this excuse, Beatrice sat down to busy herself with preparations. Let Mr. Clayton think—nay, let everyone think—she flushed because of the exercise and the warmth of the hot water.

"Come here, Tyrone," beckoned his wife. "Look at this music and see if there are others which we could try with only four of us." The two were soon engrossed, turning pages while they considered and debated, sometimes picturing the figures in their heads and other times stepping through them together.

After a minute of watching this with nothing to contribute, Clayton took the chair opposite Beatrice.

"How—how do you like your tea?" she asked, determined to stop being a ninny about him. *Treat him as you would any other gentleman of your acquaintance.* "With milk or sugar?"

"Both, please. A generous amount." He took the cup offered to him, nodding at her and taking a sip. "Perfect, Miss Ellsworth. What a treat. Molly, the maid at Number Five, for all her many excellencies, makes a rather disappointing cup of tea."

"Too strong? Too weak? Not enough sugar or milk?"

"Too weak. 'Insipid' might best describe it."

Beatrice smiled. "I will defend your poor maid and say the fault may not lie entirely with her."

"How so?"

"In the first place, you strike me as...someone who does nothing by halves. Strong tea, plenty of milk, plenty of sugar. Perhaps many things you meet with—not just your tea—disappoint you as insipid." She wondered if he classified *her* thus. Miss Ellsworth, the pleasant but weak creature who nearly drowned.

To her surprise, his own color rose. "I suppose I gave you that impression because I was rather high-handed."

"High-handed? When?" she asked, puzzled.

"When I peremptorily recommended you learn to swim," he answered. "Without knowing you at all."

"Mr. Clayton, really! I beg you will not believe that I, knowing you equally as little, would seize this early occasion to criticize your character! I meant my remark as a compliment, rather. You are decisive. In your work, in your leisure, and in your tea."

This drew a genuine smile from him, softening his attractive features, and Beatrice lowered her gaze quickly, adding in a quiet voice, "Besides—I am glad you encouraged me to learn. I can hardly wait for tomorrow's lesson."

"Nor can I. Though I am enjoying this as well."

"See?" she replied. "I would expect as much. You would either love or hate dancing." Rising, she brought Tyrone and Aggie their cups, leaving them on the spinet because Tyrone was now beside his wife on the little bench while she played.

"Did you have another reason you thought I found Molly's tea insipid?" he asked when Beatrice resumed her seat. "You said, 'in the first place…'"

"I did. I thought, if you did not come to Bognor with your own tea, the tea supplied by the owner of Spencer Terrace might not be the very finest."

"Why, you have hit upon it, Miss Ellsworth," he marveled, pointing to the cup in his hand. "*This*, I assume, is not Spencer Terrace Select then, but rather an Ellsworth import?"

"You think we travel with our tea caddy?" she laughed. "No. But we no sooner tried the 'Spencer Terrace Select,' as you call it, than we resorted at once to the tea merchant in the High Street. We will send you home with some, sir."

"But then I will only need more tomorrow," he pointed out. "In which case I will have to return, whether you Ellsworths like it or not. Perhaps it would be better if I paid my own visit to the tea merchant in the High Street after our lesson."

His teasing won a dimpled smile from her. "You must please yourself, but I think it's obvious enough that you might come tomorrow and any day thereafter to resupply."

So much for treating him like any other gentleman of her acquaintance! No sooner were the words spoken than Beatrice heard how flirtatious, how *eager* they sounded, and she shrank back, hiding herself in a long sip of tea. Longer than the little tea remaining in her cup warranted, so that she was doing no more than pretending to drink, the last few seconds.

Fortunately Tyrone and Aggie rescued her by rejoining the pair and bustling about the tea things. (Tyrone had been in no hurry to do so, but Aggie glanced over and saw Beatrice's embarrassment.)

"We have agreed at last, Mr. Clayton," Aggie announced. "Tyrone was all for teaching you one of the longways dances, with him and Beatrice rushing around us, pretending to be a fresh couple each time through the pattern, but I think that might wait. In the meantime we might do Hit and Miss, which is more complicated than Rufty Tufty and would give us practice with changes. What do you say?"

Clayton's gaze flicked to Beatrice. "By all means, let us try Hit and Miss. With two arrows in my quiver, if we can bribe the musicians to play them, I might partner youfor the one, Mrs. Ellsworth, and Miss Ellsworth for the other, and retire with full honors, having done my duty."

"Ah ha!" said Tyrone. "Then you will come to the assembly on Thursday? Never fear, I will see to it that these our favorites are performed, and all Bognor will stand agog in admiration of your prowess."

Clayton shook his head, half amused and half rueful. "Egad. So be it. I will come."

The second lesson proceeded much as the first: Aggie played the music through several times; Aggie placed them and walked them through the figures; Clayton found himself dancing nearly as much with Miss Ellsworth as with Mrs. Ellsworth. While he grasped the patterns and steps even more quickly this time, he was conscious of enjoying himself less. It was not that the Ellsworths or the activity ceased to charm. It was that his mind kept returning to Miss Ellsworth's blush and sudden shyness. Nor did she speak another word that evening, if she could prevent it.

Had he been mistaken in thinking Miss Ellsworth required no protection from him, the humble John Clayton? Only hours before he had told himself such was the case. He had told himself he might dally in the enjoyment of a young lady's company with no danger to her or to others, casting it in the light of an indulgence of his own secret whim. But now—

But now here he stood, thinking he might have been altogether mistaken.

Incredible as it would have seemed even a day ago, John began to believe he was wronging her. Wronging Miss Ellsworth and wronging her family by not declaring himself openly as an engaged man. Because somehow his impetuous rescue of her had been the starting link in a chain of unlikelihoods. Gratitude led to warmth, and warmth led to the Ellsworths' decision to enfold him, to include him in everything, to like him as a person and a friend. And that last step—the fatal one—was inconceivably leading Miss Ellsworth in turn to consider him—as a possible suitor. There was no other word for it. Though he had so little experience with young ladies, and though he could not claim to know Miss Ellsworth well, nevertheless it was hard for him to imagine her smiling and speaking playfully to him out of sheer coquetry. For if coquetry alone moved her, why would she then turn pink and hunch in discomfiture, as if she had done something reprehensible?

One thing was plain. He must either withdraw hereafter from their company—avoid them, even—on some excuse, or he must make his situation known before things went too far. Before Miss Ellsworth's innocent ideas metamorphosed into expectations.

Neither path appealed to him. Now that he had met them and been so welcomed, he hated to think of retreating to the solitude of Number Five, Spencer Terrace, to his piles of correspondence and the cold comfort of work. To meals on a tray and days spent within doors with nobody to talk to but the servants. Not to mention, any withdrawal would require a plausible reason, and here he had already agreed to both the swim lessons and the assembly!

Therefore he must speak. He must make known Priscilla's existence.

But how to go about it? He could hardly say, "See here, you Ellsworths, it's clear I've charmed the lot of you, to the point that the beautiful, wealthy, educated, well-connected Miss Ellsworth has set her cap for me. Therefore, I'd better just nip all that in the bud by informing you of my pre-existing engagement." Heavens!

It got worse.

Even if gentler, subtler words could be found, Clayton realized he did not want to speak them. He *wanted* to go on as they were, it seemed. Most reprehensible. If Miss Ellsworth had continued indifferent to him, that would have been another matter. Then they could all have gone on and on, but now—now he could not excuse himself from trying to set things right.

He would tell Tyrone, he decided, even as he took hands with each of the foursome to step through the changes. The next time he and Ellsworth were alone and conversing. At the coffee house or the library. Then let Ellsworth tell his wife and sister. They would be surprised and, perhaps, disappointed, but it would all be got over and hidden away before they saw him next.

Failing that, he would have to seize upon another opportunity to talk about his work or the role Donald Brand played in his life, saying with as much ease as he could manage, "Yes, yes, he was the most important figure to me, and my connection to him continues, you understand, for I am engaged to marry his daughter." Picturing the ladies' reactions made him twitch uneasily just as he was taking Beatrice's hand to pass in change. At the movement, her clear hazel eyes met his, and a charge of another kind flew from fingertip to fingertip.

Tomorrow, John vowed. *I will say all tomorrow.*

Because heaven help me if I don't.

CHAPTER SIX

That's a day longer than a wonder lasts.
— Shakespeare, *Henry VI, Part III,* III.ii.1601 (1591)

She might have gone farther, but Beatrice was so elated after taking her first completely independent strokes that she stood up in the surf exclaiming, "Did you see that? Did you see that?"

But it was Mr. Clayton she surfaced in front of, not Tyrone. "Goodness me," she laughed, when she pushed her streaming hair from her eyes and realized her mistake. "I thought you were my brother. I did not mean to shout at you."

"I don't mind a bit," he replied, running a hand through his own dripping locks. "I saw your last couple strokes. You were doing it, Miss Ellsworth—you were swimming!"

"Yes!" Clapping her hands and hopping with a splash, she sang, "I was swimming! All by myself." Catching sight of Tyrone she added,

"Botheration! He had his back to me and didn't see a thing. I might have drowned, for all he knew."

But her annoyance was fleeting because she was too pleased with herself, and when she smiled again, eyes twinkling, Clayton heard himself say, "I would never have let you. Drown, that is."

"Oh." She lowered her eyes to the water, dragging her fingers through the floating foam. "Thank you. I know you wouldn't."

Inwardly he groaned. What was he doing, saying such things, and with such earnestness? After the previous night's vow that he would make a clean breast of it and confess the existence of Priscilla Brand? (Not that he could do so now, though, while he and Miss Ellsworth stood in the Channel wet to the skin.)

To cover their mutual embarrassment, Clayton said, "I still haven't got the timing of the kick right. I sink like a stone between each pull of the arms. Nevertheless, with regrettable masculine overweening, I hereby challenge you to a race, Miss Ellsworth. To the shore. I'll even give you the start of m—"

Before he could complete his offer, she was off with a splash, and he shut up at once to throw himself in after her. Truth be told, they were both such beginners that a skilled child could have beaten either of them, Clayton's timing being as clumsy as he claimed, and Beatrice so eager to win that she flailed in place nearly as much as she propelled herself forward. Fortunately they were so near shore that both could stand when they ran out of breath, to laugh and stumble from the water.

The clouds were beginning to thin and the October sun to filter through, but they hurried to wring what water they could from their bathing attire before taking it in turns to change in the bathing machine's shelter.

Clayton emerged to find Beatrice wound in a shawl and peering out to sea. She raised a hand to wave back at Tyrone and Aggie, who showed no signs yet of wanting to be done.

"That Mrs. Ellsworth puts us both to shame," he observed. "Look at her go. If she and your brother were to race, she might even beat him."

"I'm not the least bit surprised," agreed Beatrice, willing her teeth not to chatter. "For she and my sister Araminta were always such tomboys. They excelled at every sport they tried, growing up. Wait till Minta hears Aggie has learned to swim, or even that I have, after a fashion. She'll be consumed by envy!"

"Perhaps your sister could be lured to Bognor herself."

"I doubt it. She likes to be wherever her husband Mr. Carlisle is, and Nicholas is a doctor and works as hard as ever you do, Mr. Clayton. But patients aren't like projects—there never seems to be a predictable gap when everyone is well or not having babies. I'm afraid Minta will just have to stay envious." There was a moment's pause before she ventured, "And—you? Have you brothers or sisters, Mr. Clayton?"

"Not a one, sadly. Which means therefore that I also lack any sisters' husbands or brothers' wives who might eat their hearts out with envy at my new skills."

"Oh, no! Then must your swimming go altogether unadmired?"

An unengaged man might have made the flirtatious reply, "Only if *you* will not admire it, Miss Ellsworth." But alas, Clayton was not an unengaged man.

No. And here they were, again, within a heartbeat of his necessary confession.

He could not and should not hide the fact any longer, he determined, his hands gathering in fists. Not when, with each passing minute, he was more tempted to do just that. It was precisely because the temptation grew that he must speak.

Therefore he swallowed, feeling his heart quicken. "But you must not think my myriad virtues have gone unnoticed," he began, striving for a teasing tone, "though I have been alone in the world in regard to family. As I mentioned, at the age of fourteen I was apprenticed to Mr. Donald Brand, the best of men and as willing as any fond father to admire and praise."

"I am so sorry for his death, then," murmured Beatrice, her heart a little wrung to think of so kind and agreeable a person as Mr. Clayton losing his dear mentor and closest companion. What did that make him now, if not alone? "I declare—it makes me glad, then," she continued, "that we might all be friends. You and we Ellsworths, I mean. Not that it wouldn't be the case—that we wouldn't like you, that is—if you had twenty brothers and sisters and as many more brothers' and sisters' spouses." Aware that she was starting to babble, she gave way to her chattering teeth and busied herself with winding her shawl tighter.

Now, thought Clayton. *Blast it, man, you must speak* now.

But he delayed one more delicious moment, taking up a second shawl and assisting Miss Ellsworth to wrap herself in it. From the corner of his eye he saw Tyrone Ellsworth extend a hand to his wife, that they might make their way in toward the shore.

Now now now. It must be now.

"Miss Ellsworth," he blurted, "I have been glad to meet with—your family as well. One can never have too many friends. But—er—while it is true that I have no family members beyond a distant cousin or two, and while it is also true that it has been some years since I lost Mr. Brand, he—Mr. Brand, I mean—er—left me with a still closer tie."

She tilted her head, waiting to hear more and clearly with no idea what he was hinting at. Clayton clenched his jaw, fighting teeth-chattering of his own, or some combination of teeth-chattering and dread. But he could hear the other Ellsworths joking with each other now as they drew nearer, and if he didn't hurry, he would have to begin all over again or wait for another opening.

"He left me his daughter."

Her brow puckered. "You—are responsible for a child? You are a guardian?"

"I—yes, she is legally my ward—"

"Why, that's splendid!" She turned to her brother and sister-in-law as they clambered up. "Isn't it cold? Here, let me help you into dry clothing, Aggie."

As he feared, the subject was lost again in the hubbub of everyone going in and out of the bathing machine and wrapping themselves for warmth, and Tyrone paying off the dipper, and all the Ellsworths questioning and congratulating each other on the morning's triumphs, but when the party at last regained the gravel paths, he was both relieved and filled with trepidation to hear Miss Ellsworth say, "Before you and Aggie joined us, Tyrone, Mr. Clayton was just telling me that he is the guardian of a child! The daughter of the man who apprenticed him."

"A child!"

"Brand's daughter, you say? Why, that's capital, Clayton!" said Tyrone. "How old is your charge?"

"That's just what I've been trying to say," he replied, giving a short, wry laugh in spite of everything. "It happens that my—ward—Miss Brand—is no longer a child. She was eighteen in April. And—she is not only my ward, she is—that is—I mean to say—Miss Brand and I are engaged to be married."

He avoided looking at Miss Ellsworth as he announced this, whether from a desire to protect her feelings or to spare himself, he could not say. In fact, he didn't look directly at any of them, instead fiddling with the corners of the blanket enfolding him. But he could not help noticing that his companions' progress halted abruptly alongside him (though they just as quickly stumbled forward again). Nor could he stop his ears from hearing the chorus of gasps, both sharp and soft. Ellsworth was obliged to feign a cough, a loud one requiring the self-administration of several violent thumps to his chest.

"Goodness," said Aggie, her voice higher than usual but steady. "We had better get you some hot tea for that cough, Tyrone, the moment we reach home. But—engaged you say, Mr. Clayton?

How—how—what very good news, to be sure. We wish you and Miss Brand every happiness."

"Every happiness," echoed Miss Ellsworth, fainter.

Despite each of them wondering desperately how it might be conquered, an uncomfortable silence fell as they came in sight of the Chapel House, and it lasted until the elegant building with its many-arched façade and spacious grounds receded behind them.

"We congratulate you," put in Tyrone then, too loudly. He clapped a hearty hand on Clayton's back. "Yes. We congratulate you. How—fortunate for you both. You and—and Miss Brand. When is the happy day, if I might ask?"

"We have not yet fixed one," answered Clayton, conscious of a cloud of misery settling upon him. "Miss Brand has just completed her education, and I have been in Worcester until recently, as you know. Then, when she and her cousin Miss Croy were considering a removal to London to take up residence, I had this touch of ill health and was ordered by the doctor to Bognor. Or, rather, one doctor recommended Bath, while the other was for Bognor." He heard himself launch into the little story with more enthusiasm than it deserved. "They got in quite the tussle about it. Mr. Yount saying what I needed was to take the waters. 'Minerals, my good man! You are short of minerals!' While Mr. Hodgkiss said nonsense—all I needed was a few weeks' reprieve from standing at all hours in the rain beside ditches, and for that purpose any place might do, from Blackpool to Bognor."

"And so you chose Bognor." Miss Ellsworth seemed to speak more to herself than to him as they turned before the Dome House.

It was not a remark requiring a response, and no one made one, though her muted voice made him want to writhe.

How gladly he would have excused himself so the Ellsworths could discuss (or curse) him in peace, but being next-door neighbors, escape was impossible. They trudged onward, Spencer Terrace never seeming farther away, each revolving in his mind what to say next. Aggie's hand on her husband's arm squeezed it significantly, and they had been married long enough for Tyrone to have no difficulty understanding her. Would Mr. Clayton still want to swim and dance with them? And, if he did, ought they still to encourage the friendship? It was clear enough that poor Bea was disappointed by the morning's revelations, and had her brother and sister not worsened the matter by throwing the two together?

He laid his own hand across hers, returning the pressure. Yes, yes, he felt the same. What a disaster. The very first person Beatrice should ever show any interest in—to be already engaged! Had there been any way to prevent such a calamity? Should Mr. Clayton have said something sooner? Should they have asked?

Both Tyrone and Aggie peeped at her, but Beatrice determinedly looked straight ahead, her bonnet brim wide enough to shield her from study. Mr. Clayton himself the Ellsworths dared not look at, for fear their chagrin would be too plain on their faces.

To the momentary relief of all, however, a distraction soon claimed their attention: there was a cart drawn up before Spencer Terrace, from which luggage was being unloaded.

"Mr. Clayton!"

Before Clayton could register what was what, a young lady was flying toward him, one hand clutching her bonnet to her head and the other outstretched—dear God—as if she were a catchpoll and he the unfortunate debtor. And like a debtor, he had the same urge to flee.

"Oh, Mr. Clayton!" she cried, scrambling to a halt before him—before all of them. "Isn't this a surprise? I hope you won't be angry, but Cissy and I could wait no longer. We had to see with our own eyes that you were improved. And I see you are. Isn't he, Cissy?" This last was thrown over her shoulder at the older woman hastening after her.

"Miss Brand," croaked Clayton, bowing like a beam under too heavy a weight. "And Miss Croy. What an—unexpected pleasure."

"It need not have been," Miss Brand answered, now hesitant. "If you were a more regular correspondent, I would have written to you for your permission, knowing I would receive an answer with the return post. But alas. Will you not introduce me to your friends?"

Those friends were still recovering from these successive blows. First to learn of Miss Brand's existence and—worse—Clayton's obligation to her, and now, within the same hour, to come face to face with the young lady herself! But despite her unhappiness, a small part of Beatrice's mind nevertheless noted the curious piece of information: "if he were a more regular correspondent"? What an accusation to level, when Mr. Clayton did nothing from dawn to dusk but correspond.

"Of course," Clayton replied. If it was an effort to master himself, he hid it well. "Miss Brand, I have the honor of introducing to you my neighbors here in Bognor: Mr. and Mrs. Tyrone Ellsworth and Miss Ellsworth. Ellsworths, may I present my—betrothed, Miss Priscilla Brand, and her cousin Miss Croy."

Proper acknowledgements followed, but it would be hard to say who was more curious to meet the other. In Miss Brand the Ellsworths saw a small, trim person with curling red-blonde hair and round blue eyes. Kittenish and sweet, without being precisely pretty, though these qualities combined with the freshness of youth served much the same purpose, especially in comparison to her companion Miss Croy, an older woman devoid of rosiness or pleasing plumpness, as if there had only been enough of these items for one person, and Miss Brand had taken it all.

It was Aggie who rose to the occasion. Seeing the shock Beatrice had received and desiring to hide it, she wound an arm through that of her sister-in-law and said, "Miss Brand, Miss Croy, for Mr. Clayton's sake, how delighted we are that you have come. We have been his next-door neighbors this past fortnight and think him too good a person to hide away from the world, always working working working. Now that you are here, he will have close friends to keep him company. And we hope we will—see much of you—if you intend on staying for any length of time."

"Thank you, Mrs. Ellsworth," responded Miss Brand eagerly. She favored her betrothed with a glance both hopeful and uncertain. "I hope Miss Croy and I will stay in Bognor as long as Mr. Clayton does."

"We will leave you, then," said Aggie. "You must be weary from your journey and will have much to discuss, I'm certain. Good day to you all." Then, with as unobtrusive a pressure as she could manage, she succeeded in nudging Beatrice into motion, and the Ellsworths made their measured retreat to Number Four.

Clayton watched them go, his mind awhirl with thoughts and feelings which would take an hour's peace to disentangle, but there was no time for that now. He looked down at his intended bride, who stood biting her plump lower lip and regarding him with doubt.

"You aren't angry, are you, Mr. Clayton?" she asked timidly. "Cissy was of half a mind that we should wait until you gave us leave to come, though we were so anxious to see for ourselves that you were restored to health."

"Yes," spoke up Miss Croy. "I said, despite the two of you being engaged, we had better not simply turn up on your doorstep, you being such an exceedingly busy man..."

"Of course I'm not angry," Clayton answered. Which was true—anger did not seem to be part of the moil. There was dismay and embarrassment—but not anger. He had made his confession to the Ellsworths, after all (in the nick of time), with who knew what effect. Miss Brand's arrival merely brought to an abrupt close a strange, stimulating, delightful interlude unlike any he had known before.

That was all.

"I promise we won't bother you a bit!" cried Miss Brand, extending a beseeching hand toward him. "We will be quiet as mice while you work, and you need not entertain us." Though at this her head turned in the direction of the Ellsworths' door.

"We were returning from a morning bathe," Clayton heard himself explain. "I *have* been doing that much. It would hardly do to come to Bognor without bathing."

"Of course it wouldn't," Miss Brand agreed at once. "I'm so glad you have. It has done wonders. I think you are in the pink of health. Perhaps—you wouldn't mind if Miss Croy and I joined you when you went next?"

"By all means, by all means." But even as he said it he felt his heart sink further. Would this mean no more swimming with the Ellsworths—with Miss Ellsworth?

Fool.

That is exactly what it means.

"Come," he said, more heartily. He gestured at the steps to Number Five. "What unpardonable rudeness, to keep you out here in the chill. Shall we go inside?"

CHAPTER SEVEN

So times are changed to and fro,
and chaunging times have chaunged us too.
— **Gervase Babington,** *A very fruitfull exposition of*
the Commaundements **(1583)**

Pidgeley was given two letters to post that afternoon: one from
Tyrone to his twin sister Araminta (with additional contri-
butions and margin notes supplied by Aggie), and the other from
Beatrice to her stepmama Mrs. Wolfe.

"So you wrote to dear Mrs. Wolfe, did you?" began Aggie at
dinner, between sips of her fish soup. "We must write to her as well,
Tyrone, since she and Mr. Wolfe are in Kent and will not be able to
read the letter you sent to Minta."

"Indeed," he replied. "Though I suppose Bea's letter will serve the
purpose. Wouldn't want us all to be repeating ourselves." He winced

as his wife pressed his foot under the table with rather too much vigor, but fortunately Pidgeley was ladling more soup into Beatrice's bowl, his shaking hand providing a disconcerting distraction.

Once the footman made his creaking retreat, however, Beatrice replied, "No, I don't suppose my letter to Mama left anything out. I even told her how Joanie pinched her finger in the door and what Margaret said to Nurse."

"Then you—also told her about—er—your bathing accident and the swim lessons?" ventured Aggie.

"Of course. But not in a way to cause her anxiety, I hope. All being well that ends well." At this last, her voice shook the slightest bit, and she hastened to clear her throat. (Which caused Pidgeley to spring forward with a popping of knee joints to deposit a roast partridge breast upon her plate.) "Oh. Thank you."

They all three chewed and sipped quietly for some minutes, Tyrone now nudging his wife's ankle with his own foot, but then finally Beatrice set down her knife and fork and said boldly, "I told Mama about Mr. Clayton, naturally, and how very much we liked him, but—but I said I was afraid we would not see much of him anymore, now that his—friends—his intended bride and her companion, that is—were come to Bognor."

"Are you sorry about that, Beatrice?" asked her sister-in-law. "I know I am."

"We don't *know* for certain that we will not see him anymore," pointed out Tyrone. "Though perhaps we should have invited Miss Brand and Miss Croy to join us in anything they liked. We might have said, 'the more the merrier,' or something to that effect."

"I suppose we could still send a note," his wife answered dubiously. Privately she thought it would hurt Beatrice more, to have Miss Brand about and to witness the engaged couple's bliss, if bliss it proved. Though she would never say so to Beatrice, to Aggie's mind, the appearance of his intended had not seemed to fill Mr. Clayton with overmuch elation.

Before Tyrone could answer, Beatrice interjected, her chin lifting. "I think Mr. Clayton would already know *he*—and therefore *they*—would be welcome, so...we had better leave it up to him. We mustn't—chase him, you know. It would appear...odd. Extreme."

Aggie made a helpless gesture. "Certainly that is not the impression we wish to make, dear Bea, but would it not appear equally suspect if we were to drop his acquaintance altogether, now that his friends have come and we have learned he is engaged? That would look like we only wanted his company because we—because we thought—"

"Because we thought he and I might like each other," finished Beatrice, her cheeks flaming. "You may as well say it, Aggie."

"May we have the apple tart, Pidgeley?" Aggie blurted. She fidgeted while the ancient footman pottered from the room before resuming, "Now that you mention it, Bea, we have nothing to be ashamed of for admitting it. A kind, congenial, talented young man. Of course Tyrone and I liked him! And it would have been unnatural if it never crossed our minds that you might like him as well."

Beatrice pushed her partridge to the edge of her plate. "Though *my* liking him is not the same thing as you and Tyrone liking him."

"No," said Aggie meekly. "Which is why we have guilty consciences. For...pushing the acquaintance."

"Guilty consciences? Don't be ridiculous." Beatrice pushed the partridge back to the center of the dish and studied it, her lips pressed together to prevent any trembling. "Even if Tyrone had not invited him to everything under the sun, I suspect I would have liked him in any case. But—it doesn't signify now. We—we did not then know he was engaged, and now we do. And now Miss Brand is here in Bognor, and as I said, I would be—greatly surprised if we see any more of him."

Beatrice was doomed to be surprised then, as it turned out, for the very next morning, as Tyrone negotiated the use of a bathing machine with one of the dippers, a quiet voice addressed her.

"Good morning, Miss Ellsworth, Mrs. Ellsworth."

Beatrice shivered, though she was well bundled and the morning air was still.

"Mr. Clayton. Good morning to you," the ladies replied, Aggie stifling a nervous giggle and Beatrice scarcely audible.

His gaze touched hers fleetingly, like fingertips probing a sore spot and shying away again. Then he turned toward the promenade. "Here they come. I hope you will forgive me for not joining the swim lesson this morning. Miss Brand and Miss Croy are eager to try bathing."

Making a magnificent effort of which she would later be proud, Beatrice replied with seeming ease, "They could not have been favored with a more beautiful day for it, sir." And then, "Good morning to you, Miss Croy, Miss Brand."

Miss Brand gave a little hop, clapping her mittened hands together. She was, Beatrice thought with an inward sigh, a rather adorable creature. "Good morning, good morning! Ooh! I am frightened, I confess. Mr. Clayton tells me you are all 'old hands' at this, but Cissy and I are filled almost equally with avidity and fear."

Beatrice thought the ratio of avidity to fear in Miss Croy far from equal, for the older woman was pale and twitching, but the sight of the woman's dread contrarily bolstered her own courage. "I think you will both enjoy it very much," she said. "And Mr. Clayton will secure you a competent dipper."

"I know it," answered Miss Brand with a little smile directed at the man in question. "Mr. Clayton is supremely capable."

It was not a proprietorial smile, per se, nor would Beatrice even categorize it as confident. It was meant to be...pleasing. It made her wonder how intimate Mr. Clayton and his betrothed were. How well they knew each other.

And Mr. Clayton smiled in return, but his was vague, polite. Beatrice thought she had seen more easiness when he challenged her to swim to shore or when they spoke over the teapot.

Stop it, she ordered herself. *However Mr. Clayton and Miss Brand feel toward each other is not only none of your business, Beatrice Ellsworth, but it hardly matters. All that matters is that the deed is done. Mr. Clayton is engaged, and he is* not *engaged to you.*

As if to reinforce this argument, when Mr. Clayton stalked off in the same direction as Tyrone toward the row of bathing machines, Miss Brand said, "I am so glad Mr. Clayton made friends in Bognor. I was a little afraid, coming unannounced, I should find him quite surly and drudging—he and Papa always worked so hard and so continuously, you understand. It required some effort on my part to wrest information from him, but I learned that he has been to supper at your house and to the library with Mr. Ellsworth and even that he has promised to try the assembly. You cannot imagine how my heart took wings to hear that last part! Because I told myself, if Mr. Clayton were recovered and were only going to sit at his desk and answer my questions Yes or No and silently wish me back to town, I would not long withstand such treatment. Surely it would end in Cissy and me returning to town in a week, and how uncomfortable that would be, when we have only just arrived, and Bognor took some getting at."

"Then Mr. Clayton still intends on being at Thursday's assembly?" asked Aggie.

"He does. He said he hoped I would pardon him, but he had already given his word that he would partner both you and Miss Ellsworth at least once, as if I would have any objection to that at all!" Another clap of the mittens. "I adore dancing, and it has grieved me in the past to think that Mr. Clayton did not dance. And now—!" Clap, clap. "I told him as well that, now that he has a hostess, he must return some of your family's kindness. Is it wrong of me to say he required convincing? But I insisted it would be no trouble at all to him—Cissy and I would arrange matters. He need only rise from his desk and repair to the dining room at the appropriate hour. So won't you come for supper tonight at seven?"

With care, Beatrice and Aggie managed not to exchange glances. If Mr. Clayton required convincing, how could they possibly impose on him and accept? To which Beatrice added the silent postscript to herself, *You see? He has decided the friendship must be given up. Oh, please heaven, may it not be because he guesses I have feelings for him!*

But then the gentlemen returned, Tyrone with the chosen bathing machine following behind and Mr. Clayton beside him.

"...It would be a pleasure, Clayton," Tyrone was saying. "I may speak for all of us and say we are at liberty to accept."

"Oh!" The little exclamation escaped Aggie, even as Miss Brand gave another of her hops and cried, "Oh, goody! You Ellsworths will come, then? You will see, Mr. Clayton, how painless Cissy and I will make things for you."

"Perhaps I ought to return to Spencer Terrace and tell Barnstable and Molly of our plans," suggested Miss Croy, eyeing the surf with some trepidation.

"Nonsense," declared her charge. "There is plenty of time for that later, Cissy. You are trying to avoid bathing. You had better lead the way, Mr. Clayton, before Cissy runs off altogether."

This was the signal for the group to split up, the Ellsworths heading toward the rocks where the swimming lessons took place and Miss Croy and Miss Brand remaining to trail after Mr. Clayton toward the bathing machine some yards in the opposite direction. And though he did not look over his shoulder, it made no difference—whether he would or no, he pictured what the morning might have been, had his intended and her cousin not come.

But they had come.

It had been perhaps three months or more since he had last seen Miss Brand, and that had been but an afternoon call. Before that, it had likely been the previous Christmas season. They had corresponded in the meantime, she diligently and he in his more desultory fashion, but he could not now recall any specific item communicated between them. She wrote to him of finishing her schooling and the summer spent with friends in Cirencester; he wrote to her of the completion of the Worcester project and negotiations for the next. Had their letters fallen into other hands, they might have been taken for messages between siblings or between an uncle and niece, but certainly not for love letters. Not once had mention been made of their arrangement or what the future held.

And now she was here, literally on his doorstep. The future had come to him. The cloudy future had become the all-too-distinct present.

"I am so glad they will come tonight," Miss Brand was saying, the slightest bit breathless from the effort of walking in the loose sand. "I like the looks of them very well. And I hope they will invite us to Number Four again in return, for I would like to see the Tyrone Ellsworths' little girls. Have you seen them?"

"I have." He gestured toward the chosen bathing machine which the ladies might share. Taking a deep breath, Miss Croy set her shoulders and entered, like a *comtesse* mounting the steps to the guillotine, but Miss Brand hesitated.

"Mr. Clayton—*John*. May I call you John? I wish you might call me Priscilla now. At last, I mean. Now that I am grown."

He bowed his head in acknowledgement.

She gave a wavering smile. "Thank you. *John*. I realize we don't know each other very well...yet. Somehow writing letters is not the same as seeing another person face to face, is it? But it is all right that Cissy and I are here, is it not? You aren't angry, that is?"

"I am not angry," he replied gravely. It was the truth. He was not angry with her. Only with himself.

Her smile flickered and then faded, and she turned to follow her cousin up the steps of the little cabin.

Clayton gave a sigh of his own. He must do better than this. He *must*. It was not fair to Miss Brand, who had every right to expect not only courtesy but even enthusiasm from him.

It was this gap between what he knew was expected of him and what he had so far been able to muster which led to him agreeing to the supper. In the context of his work, John understood that, when a strut in a framework gave way, it must not only be replaced, it must be reinforced. It must be shored up, if it was not to break again. In the same way, entirely without conscious effort or forethought, he knew he had placed too much weight on the untried structure of his engagement, only to find it failing beneath him. He had believed, because he had never been in love, that he might then never be. He had believed he should and would work on developing affection for his betrothed when the time came, only to find that affection could develop on its own, unasked for, and with no regard for convenience or propriety.

And for this mistake in judgment he must punish himself. The engagement must be rebuilt, strengthened, tested. Which meant he must apply the pressure of Miss Ellsworth's presence to ensure the repair would hold. Because he had been so wrong to indulge himself, moreover, he must be absolutely proper now. He could only hope, when Priscilla had appeared, bringing everything figuratively down about his ears, Miss Ellsworth had suffered no injury. That too must be tested.

Therefore, the supper. The supper and, heaven help him, the assembly.

Squaring his own shoulders much as Cissy Croy had, John Clayton took up his invisible burden and headed for the neighboring bathing machine.

"Why did you say we would go, Tyrone?" Aggie hissed at last, when she saw Beatrice swimming back to shore. "After Bea told us this morning of her feelings for Mr. Clayton?"

"It could not be avoided," he returned. "I hemmed and hawed and looked a fool when he issued the invitation, as you might expect, but Clayton told me we had entertained him so much that he must return the favor."

"I don't like him anymore," his wife declared unreasonably. "Mr. Clayton. Given his circumstances, he oughtn't to insist and cause her pain."

"But that's just it, Aggie—he doesn't *know* he's causing her pain. He means to be friendly and generous, I daresay. It's our own fault for nursing the idea and passing it to Bea like a bad cold. Certainly that wasn't Clayton's intention! How could it be, when he always had Miss Brand in reserve?"

His wife scowled and made no reply, but Tyrone knew her to be a rational creature, however disappointed she might be in the moment. Under cover of the water he gave her a fond pinch. "Come on, then. Smile, my love, and promise you won't take a bite out of Clayton tonight. Beatrice is looking this way, and having managed to infect her with fondness for our neighbor, now we must try for the cure."

"You mean, try to make her dislike him?"

"Nothing so ambitious, I'm afraid. But unless either he or we decamp from Bognor posthaste, we had better learn to practice indifference."

Having emerged from the bathing machine in her dry clothing, Beatrice nodded to the dipper perched on the rocks. She suspected the Ellsworths must be favorite customers by this point, since whomever they employed was excused from actual dipping and had only to wait while they swam.

Tyrone and Aggie were still frolicking in the waves, and her gaze drifted up the beach toward where they had left Mr. Clayton and his party. She could not tell which machine they used, each one having its own canvas shelter for privacy, but, squinting, she picked out a dark spot bobbing outside of one. It might have been a seal, but when, after another bob and duck, the spot rose and became a dark head of hair above a lithe form, to which a linen shirt clung damply, there could be no doubt.

Even at this distance, she blushed fiercely and half turned her own head away, in case Mr. Clayton should see her watching him. So he was still working on his swimming, though he must stay with Miss Brand and Miss Croy? Somehow the thought acted as a balm on her wounded heart. He might be engaged to Miss Brand—nay, he *was* engaged to Miss Brand—but he had enjoyed learning to swim all the same. And perhaps the tiniest, most infinitesimal part of that enjoyment had been her company.

CHAPTER EIGHT

**...Here is your pretty Ward and mine;
let us try to make her Time with us easy.
— Samuel Richardson, *Pamela* (1740)**

When the supper hour came, though they mounted the steps of Number Five quiet and uneasy, the Ellsworths found the ice broken at once and most unexpectedly.

"Why, look at this, Aggie," said Beatrice, rising from her curtsey. With her fingertips she indicated the bow porcelain figure of a goldfinch with bulging eyes on the table. "It's the same one we have in Number Four!"

"Heavens," Tyrone laughed, snatching it up to inspect. "You can't tell me they made more than one of these hideous things! If ever the occasion warranted breaking the mold, this would have been it."

"It's not only the ugly goldfinch—look!" Beatrice's gaze swept the drawing room. "It's the paper too, with the scrolls every few feet—though this one is striped with gold and ours with ivory—and then there are the candlesticks and even—" breaking off, she took a few steps nearer the portrait on the wall— "It's him! the gentleman in the tartan waistcoat!"

"Gracious me," said Aggie over her shoulder. "You're right! I suppose it's far less trouble for the owner to furnish everything similarly, though why anyone would request multiple copies of this particular picture confounds me. I wonder if Numbers 2 and 3 share the same household effects."

"If they do, imagine how the poor gentleman in tartan feels," Tyrone chuckled, "to witness the goings-on in every drawing room in Upper Bognor Street."

Beatrice threw their host a look both teasing and shy. "You didn't mention the curious uniformity, Mr. Clayton, when you visited us at Number Four."

He gave a sheepish laugh. "I'm embarrassed to confess it, given how it struck you Ellsworths at once, but I entirely failed to notice."

Inexplicably, he colored as he said this, and Miss Brand hastened to say, "John is just like my father was, in that respect. That is, if something has anything to do with *work*, then not a jot nor tittle goes unnoticed, but otherwise..." She gave a little shrug and nudged her intended coquettishly, at which his color only deepened. Poor Miss Brand could not guess the true cause of his discomfiture, which was his realization that, when calling at Number Four, he had apparently been too busy observing Miss Ellsworth to spare any attention for porcelain goldfinches or tartan-clad men.

With his sudden confusion, the easy tone of the gathering evaporated as quickly as it had come.

Beatrice felt her own face warm to hear Miss Brand call Mr. Clayton by his Christian name, and she turned to choose a seat. So that was how it was now? Even in the short time since her arrival, Miss Brand and Mr. Clayton had found a more intimate footing for their relationship?

Nothing more than a restless movement of her hands gave her unhappiness away, but even these disobedient limbs were ruthlessly subdued. She folded them in her lap and pinned a pleasant expression on her face.

The motion failed to escape Tyrone and Aggie's notice, however, and those two, in their determination to protect her, began pelting Mr. Clayton and Miss Croy respectively with comments and questions about their day. The bathing, the aftermath, their further activities, what Miss Croy thought of Bognor, and so forth.

Rather than listen or contribute to this, Miss Brand placed herself on the sofa nearest Beatrice, her gaze open and eager. "Miss Ellsworth, how glad I am to find a young unmarried lady near my own age here! It will greatly enliven my stay, I hope. John can be good company, of course, but he is so very busy, isn't he? Cissy and I must occupy ourselves much of the time, I suppose, so as not to try him by being always underfoot. And you will understand that Cissy and I welcome any novelty, having long been together. However much one might like a person, there always comes a point when everything has been said more than once, don't you think?"

"Yes, I suppose that's true," answered Beatrice with a somewhat fixed smile.

Undeterred, Miss Brand leaned forward to add, "Not that I haven't already heard a few surprising things from John himself. For instance, he tells us that your brother Mr. Ellsworth is teaching you all to swim. How envious I am of your bravery!"

"Did you not enjoy bathing this morning?"

"Oh, it was both alarming and delightful, Miss Ellsworth. I felt helpless as a rag doll in the waves, and my dipper was so *massive* that I was almost as afraid of him as I was of the sea's power."

For an instant Beatrice remembered her gown pinned by the bathing machine wheel and the water closing over her head. With a shudder, she felt her first twinge of sympathy for the girl. "I was afraid of my dipper the first few days too, but you're better off with a strong one, I daresay." But it was not any recollection of the burly dipper's arms which caused her blush the next moment. Against her will, her gaze flicked to Mr. Clayton, who was replying to Tyrone, but she had the sense that his own had just been withdrawn. Could he have mentioned her bathing accident to Miss Brand?

Surely not.

Not because it was a secret or because Beatrice would have asked him not to, but because it painted him in the light of a hero. He could not mention her being held beneath the waves, in danger of drowning, without also confessing to having saved her.

When Barnstable the footman entered to announce the supper, the party rose, Mr. Clayton offering his arm to Aggie and Tyrone to Miss Brand, leaving Beatrice and Miss Croy to follow behind. The similarities of the dining room to Number Four's must also be catalogued and remarked upon, but when this was accomplished, Miss Brand took her place at the foot of the table and invited Beatrice to sit at her right.

"John has promised we will attend tomorrow's assembly," she began again when the soup was served. She pitched her voice low for Beatrice's ears, though Tyrone had valiantly thrown himself into a speech about some person he had seen at the coffee room that day, who in appearance was not unlike so-and-so, whose new poetry book was such-and-such.

"Yes," said Beatrice, angling herself to face her hostess and speaking as quietly. "We too." Across from her, Miss Croy gave a meaningless smile and continued to sip her soup.

"I cannot tell you how delighted I was to hear him say so," Miss Brand all but whispered. "You will scarcely credit it, but I have never once danced with him, though we have been engaged these two years!"

In response to this, Beatrice only widened her eyes. But when Miss Brand mirrored her, with the addition of an emphatic slow nod, as if to say, *Indeed, it is so—doubt it if you dare!* Beatrice was forced to murmur, "Yes, that does surprise me."

"I knew it would. And I have a further confession for you, Miss Ellsworth." Again she stopped expectantly, and again Beatrice was obliged to make some response to jog her into continuing. Miss

Brand toyed with her spoon a moment before hunching lower to share her confidence. "To tell the truth, I am a little afraid of my John, because he is older and because he worked with Papa, so I've never dared to ask him what he thinks of dancing or if he even *can* dance! I do hope he can and will. For dancing lessons were my very favorite at school. I am not much for book learning or arithmetic, sadly, and I always mix up my Italian and my French. I suppose you speak beautiful French and Italian, Miss Ellsworth?" Before Beatrice could demur, Miss Brand fluttered her fingers and went on. "But I comforted myself that there would seldom be an occasion when such things were necessary, for heaven knows John never speaks anything but plain English, and for him to have a wife who gave herself airs would be silly, don't you think? He wouldn't like it, I imagine, because he is always matter of fact." She sighed. "Still, John does meet with important people from time to time—not that I would be present. But then again, I might! Suppose he were called to a ribbon cutting, to open a canal? Or called to stand beside another person who cut the ribbon—mightn't I be there as well?"

"At any rate, I daresay neither Mr. Clayton nor any other person at a ribbon cutting would ask you to speak French or Italian, much less work sums," pointed out Beatrice, but Miss Brand barely paused to acknowledge this.

"I would just have to tell John to warn me far in advance, so I might prepare," said the young lady, smiling. "Can you see me standing beside the mayor of London or the prime minister or some such and having to *perform*, as if I were on a stage?" She tapped her temple with a stubby finger. "Let us pray all that learning is in there somewhere. Papa paid *handsomely* for my education, after all, as if I were going to marry a duke or something!" When her listener only smiled, she added, "Isn't that amusing?"

Left with no alternative, Beatrice forced the desired chuckle, but she was beginning to feel mildly resentful of having particular responses coerced from her. What would happen if she were to ignore Miss Brand's cues? Would the young lady rattle on as if nothing was amiss?

But perhaps she was being too hard on her, for the next moment Miss Brand leaned still closer toward her, conspiratorially. "I am talking too much of myself, aren't I? Mrs. Archer—the headmistress at my former school—would say I was. I can see her raising her lorgnette and saying, 'Miss Brand, must I remind you of the existence of those around you? A well-bred young lady listens twice as much as she speaks.' Therefore, in honor of Mrs. Archer..." Miss Brand motioned that she was sealing her lips. "You must talk of *yourself* now, Miss Ellsworth."

"Oh! I—er—haven't any idea where to begin."

"Haven't you? Let me help you, then. I will tell you what my friends and I like to talk of, world without end: beaux and *beaux yeux,* if you understand me." (This with a self-conscious giggle.) "Have you a beau, Miss Ellsworth?"

"I'm afraid not." Beatrice glanced across at the stolid Miss Croy in search of rescue, but that good woman merely signaled Barnstable for more soup.

Miss Brand frowned at her, and Beatrice suspected she found her deficient in the art of pleasing. It was probably true in the main. Beatrice's friend Mrs. Coningsby, née Emmy Wright, had often sighed over Beatrice's indifference to "beaux and *beaux yeux.*" Fidgeting in her chair and wishing the tête-à-tête might end, Beatrice peeked next up the table, envying the laugh Tyrone and Aggie were sharing with Mr. Clayton.

"What about an old beau?" Miss Brand prodded. "Someone you already considered and rejected."

"I'm sorry," Bea apologized again. "There's no one at all to speak of."

"Well then, what about a beau *ideal*?" prompted her new friend impatiently. "Surely we girls ought to be able to conjure up an ideal! Why, if I were not already engaged, I would tell you mine was a lord with golden hair and sapphire eyes and a brooding manner."

Now it was Beatrice's turn to scowl. Imagine Miss Brand dreaming of such a creature, with such a paragon as Mr. Clayton already in her pocket!

"I can't say I prefer blond hair to brown or black, or blue eyes to green or brown," she rejoined with spirit, "but what use would a brooding manner be?"

Miss Brand's eyes widened at such ignorance. "A brooding manner like Sir Ralph De Wilton, brooding 'on dark revenge and deeds of blood,' of course! Did you never read the poem? It was the rage at Mrs. Archer's when I was younger."

While Beatrice had herself not pored over *Marmion,* Tyrone had read it to the family. And though at the time she had liked the hero of that poem as heartily as any girl in England, something contrary in her made her reply, "Pooh. De Wilton aside, nine times out of ten, a brooding manner simply means a gentleman has a peevish disposition."

"Well, aren't you something!" declared Miss Brand, her voice rising. "Next you will tell me that, if a dashing, poetical duke asked you to marry him, you would refuse!"

"I would not be the least tempted to accept," answered Beatrice roundly. "Such a person sounds alarming. Besides, I've only ever seen one duke in my life, and not only was he *neither* dashing nor poetical (much less golden-haired or sapphire-eyed), but he was in fact quite old and bald and regarded every young lady most improperly through his quizzing glass. No, indeed! Myself, I would far rather have a modest, respectable, gentlemanly husband who spoke plain English and gave himself no airs." As soon as she heard herself unintentionally echo Miss Brand's earlier description, embarrassment seized her. She gulped, coloring, and hurriedly returned to her soup. But this haste bore terrible consequences, for she ended in half inhaling it. Beatrice had but one fraction of a second to perceive her mistake before a fit of explosive coughs reduced her to burying her face in her napkin.

"Mercy!" cried her brother, turning toward her at last. "Did you swallow a fish bone?"

Of course Beatrice could not answer and only coughed the harder, feeling her face on fire, while Tyrone pounded her between the shoulder blades. To her increased mortification, all conversation ceased, though Bea waved a hand to indicate she would be perfectly well in a moment and that Tyrone need not beat her to death, but she had no breath to urge them all to carry on and leave her to asphyxiate in peace.

Nevertheless, Aggie understood. "I daresay we are all tempted to drink our soup too quickly," she blurted. "And what a delicious one this is! We never enjoy a fish soup in Winchester, do we, Tyrone? Though I imagine our cook Wilcomb could make a tasty one, if given the chance."

"So she could," he agreed, catching her hint and leaving off pummeling his younger sister. "A boast which you must put to the test, Clayton, by calling at Hollowgate the next time you are in Winchester." Belatedly he bent his head toward Miss Croy and Miss Brand, adding, "And you as well, of course, ladies. With the impending nuptials, I consider you all one party."

Miss Brand clapped her hands together. "I should love to see Winchester! I have been so few places. Of course, it is up to you, John," she added belatedly, with a duck of her head. It surprised Beatrice that there was no coyness in the action, considering how intently Miss Brand had managed their own intercourse.

Mr. Clayton only nodded in a way hard to interpret, raising his glass in acknowledgement of Tyrone's invitation. "I have never been in Winchester myself."

"Tell us about your home," urged Miss Brand.

When Tyrone and Aggie combined to offer a description of the town's history and notable features (Beatrice still trying to clear her throat quietly), Miss Brand heard them politely for a minute before giving a little hop in her seat. "Yes, yes, how interesting. King Arthur and such. But I meant, won't you tell us about your *home*? Do you live in the town or without?"

Such a question led to a discussion of Hollowgate, naturally, and the complicated circumstances which resulted in the Tyrone Ellsworths living there but not owning it, and the Robert Fairchilds owning it and only beginning to live there.

"How curious!" exclaimed Miss Brand. "Mr. Ellsworth, you mean to say that your elder sister Mrs. Fairchild inherited Hollowgate over a son? I understand she had a different mother, but however did she manage it?"

"My brother-in-law Robert Fairchild could explain it best because he is the family lawyer," replied Tyrone, "but it all has to do with the mother of my two older sisters being a Baldric. The Baldric name in Winchester was once great, but it has sadly died out. Nevertheless, the last male Baldric, Flossie and Lily's grandfather, was wily enough to ensure that Hollowgate would remain in his daughter's line, unless she had no issue whatsoever. Only then could my formerly penniless father William Ellsworth inherit. Fairchild describes the Baldric-Ellsworth marriage settlement as 'remarkable,' and I suppose he would know."

"So no Hollowgate for younger half-brother Tyrone," laughed Aggie, "unless he had chosen to murder his two older sisters before they had children themselves."

"Don't think I didn't consider it," he returned with mock solemnity, "but sadly we all get along too well. Flossie goes so far as to allow me and mine to live on at Hollowgate, as long as I manage it for her. Therefore, landless and not sufficiently bloodthirsty, I resorted to marrying an heiress of my own." This last he said with a wink at his wife.

"Not that I brought you an estate either," said Aggie archly. To Miss Brand and Mr. Clayton she added, "I am the youngest of three daughters, so The Acres—my father's estate—will go to my eldest sister—or to her husband, I should say, since, unlike the old Mr. Baldric, Papa had no objections to Phronsie's Philip and made no unusual stipulations in the marriage settlement."

"Flossie—that is, Mrs. Fairchild—is generous, to be sure," put in Mr. Clayton, "sheltering not only your little family, Ellsworth, but also her youngest sister Miss Ellsworth."

"Oh, I don't live with Tyrone and Aggie," spoke up Beatrice, finally having regained control of her voice. "I live with my stepparents nearby at Beaumond." In spite of her recent embarrassment and Mr. Clayton's regard, she almost laughed. "Not that that clarifies matters, for Beaumond belongs to Aggie's father Mr. Weeks."

"Who got it from Aggie's former suitor's family," grinned Tyrone. "On second thought, Clayton, perhaps you had better stay away from Winchester. It's a veritable thicket of reciprocal relations and obligations."

"So it is," Clayton agreed. He favored his intended with a rueful smile. "And we would be babes in the woods, wouldn't we, Miss Br—Priscilla, rather—having so few remaining family members ourselves."

"We would!" she seconded, brightening visibly to be addressed.

She is not yet confident of his affections, Beatrice thought. The realization hardly cheered her, however, for Miss Brand would have the rest of her life to grow more confident and to win those parts of Mr. Clayton's heart thus far unconquered.

If he addresses me, *I must remember to hide my delight.* It would not do at all if her own countenance lit up as Miss Brand's had, were Mr. Clayton to speak to her. *Everyone would guess—everyone would* know, *that I have begun to care for him.*

Beatrice need not have feared.

Mr. Clayton did *not* address her during the whole course of the meal, nor when they removed to the drawing room, leaving at last only her disappointment to be hidden.

CHAPTER NINE

Lead in your ladies, every one: sweet partner,
I must not yet forsake you: let's be merry.
— **Shakespeare and Fletcher,** *Henry VIII,* **I.iv.807**
(1623)

B anniker," said Beatrice to Aggie's maid, when the woman
came to dress her, "what would you say to some curls?"

Banniker might have come to The Acres years earlier as a raw
young servant barely older than her mistress, but she was polished
enough now. Barely a hitch in her step betrayed her amazement at
Miss Ellsworth's request, the latter having consistently disdained the
services of the iron.

"Of course, miss," she replied evenly. But when she withdrew
once more to fetch the iron from Mrs. Tyrone Ellsworth's chamber,

she could not forbear announcing, "I've come to fetch the iron at Miss Ellsworth's request."

Aggie looked up from where she was disentangling little Joan's fingers from the lace at her hem to hand her off to Nurse. "Beatrice wants curls?" She had known Banniker long enough to suspect the maid's barely-disguised triumph, but the news filled Aggie herself with alarm. When the two servants were gone, Banniker with the iron and Nurse with their daughters, she turned on her husband, who had shut his book with a snap. "Oh, Tyrone! What shall we do? If Beatrice wants curls, she must be in love with him, and it is all our fault."

"I don't know that we can determine that. She did not pay him undue attention last night."

"Of course she didn't! But don't you see? They had become fast friends—we all had—before we learned of Miss Brand's existence, but last night the two of them hardly spoke."

"Well, whatever her feelings, she could hardly chat with the man under the nose of his betrothed without opening herself to criticism," he replied reasonably, "and I commend her for putting a brave face on the matter, of which *curls* are a good indication."

Heedless of her own hair and dress, Aggie came to perch on the arm of his chair. "I do hope you're right, Tyrone. I would feel far less guilty. Only think if we were to return to Winchester, not only having failed in introducing Beatrice to someone eligible, but having encouraged a doomed attachment!"

He lifted her hand to his lips before clasping it between his own. "I know she likes him. We all do. But how attached can she possibly be, on so short an acquaintance?"

"You, my good lad, are simply trying to persuade yourself. You know very well that the acquaintance might be short, but it began in intense and unusual circumstances, ones which would have made a deep impression on a far flightier girl than your dear sister, and Beatrice is not the least bit flighty. Suppose the curls are an attempt to make Mr. Clayton regret his engagement?"

"Do consider what you're saying, Mrs. Ellsworth," he answered with a teasing frown. "You say in one breath that my sister is not flighty, and in the next you accuse her of trying to excite gnawing envy in a man's heart?"

"No—you're right. It must be what you said—putting on a brave face. Therefore, I had better go see how she fares. We must all be brave, I suppose, having had our hopes dashed. But there are plenty of fish in the sea, as the saying goes. It's our communal misfortune that we all set our hearts on the first one to swim by."

What neither Aggie nor Tyrone voiced was that it remained to be seen whether so steadfast a girl as Beatrice Ellsworth could succeed in detaching her heart from that first shining fish to settle it on another.

In the slower seasons, the Bognor subscription room offered but one assembly per month, and it would be folly to expect anyone there but those already seen in town and at the shore. When the

Ellsworths entered, it was precisely this collection of doddering old gentlemen and the occasional pale and wasted lady of certain years with her equally desiccated companion. Here and there, like flecks of gleaming quartz in otherwise uniform granite, shone more youthful parties, and the (doddering) master of ceremonies hastened forward to make introductions.

"There may be a sad shortage of partners for the young ladies, I'm afraid," Mr. Haddon apologized with a bow to Aggie and Beatrice. "Mr. Ellsworth, I am certain you will do your duty, as will Mr. Worsley and Mr. Phipps, but the older men are more for cards than dancing."

"It so happens, Mr. Haddon, that we expect another friend, a Mr. Clayton and his betrothed," Tyrone informed him, "thus bringing the number of male partners to four. Mr. Clayton knows but two dances, I believe, so perhaps under the unusual circumstances, when he arrives, the musicians might confine themselves to *only* those dances? It would allow Mr. Clayton to dance with my wife, my sister, his intended, and his intended's cousin and therefore make the most of his services."

"Splendid," agreed the relieved man. "But perhaps in the meantime we might begin with another...?"

Before Beatrice could wonder whether it was more appropriate for Tyrone to ask her or his wife, Mr. Worsley thrust himself in front of Mr. Phipps and begged for the honor, leaving Mr. Phipps to turn to Aggie. Being as full of human weaknesses as any other young lady, she could not help wishing it had been Mr. Phipps who won the day because Mr. Phipps, if not a handsome man, was at least handsomer than Mr. Worsley. The latter was nearly bald, save for a tuft of ginger hair sprouting above either ear, and he had one eye which did not look at the world straight on. That feature might have been a blessing in disguise, however, considering how his other was disconcerting in its fixedness on her.

For his part, Mr. Worsley found no fault in his partner, for Beatrice was looking her best. She had not aspired to exciting Mr. Clayton's envy or chagrin, but she had indeed hoped to disguise her own heartache with a good show. Banniker had dressed her golden-brown hair atop her dainty head, twisting the sides in lustrous ropes and curling what escaped the chignon. The faint pink of her simple dress found its complement in her cheeks and the apprehension of her parted lips.

"To think such fair English roses bloom even in autumnal Bognor," effused Mr. Worsley when the music began. As his divergent eye encompassed Aggie and his direct eye Beatrice, Beatrice hoped his compliment was meant to be applied generally, and she gave only a noncommittal *hmm* in response. But no, for he distinctly pressed her hand more firmly than the occasion required, adding, "Certainly your steps are light as falling petals, Miss Ellsworth."

Another *hmm*, this one more grunt-like. *Must he?*

With Beatrice being the only single lady in the room under the age of fifty, it seemed he must. Finding his partner as reticent as she was fair, Mr. Worsley took it upon himself to deliver what information he deemed vital in the time granted him, beginning with his origins (ancient), his family connections (respectable), his education (typical), hints at his income (more than adequate), his health (middling), his prospects (bright). Had she been attending, she might have learned more of Mr. Worsley in ten minutes than she had of Mr. Clayton in ten days. But it was Mr. Worsley's additional misfortune that, before he was halfway through his monologue, a new party appeared in the doorway which consumed what little attention Beatrice had allotted him. Not that she betrayed it by a glance or a remark, but her pink deepened. Abruptly she looked in her partner's most likely eye. "Yes. The bathing at Bognor is most invigorating."

Blinking at this non sequitur, Mr. Worsley scrambled to respond, but he might have saved his breath. Beatrice heard nothing but the pounding of her heart in her ears. And though she did not turn her head, she knew Mr. Clayton and Miss Brand and Miss Croy had joined Tyrone. How was it that she could simultaneously envy Tyrone their company and wish that they might turn right around and leave? How was it that she could picture Mr. Clayton—his firm, upright person and the noble carriage of his head—when her eyes took in only Mr. Worsley's right ear capped by its unfortunate ginger whisp? But so it was.

Only years of repetition and practice carried her through the figures, and four times more through the pattern passed in a twinkling. The next thing she knew, Mr. Worsley was executing his bow (and presenting her with his sparse-carpeted pate. Then he took up her hand to return her to Tyrone, Beatrice biting her lip and bracing herself inwardly.

Naturally, he will dance with Miss Brand first, but will he ask me after that, or will it be Aggie or Miss Croy? I ought not to look forward to it, but I can't help myself. But no—it will be better to dance with him and have done with it, for then I may show him how perfectly calm and indifferent I am, and he will never, never, never imagine how silly I have been. How foolish. For it is foolish, to think him the best of men. Just because he...saved me.

Lifting her gaze, she did indeed see Mr. Clayton leading Miss Brand to the floor, face impassive, while the young lady beamed. If only Tyrone or Mr. Phipps would hurry over and ask her—they might stand near Mr. Clayton and Miss Brand! As if she had breathed the thought aloud, Mr. Clayton looked her way, and Beatrice forgot all her resolve to pretend indifference. Her lips curled upward and her eyes lit—

"If I might have the honor?" croaked a voice, one issuing from a long and stooped and creaking body which swung before her and Mr. Worsley like the fall of the executioner's axe. Poor Beatrice nearly yelped in horror, being reminded of one of the illustrations in Tyrone's books: the ghost appearing to Athenodorus. "Worsley, you might introduce me."

Mr. Worsley was only too willing to comply, thinking such a contrast between his (relative) youth and this walking mummy would make him shine the brighter in Miss Ellsworth's estimation. "Miss Ellsworth, may I present Mr. Herman Boydell?"

Mr. Herman Boydell was a hundred, if he was a day, it seemed to Beatrice, and she wondered why being in the presence of Mr. Clayton always required her humiliation, whether by drowning, choking on fish soup, or dancing with revivified corpses.

Mercifully Mr. Boydell was no mind-reader, so he was spared the unkind aspersions of youth. With ancient gallantry, he bowed her into the line, three up from Mr. Clayton and Miss Brand, as the fiddler and pianoforte player began to run through the melody of Rufty Tufty at double time so the dancers might review the steps in their heads before being called upon to perform. When she recognized the tune, Beatrice could not repress a sigh. Ah—then she and Mr. Boydell would not interact with Mr. Clayton and Miss Brand, confined as they were to their own foursome.

It's better this way! she reminded herself ruthlessly. *Far better. Remember: you are to be calm and indifferent.*

Perhaps in deference to Mr. Boydell's age or because Tyrone had requested it for Mr. Clayton's sake, the musicians played at a languorous pace. Which meant Beatrice had ample time to make and break her resolution throughout. Because it would be odd *not* to glance Mr. Clayton's way, would it not? It would be as if she were disturbed by him. Only see how Aggie not only looked but also praised and encouraged—Aggie and Tyrone being fortunate enough to make up Mr. Clayton's foursome.

The universe made one concession to her, however, in that Mr. Boydell refrained from making fulsome compliments or droning on about himself as Mr. Worsley had, and he moved well for his age. If Beatrice could not be proud of her partner—if she could not glow up at him and flush prettily, as Miss Brand did with Mr. Clayton—at least they need not attract undue attention.

She was mistaken there, though she did not know it, for Clayton had marked her presence the moment he entered and was himself wrestling with guilt and uncertainty. Guilt because his heart leapt within him and uncertainty over what must be done.

"Oh!" cried Miss Brand—*Priscilla*. His intended was still too in awe of him to address him frequently, as if guessing it sometimes tried his patience, so she addressed her remark to Miss Croy. "There are the Ellsworth ladies, already dancing. See them? What do you think, Cissy? Miss Ellsworth has curled her hair."

"Very nice," said Miss Croy. "Very pretty."

"Yes, she is pretty," Priscilla half-sighed, and Clayton felt her glance at him even without turning his head. He ought to say something about how she too was looking well. He knew he ought. *But I have never in my life paid a woman a compliment and don't know how to go about it,* he excused himself, only to have another, more honest thought streak through his head: *you don't want to make the effort. Not when Priscilla is going to fish for it like that. And not when it was Miss Ellsworth you really were admiring.*

Soon after they came to stand beside Tyrone Ellsworth the master of ceremonies scurried over again to do his duties, which included assuring Mr. Clayton *sotto voce* that the musicians would gladly accommodate him by playing Rufty Tufty next, followed by Hit or Miss, then Rufty Tufty, then Hit or Miss.

"I suppose I have you to thank for this arrangement," Clayton said wryly to Tyrone, when Mr. Haddon strode away again, summoned by a table of card players.

"Indeed you do," he replied. "But trust me—it is better than you sitting out the dances you haven't learned and earning the ire of any ladies hoping to partner you. Ah. This one is winding down, and I had better snatch up my wife before Beatrice's fellow forestalls me. If you would pardon me..."

"Shall we—Priscilla?" Her name lurched ungracefully off his tongue, but she did not complain, taking his hand eagerly and waving farewell as they abandoned Miss Croy.

It was only natural then to glance up the set as they joined it, which was how Clayton's gaze caught Miss Ellsworth's. A smile bloomed on her face, a smile which did funny things to him and which would likely have caused him to bumble into someone, had she not been hidden from view the next moment by someone else asking her to dance.

Having the entirety of Rufty Tufty, played at a most leisurely tempo, to consider and reconsider the fleeting encounter, Clayton arrived at the conclusion that he need not be anxious for Miss Ellsworth's sake. His unguarded friendliness toward her must not have wrought any havoc after all, if she could throw him such an ingenuous smile. No—her own friendliness to him had been simply that: friendliness. If he feared it had been more, it was only the mistake of his own inexperience.

Mere friendship.

And now the existence of Priscilla and the actual presence of Priscilla required that either all his friendships become *Priscilla's* friendships as well, or that those friendships be effectively given up. Not that any such sacrifice was demanded, for Priscilla showed herself more than willing to embrace anyone and anything her intended embraced.

Thus, a happy ending.

So why did he not feel happy?

It could not be that he wished in truth he had broken Miss Ellsworth's heart! No, no...he could acquit himself of such selfishness. But he was sorry to realize that she had not developed any particular fondness for him.

Again he corrected himself. No, that wasn't it—He was sorry that this realization made him sorry. Because that sorriness indicated to him, as plainly as if it were written in black and white, that *he* had developed a particular fondness for *her*. *He,* John Clayton,who had no business developing particular fondnesses for anyone save the young lady he was promised to.

That same young lady who even now looked at him with such determination, as if to will him into speaking (which, in fact, was exactly her hope). He suppressed a sigh.

This would never do.

He must try. Try, or relinquish any claim to honor.

"Did you learn this dance at school?" he asked, somewhat stiffly.

At once she swelled with delight. "Yes, this one and many others. You—are managing quite well, John. Where did you learn? I did not know if you danced or not, and I never dared to ask you."

"You mustn't be afraid of me," he replied vaguely. "I know I can be preoccupied, but we must...learn each other's ways."

"All right." She took a deep breath, but his bare statement of the fact did not make the process any easier, and they danced in silence, each grateful for the constant motion and frequent changes in direction which made their awkwardness less apparent.

"I wish you might dance with Cissy at least once," Priscilla said after a minute.

"I will ask her. I told Ellsworth I would partner each of you ladies one time. I'm afraid I know only two dances, but the master of ceremonies said that with so few of us we might repeat them."

She frowned in disappointment then. Only four dances in total? Then this would be their only one together. If only he were easier to talk to! If only he would smile, to show he enjoyed himself and her company. Why must she prod him? Why did he not say something pretty? Or anything at all?

And then even their one dance drew to a close.

Once again the dancers bowed and curtseyed, shuffled and re-arranged. Hit or Miss followed Rufty Tufty; Clayton partnered Miss Croy. Rufty Tufty (reprise) then followed Hit or Miss; Clayton partnered Mrs. Ellsworth. And then, when the musicians played once more the opening notes of Hit or Miss, and it could no longer be avoided, he plucked up his courage and approached Miss Ellsworth.

Strive for unspecific friendliness, he exhorted himself. *Bland courtesy.*

And she, curtseying in response to his bow, thought, *Be calm and indifferent.*

CHAPTER TEN

The fifth and last of our Senses is Touch; a sense spread over the whole body, tho' it be most eminently plac'd in the ends of the fingers.
— **John Locke**, *Elements of Natural Philosophy* (1720)

G loved hand met gloved hand. Tentative gaze met tentative gaze.

Beatrice gave him a smile, but it was not the spontaneous one which illuminated her countenance earlier. This one was measured and contained, but still Clayton could not speak right away. It was all he could do to ensure his own face revealed nothing, for the other couple in their quartet was Miss Croy and Mr. Phipps.

"Can't think why we're doing this one again," rumbled Mr. Phipps. "Haddon must be distracted."

Neither Clayton nor Beatrice felt the need to enlighten the man, if they even heard him.

"You have acquitted yourself well, Mr. Clayton," said Beatrice boldly, determined to begin her new program at once. "One would never guess you were new to this."

"I had the best instruction."

Though there was nothing of flirtation in his voice, she still took a moment to recover, gladly parting to step forward and back with Mr. Phipps. Then she managed, "Tyrone and Aggie *are* good instructors, he in swimming and she in dancing."

"To be sure." They took hands again and turned outward. "Though finally one is only as good as one's partner."

Feeling his light grasp of her fingers to every nerve end, Beatrice's next comment was a little breathless. "In any event, I hope you will have many more occasions to dance in the future, Mr. Clayton, if not at Bognor."

"Why not at Bognor?"

"Tyrone says there is but one assembly per month, and—and we will be gone back home before the next occasion."

"Yes, of course. In that case, I suppose I will be gone as well. That is—*we* will." He must begin to think of Priscilla and himself as a team. A pair.

So this would never happen again—this dance together, this innocent touching of hands. In the face of this truth, silence fell briefly between them. They continued to step through the figures together and in turn with Mr. Phipps and Miss Croy, but some invisible alchemy was at work. Beatrice was telling herself, *If this will all end soon, and I will never see him ever again,* must *I hold myself under such tight rein? Soon enough I will be back in Winchester, and nothing will happen to me—nothing like this. Not to the end of my days.*

And Clayton, holding those delicate fingers of hers, was seized with an irrepressible desire to explain himself. To be understood. She might only feel toward him as a friend, but selfishly he wanted to seize upon the chance—perhaps the only chance he would ever have—to be heard by her. And though the constant movement of the dance would limit him to expressing himself in fits and starts, it would have to serve.

"Miss Ellsworth, however few occasions henceforth I might have to dance or swim or—or talk about books in pleasant company—the best company—I will never forget—my time in Bognor."

She might have replied in a dozen ways. She might have chosen to acknowledge only the most superficial level of his words and spoken of the marvels of the sea or the thrill of sea bathing or the educational value of travel. But she only said quietly, "Nor I."

"You might have surmised, from my history, that I have not often been thrown together in—social situations with people as—as pleasant as you Ellsworths." Clayton flushed at his own inarticulateness.

"Thank you. We too have enjoyed your company. *Relished* it," she answered, in a burst of honesty. Politeness dictated she add some sop regarding Miss Brand's arrival, something like, "And Miss Brand's acquaintance promises more of the same," but Beatrice felt her throat close on the words. On the lie it would have been.

Nor could Clayton muster the expected compliment to his intended, saying rather, "I understand now why people are so eager for holidays. To this point, any satisfaction I have enjoyed following my dear mentor's death has derived entirely from my labors. Yet—yet—it has only been in ceasing to labor that I discover...everything I have been missing. I had never met anyone like—you Ellsworths."

What was there possibly to say to this?

But no reply was necessary, for he began again. "And I—regret—if, in forming our acquaintance, I did not mention—er—the existence of Miss Brand and my engagement to her until relatively late."

"It was none of our business," Beatrice excused him hastily, her pulse speeding. "And it never came up. Therefore, it would have been...odd, if you introduced the fact without rhyme or reason. It would have seemed as if you suspected us of—as if you thought we might be—might be—"

"Yes—"

"—Might be harboring—*designs* on you—"

"Yes! Exactly," he agreed, relief at her comprehension flooding him. "Which of course you were not—it sounds ridiculous even to have to say so—"

"Ridiculous," she echoed faintly. "So you did not think it a subject needing introduction. Certainly I understand. Please—say no more about it. It's dreadful that one cannot form friendships without arousing suspicions of this sort. Even if no one were to speak such suspicions aloud, just knowing *someone* might be thinking such a thing is enough to make one feel defensive."

She was protesting too much, and she knew it. Pressing her lips shut, she cast about for something new to talk about.

"Well, sir, what next for you?"

"After Bognor, you mean?"

"After Bognor, when your holiday ends."

"Why, after this I will return to work and...start the next chapter of my life."

A next chapter which contained his marriage, Beatrice supposed, her shoulders drooping a fraction. He had said days earlier that no date was set, but she wondered if that lack had since been remedied.

With an effort, she rallied. "Tyrone tells us your next project is the Cumberland Arm of the Regent's Canal. I'm afraid I have no clear idea where the Regent Canal's is, other than somewhere in the environs of the capital."

"Have you been to town recently, Miss Ellsworth?"

This drew a laugh, and he felt himself smiling in return. "Mr. Clayton, I don't know about 'recently,' when I have only ever been there once, and that time my parents and I were merely passing through on our way to Kent. But that was a year or more ago, so perhaps it counts as 'recent'?"

"It does, thought the city changes so rapidly that even a native might not recognize it from year to year. And the area around the new Regent's Park is a constant scene for construction. Eventually the Canal will connect the Grand Junction to the Thames at Limehouse, but that is many years away. At present they work to build the section from Paddington to Camden Town."

"And your proposed Cumberland Arm...?"

"Will branch from the Canal and run down behind the barracks on the east side of the park, paralleling the Albany Road." They turned in place and took hands again, Clayton adding after a hesitation, "If you Ellsworths ever come to town, I will give you a tour."

"Oh," she breathed, hoping she did not sound too wistful. "Thank you. I will tell Tyrone and Aggie, but I don't imagine it likely any time soon."

He guessed as much but was nevertheless aware of a swoop of disappointment. No, of course not, unfortunately. Though London during the season never suffered from any shortage of young ladies, not a one of them would be Beatrice Ellsworth.

With another effort: "When you leave Bognor, then, you will return to Winchester. Ellsworth to managing your sister's estate, and you to...whatever life holds next." Marriage, he supposed, with an inward wince. She was too lovely a person for it to be otherwise. The real question was how she had remained single this long.

Her eyes lifted to his. "I'm afraid a young lady's life has a great deal of sameness to it. At least, mine does. Not that I don't like it very well. I have—to this point—always liked—*loved*—my life. Never wished for the least change." (*So this is what is meant by, "Be careful what you wish for"!* she thought with a grimace.)

"It must be a pleasant life, then," he rejoined. "And if it is always the same, tell me what a young lady like you does in the late autumn and early winter in Winchester. Is it a whirl of assemblies and balls?"

Beatrice thought of her quiet days and gave a slow shake of her head. "If it were left to my dear mother and sisters it would be. They are forever encouraging my attendance on such occasions. Perhaps because they are all so happily married." Her color came and went when she heard the too-candid words escape her. "But truth be told, I prefer dancing at home with my own family. Dancing at home, working beside my mother to keep the house, practicing my music, reading, visiting my siblings and nephews and nieces. When my younger brothers are home from school—I have a half-brother and a stepbrother at Winchester College—Beaumond is lively enough, but otherwise I am sure you, with your active life and important work, would find my life quite dull."

Her chin lifted with a touch of defiance, but she found no mockery in his eyes. If anything, they were rueful. "While it's bad manners to contradict a lady, Miss Ellsworth, I fear I must. You cannot imagine what a heartwarming picture of home and repose you paint, to someone who has never experienced the like. While I have never lacked a roof to shelter me, 'home' for me has meant lodging houses of varying degrees of cleanliness, apart from the holidays I spent with the Brands. But Mr. Brand was a widower as long as I knew him, and I daresay a house without a mistress cannot compare for comfort and pleasantness. No, no, Miss Ellsworth, I see nothing to scorn in your life and much to envy."

For a bad moment Beatrice thought her eyes would fill, and she quickly looked off to where Tyrone partnered an unknown matron while Aggie danced with the hundred-year-old man. But Mr. Clayton's kindness brought a lump to her throat nonetheless, and her voice was low when she managed to reply, "Thank you, sir. And—I do not forget the fact that it is because of you I still have my beloved life to return to."

While her voice did not tremble, her hand did. Or perhaps that was his own.

Clayton swallowed. Then, with an effort he said, "I thank God I was there."

Suddenly the light joining of their hands became a grasp, lasting no more than a few seconds but unable to be recalled afterward by either of them without a blush. Their fingers threaded and tightened, warmth flooding through two layers of silk gloves, even as it flooded their persons.

At the next change in figures they broke apart with a wrench. The closing notes sounded, Beatrice sinking into her curtsey, heart hammering, as Mr. Phipps lurched forward to claim her.

Then there was an outward rush to mirror her inward tumult, as the master of ceremonies announced the longways dance Childgrove (to the approbation of those not acquainted with Mr. Clayton and his choreographic limitations), and all rearranged themselves. A longways dance! Ah, then she could not even touch him again in passing as they progressed with new partners...

Beatrice ventured one final, longing look at his retreating figure before Mr. Phipps carried her off toward the top of the room.

"What is it, John?" asked Priscilla, appearing at his elbow when her partner returned her. Clayton had been pretending to observe a card game throughout Childgrove, though he saw little enough, being too occupied with upbraiding himself. The sight of his betrothed's eager face, glowing with the exercise and with delight, only made him feel worse.

Hating the mask he must wear, he lifted questioning eyebrows. "To what do you refer? I had to sit out the dance, having already dutifully performed the ones I know."

"Yes, it's too bad! Oh, John—I wish—I wish you might learn more dances," she urged shyly. "Mrs. Ellsworth tells me this will be the only assembly in Bognor until November, but perhaps if—we enlisted the services of a dancing master in the interim..."

"We won't be here in November," he returned, more curtly than he had intended.

Nodding, she turned her head to hide her dismay at the rebuff, but the subject was important enough to her that she persisted. "But it would be so amusing, just the same! And there is plenty of dancing in London, so the lessons would not be wasted."

"You would want to dance in London?"

She steeled herself to meet his gaze. "Yes. I would. Please. I enjoy it very much." Not much encouraged by his grim nod—what did that mean?—she persevered, laying a tentative hand on his sleeve. "Don't you? And here you might practice among friends because we could invite the Ellsworths to join us—"

The sudden stiffening of his arm startled her, though he relaxed it the next instant. (Priscilla might have dismissed it as a start of his own, had she not then observed the working of his jaw muscle.) "Dear me!" she fretted. "What have I said? Of course we needn't, if you don't like—"

"Forgive me—Priscilla," he uttered. The corners of his mouth turned up in the approximation of a reassuring smile. "But I have been on holiday too long."

"I...see. You mean you intend on returning to town soon?" The idea made her heart beat faster, for, if she were finished with school and they were both at last to live in the same place, their wedding day drew that much nearer.

He was staring again at the cards laid upon the green baize surface. The old man nearest him squinted at what had already been played before sighing and tossing down the knave of clubs. Across from him, his whist partner groaned, leaving the offender to sputter, "I had no alternative! No trumps, nor anything which could take the trick."

"For pity's sake, man," hissed his partner. "Say no more, or everyone will know your hand."

It wasn't bad advice, Clayton acknowledged with a twist of his mouth. Not bad at all.

He could not hope to win with the hand heaven had dealt him, but it remained his duty to play it out and to do what he could for his partner. *If only*— But he stopped the thought before it could streak out. Nothing helpful ever began with the words *if only*.

Taking a deep breath and squaring his shoulders, he turned to smile down again at his intended bride, and while the smile may not have reached his eyes, Priscilla was glad it held no darkness this time.

"I intend on returning to town as soon as arrangements can be made," he answered. "But once there, if you like, I will take up lessons with a dancing master."

"Oh, John!" She could not prevent a hop of excitement and a convulsive squeeze to his forearm. "Oh, John, thank you! I won't mind going back even tomorrow, if you truly will take lessons! But I suppose it won't be that soon, will it—because you will have to find lodgings nearer Papa's house in Marlboro Street."

"No—I will return to my rooms in humbler Warren Street—the better to keep an eye on the work progress."

"So far north? Papa never liked me to venture north of Oxford Street, even with Cissy beside me. He said the workers in Marylebone could be troublesome."

"And so they can, which is why I should keep a lookout."

"But we will see plenty of you, I hope?" A childish pout crumpled her features. "You won't simply disappear into your work?"

"You will see me. What use would my dancing lessons be, if they were never to be put to the test?"

The question of setting their wedding date hove into view, but there was only so much he could deal with at one time, and he knew Priscilla would be hesitant to mention it if he didn't. It was cowardly of him to avoid it, he knew, but the pain of giving up Miss Ellsworth was still too fresh. Wait a while. When she was miles and miles away from him, instead of merely across the subscription room, then he could lay the memory of her in tissue paper and put it away for, oh, who knew how long, perhaps never to be taken down, unwrapped and examined again until he was an old, old man.

CHAPTER ELEVEN

**Then I said, I will not make mention of him, nor speak
any more in his name. But his word was in mine heart
as a burning fire shut up in my bones, and I was weary
with forbearing, and I could not stay.**
— Jeremiah 20:9, *The Authorized Version* **(1611)**

For only the second time in her life, Beatrice kept a secret from
her dear mother. And really it was only a partial secret, for in
her letter she had given a full report of the doings at Bognor to that
point, if not of her subsequent feelings. But she suspected Tyrone
and Aggie had made a more thorough account.

A much more thorough one.

If she required any confirmation of this, it came in the form of her
parents and siblings showing an almost insulting lack of curiosity
about her holiday. They questioned her about the sea and bathing

and learning to swim and what the views and town amenities were like, certainly, but in every case, even if Beatrice deliberately mentioned Mr. Clayton or Tyrone or Aggie *accidentally* did, no one ever pursued the subject, despite their compressed lips and glinting eyes declaring their desire to do so. It was not as if Beatrice went out of her way to mention him—of course not—she had not meant to mention him at all. But to avoid mentioning him altogether proved impossible, and the more she tried to do it, the more frequently she found herself tiptoeing around him. For, honestly, how *could* Bognor or bathing or swimming or the assembly be spoken of without speaking—if only in passing—of him? To erase his presence would leave puzzling pauses and awkward narrative gaps. Her perseverance paid off eventually, in that Tyrone and Aggie ceased to flinch if Mr. Clayton came up, and once even Beatrice's stepfather Mr. Wolfe read something from the newspaper about the Regent's Canal without everyone else in the family immediately leaping upon him to administer a figurative rap of the knuckles.

But no one, not even Tyrone and Aggie, knew about Beatrice's last conversation with Mr. Clayton. And no one knew about that last clasp of their hands.

It had indeed been the last of everything. For not two days afterward a wagon drew up before Number Five, Spencer Terrace, to cart the trunks and persons of Mr. Clayton, Miss Brand, and Miss Croy to the coaching inn in Chichester. There followed warm but stilted farewells between the inhabitants of Numbers Four and Five. Tyrone spoke of seeing the progress on the Cumberland Arm when next he was in London, but all was left general and vague.

The Ellsworths remained another ten days, each determined not to admit to the others how flat things seemed after Mr. Clayton's departure. And then, as October drew to a close and word came that Beatrice's parents the Wolfes were once more at Beaumond, the Ellsworths packed their things and returned to Winchester.

But home had changed.

How was it, Beatrice wondered, that everything so familiar appeared in a new and strange light? Here was her sweet, rose-papered bedchamber; here were her dear parents and beloved extended family; here was the plump and sleepy cat Cupid which her mama had given her when they removed from Hollowgate. Here, in fact, was exactly the calm and peaceful life she had described to Mr. Clayton, and which he had admired. So why did it feel...why did *she* feel...restless?

And when discussion of her trip to Bognor naturally diminished, giving way to newer tidings like her younger brothers' school adventures or her niece losing her first tooth, Beatrice began both to hope and to fear she would never hear Mr. Clayton spoken of again.

Something so momentous has happened to me, she thought. *Can it possibly be invisible to those who love me best?* Equal parts doubt and remorse consumed her. After all, was it not better that her struggles be invisible? That they be buried in oblivion? Even as she sat at her needlework, Miss Brand and Mr. Clayton might be preparing for their wedding, after all. They might even be already married by license. To talk of him or her feelings toward him would not only be fruitless, it might even be wicked.

But as the days passed, the burden Beatrice carried grew heavier, until at last, one Sunday after church, she begged her mama Mrs. Wolfe to accompany her on a walk.

Raising a dubious brow as he regarded the November rain speckling the windows, Mr. Wolfe said, "If it's privacy you're after, Beatrice, I can easily retreat to the library. No need for you two to risk a chill."

"If you please, then," said Beatrice meekly.

With his back to her, her stepfather bent to drop a kiss on his wife's hair, giving her the barest wink as he straightened. For while it seemed to Beatrice that her unhappiness escaped notice, her mama had been wringing her hands over it throughout, requiring several times her husband's patient soothings.

As soon as they were alone Beatrice flung herself at her stepmother. "Mama," she moaned into Mrs. Wolfe's neck, "I have a dreadful confession to make."

Wrapping her arm about her daughter's shoulder, Mrs. Wolfe murmured soothingly. "There, there, darling. Shhhh…You know I will love you all the same, but let us hear it."

"It's—about the Mr. Clayton we met at Bognor," she whispered. "You remember—the man who saved me when my gown was pinned beneath the bathing machine wheel."

Miranda could not repress a shiver, but she said simply, "I remember."

Once begun, Beatrice told the whole tale from the moment he wrenched her upward to air and life, only pausing from time to time to dash away an embarrassing tear or to wait for the heat in her face to subside. And her mother did not once interrupt, though sometimes she would nod or her arm would tighten around her.

"So you see?" her daughter choked. "It is all hopeless, and I will never see him again. Or if I do, he and Miss Brand will be married, so it's all the same. He was never anything but friendly and kind—oh, perhaps if Miss Brand had not existed, I might have won him in time—" Here she broke off, flushing again and hiding her face. "No, Mama, you can see I haven't repented because I think he *could* have loved me, if he were free, and I take comfort in the thought, though I shouldn't! And—and—worse, I—still love him, though I shouldn't do that either, only I don't know how one stops!"

Miranda rested her cheek again Beatrice's tumbled hair. Ah, poor girl. Poor darling. Finally to have the miracle happen to her, and to have it be doomed! And how lovely this Mr. Clayton sounded! Miranda would have loved him already for rescuing her girl, but to hear how he had suggested her learning to swim, to overcome her fear...To hear of his hard-working and lonely life which had somehow neither embittered him nor made him unwilling to try things outside his purview. Nor was Beatrice alone in praising John Clayton. Both Tyrone and Aggie had confided in her, making their own guilty confessions for having sought the man's company before they knew he was engaged, not only for Beatrice's sake but because they themselves liked him so well.

If there was one criticism Miranda could level, it was that *he* ought to have held himself aloof from the Ellsworths, knowing his situation. But would that even have been possible? She frowned, considering. In the aftermath of the near-drowning, of course, the

Ellsworths had embraced him without forethought, in gratitude and high emotion. And Mr. Clayton, alone as he was, could he be blamed for being willing to be thus embraced? Miranda couldn't see it. And, then, once the acquaintance was begun and so thoroughly enjoyed all around, when would have been the moment for Mr. Clayton to issue a warning?

She sighed. No. It was a tragedy, but one which could probably not have been avoided. And being a very fond mother, she did not doubt Mr. Clayton might have loved Beatrice, had he been a free man. Perhaps, if Beatrice's description of the grasp of her hand at the assembly had not been her own wishful thinking, he had even been tempted to.

But that was neither here nor there. Mr. Clayton was *not* a free man, nor did he seem a dishonorable one who would break his promise to the fortunate Miss Brand. Therefore he must be rooted from Beatrice's heart, quickly and completely, lest her suffering begin to tell on her health or cost her any future happiness with another person.

"Mama," Beatrice was sniffling to her conclusion, "the worst of it is, since we have returned, everything seems so—so 'weary, stale, flat and unprofitable'! I am restless and unhappy, though I try not to be, honestly I do. I continue to do all the things I have always done, which used to bring me such satisfaction, but at the end of the day I still feel like crawling into my bed and sleeping for a hundred years. Am I hopeless? Ungrateful? To have so much, yet appreciate it so little?"

"No, my dearest girl, you are doing everything you ought to, to overcome your heartbreak," said Mrs. Wolfe decidedly. "And I am proud of you for the efforts you have made. I know how steadfast you are in your loyalties—a quality I would never wish changed in you—but in situations like these, such a trait can...impede the recovery of your usual tranquility."

"Yes," Beatrice sighed. "It will just take time, I suppose. Time and time and time, and nothing can be done to hasten it."

Here her stepmother paused, weighing a decision. Her husband Colin had been in favor of it and she herself undecided, but now Beatrice's confession effectively turned the scale.

"There is...one thing which might hasten it," she murmured.

Beatrice straightened, her eyes red and hair disheveled. "What, Mama?"

Taking a slow breath, Miranda answered, "Mr. Wolfe received a letter from his sister Lady Hufton yesterday. You remember Lady Hufton, of course."

"Of course," said Beatrice. "She visited Mr. Wolfe before you and he were engaged."

"Yes. Well, she and her husband Sir John have two daughters, if you recall, and they had originally thought to take the elder, Miss Marjorie Hufton, to London in November for the season, now that she has finished school, and Miss Hufton always expressed herself eager to go."

"But she fell suddenly ill, did she not, and the plans were cancelled? I remember you and Mr. Wolfe talking about it shortly after I returned from Bognor."

"That was indeed what Lady Hufton told us, but now—" Miranda swallowed. "I tell you this in confidence, Bea. But Lady Hufton now writes to say that Miss Hufton was only feigning illness."

"Feigning! But whatever for? Did she not want to go after all?"

A sigh. "She was feigning illness because she formed a most regrettable attachment to one of the Stourwood Park grooms. A man who, besides being one of the Huftons' own servants, is much older and sadly given to drink. Therefore they will be smuggling their daughter to London after all—over her protests—and Lady Hufton has asked us if we would like to send you as a friend and companion to her."

Beatrice's eyes widened in alarm. "Send me to London? But I have never even met Miss Hufton! Why would they ask for me? Or do you mean they want all three of us to go, you and me and Mr. Wolfe?"

"It happens they particularly would like *you,* Beatrice," Miranda answered with a smile. "In fact, Lady Hufton said that, while she would delight in seeing Mr. Wolfe and me as well, it is your company they especially covet. You see, you and Miss Hufton are now cousins of a sort, by marriage, and you are the closest cousin of any kind in age to her. Moreover, Lady Hufton praised your calm, sensible demeanor, Beatrice. She thinks you might lift Miss Hufton's spirits—in addition to amusing yourself."

But Beatrice was already shaking her head in panicked refusal. "Oh, no, Mama! I am sorry to disappoint Mr. Wolfe's family, but I simply couldn't! It's impossible—go to London? What if I were to encounter Mr. Clayton again? Oh—no—no. I'm sorry, but no."

"Of course I thought of all that when Mr. Wolfe and I discussed the invitation," replied Miranda. "He and I had already agreed we ourselves would not go, so soon after having been absent in Kent, but whether or not *you* should go required more thought. The possibility of your meeting Mr. Clayton again was my chief qualm, of course."

Beatrice drew back to look at her. "What qualms should you or Mr. Wolfe have had, if you did not yet know I cared for Mr. Clayton? No—don't tell me! Did Tyrone and Aggie say? Or was it so obvious?"

"Tyrone and Aggie only said they were sorry for not having been more on their guard—not that Mr. Clayton had done anything wrong—and—oh, Beatrice—it has been plain to me, at least, that you have not been...as you were. Not that it does not relieve my heart somewhat to have you confide in me. Therefore I too disliked Lady Hufton's proposal. For how could we hope and pray for you to be made heart-whole again, while at the same time putting you in danger of being wounded anew?"

"And—what did Mr. Wolfe say?"

Miranda's expression was wry. "He said that, firstly, the most recent census of the capital reported a population of over a million people, which made the odds of a chance encounter low. Of that million people, he went on to say, perhaps five hundred to a thousand make up the fashionable world where, presumably, the Huftons intend to take their place. Therefore, the question would be, from what we knew of Mr. Clayton and Miss Brand, would they be expected to join this set?"

With a mixture of chagrin and faint amusement at her stepfather's matter-of-factness, Beatrice once again shook her head. "I think not. Miss Brand once spoke half in jest of wishing to meet a duke, but certainly Mr. Clayton never said anything of the kind. Any 'important' people he meets with would be in the course of his work, I suppose, and not in social settings. Nor did he seem troubled by that, as if he would change it, if he could."

"Yes, we arrived at the same conclusion: that your paths would be unlikely to cross." Miranda took Beatrice's hands between her own. "Now that was the first thing Mr. Wolfe said regarding the matter. The second was that it was one thing for the Huftons to kidnap their daughter to protect her from a drunken groom's company, but quite another for us to hide you in the country, to 'protect' you from an honorable man whom you likely would not even encounter. Mr. Wolfe asked if it would be advisable for you to forego this opportunity for amusement and novelty and education out of fear of something which might not even happen." A squeeze of the hands. "Before you went to Bognor I would have dismissed this latter argument and said you were content at home, with neither desire nor need to seek distractions, but now I wonder..."

Beatrice was silent, her gaze abstracted. She was remembering Mr. Clayton after her bathing accident, in the drawing room of Number Four, Spencer Terrace. They had barely known each other at the time, but she could hear again his low, pleasant voice saying, "While your brother and sister might deem wrapping you in cotton wool for the remainder of your stay a comfortable resolution, I have always thought it advisable to face a fear, if one hopes to overcome it."

The Beaumond parlor was quiet, save for the tapping of the rain on the windowpanes and the solemn ticking of the mantel clock. As she waited for her daughter's decision, Miranda felt tempted to yield, to assure Beatrice she might do whatever she pleased, no matter what her parents thought, but she held her peace.

Finally Beatrice spoke. "It would not be out of desire for amusement or novelty or the like that I would want to go, Mama, though—" with a mirthless chuckle "—I suppose it would be a novelty to think of somebody other than myself for a change! I would want to go because—Mr. Wolfe—is right. I should not let fear prevent me from...experiencing life."

"Ah," breathed her mother. She raised Beatrice's hands to her lips and then pressed her cheek against them. "That's my brave girl. You shall conquer this, Beatrice. See if you don't."

Chapter Twelve

Lowlynesse is young Ambitions Ladder,
Whereto the Climber upward turnes his Face.
— Shakespeare, *Julius Caesar,* II.i.23 (1599)

"What do you mean he has decided not to purchase the five hundred shares?" demanded Clayton. "I thought the matter settled and the funds secured."

With a rusty sigh, Alan Braham, formerly Donald Brand's lawyer and man of business and now John Clayton's lawyer and man of business, held out a letter. "His lawyer Keele says, in so many words, that Lord Stanley hasn't time to read through all the shareholder information we sent. Moreover, he has a daughter to marry off and is therefore of a mind at present to reduce unnecessary expenditures and avoid speculation altogether."

His eye running down the page, Clayton confirmed the accuracy of Braham's summary, and he sank into the chair opposite the lawyer's desk. "Stanley was the chief investor, by heaven. With his permission I've been using his name to persuade others to buy shares. Do you know what this means, Braham? If the man withdraws his support, it might well create a panic."

With a nod the lawyer took the sheet back from his client's numb fingers, folding it carefully and hooking it once more on the file. "I know it. But it happens Keele is an old university friend of mine, and our cousins are married, so he told me confidentially that all may not be lost."

"Indeed? How good of a friend is this Keele?" asked Clayton with grim humor. "Does he offer to filch the money himself from the earl's account?"

Braham gave the dry cough which served him as a laugh. "Nothing so risky, Mr. Clayton. But he tells me it will be no use sending Lord Stanley pleading letters about the matter. The man will simply ignore them and leave Keele to write the placating replies. Keele says the trick is to find the earl in person and drive him into a corner. It seems Lord Stanley is far more susceptible to persuasion when it is done face to face. Furthermore, if he gives his word in person, he will find it impossible thereafter to wriggle out from it. A matter of pride, you see."

Groaning, Clayton ran a hand through his hair. "So I'm to go wait upon the earl wherever he lives, hat in hand? What's to stop the man from saying he is not at home?"

"No, you're right. He can't be caught at home. Keele agrees that won't work. You'll have to spring yourself upon him, or he'll dodge you like a creditor."

"What? I'm to chase Lord Stanley around London, then? Perhaps I should simply kidnap the marriageable daughter and hold her for ransom. What exactly does Keele advise?"

Another dry cough, and this time the lawyer's parchment face cracked in a smile. "He advises—and I second it—a two-pronged approach: seek Stanley where he may be found, while simultaneously working to widen your investment base, so that the construction of the Cumberland Arm is not entirely dependent on 'this bruised reed,...on which if a man lean, it will go into his hand, and pierce it.'"

This drew a grin from his client. "Stanley has proven a bruised reed all right. Very well, then. But how do you two recommend I implement this plan? Shall I spring from the hedges beside Rotten Row and hang from the harness of Lord Stanley's mount until the man yields? Then once he has yielded (or failed to yield), I could beg the entree to Watier's to entrap the capital's most daring or foolhardy venturers to make up the balance. Come to think of it, if Lord Stanley himself is a member of Watier's, I might omit altogether the highwayman act in Hyde Park."

"I am quite serious, Mr. Clayton," said Braham, with a hint of reproach. When Clayton only eyed him skeptically, the lawyer slid across the desk an engraved card.

"What is this?"

"It is an invitation."

"I see it is an invitation, but I don't know this person, so it can't have been sent to me."

"I know for a fact it was sent to half of Mayfair and the better portion of Marylebone. But this particular card was sent to a Mr. Dodson. Another client of Keele's with connections of his own."

"Won't Dodson miss it?"

Braham shrugged. "Dodson will be welcome on his own merits, so his presence would never be questioned. The point is, Lady Aurora Robillard intends for every name in London to be at her rout, and to secure the outcome, she has managed to pin down the attendance of the latest mushroom millionaire, a certain St. John Rotherwood. Trust me: your Lord Stanley will be there, as will every man worth canvassing in town, including Rotherwood himself."

"All right, Braham. *They* will be there," conceded Clayton, "but you still haven't explained how *I* would be."

"You will be there because, in that crowd, the presence of one more man, give or take, will entirely escape notice."

Clayton stared. "But—even if I had to audacity to force myself upon them, there would be no one to perform the introductions. I cannot simply plant myself in front of every rich man and ask him if he would please purchase five hundred shares."

"You have met Lord Stanley, at any rate," returned the lawyer, "and if you cling to him, he will have motive enough to perform any and all introductions. Because not only will he wish to extricate himself from a ticklish tête-à-tête, but he will recognize that the more wealthy investors he can bring into your orbit, the fewer shares he will end in having to purchase. If you can't get close enough to

Stanley, look for Dodson. He won't stand on ceremony and has his own reasons for wanting to appear a man of influence."

"And how would I know this Dodson?"

Braham waved a hand. "Young man with dandyish leanings. Waving brown hair. A goodly amount of money which he will likely run through in a shockingly short time because Keele says he's acquired a taste for gambling. You might solicit Dodson himself for a few shares—only tell me at once, so I may secure the funds from Keele while they yet belong to his client."

Braham knew he had carried the day when Clayton didn't answer, falling instead into a brown study. The lawyer let him think while he quietly arranged unanswered correspondence in order of urgency. At last Clayton said, "Very well. I will go, though I doubt I can strike any bargains in such an environment."

"It will be a beginning. Will you take Miss Brand with you? I daresay she would enjoy it, and her presence would give you someone to speak with while you wait for Stanley."

While Clayton could see the advantage of this, his heart sank. For he could also see the disadvantages. Supposing he did manage to attach himself to the earl? How could he then discuss business with the childish Priscilla at his side? Could he ask her beforehand to hold her tongue if he found those he sought? Taking everything into consideration, he probably could make such a request—she was ever anxious to please him, and she would be dazzled to attend a rout alongside such guests—but the realization did not lift his spirits. Rather it only added to the guilt which had niggled at him, mounting steadily as the days passed without him calling at Marlboro Street. For pity's sake—what a boor he was. It wasn't Priscilla's fault he had agreed to marry her. He had done it to himself. Nor was it her fault she was who she was and was not who she was not.

Don't think of who she is not.

Matters stood where they stood, and ignoring them would not make them disappear.

Stifling a sigh, he rose and took up his hat, giving Braham a nod. "It's a good idea. I will ask her."

Across from him in the Brands' landau, Priscilla fairly trembled with excitement. She had taken Clayton's instructions to an extreme, however, and seemed to think she should address him as little as possible the entire evening. Therefore she whispered constantly to Miss Croy beside her. A whisper just loud enough to affect Clayton like the buzzing of an insect but not quite loud enough to be intelligible. Therefore he was left to deduce her remarks from Miss Croy's responses.

"Indeed, your pins are still in place." "I do hope we recognize someone as well." "No, I am not sitting upon your skirts. Pull them free—see?" "I daresay you had better bring your shawl. If it is very warm within, you might let it hang down, but you will want it when it is time to leave."

The rout had begun a half hour earlier, but Clayton having no desire to be among the first arrivals had only made his way to Marlboro Street by then. Now he found the crush of carriages surrounding the approach to Portman Square would likely delay them at least another half hour. Perspiration prickled, despite the November chill. If Lord Stanley put in only a passing appearance and was gone before they arrived, Clayton would be left with no acquaintances at all, in which case he might as well turn right around and leave, however Priscilla might protest.

But it was Priscilla who carried the day, for the moment the footman unfolded the steps and assisted her to alight, she gasped and turned back to the descending Miss Croy, crying, "Cissie! Look there! I declare it's my schoolmate Audrey's cousin—what was her name...?—I have it! Miss Kempshott! It's Miss Kempshott!"

The tall young lady, hearing her name spoken, turned, her narrow countenance lighting with pleasure. "Ah! It's you, is it? Audrey's little friend. Miss—Miss—Burnside?"

"Miss Brand," corrected Priscilla eagerly. In her excitement her curtsey was little more than a jerk. "How lovely to see you again—to see any familiar face. I am so delighted you remember me."

"Of course I remember you," said Miss Kempshott. "When I visited Audrey, the three of us spent that pleasant afternoon in Kentish Town. May I introduce you to my aunt Mrs. Dodson?" She gestured to the imposing older woman behind her with a bust like a ship's figurehead, but one encrusted with diamonds. At the name, Clayton drew a sharp breath, his eyes darting behind them, but he saw no dandyish young man with waving brown hair.

Priscilla gave a more graceful curtsey this time, beginning to remember herself and the injunctions given by her intended. "Er—Mrs. Dodson, Miss Kempshott, may I present my cousin Miss Croy and my intended Mr. Clayton? Cissie and John, this is the Honorable Miss Kempshott, whose cousin attended school in Hampstead with me."

Mrs. Dodson's initially frosty demeanor thawed considerably when she heard this eager and winsome little creature was already engaged, and she became quite affable. "What a crush we have here! Lady Aurora will be triumphant, but I do not know how Kitty and I will find my son Edgar who promised to meet us."

"He won't miss it," Miss Kempshott assured her. She grinned at them. "Ridiculous, really, how all Mayfair is here, hoping to catch sight of the 'Marble Millionaire' and secure an introduction."

Priscilla bit her lip and could not prevent a little hop, so eager was she to ask a dozen questions, but fortunately Clayton had his own reasons for wanting to learn more.

"Mrs. Dodson, I am afraid we are only recently come to town," he began, "and therefore know but few souls as yet and certainly not this millionaire person, though I might have heard him mentioned. How did he come by the nickname you gave him?"

With the glee of being the first to impart news and the satisfaction of boasting a more extensive acquaintance than the newcomers, the matron now beamed upon them. "If you are but recent arrivals, I will be pleased to perform any introductions you like this evening, Mr. Clayton. It will be no trouble at all, for I daresay Kitty and I have at least a bowing acquaintance with many we will meet. And as for the Marble Millionaire Mr. St. John Rotherwood..." With relish, Mrs. Dodson told them of his descent from the now-extinct Holt baronetage and his rapid rise to heir apparent of millions upon millions. "Can you imagine? After being raised in obscurity and having to work for his bread as an Oxford tutor, now to become the catch of the season!" she concluded breathlessly. "Oh, I do so hope he will be here tonight. And his mother Mrs. Rotherwood, of course. Perhaps if he cannot be got at, *she* can."

"How lucky you are to be already engaged," Miss Kempshott told Priscilla drolly. "You cannot imagine the pressure placed upon us single girls and how Mr. Rotherwood's name has been drummed in my ears. If the man and his fortune could only be cut into shares and doled out equally, then there would be plenty of him to go around!"

Clayton twitched at the word "shares," and he said, "In truth, this Rotherwood can hardly be called a millionaire, when he only has the *expectation* of great fortune. Rather, it is his mother Mrs. Rotherwood who is the millionaire-ess, if there is such a term." Could he possibly talk to the woman about purchasing canal shares?

"And don't think every fortune hunter in London is not aware of that," rejoined Mrs. Dodson with good humor. "My son Edgar was even telling me the latest odds in the club betting books, mischievous boy! But there are several good reasons to be confident the young man will eventually have the money for himself: the first is that he is unquestionably the apple of his mother's eye, leaving no room in her heart for love of any other kind; the second is that they are in town together, where the son may quash any amorous attempts to win the mother; and the third is that Sylvester Pinckney has the management of their fortune, and a sharper agent is not to be found in the entire capital."

This last titbit was discouraging from Clayton's perspective. Would there be any point in meeting or wooing either Rotherwood, if it was in fact the agent he must make up to?

By this point they had forced their way into the entrance of the Robillard home, though really it was more a matter of the numbers who arrived after them swelling and pushing them forward. Before them rose a grand staircase, packed cheek by jowl with every person in the capital with pretensions to wealth or fashion, and by the direction in which every head was turned it was clear that the Marble Millionaire had indeed graced the gathering with his presence.

But it was not the muted gasps and squeals and whisperings of his party which claimed Clayton's attention; nor the sight of Rotherwood himself at the top of the staircase, sculpted, aloof and handsome; nor even that of the much-sought Lord Stanley, riveted to Rotherwood's side, gazing up like a suppliant at his incense-shrouded idol. Indeed, Clayton's gaze did not reach the cynosure of all eyes, but instead snagged on the lovely head of a young lady halfway up the flight. Lustrous golden-brown hair, a sweet face in profile with lips slightly parted, bent a degree or two to catch the words of whoever stood next to her—

No—Clayton saw nothing and no one else. His heart pounded so suddenly and irregularly he thought for one terrible moment he would collapse.

Or combust.

Or cry out.

For what was she doing here?

He shut his eyes. Surely it was his imagination playing tricks. Miss Ellsworth crossed his mind so frequently, whether he willed it or not, that his mind must now be greedily seizing upon this young lady of similar coloring and proportions. There could be no other explanation. And he must breathe deeply, as if he were about to plunge his head beneath the waves at Bognor, so that, when he mastered himself again enough to rejoin the world, the apparition would have vanished, leaving behind some other young lady. A perfect stranger who, upon closer inspection, would prove to look not a thing like.

When he did open his eyes again, he forced them to remain on the head directly before him, one swathed in a magnificent silk turban pierced with a feather.

Gradually Mrs. Dodson's words penetrated his consciousness. "...That's him, to be sure. Oh, gracious, Kitty, we have been forestalled. For that vision before Mr. Rotherwood is Lady Sylvia, daughter of Lord Stanley."

"Dear me, she's beautiful," said Miss Kempshott, sounding not at all chagrined. "Looks like the game is up before it's fairly begun, Aunt Ruth."

"It may be, child, but if ever a game was worth the candle, this would be the one. Gracious, it's hot in here, and it may be an eternity before we reach Lady Aurora, much less the Rotherwoods." She plied her fan languorously, letting her gaze wander to lesser mortals.

Then it was Priscilla's turn to pipe up. "John!" A pluck at her betrothed's sleeve. "Look up there! Can that possibly, possibly be Miss Ellsworth? What do you think, Cissy?"

"Why—I do believe so," returned Miss Croy after careful scrutiny. "I wonder what she can be doing here."

Mercy, Clayton thought. Then she had not been an illusion?

Slowly, his breathing uneven, he raised his eyes and looked again beyond the turban in front of him, just as, some dozen steps above, the young lady in question turned to assist her companion with the clasp of her necklace.

"It is! It is, John!" insisted Priscilla, when her intended made no reply.

"Who is what?" demanded Mrs. Dodson.

"The young lady with the light brown hair is Miss Beatrice Ellsworth of the Winchester Ellsworths," answered Priscilla, hopping again. "We knew her in Bognor last month, didn't we, John?" She glanced at her still-silent companion, willing him to speak, but at the sight of his thundercloud brow she drooped, pressing her lips together. That was right. He had invited her to accompany him to this glittering event but warned her that it was for business purposes, and if she would be so kind as to follow his lead in conversation...? But surely he would not accuse her of letting her tongue run away with her, simply because she remarked on their mutual acquaintance?

"I do believe the older lady with her is Lady Hufton, wife of Sir John Hufton," Mrs. Dodson said thoughtfully. "We were introduced once. And the other young lady must be her daughter Miss Hufton for they're alike as two peas. Ah! See there? Lady Hufton has caught sight of me. Let us force our way to them."

Before the others could object, Mrs. Dodson thrust her magnificent bosom between the guests above them like the icebreaker on a bridge pier, and just like river ice, the crowd parted. Miss Kempshott followed in her wake, chuckling at her aunt's tactics, tugging Priscilla by the hand, who in turn tugged Miss Croy. It was left to Clayton in the rear to make appropriate apologetic mutterings, but he was so discomposed by the crisis of meeting Miss Ellsworth again that he later had no memory of what he said or how anyone responded.

But even this blurred blink of time gave Clayton the advantage over Beatrice, for she did not see Miss Brand or him until they were two steps below her, at which point her sharp breath was audible even over the buzz of the throng. "Mr. Clayton! Miss Brand. Miss Croy. What a—pleasure. I mean—what a surprise. That is, what a-a pleasurable surprise."

She shut her lips abruptly on this babbling, but Priscilla was still too abashed to do more than smile at her widely in answer and Clayton too perplexed. As the two varied parties were clustered on three different steps without enough space to bow and curtsey properly, introductions proved a challenge, but at last they were accomplished.

For her part, Beatrice was forcing down panic. It was one thing to be brave and to tell her stepmother she would risk a chance encounter with Mr. Clayton in the capital and quite another to meet him at the very first social affair. She had pictured it happening very differently: she would be driving with Lady Hufton and Miss Hufton in Regent's Park and glimpse the man standing beside a ditch, open plan in hand while he directed the workers. (Having never in her life seen the unfinished park or any canal, finished or unfinished, Beatrice must be pardoned for the vagueness of her fancies.) But this! Mr. Clayton at the rout of a fashionable viscountess? A beautifully tailored Mr. Clayton, no less, in black and buff, his dark hair dressed, flanked by not only the fetching Miss Brand but also an Honorable and a woman sparkling with diamonds! Beatrice was simply dumbfounded.

And Clayton—he was equal parts confusion and mortification. Confusion at the sight of her whom he had pictured a day's journey away, and mortification to be found in such a setting. What must she think of him? That he had posed in Bognor as the modest engineer to mask his social ambitions? Or that he had acquired a taste for such things after a fortnight in that place and the more exalted company he kept there? Even if she did not think such things yet, she certainly would, once she saw him pursue Earl Stanley or the embryo millionaire Mr. Rotherwood.

"There they go," hissed someone nearby. "The Stanleys are carrying him off!"

Every head on the staircase tilted upward, like so many sunflowers at midday, in time to see the triumphant earl and countess with their beautiful daughter march away beside the Marble Millionaire, trailing various hopefuls and hangers-on. A collective sigh issued from the staircase mass, but the departure of the Golden Ones had at least the positive effect of unstopping the plug and allowing a freer flow of traffic to greet the hostess.

Chapter Thirteen

...Speake her pardon or her sentence;
Onely break thy Silence.
— Richard Crashaw, *Steps to the temple: Sacred poems,*
with other delights of the muses (1646)

I f Mrs. Dodson had hoped to impress Lady Hufton by introducing the handsome John Clayton and unexceptionable Miss
Brand to her acquaintance, the fact that Lady Hufton's charge already knew them robbed her of this satisfaction.

"It was but a brief acquaintance," Miss Ellsworth said almost
apologetically, after referencing the time in Bognor. Mrs. Dodson's
jeweled bosom and social confidence cowed her in her flustered
condition, and she thoughtlessly added, "I daresay you and Miss
Kempshott know them quite as well as I do already."

To Clayton's anxious ears, this was a scoff, as if she had added, "They have turned out so different from what I was led to believe." She could say this, after what had passed between them at the seaside? Not the rescue—he hardly thought of the rescue—but the laughter and dancing and friendship and talk?

A hundred possible responses occurred to him, none finding utterance, and he was grateful when Miss Croy spoke up (a result of Priscilla poking her and whispering).

"But Miss Ellsworth, how do you come to be in London?" asked the unprepossessing woman. "You never mentioned such a plan in Bognor."

Beatrice colored, in dread that Mr. Clayton should think she had followed him, to force herself once more upon his notice. "I said nothing of it, Miss Croy, because at the time I had no notion of taking another trip."

"As a matter of fact, it was I who begged Beatrice to join us," spoke up Lady Hufton, squinting her eyes and tipping up her chin. "I thought my Marjorie would enjoy the capital so much more with a friend her age. They are stepcousins, you see. My brother is married to Beatrice's stepmother."

"Goodness, I hope you will admit me to your company," said Miss Kempshott cheerfully, "if Miss Brand and Miss Ellsworth are already acquainted, and Miss Hufton and Miss Ellsworth nearly cousins. Miss Brand must vouch for me, Miss Ellsworth. I am harmless. We may all band together, I hope, to carry the day and conquer London."

Mrs. Dodson could not pretend to share her niece's delight and seconded this with a chilly smile. Four young ladies! What was Kitty thinking? The girl had no more awareness of danger than a goldfish. A *herd* of four young ladies would scare away every eligible young man in sight! And though Miss Brand was already engaged and Miss Hufton looked only a younger, grimmer version of her mother, Miss Ellsworth was a horse of another color—

"We might be too late, however," continued Miss Kempshott in the same blithe manner, "because it seems Lady Sylvia Stanley has already made off with the prize of the season. Let us pray some other worthy appears to practice our wiles upon."

"Kitty, honestly," chided her aunt, even as Miss Hufton's face darkened.

With a sniff the latter declared, "You may have *my* share of gentlemen, Miss Kempshott, for I have no intention of *ever* marrying."

Then it was Lady Hufton's turn to cluck, "Oh, Marjorie, my dear! Such vehemence."

"You would be vehement too," muttered her daughter, "had you been kidnapped against your will as I have."

"Ha ha, dear girl!" tittered Lady Hufton. "'Kidnapped,' indeed! As if a thousand girls would not give their eyes to be in your place."

"There would be no need for them to make such a sacrifice," scowled Miss Hufton, "when rather it is I who would give anything to return to Kent."

An awkward pause succeeded this, into which Clayton eventually dropped, like a pebble in a pond, "It appears then, if eligible London is to be conquered, Miss Kempshott, it must be you and Miss

Ellsworth in the vanguard, and I do not doubt you will prove equal to the task."

"Behold—a gauntlet thrown down!" cried Miss Kempshott. "Miss Ellsworth, shall we take it up?"

Beatrice smiled tightly, despite a flare of vexation. What did Mr. Clayton mean, saying she must be in London to catch a husband—as if she were a flirt, a butterfly? As if Lady Hufton had not just explained the reason for her presence? (And keeping Marjorie Hufton company so far had certainly proven more a chore than a pleasure.) Mr. Clayton had no right, no right at all, to assume her presence at this rout bespoke some other hidden motive!

"Mr. Clayton makes it sound as if conquering London was something only attempted by young ladies," she said with dangerous sweetness. "But for every young lady here who dreams of courtship, surely there is also a young man who dreams of *climbing*."

There, she thought, seeing him redden. But the next instant she felt ashamed—the man had saved her life, after all, and she begrudged him one little, half-teasing, critical remark? If it could even have been called critical. For there was no denying that many—most—young ladies did come to town to catch husbands. Had Mr. Clayton discovered her in Hounslow Heath holding a pistol, he would be excused for thinking her a highwayman—how was this any different?

Each felt misunderstood. Each longed for an opportunity to explain.

At the top of the stairs, the hostess Lady Aurora Robillard welcomed them, though she blinked in surprise at the unknown Clayton party.

"Who is this with you, my dear Mrs. Dodson and Miss Kempshott?"

"Miss Brand here is a school friend of Miss Kempshott's cousin," Mrs. Dodson explained, a little startled herself to realize the Clayton party had no acquaintance of their own with their august hostess. Had she been currying favor with an *umbra*—an uninvited guest?

"Which makes her my friend as well," put in Miss Kempshott, smilingly.

"And I too consider Miss Brand and—Mr. Clayton and Miss Croy friends," blurted Beatrice from the step below, scarlet flooding her face even as she spoke. The eyebrows of Lady Aurora rose at these bold interjections, but Lady Hufton scrambled to regain control of the situation. "Yes, indeed, Lady Aurora. Do pardon the *informality* of my dear step-niece. You know how eagerly the younger people take to each other."

"I do indeed," Lady Aurora returned. There was no doubt this Mr. Clayton was a handsome addition to her gathering, whoever he was, so she let the irregularity pass, giving them a parting nod.

If Beatrice hoped to catch Mr. Clayton's eye at that point, she was disappointed, for Mrs. Dodson swept her niece and the Clayton party away with a breezy, "Would you excuse us, Jenny? I promised Mr. Clayton I would introduce him to as many noteworthy people as I could manage."

Not knowing Miss Ellsworth's feelings on the matter and glad to have escaped a ticklish situation, Lady Hufton raised no objections, instead taking firm hold of her daughter's elbow to steer her behind some palms and tell her a piece of her mind. Beatrice had no choice but to accompany them, though she would have preferred not to hear what followed.

"A word with you, young lady," Lady Hufton hissed.

"Don't you want a word with Miss Ellsworth too?" demanded her daughter. "I can see you mean to criticize my conduct, but it was Miss Ellsworth who just *accosted* our hostess when nobody was addressing her!"

"Never mind about Beatrice," Lady Hufton said, not to be distracted. "Listen to me: your papa and I have your best interests at heart, and I would have you hold your chin up and remember yourself. What would have become of you, Marjorie, if we allowed you to elope with Hughes? You would have lost your rank! Your place in the world! All to be the wife of a drunken groom, growing poorer and more slatternly by the year!"

Such home truths only caused Marjorie to burst out in sobs, which her mother tried to hush and Beatrice to mask with a coughing fit.

"But I love him, Mama! And he isn't drunken—that is, he doesn't drink *too* much, and he tells me he will not touch another drop, if only I will marry him! *Can't* we go home again?"

"We absolutely cannot. If you ever wish to see Kent again, Marjorie, you must prove to your father and me that you can behave sensibly. Here you are surrounded by your kind. You must not complain at where God has seen fit to place you in the world. That dreadful Hughes has probably already given up and begun to chase someone more within reach—"

This drew new wails, and Beatrice was forced to utter, "Madam, we will be overheard!" Ducking behind the potted palms, she put an arm about the girl's shaking shoulders. "Miss Hufton, I am so sorry for your distress. It must be very difficult to be asked to—put aside and-and forget someone you care for." This was by no means the first time Beatrice had tried to express timid sympathy (though from the bits and pieces her unhappy stepcousin shared of the groom Hughes, Beatrice could not begin to understand his appeal). On every earlier occasion, however, Miss Hufton had snappishly told Beatrice to keep her breath to cool her porridge. But now, a fortnight onward, as water wears away the stone, the girl gave way like a rotting wall and slumped against her. Lady Hufton's eyes met those of Beatrice. *Here was progress!*

Beatrice nodded at her step-aunt, mouthing, *Leave her to me a while.*

"I will fetch us some refreshment," announced Lady Hufton loudly. With a last glance at her still-sniffling daughter, she marched away.

Miss Marjorie Hufton might be quieting, but her tears continued to flow in abundance, as Beatrice could attest, feeling the damp spot on her shoulder spread toward her bodice. This must be what the cisterns felt like when the gutters from the eaves emptied rain into them.

"Miss Hufton," she murmured.

"Ermjree," wept the latter, her words unintelligible. "Kermer er-mjree."

"Miss Hufton," Beatrice said again. "Again, I am sorry for your heartbreak. If it—if it is any comfort, I know what it is like to—form a doomed attachment."

Miss Hufton's head came up so quickly she nearly knocked Beatrice in the chin. The girl looked considerably the worse for wear, her small eyes now red-ringed and her complexion blotched. "Y-You do?"

Much as she wished to comfort her companion, Beatrice shrank from making a detailed confession, especially with the object of her affections somewhere nearby. She cleared her throat. "I do. There was—someone I met once whom I liked very much."

"But your parents objected?"

"No...my parents never met him. But he—shortly after I met him, he went away, and later I heard he—had been engaged to somebody else all along."

"Wretch!" cried Miss Hufton. "Leading you to believe—when he was engaged the whole time! Then he was not deserving of your affection," she declared, not giving Beatrice a chance to defend Mr. Clayton, even if she had known how. "He was not like—not like—my—my—darling Sam." Another wail began to wind up, like the whistling approach of a cannonball which would blast them to pieces, but Beatrice jammed the girl's face against her again, administering hasty pats and susurrations to cover the urgency of the measure.

"In any event," Beatrice continued, "we must rally, Miss Hufton."

"Ermjree."

"What?"

Miss Hufton's head rose again, and this time she shrieked before Beatrice could do anything about it, as her earring had snagged in the lace trim of Beatrice's dress and jerked her back.

"Shh—shhh—here—let me untangle it," said Beatrice, fumbling to detach the whimpering girl. Their nearness and her slippery silk gloves made it a tricky business, but at last it was done. "There. Heavens, Miss Hufton."

"Marjorie," said the latter with a long sniff. "Thank you. Won't you call me Marjorie?"

"Yes, of course I will, if you will call me Beatrice. But I mean to say, we must rally. We must. For our own sakes and for the sake of those who love us. Leaving aside the question of their worthiness, we must try to—forget those persons we—liked—and carry on."

"Oh, Beatrice. I don't know if I can." Marjorie's face screwed up again alarmingly, but then, just as quickly, it unscrewed, and her mouth fell open. "Dear me! What a mess I have made of you, when you have been so kind. You look like you've been ducked head foremost in a barrel and swished about."

Dismayed, Beatrice looked down to see it was so, the fabric of her sleeve and upper bodice darkened with moisture and her lace now trailing several threads.

"Here," said Marjorie, snapping open her fan and beginning to wave it energetically. "We will dry you. Where is yours? Quickly, before Mama returns."

"There is no way I will dry before Lady Hufton returns," protested Beatrice, but she plied her own fan all the same.

"Good gracious!" came Lady Hufton's voice. The rest of her followed soon after, bearing two glasses of lemonade. "Well, I am relieved to see you have mastered yourself, Marjorie, but what have you done to poor Beatrice? No, no—stop that, girls. All that fanning is only making her hair untidy. Here, Beatrice, take your glass of lemonade and hold it with both hands in front of you. Perhaps no one will notice. But in the next drawing room where I got these, one of Lady Aurora's maids was putting drops of sal volatile in water for old Mrs. Sloane. If you hurry, you can catch her and tell her to bring you one of Lady Aurora's muslin shawls to cover yourself with."

Beatrice obeyed. Shoulders hunched and lemonade held before her like a ceremonial chalice, she threaded her way through the gathering until she reached the passage, where she peeped into the rooms opening to either side.

There was no sign of Lady Aurora's maid, but without any better ideas, Beatrice ventured into the refreshment room nevertheless. Perhaps she might tuck her handkerchief into the top of her dress while she waited? If she ate something at the same time, her action would seem only gauche, rather than bizarre.

Replacing the glass of lemonade on the table, Beatrice snatched up a biscuit and retreated to a chair behind more potted palms in the farthest corner of the room, where she might wait for the reappearance of the maid. Whether from economy or the wish to provide private corners of retreat, the candles in the nearest sconces were not lit, lending a welcome dimness.

Thus hidden from view, Beatrice did not bother with getting out her handkerchief and absently began to eat her biscuit, seizing upon the moment of peace to return to thoughts of Mr. Clayton. If she could find him again, she would apologize for her unpleasant insinuation. To call him a climber! Why, he might have a dozen reasons to be at this rout. Miss Brand had said he met often with important people, after all. Perhaps one of those important people had asked to speak with him here, especially since his latest project was found right here in the capital, rather than the more northerly hinterlands. Yes, that must be it—Mr. Clayton hoped to meet someone for business, but had not yet found him and was thus placed in the awkward position of attending the rout without prior acquaintance of the hostess. Hardly an approach he would have chosen, if his primary goal was to ingratiate himself with the fashionable world! Oh—it was all too, too plausible, and she had accused him of making up to people for ambition's sake!

"Please," she prayed under her breath, "please may I have a chance to beg his pardon?" She could not even revive her earlier resentment toward him, when he had joked about her conquering London. Indeed, now it struck her as a blessing. For wasn't it better for him to think she was in town to catch a husband, than for him to suspect she came in hopes of seeing *him*?

Providence soon smiled upon Beatrice's prayer, with the appearance of the very man she sought in the doorway, accompanied by Lord Stanley, but like all answered prayers it proved a mixed blessing, for her pulse accelerated so violently in response she thought she might swoon. Gracious! Would they come near? And if they did not, should she approach Mr. Clayton? But how could she, when he had the earl beside him and the two of them were conversing so intently, and her dress was in such disarray?

The two gentlemen seemed more in want of privacy than refreshment for, to Beatrice's consternation, they strolled slowly in her direction.

"...You saw one of the chief reasons for my hesitation beside me, I daresay," Lord Stanley was saying. "My daughter Lady Sylvia was still in school when Parliament approved the Cumberland Arm and Brand approached me to invest. But now over two years have passed. Brand has died, God rest him, and my Sylvia must take her place in the fashionable world. And when she marries there will be the matter of her settlement. I would not have you believe I am a poor man, Clayton, but of course my money does not sit around in bags upon my desk, waiting until I have need of it. What I had ready at hand two years ago has since been allocated elsewhere. That is the long and short of it."

They had stopped some feet away, on the other side of the potted palms, and Beatrice hunched accordingly deeper into the shadows, hardly daring to breathe.

"Sir." Mr. Clayton's voice was heavy. "What you say makes perfect sense, I assure you. But I hope it will make sense to you as well when I observe that the loss at this stage of our chief investor, no matter how plausible the reasons for his withdrawal, will come as a crippling setback to the project as a whole."

Stanley grunted, unwilling to concede the point, and after another pause, Clayton continued. "I wonder if you could not...speak to your man of business and perhaps...find some portion of the original pledge? Not five hundred shares, to be sure, but possibly four hundred or three hundred. It would be far easier for me to persuade other investors to take up the necessary shares if I could still speak of you as the driving force behind the project, not to mention, filling the gap of one or perhaps two hundred shares is more easily done than the alternative."

"Hmm."

In the gloom Beatrice could not be positive, but she thought the earl frowned and twitched with annoyance.

"Hmm," Stanley grunted again after a minute, giving a wave of his gloved hand idly mid-air, as if chasing away a cloud of gnats. "Let me think on it and let you know my decision at another time."

With sinking spirits, Beatrice thought Mr. Clayton would be lucky if Lord Stanley handed over so much as three or four shillings at this rate. But though she expected Mr. Clayton to admit defeat and let the earl flee, he surprised her, drawing a deep breath and straightening. "Thank you, sir. If you would allow me one last observation...?"

A grimace from the earl met this persistence, which Mr. Clayton wisely or foolishly pretended not to see.

"This arm off the Regent's Canal is too valuable an enterprise to be left undone," he resumed, "and it *will* be completed, by hook or by crook, as the saying goes. You see how the Grand Junction Canal has already proven its value—and rewarded its initial investors—a hundred times over, but how much more valuable will a branch be, which joins the Grand Junction to the capital itself? For at present everything conveyed on that mighty canal can only be brought the final miles to the markets and warehouses and barracks of London with great inconvenience and expense. Imagine, then, the golden day when those same things float easily and cheaply from the farther reaches of the kingdom or the ends of the earth all the way to the heart of the capital, stopping only to pay a few tolls. Tolls which will line the pockets of those who first made such a miracle possible."

Beatrice had a sudden vision of barge after barge heaped with goods, floating along a glimmering waterway—a vision which admittedly drew more inspiration from Enobarbus' speech in *Antony and Cleopatra* than reality—but something similar must have struck Lord Stanley because this time his grunt was more of an "ah-ha."

For the first time since entering the room, the earl looked directly at his petitioner. "Ah-ha," he repeated. "Hmm. I understand. Yes, Clayton, your point is a persuasive one. Let me talk to my man. Perhaps some portion may be recovered."

"Then—I may continue to name you as one of the investors?" pressed Mr. Clayton.

"...You may," conceded Lord Stanley at last. "Not the principal investor, but you may name me. And, in the meantime you must give such a speech to as many as you can. Here you stand, my good man, in the financial and social capital of all the world. Surely you can turn that to your advantage."

With that he swept away, leaving Mr. Clayton to regard him thoughtfully. Beatrice thought he would follow, but he must have wanted to afford the earl some space, for he lingered, wandering after another moment toward the table of refreshments.

Now, Beatrice! she urged herself. *Go to him.* Let her damp and straggling condition be, for she might not find another opportunity, and even this occasion could not last. She was surprised, in fact, that Lady Hufton had not already come in search of her.

"Mr. Clayton."

He startled at her voice. "Miss Ellsworth!" In a glance he took in her appearance, and the corners of his mouth twitched. "Did I miss another swim lesson?"

She made a hasty, dismissive gesture. "Never mind my appearance. Mr. Clayton, I may only have a second to tell you, but I wanted to—to beg your pardon for my—my—my discourteous and—unjustified remark earlier this evening. When I called you a 'climber,' I mean. Or—I did not call you that, exactly, but I might have implied—*did* imply. It discomfited you, I'm afraid, and it was wholly undeserved. You have shown me nothing but kindness, you know. And I don't believe it of you at all! Not a bit. I cannot think what possessed me—therefore I have been so embarrassed this evening. So regretful—"

He was already holding up his hands to stem her outpouring. "Miss Ellsworth—please. I assure you, if there was anything to pardon, I have long done so. It was natural you would be astonished to find me here—I'm rather astonished myself. Though not as much as I was to find you here as well, until your—'step-aunt,' would she be called?—explained the circumstances."

Beaming, Beatrice clasped her hands to her soggy bosom. "Yes—what an unexpected occurrence. When I learned I was coming here, I—thought the odds very small that we would meet..."

"And I thought when I left Bognor I would never see you again," he said quietly.

A weighty pause followed, where neither knew quite what to say.

You have apologized, Beatrice reminded herself. *You may go now.* But she didn't move.

With a wrench, Clayton tried to turn the conversation in an easier direction. "Yes—that is—in Bognor I gave you no indication that I intended to live the life of a swell in town—"

"Nor *do* you intend to live such a life," Beatrice broke in, glad of another opportunity to assure him of her good opinion. "For I must also confess I overheard your discussion with Lord Stanley just now. I could not help it. I was seated behind the palms in the corner, trying to repair my state." She held out her arms, as if he had not seen the dampness of her dress. "You can understand why I hesitated to spring from my hiding place. I suppose you must have come tonight in hopes of speaking with him."

"I did."

"I am sorry, Mr. Clayton—it sounded like trouble with your canal project."

He regarded her a long moment, his lips pressing in a line, as if to hold back words. But then he nodded. "I'm afraid so."

"Oh, my." Beatrice extended a hand toward his sleeve but stopped short. "If I understood correctly, you will require additional investors to...make up for Lord Stanley withdrawing."

"You have hit the nail right on the head, I'm afraid." His eyes fell to her outstretched hand and then swiftly looked away.

Self-consciously, she drew it back and wound it in her skirts. "I found your description of what the Cumberland Arm can be—*will* be—so powerful," she went on. "So persuasive. Why, I decided two things on the spot from hearing it."

That drew a smile. "Did you? Pray enlighten me. What two things did you decide so impulsively, my dear eavesdropper?"

Feeling her face warm to be called dear, even in jest, she hurried on. "For one thing, I would write to my family of it. You remember Tyrone showed interest? As for myself, I have only my pin money ready to hand, unless I speak to my brother-in-law Mr. Fairchild, but perhaps he would agree to advancing me a portion of my inheritance—"

"Miss Ellsworth," he interrupted, his expression alarmed. "I beg you not to speak to your Mr. Fairchild."

"But why not? You believe it a worthy investment, so what would I lose by it?"

"Please. It is indeed a worthy investment, but all the same, it would not be proper to ask a young lady to draw on her own funds." He gave an expressive shudder. "To be honest, I wish you would not mention it to your brother, either. It would seem as if I had...preyed upon your goodwill at Bognor."

"How, 'preyed upon'?" she demanded, indignant on his behalf. "Why should you praise the enterprise, when speaking to Lord Stanley, and then act as if it were some—some *swindle* if I propose to participate?"

"Because it would be a swindle of sorts, Miss Ellsworth," he replied, his rueful smile returning. "It would be taking advantage of—of your family's kindness and friendship, when the idea to invest would never have occurred to any of you, had you not met me. But come—do not look so downcast. Tell me the second thing you 'decided on the spot,' and let us hope it is not similarly objectionable."

His tone had become teasing with this last, and Beatrice at first could only blush and stammer a little in response. How she longed to come to his aid, if only he would allow it!

"Well, whether you find my second idea objectionable, I daresay you can do nothing to prevent me acting on it," she began, with a touch of defensiveness.

"Dear heavens, what can it be? A sign? An advertisement published in the newspapers? A shop card you will hand out in Bond Street?"

Her hazel eyes flashed at him. "It is neither kind nor friendly of you to mock me, sir, when I mean to do you a good turn."

"You're right," he said solemnly. "Forgive me, Miss Ellsworth, and let me hear you in good earnest."

"I simply thought that, if I am to be in London for the time being, meeting all sorts of people, perhaps I might have occasion to talk about your project and—how beneficial it would be." In shyness she spoke to the top button of his waistcoat. "I have heard your speech and think I could manage to reproduce a version of it when called upon. Only—if I do find any of my new acquaintance showing interest, to whom should I direct them?" Raising wary eyes and clearly expecting him to find fault with this plan as well, she was glad to see him wrestling with the notion.

And Clayton was indeed wrestling. He could not help but remember how, only a few hours earlier, he had effectively asked Priscilla to let him do the talking to their new acquaintances that evening. Leery of her youth and naïveté, he had feared she might blunder and jeopardize his own efforts. Having thus bid his intended bride to guard her tongue, how then could he give Miss Ellsworth permission to speak on his behalf, to whomever she thought fit?

Miss Ellsworth is cleverer than Priscilla, may heaven pardon me for saying so.

He tried to rationalize it to himself. Miss Ellsworth was a few years older, and when one was so young, each year of additional maturity made a difference. But, no, that was not all of it. Miss Ellsworth was by nature more reserved, more contained in company than Priscilla. He trusted her discretion. She would never fidget or prance or baldly yearn for attention as Priscilla did, poor girl. Twice-poor Priscilla Brand, whose soon-to-be husband could tally up her weaknesses so coolly! Indeed, though Clayton would have been a far happier man to overlook such things, it was impossible for him, as impossible as overlooking engineering flaws in a work project.

Finally, slowly, he said, "I have no authority over you, Miss Ellsworth..."

"Not a shred of it," rejoined Beatrice promptly, with more confidence than she felt. Inwardly her spirits danced. He was going to let her help him! He trusted her not to bungle things! (*Oh, please, dear Lord, may I not bungle things—*)

"And I suppose I have already pushed my luck in asking you not to invest personally in the Cumberland Arm." He shook his head, but he was smiling. "Therefore, if you find any fish nibbling at your line, you had better direct them to Alan Braham, Cursitor Street."

CHAPTER FOURTEEN

And so the grand scheme and contrivance of...redemption...must only be the fruits of his own disappointment, and contrivances of his to mend and patch up, as well as he could, his system.

— Jonathan Edwards, *A careful and strict enquiry into the modern prevailing notions of that freedom of will* **(1754)**

The following day found Clayton in Cursitor Street himself to relate the results of his efforts to the lawyer.

"You have made a promising start," Alan Braham declared, "in getting Stanley to reconsider. I doubt you will get the five hundred shares from him, but you might recoup a hundred."

"A hundred," repeated the young man grimly from where he sat across the desk. Throwing himself back in the chair, he contemplated the ceiling, darkened from the smoke of the oil lamps. "Leaving a shortfall of four hundred shares. Not that the earl can be counted on for even the hundred. I will have to pursue the man until he gives me the money just to be rid of me."

"Your persistence will yield another benefit or benefits, Mr. Clayton. For I daresay Stanley will begin to recommend the canal shares to his own acquaintance, simply to be rid of you. Between his persuasion and your own, you should be able to find at least another couple rich men in Mayfair. After that it may be a tedious matter of pursuing individual, smaller investments."

"Mm." With a wry grimace, John thought of Miss Ellsworth and her pin money. If fifty or a hundred such young ladies bought a share or two...

"There is, of course, another source of funds," resumed the lawyer after a minute.

Clayton raised his head, his look enquiring.

"Your own."

"Mine?"

"Well—effectively your own."

"Do you mean the £200 per annum Brand designated for me until the completion of the project?"

"That would not go far, to be sure," admitted Braham with a courteous cough. "No—I had something else in mind: you might marry Miss Brand sooner, rather than later. Before the ink was dry on your marriage license, her fortune of ten thousand pounds would be *your* fortune of ten thousand pounds, to dispose of in whatever manner you saw fit. And while I would not advise using the whole of it to purchase shares—you will need something to live on until they begin to pay out—some considerable portion of it could go toward the purpose."

Rising, Clayton began to pace the room, pausing before the window to peer into narrow Cursitor Street. He had thought of the possibility, of course. Thought of it and dismissed it. Although he had given his word to marry Priscilla, he could not bear to do so yet, when they still hardly knew each other and did not yet love, and when his mind still lingered on Miss Ellsworth. And while he knew it fruitless to think of that young lady, he was not cold-blooded enough to pretend love for Priscilla for the convenience of plundering her inheritance.

"Thank you, Braham," he said after a long pause, turning back to face him. "I will think on the matter. But while I do, I will persevere in the course of action already proposed. To which end I must leave you now." The shadow of a grin appeared on his face. "To wit, a dancing lesson. For, if I am to chase these people about, I cannot let them escape me in the ballroom."

The dusty lawyer returned his grin. "The next time you see Stanley, tell him the least he can do is procure you vouchers for Almack's."

Mr. Wilson's Academy of Dance was located in Wells Street, an easy walk for Miss Brand and Miss Croy from their home in Marlboro Street but requiring Clayton to hail a cab if he wished to be there in time.

Priscilla was in a flutter when he arrived. "Oh, John, there you are. What a dingy place this is! We hesitated to go in without you."

The academy shared a building with a drawing-master and a printer, and the plate which marked it was by no means the largest or shiniest. This dancing lesson would be a far cry from running up the stairs of Number Four, Spencer Terrace, anticipating coziness and good company, but there it was.

"You will never guess who Cissy and I received a card from," Priscilla said as they climbed the stairs.

He looked back to show his attentiveness, but when she did not go on he was obliged to prompt her. "Was it from Mrs. Dodson?"

"Yes! I was so glad of it, John. It was lovely to know she was willing to continue the acquaintance. Miss Kempshott even signed her name underneath her aunt's printed name. You may ask Cissy, but I was all a-tremble, and why do you think that was?"

They had reached the landing, where the door lay open. Mr. Wilson's school consisted of one vast and bare great room, holding only hooks along the wall on which the students hung their cloaks and coats and a spinet in the corner.

"You had better tell me everything you wish to, all at once," he answered, "because when the lesson begins you may not have another chance."

Her brow knitting at his uncourtly manner, she said with a touch of sulkiness, "I only wanted to say that I do hope it means we will see them again! I mean, Cissy and I can call and leave our own card, but that's not the same as going to a ball or something. Oh, John, how I would like to dance in London, but do you suppose we will ever do so outside this room? Will we ever be invited to a ball with lords and ladies?"

"I hope so, for your sake," he returned, lowering his voice. "But it wouldn't do to expect or become accustomed to such things. Because once I succeed in finding investors to replace Lord Stanley and work begins in earnest—"

"Yes, yes," she interrupted, surprising him with the first sign of temper she had shown. "I know. When you have your precious money, you will be too busy digging ditches to squire me about town. You need not say so again."

"Priscilla," Miss Croy remonstrated feebly.

But there was no time for more because a slender young man with rather beautiful golden locks and mournful blue eyes approached. "Are you here for the three o'clock lesson?" he asked, in a tender voice which reminded Clayton of a cooing dove. "The others are waiting." He indicated a handful of pupils ranged against the far wall, keeping each to himself, and Clayton was relieved to see they were all adults. It would have added a level of mortification to partner children.

"You are Mr. Wilson?" asked Priscilla, following him without a second look at her intended. Clayton suspected she meant him to feel snubbed.

"No, no. I am Mr. Hubert Saint-Cloud, Mr. Wilson's assistant. And you are...?"

Introductions followed. Of course Clayton had not expected to meet with any of the people whom he had encountered at Lady Aurora Robillard's rout—everyone of that class having likely begun dancing lessons once out of leading strings. No, their fellow students at Wilson's academy hailed from a stratum or two below the rout set, as many made no secret of. Perhaps Miss Ellsworth would call them "climbers" for aspiring to imitate those above them. Or were they like Clayton himself, hoping merely to comport themselves without disgrace if called to mix with the Lord Stanleys and Lady Auroras of the world? Probably a mixture of both. Before Miss Ellsworth applied the offensive word to him, Clayton would have said both she and the Tyrone Ellsworths seemed oddly indifferent to such classifications, perhaps from being what the smart London set would call "provincial," which had made her accusation sting all the more. But the memory of her barb led naturally to the sweeter memory of her apology, and he found himself seeing again, hearing again, reliving that delicious moment.

"Mr. Clayton, are you attending?" the soft-spoken dancing master broke into his thoughts. "If you could take your place..."

Rousing himself, he discovered the other pupils had formed a set, and with a muttered apology he hurried to stand across from

Priscilla. Miss Croy had been paired with the insurance broker, the shipbuilder's daughter with the jeweler, and so on down the line.

Despite his quietness, Mr. Saint-Cloud ruled absolutely, with no need for an iron fist. On the contrary, his students hung on his murmured instructions, and when Saint-Cloud needed to address the accompanist the languorous lift of his gloved hand would cause her to break off at once.

The lesson could not have contrasted more sharply with the one Clayton received in Bognor, nor did he perform as well as he had for the Ellsworths, but it would suffice, and he would suffice. Another fortnight of this, thrice per week, and he could certainly lead Priscilla and Miss Croy to the floor without mishap. Moreover, this style of lesson had compensatory amusements, namely the dancing master.

Holding himself aloof and bestowing favor with the lift of an eyebrow or censure by the curl of his lip, Hubert Saint-Cloud commanded the room as if he were a king and they courtiers. When he demonstrated the figures, he would insert himself in place of one of the men and walk through the steps with the man's partner, causing noticeable flutters in the women: blushes, stumbles, titters.

At one point he said, "Miss Brand, you dance admirably. This cannot be your first lesson."

It was the only praise he had bestowed on any of them, beyond a clipped "good" when they finally managed to get through the pattern without blundering, and Priscilla was correspondingly elated. "I confess, Mr. Saint-Cloud, I have had many dancing lessons in school! But I promised John—Mr. Clayton here—that Miss Croy and I would come with him while he learned. Mr. Clayton and I are engaged to be married."

Saint-Cloud made him a half bow. "I congratulate you. With continued instruction and practice you may eventually be a credit to your bride."

"Thank you," said Clayton dryly.

Raising his gloved hands, Saint-Cloud clapped them together once, and the lesson went on.

"Oh, John!" cried Priscilla when they emerged again into Wells Street two hours later. "I cannot think when I have enjoyed anything so much! Wasn't Mr. Saint-Cloud splendid?"

"*Monsieur le vicomte?* He was a good teacher."

Her mouth made a little round O. "What do you mean, calling him such a thing? Did he really tell you he was a viscount?"

Clayton managed not to pull a face and courteously offered an arm to either lady. "Pardon my facetiousness. It was only a joke. I'm afraid he said nothing of the kind, though it wouldn't surprise me if there were some *emigré* nobleman's blood in him. He carried himself like at least a chevalier. And why shouldn't he? Within the confines of Wilson's Academy of Dance, Mr. Saint-Cloud reigns supreme. Unless the alleged 'Mr. Wilson' appears, I suppose."

She frowned at him and gave a pettish shake of her head before leaning to consult Miss Croy. "What did you think, Cissy? Did you enjoy the lesson?"

"Very much so, my dear, though I confess I was intimidated by Mr. Saint-Cloud."

"Intimidated? Ridiculous Cissy, How could you be intimidated by such a quiet, elegant man?"

"You were not afraid of him, Priscilla, because Mr. Saint-Cloud praised your dancing. But the rest of us…"

Priscilla smiled broadly to hear again the compliment to her skills and gave a little hop and a squeeze to her intended's arm. "He *did* like my dancing! Oh! If only it were time already for the next lesson. But you and John did very well yourselves, Cissy," she added generously. "Mr. Saint-Cloud was not obligated to correct you as often as the others."

By this time they had paused at Oxford Street. Before Clayton could open his mouth, Priscilla anticipated him. "John, won't you accompany us back to Marlboro Street? You might have a cup of tea or even stay as late as supper. I have a new piece of music I have been practicing."

"That sounds lovely, but I beg you and Miss Croy to excuse me," he demurred. "I met with Braham earlier and would like to work on condensing the information about the project so that it might be imparted in ten minutes, five minutes, or one minute, as opportunity affords. As we go forth to meet the Lord Stanleys and Mr. Rotherwoods of the world, I must be ready. All activities bend thitherward, you know. Even these dance lessons share that sinister purpose."

"'Sinister'? I am sure you are too hard on yourself, John," returned Priscilla, missing his joke as she usually did. "Will we not see you until the next lesson, then?"

"You make it sound as if it were next January instead of two days from now," he said, smiling more broadly to remove any sting from his words.

But the young lady could not be blamed for thinking what Clayton himself thought, after he had taken leave of them: that if he truly loved her, he would have counted each day apart as time lost, rather than gained.

Am I a fool for delaying marriage to Priscilla? he wondered, as he retraced his steps up Wells Street. If it could not be avoided, what point was there in putting it off? Braham, for one, could not understand why he did not leap at the chance to kill two birds with one stone. Why not set the date and, when the deed was done and her fortune in hand, abolish much of the project's budget deficiency?

"I can't," he muttered aloud to the passing traffic. "I cannot be so cold-blooded about it. Better to jilt her altogether than to let her money rush me into what I would otherwise defer." Though it was not true, of course—that it would be better to jilt her. Jilting Miss Brand would only plunge her in humiliation and scandal, not at all what her father Donald Brand had in mind when he exacted his promise.

But if Brand were still alive, would he still have encouraged Clayton to marry his daughter, if he knew Clayton cared for another? Much as Brand had loved his only child, Clayton did not think he flattered himself to believe Brand had also loved *him*. Surely the man would have seen the two were not an easy pairing; he would have seen and mistrusted Clayton's politeness and Priscilla's uneasy eagerness to please.

But Donald Brand was not alive to undo the mischief he had created. If anything at all could be done, it must be done by Clayton himself. Would such a thing be possible, however? And, if possible, would it be moral?

So deep in thought was he that he reached Fitzroy Square before he knew it and, with a shrug, he continued on to cross the New Road. For what better place to sort out his thoughts than looking out upon the slowly developing Regent's Park? All the villas originally planned by John Nash might never be built, but in the meantime the spreading development of London began to press against the parkland's borders, a crowding which would increase rapidly when the canals were complete and business and transportation throve.

A few heads turned, drawn by the upright figure of the young man, with his appealing looks and preoccupied air, but Clayton walked on, oblivious.

He had his plan for attracting new investors, and if it succeeded only in part, or if it failed altogether, he must set his mind to his wedding. *I'm like a shipwreck victim, clinging to spars while I look in vain for rescue.* For Donald Brand was dead and there was no way out. Only a young lady might end an engagement without unwelcome social and legal ramifications, and however uncomfortable each might find their arrangement, it was plain that Priscilla was content to make the best of it and still had hopes of true attachment growing between them. While Clayton was fairly certain she did not yet love him, no gentleman could possibly say anything to the effect of, "We had better call a spade a spade. Whatever you might come to feel for me, I begin to believe I will never love you in return, and I doubt we could make each other happy. Therefore would it not be best to give each other our freedom?"

Nor could he seek rescue at Priscilla's hands. Even if, by some miracle, she came to prefer another—

His step halted a moment. But *would* it be a miracle? Only see how she responded to the praise of a French dancing master! Not that destitute Hubert Saint-Cloud could be considered eligible. Given Priscilla's youth and inexperience, she might easily leap from the frying pan into the fire, and Clayton could not in good conscience allow her to marry unwisely, even if it gave him blessed liberty.

No, Saint-Cloud would never do. Only imagine what Donald Brand would have said, to see Clayton cast Priscilla and her sizeable fortune on a penniless nobody!

Reaching the first bridge overlooking the new ornamental water, he leaned against the parapet. "There is no use in mincing matters," he said under his breath, though there was no one to hear him. "You have made your bed, John Clayton, and now you must lie in it. Yes."

Still, his head dropped as if he had sustained a physical blow.

It might be true. It might be inevitable. But how it hurt! To think he must shoulder this burden as he had every other one in his life.

And what of Miss Ellsworth?

His face twisted, and he felt the sting of tears rising.

Leave her. Her reappearance in his life complicated matters, but perhaps their paths would not cross again. Perhaps. Could he go on pretending she was still miles away in Winchester, never to be seen again? Impossible. Heaven help him if she was not uppermost in his thoughts—if she hadn't been uppermost, even when he *had* believed her everlastingly divided from him. Her reappearance meant nothing—should mean nothing—because he was no freer to court her than he had been in Bognor.

No.

All that remained in honor would be to gather up any crumbs of her words or smiles—or dances?—which might fall to him. *Crumbs*? That brought a humorless smile. The metaphor was inadequate, for ordinary crumbs would be scooped up and consumed, while these would be hoarded. Treasured. His smile became genuine as he remembered her determination to help him. Whether or not she had any success, he could look forward to reports of her progress. Ah...indeed. Instead of dreading the next function to which he could inveigle an invitation, Clayton found himself impatient for it, wrong though such a feeling might be. He needed to write to the earl in any event, and the guilty desire to see her again spurred him.

Dusk was falling when he reached his plain and spare lodgings in Warren Street, already mentally composing the note he would send to Stanley.

But the earl had anticipated him.

"Mr. Clayton!" gasped his landlady Mrs. Oakes, the moment she opened the door. "There you are. I've been that anxious for your return."

"What can it be, Mrs. Oakes?" he asked, grinning at the tiny old woman who nevertheless kept a quiet, orderly, and spotless house with the help of her burly son. "Did I forget to pay my rent?"

"You may joke, sir, but while you were out, a fine black carriage came with a crest on the door, and a footman all fine, fine in livery and gold frogs leaped down to deliver this note."

She whipped it from the pocket of her apron, and one glance at the scarlet seal confirmed John's suspicions: while he had been thinking of the earl, Lord Stanley had simultaneously been thinking of him. Taking the stairs two at a time to his room, John lit a taper in the fire and jammed it in its mirrored sconce. Then he removed his gloves and worked a finger under the wax.

20 November 1814

Cavendish Square
London

My dear Clayton,
After consulting my man of business, I must regretfully confirm my inability to make the full purchase of five hundred shares which I hoped to, two years ago. In the present circumstances, as I outlined to you, it even took perseverance on my part to insist on the feasibility of the partial investment of one hundred. You may thank your persuasive powers, Mr. Clayton, that it is done. Please have Alan Braham write to Timothy Keele of Middle Temple with the terms of sale.

I wish you continued success with securing funds for

the project and, to this end, will do what I can to expand your acquaintance and ensure you meet with open doors. Enclosed please find a short list of occasions where I will be present and which you may also attend under my aegis, in lieu of a specific invitation. These include, should you be interested, attendance at Almack's. I must beg your Miss Brand's pardon that Lady Stanley could not secure a Strangers Ticket for more than one guest, it being against the rules.

Yours, etc.
Stanley

CHAPTER FIFTEEN

This is no very great mistake, but it is always ominous to stumble at the threshold.
— Thomas Baker, *Reflections upon learning, wherein is shewn the insufficiency thereof, by a gentleman* (1699)

U ntil the night of Lady Aurora Robillard's rout, Beatrice's stay with the Huftons had been no bed of roses. The redbrick townhouse they had taken in Green Street was both elegant and convenient, to be sure, and Beatrice was given her own pink-and-yellow papered room overlooking a pocket handkerchief of a back garden, but these domestic pleasures had been counterbalanced by the shock of London itself and her stepcousin's hostility.

Lady Hufton called the West End the "quiet part of town," but to Beatrice's provincial ears they were nothing of the sort. All through the night the watchman's voice called the hour, giving way in the early morning to the coal wagons, bumping along and stopping at every house to shovel out the day's rattling load. Then came the milkmen, followed by the tradesmen's carts along Oxford Street heading for the markets. In between jolted the mail and flyer coaches delivering their burden of post and people. While the residents of Mayfair rose late following their nightly entertainments, when they were at last ready to face the world, they swept into the streets, walking, riding, driving, observing, shopping, and talking talking talking. Beatrice had never seen so many people in so small a compass, nor heard such a din which never fell completely silent. It was alternately stirring and irritating, depending on her mood; nor could she prevent herself from wishing to take part in the social mill, though she both dreaded glimpsing Mr. Clayton and hoped for it. A dozen times a day she thought the moment upon her, imagining him in every tall figure which strode by or emerged from a hackney coach.

But more trying when they first arrived had been Miss Hufton's conduct. The young lady obeyed her parents, but only just, her demeanor sulky and speech gruff. Beatrice's timid but friendly overtures met with the minimum of courtesy, and this unaccustomed coldness made her more than once wish herself back in Winchester, even as she grew more used to the noise and hubbub of the capital. Therefore her stepcousin's sudden warming at the rout had been as welcome as it was unexpected, but Beatrice did not dare to hope it had outlasted the night.

"Good morning, Beatrice," Lady Hufton greeted her when she descended for breakfast. "You look rather pale today. Did you not sleep well?"

In fact she had not slept much at all, being too full of excitement from seeing Mr. Clayton again and from revolving plans to save his canal project, but Beatrice assured her hostess she was perfectly well. Accepting a cup of chocolate and several slices of toast, she took her usual seat across from Marjorie, gaze lowered because she had learned the girl was more apt to snarl than to smile in the mornings.

But not this morning.

"Mama proposes we go shopping again," Marjorie accosted her. "What do you think?"

Beatrice lifted her head, lips parting. But her cousin sustained her gaze stolidly, as if she had never scowled a day in her life. "That would be pleasant," Beatrice answered.

"Well, *I* would rather go for a walk," said Marjorie.

"One might walk to the shops," answered her mother.

"I mean a *walk* walk. And one with just us girls. That is, if Beatrice is willing."

"I am. Yes." Beatrice said at once. For unknown to anyone, that very moment in her pocket she carried a list of the most promising gentlemen to whom she had been introduced or who had been pointed out to her. If they went walking, who knew whom they might encounter?

However Lady Hufton might have preferred to keep an eye on her charges, Marjorie's improved spirits were too novel to be put to the test. With a glance at her husband Sir John, who merely cleared his throat and frowned over the post, she yielded the point, and within the hour the two young ladies were dressed against the November chill and proceeding up Green Street toward North Audley, Marjorie's arm most unexpectedly wound through Beatrice's.

"How glad I am Mama did not insist," she said, when they paused for a sedan chair to pass. "Because since last night, when you told me of your own heartbreak, I have most particularly wanted to speak to you. To unburden myself. I thought, 'If she too has suffered, she will understand why I have been so unhappy and, I daresay, *unpleasant.*' Therefore do tell me how long it took you to feel yourself again?" She asked this with her bonnet brim upraised and such pleading in her beady, deep-set eyes that Beatrice could not help but think of a little shrew peering from its underground nest at a burrowing fox.

"I—hardly know how to answer," said Beatrice, "except to say that my own mama hopes the same as yours: that this interlude in town will...help me to forget. But forgetting does not just happen, Marjorie. We must cooperate with it." Perhaps Beatrice was a hypocrite here, having not made much progress in forgetting Mr. Clayton and having now promised to assist him, but she still did think it good advice. Marjorie's previous sullenness certainly was no remedy for a broken heart, in any case—that much Beatrice knew. Nevertheless she hoped Marjorie would not press her for more details.

To her relief the girl clung more closely to her and whispered, "You're right. I know you are. Beatrice, you must not think badly of me for how I have behaved. If you knew the worth of the man my parents deny me!"

Managing to hide her incredulity, Beatrice answered, "I suppose discovering the best qualities in a person takes study, and perhaps we all are guilty of not taking the trouble, unless it interests us."

"Perhaps. I only know that Sam was attentive and respectful and carried himself with such an air!" She sighed, remembering the drunken groom's charms, while Beatrice wondered how it could be called "respectful" for a man to make up to his master's rich daughter. But then Marjorie prodded, "Do tell, Beatrice—what were the best qualities in your young man?"

"Oh...er..." While she could have named a hundred qualities, she would rather her stepcousin not draw any conclusions, lest they see Mr. Clayton again during their stay. The thought of him, however, spurred her to remember the note in her pocket, and her steps slowed. Could she use this situation, this conversation, to her advantage?

"Er—I would say much the same," Beatrice replied hurriedly. "That is, he was kind and—and respectful."

"How can you say so when he was *engaged*?" wondered her cousin. "He misled you! I thought you would say he was charming and handsome, which was why you were deceived."

"He was that too. Never mind. I don't want to talk about it, if you understand. In fact, I have made a plan to—distract myself from my—sorrows—and, Marjorie, perhaps it might do the same for you."

"What plan?"

"Well, I was thinking there were many—er—promising gentlemen at the rout last night. I even made a list of them before I went to bed."

Miss Hufton's beady eyes widened. "You made a list of men to fall in love with?"

"I don't know about that," Beatrice bristled. "I just meant men to...consider."

"Have you the list with you? Let me see it!" She thrust out a gloved hand and, after a pause, Beatrice handed it over.

"I don't know where they may be found," she said, "but I thought I might keep an eye open because they're most of them sure to live somewhere nearby. Mayfair isn't terribly large, nor Marylebone, if they live farther afield."

But Marjorie tapped the page. "North Audley Street. Grosvenor Square. Hmm...was it Berkeley Square for Hemings? And Chisholm was somewhere near Piccadilly because Mama said it must be so noisy there."

Beatrice stared. "You know where these gentlemen live? But how?"

Her cousin shrugged. "While you were off seeing to your dress, people chatted with Mama. I wasn't really paying attention, but some things just stick in my head whether I want them to or not. We could walk up and down every last one of these streets if you wanted, just to see if any of your candidates emerged. But what would you do if one did?"

"I hadn't thought that far ahead," admitted Beatrice. "It's far easier to speak to a gentleman when you are dancing with him or sitting beside him at a supper. But at least if I passed by him, he might address *me*. Or, at the very least, as I grow more familiar, he might address me on another occasion."

"Oh, but that will take forever! I tell you what you should do instead—it worked marvelously well for me with Mr. Hughes. If you see one of these gentlemen, you must require his assistance. Suppose we were to buy something, and then you could pretend to drop your parcel, so that he must pick it up. Or, if we are crossing the street, you could nearly be run down by a carriage, so that he must seize you and drag you out of the way. Or—"

"You mean to tell me you tried one of these methods on your Mr. Hughes?" demanded Beatrice, aghast.

"I don't see what you're so shocked about if I did," Marjorie countered. "But yes. Once I dropped my riding crop for him to pick up, and another time I pretended to fall from my pony, and then once I lost my footing on a bridge. In every instance, he swooped to my rescue!" Here she hugged herself at the blissful memories.

Well! marveled Beatrice. No wonder the groom came to have ideas above his station!

Marjorie thrust the sheet back at her. "Mr. Rotherwood is the nearest of these, for he and Mrs. Rotherwood live somewhere here on North Audley Street. We might march up and down a time or two, but I think it would be a waste of time. He seemed quite captivated by Lady Sylvia last night."

He might have been captivated, but he was also enormously wealthy, too tempting a target for Beatrice to ignore. Thus she replied, "He only just met her, so all is not yet lost. But if he doesn't appear after a turn or two, we'll go on to the next. Who would that be?"

"Probably Lord Romney in Grosvenor Square. He's rather old, Beatrice—are you certain about him?"

"I don't have to marry any of them," insisted Beatrice. "I simply have to be distracted by them. It's part of the forgetting process." But that was a lie, and she felt bad enough that she shut up and pressed her lips together.

Fortunately Marjorie interpreted her expression as stifled anguish, for she folded the note up, returned it, and looped her arm again through her stepcousin's. "Say no more. I will back you in all endeavors. Come. Let's start our Tour of Distraction."

The pair marched up and down North Audley Street twice, but when they admitted defeat and entered the north side of Grosvenor Square, whom should they see approaching but the Marble Millionaire, Mr. St. John Rotherwood himself! The stern man looked sterner than ever, his brow creased in thought and his shoulders hunched in the frigid air. Alarmed, Beatrice and Marjorie exchanged glances. *Good gracious!* Beatrice thought, her courage deserting her. *If I'm not going to try one of Marjorie's ruses, what* am *I going to do?*

Before any decision could be made, much less communicated, fate intervened. For, in looking to her companion, Beatrice's toe caught an unevenness in the pavement. That leg came to a sudden halt, the other still swinging forward. She stumbled—staggered—stepped on the hem of her cloak—and then sprawled face-down at Mr. Rotherwood's feet.

"I say," murmured Miss Hufton. "Admirably done."

Mr. Rotherwood stopped short, hardly able to do otherwise. From his great height, he regarded the prostrate Beatrice as if she were a variety of groundworm before shaking off his preoccupation and extending a hand.

"Good heavens, are you injured?"

Despite her embarrassment and the dirt now daubing her cloak, the greater portion of Beatrice's dismay stemmed from the thought that she had squandered any future opportunity to speak to him sagaciously of canal shares. What opportunity could there be, if he deemed her a clumsy clodhopper?

Had Mr. Clayton's welfare not been at stake she likely would have abandoned her plan and fled as soon as possible, but his welfare *was* at stake, as was her promise to him. *I must make the best of a bad bargain,* she told herself firmly. *And though I begin at a disadvantage, it only means I must work the harder to impress this man.*

"I am unharmed," she replied, with a smile her family members would have called pained. "But I thank you, sir, for your concern."

Courtesy satisfied, Rotherwood made her a bow and would have gone on, but instantly Miss Hufton's brows shot up and telegraphed, "What are you thinking, letting him get away so easily? Go to it, girl!"

"You—have something on your shoulder," blurted Beatrice, pointing a finger and stepping to block his escape. It worked! But just as she sprang forward to swipe at the nonexistent something, he glanced down to inspect it, with the unfortunate result that her hand smacked him squarely in the nose.

Both Beatrice and Mr. Rotherwood yelped, Beatrice retracting her fingers in horror and Rotherwood's own hand flying to his face to ensure his nose was still attached.

"Oh, dear me!" cried Beatrice, crimson as a poppy. "Do forgive me, Mr. Rotherwood! That is...er...you are Mr. Rotherwood, I believe? I-I'm afraid I did not have the pleasure of being introduced to you at Lady Aurora's rout."

There was a wretched pause which felt like half an hour to Beatrice, but at last Mr. Rotherwood determined that his nose was neither detached, nor broken, nor about to gush blood, and he carefully lowered his hand.

"You were there, at the rout?" he asked mildly. "Are you certain it wasn't at Gentleman Jackson's?"

Beatrice stared blankly at this, but Miss Hufton smothered a snort.

"Mr. Rotherwood, if I might be so bold—" she declared, striding forward and giving a jerk of a curtsey. "We were indeed at the rout, but in all that crush we did not have the good fortune to be introduced to you. We are acquaintances of many of those whom you did meet, however, including Lady Aurora. I am Miss Hufton, and this is my pugilistic stepcousin Miss Ellsworth."

Rather awed by Marjorie's daring, Beatrice sank into another curtsey, as gracefully as she could manage, her attempt at a smile now reduced to a wince. "Again, I do beg your pardon, sir. I am not usually so...absent or careless and—I hope you will not hold this morning long in memory."

That drew the beginnings of a smile. "You must have much on your mind, Miss Ellsworth. Fortunately, so do I. I do not doubt this will all have grown quite hazy by the next time we meet. Now, if you ladies will excuse me…"

Even if she had any courage left to her, short of clutching him around the ankles Beatrice could not prevent him going, and he was permitted to pass. The girls didn't continue on straight away, however. Instead they lingered to watch Mr. Rotherwood disappear into one of the elegant townhomes of North Audley Street.

"Well," Miss Hufton began, her lips twitching, "that went about as well as might be expected. He may not want to marry you, but you certainly provided us with a distraction. Though I must say, I rather liked him. He didn't seem conceited, as I thought he would be, being so rich and popular. What did you think of him, Beatrice?"

Sighing, she made a helpless gesture. "I may not want to marry him, but could any girl be pleased to have so humiliated herself?"

"What do you mean? You didn't trip on purpose, then?"

"Of course I didn't! It was purely an accident. But now he thinks me a bungling bungler and will keep far away."

Marjorie pulled a face, as if Beatrice's response defied understanding. "Well, all right then. If you would like to redeem yourself in Mr. Rotherwood's eyes, I will do what I can to help you, for I feel somewhat responsible for your mishap. But how was I to guess you were so susceptible of suggestion? I darcsay we will meet him again, so you need not reproach yourself. Now come—perhaps you'll have better luck and keep on your feet with old Lord Romney."

CHAPTER SIXTEEN

I was at Almack's last night, and such sort of doings [to] which you will say pish, was I to give you account.
— Mary Cornwallis, Letter to Admiral Cornwallis
(1763)

Until the moment his Stranger's Ticket was accepted by Mr. Willis, Clayton feared he would be turned from the doors of Almack's. To be sure, Lady Jersey's lip curled and her nod to him was infinitesimal, but she could not refuse him entry, arriving as he did on the heels of Earl Stanley's party and dressed in the required costume of knee breeches, snowy white cravat, and chapeau bras. Nor could fault be found with his manner, though Lord Stanley's beautiful daughter Lady Sylvia merely curtseyed wordlessly in response to his bow and thereafter paid him little heed.

In truth, John Clayton's entrance at the exclusive assembly room was the second obstacle overcome, the first having been informing Priscilla. "Crestfallen" would not have been too strong a word, though she struggled to repress her complaints. "Almack's! Oh, Cissy, to think of it—! *Almack's!* How—how kind of the earl to secure you a ticket, John."

"I go to woo potential investors, Priscilla," he repeated, to which she nodded, but he feared she might begin to weep.

"I know. It's just—you don't even *like* dancing, John."

It wasn't true, but he doubted arguing the point would mend matters. Instead he answered, "Even if that were the case, I don't go in order to dance."

She nodded again, her lips disappearing into a line, and he soon took his leave. But the door had barely shut behind him before he heard her muffled wail: "Oh, Cissy! It isn't *fair!* Mr. Saint-Cloud said I would grace the ballroom of a duchess, but what is the use? I will never, never be seen by anyone anywhere!"

Clayton sighed, avoiding the footman's eyes. There would be other occasions for Priscilla to shine, if he could arrange them, but he suspected this supposed snub on his part would not be soon forgotten.

As he stood on the edge of the earl's party, he gradually became aware of a crowd of gentlemen growing around them. Young, old, tall, short, handsome, nondescript. Those sporting rumpled locks à la Titus and those entirely bald. But all of them come to pay homage to the earl's daughter and to beg a dance from her. Lady Sylvia received them calmly enough, granting the boon with signs of neither eagerness nor dread, and to the earl's credit, Lord Stanley made convenient use of the men's proximity to introduce them to John.

"Fascinating fellow," pronounced the earl repeatedly. "I look on him as quite a rising man. Chief engineer and secretary of the Cumberland Arm, Regent's Canal, don't you know."

Being eager to win the earl's approval and to improve their chances with his daughter, most of the new acquaintances feigned some degree of interest, and Clayton's presence and credentials were allowed to pass unquestioned, if they were not outright embraced. A few of the would-be suitors even loitered to make desultory conversation while their gaze followed Lady Sylvia and partner.

"Stanley's pet, are you?" said one of them with a note of belligerence (middling age, middling height, middling looks, middling amount of hair—his name might even have been Middleton).

"Nothing of the sort," he returned, vexed to feel himself coloring. "More of a—business acquaintance." He would have called Stanley a partner, had the man honored his original pledge of five hundred shares, but such a description seemed a stretch under the current circumstances.

Middleton, or whoever he was, made a humphing sound. "Too bad you don't appear to be a pet of Lady Sylvia. She hardly noticed you."

Nor I her, Clayton wanted to reply waspishly, but he swallowed the retort.

"I suppose she'll be snatched up by Rotherwood. We ordinary mortals haven't a chance against him," Middleton continued, his sigh breaking off mid-breath when he added, "Talk of the dev-il—there he is."

There he was indeed. And Clayton's heart sped, along with the hearts of every marriageable young lady in the room. If he could succeed—and if Rotherwood and his mother were a fraction as wealthy as rumored, the needed four hundred shares would be as a drop of a bucket to them! But whom should he try first, the son or the mother? For on Rotherwood's arm was the elegant woman, clad in blue-black like a raven. Both Rotherwoods surveyed the gathering, the son's countenance unreadable but the mother's brightening when she caught sight of the Stanleys. A tug on her son's arm and a word in his ear and they were in motion.

Unconsciously he straightened, smoothing his cuffs and trying in vain to remember the opening lines of his speech.

"Lord Stanley, Lady Stanley," murmured Mrs. Rotherwood as the group saluted each other. "And I see our dear Lady Sylvia is already in great demand. I do hope St. John has not arrived too late to partner her." She smiled up at her son, who looked (in Clayton's opinion) as if it were all one whether Lady Sylvia danced with him next or never at all. And as for the young lady? She performed an admirable series of rights and lefts in her foursome, not betraying by so much as a flare of her nostrils that she even noticed Mr. Rotherwood's arrival.

Well, thought Clayton, if that was the fashionable world's idea of love, they were welcome to it.

Lady Stanley was shaking her head ruefully. "My Sylvia is so popular! But I am certain she will have kept at least one dance free, if only in hopes of resting or having some refreshment. Here she comes—that was the last time through the figures. Sylvia, my dear girl, only see who has come!"

"Lady Stanley tells me I am likely too late to have the honor of a dance," said Rotherwood blandly.

His mother looked pained by his manner, and the faintest twitch of displeasure flickered over Lady Sylvia's glorious features.

"No," she said. "There is La Strasburgoise."

He bowed; she curtseyed and was carried off by another partner. Rotherwood stalked away.

His mother turned to the earl and countess with an apologetic expression. "How disappointed he must be, to wait!"

"I'm certain Sylvia would have given him two dances, if she were able," returned Lady Stanley.

With Rotherwood gone, that left his mother, and Clayton was both relieved and discomposed when the earl said, "Madam, may I have the pleasure of introducing you to Mr. John Clayton here, chief engineer and secretary of the Cumberland Arm, Regent's Canal. Quite a rising man."

Mrs. Rotherwood curtsied, and for a minute or two Clayton made fumbling attempts to engage her in conversation, to which she replied with flawless but cool courtesy. Too soon, however, she herself was surrounded by her own group of hopeful swains and carried away just as Lady Sylvia had been.

He repressed a grimace. Now what?

It was tempting to scorn the Marriage Mart proceedings in which he played no part—*nothing on anyone's minds but who might bring what, to which partnership!* But no sooner did he have the thought than chagrin filled him. In what way were his aims different from, much less superior to, anything happening here? Was he not after money as well? Money, money, money. Indeed, the matchmaking efforts could at least claim a second goal, that of finding love.

If I'd had any sense, I would have asked Mrs. Rotherwood to dance.

Well, it was what it was, and there was nothing to be gained by standing blockishly beside the earl and countess all evening, upbraiding himself. He must cast the widest net possible by cultivating not only the Rotherwoods, but *all* the gentlemen of means. Nor should the young ladies be overlooked, for they could lead to conversations with fathers and brothers and cousins and uncles. Giving himself a mental prod, he redoubled his efforts. He bowed when introduced. He murmured his *good evenings* and *honoreds* and delivered whichever length of speech about the canal—a few words, a few sentences, a few paragraphs—would be tolerated.

He was in the middle of one of these speeches when his auditor interrupted, "Oh, I say. There's my cousin Kitty. See here, Clayton—may I introduce you? If you get her to dance with you, I'll buy ten of your shares. What do you say?"

Perplexed by this unexpected turn of events, he sputtered. "But—what? Why?"

"Because it will be a prime joke," answered the young man promptly. "Kitty tells me she never wants to marry, so she is trying to thwart my aunt's matchmaking efforts. But I bet her she would dance at least five dances at Almack's because she wouldn't be able to avoid it. If I win, Kitty must buy me a new cart whip."

"And if you lose?"

"Then I must accompany her and my mother to *Macbeth* at Drury Lane and sit in their box with them, when Lord knows no fun will be found that way. Come on, then. Ten shares for a quarter-hour of your time."

For heaven's sake. If this stripling could speak so easily of spending a hundred pounds to win a bet—?

Still.

Conscience prompted Clayton to say, "Er—I probably should tell you, Dodson, that I'm already an engaged man."

Dodson brightened further. "Are you? She'll like you the better for it—no risk to her whatsoever, you see."

"And if she refuses to stand up with me?" he asked.

"She can't. She won't. It wouldn't be polite. Follow me, Clayton."

Ten shares being nothing to sniff at, he obeyed readily enough, trailing after the young man. They skirted the fireplace to reach the enormous doors opposite the musicians' gallery, only to have Clayton's companion halt suddenly and fling up an arm to stop him.

"Good Lord! Kitty's talking to Rotherwood!"

Peering over Dodson's shoulder, Clayton spied the same tall, cheerful, narrow-faced young lady introduced to him at Lady Aurora's rout as Miss Kempshott, and she was indeed speaking with Rotherwood. But it was not only those two whom he recognized, for on the far side of Miss Kempshott was the little creature with shrewish features whose name he'd forgotten, and on the near side—none other than Miss Ellsworth. Miss Ellsworth, pretty as a picture in snowy muslin, face alight as she gazed up at Rotherwood.

The man had his back to them almost completely, so that Clayton could not tell how he received such a look, but he heard him say, "I rejoice to see you suffered no lasting injury from your mishap."

"Thank you, sir," she replied, flushing, her voice just carrying to Clayton's ears over the hum of the gathering. "You are very kind."

"Shall we, then?" He held out an arm, upon which Miss Ellsworth laid her gloved fingertips, and led her away to join the set.

Dodson gave a low whistle. "I say! How do you like that? All the odds in the books heavily favor Lady Sylvia Stanley, but if we were at Newmarket, some at the betting post would be calling that pretty one there an *outside*." When his companion only frowned, Dodson added, "Not a racing man, Clayton? An 'outside' is an unknown horse with unknown abilities. But never mind. Come."

Tearing his gaze from the departing couple, Clayton found himself at once very keen to dance with Miss Kempshott. Or the other one, if Miss Kempshott wouldn't have him. Anything to position himself where he might observe Miss Ellsworth and Rotherwood. Through the blood rushing in his ears he was dimly aware of Dodson speaking, and he bowed when the ladies curtseyed, managing to say, "Miss Kempshott, if I might have the honor of standing up with you...?"

She gave a chuckle. "Let me guess—Doddy put you up to this."

Her cousin made a show of pretending not to hear, saying loudly, "Miss Hufton, what about you? Shall we 'trip it as we go on the light fantastick toe'?"

Marjorie might not know her Milton, but Mr. Dodson could have invited her to a gin house and found her willing, for unbeknownst to anyone in the room but her mother (who was too far away to note), with his waving brown hair and blue eyes, Mr. Dodson bore a remarkable resemblance to a certain family groom, far off in Kent.

"That's torn it," said Miss Kempshott as they sailed away. "I commend you, Doddy, you wily creature. This will make One." To Clayton she made an exaggerated curtsey and took hold of his arm, that he might lead her out.

So intent was Beatrice on her self-appointed mission that Mr. Clayton's approach altogether escaped her notice. She was too busy girding herself. *Don't trip over your own feet, Beatrice Ellsworth! Engage him in conversation and somehow lead it around to the wonders of London and how he might contribute to them.*

She did succeed in the staying-upright part of her task, but if only he were not so unapproachably marble! He moved through the figures automatically and correctly, but his eyes were more often fixed over Beatrice's head. Was he looking for Lady Sylvia? But, no. When Beatrice craned her neck as unobtrusively as she could to peek around, she saw that Mr. Rotherwood's gaze did not linger on the beautiful earl's daughter either.

But he is certainly looking for someone, she decided. *Someone who isn't here.* Well, that person, whoever she was, would likely absorb the man's attention whenever she did arrive, so it would behoove Beatrice to make use of the time she had.

"How do you like town, Mr. Rotherwood?" she ventured, when the figures brought them together. "Are you much for balls and dancing?"

He blinked, as if a beetle on the floor had addressed him, before bending his stern countenance to regard her. "Not particularly."

"Oh?" Beatrice hoped it wasn't her company or dancing which he found a chore, but so what if it was? She must press on in any case. "But—how about London then? How do you like London? Apart from the balls and dancing, I mean."

Something flitted across his sculpted features which softened them for a moment. "I visited the Tower. I liked the Tower."

Here was progress! She glowed up at him. (He didn't notice.) "I would dearly like to see the Tower myself," she said. "My brother loves everything of that nature: history, art, books, pageantry, and the like, and he told me I must go, but I don't know if my cousin Miss Hufton would be interested."

"Ah."

When this was all the response she received, Beatrice blew out a breath. Thank heavens she only wanted money from the man and not love!—trying to penetrate his aloofness was uphill work. Nevertheless, she once more applied her metaphorical shoulder to the wheel: "I wonder if, when they were building the Tower, they knew how long it would stand."

"It's been more than nine hundred years," he replied. "It would be as if those now building the Regent's Park tried to imagine its existence in the year of our Lord 2764."

Regent's Park? *Building*? All on his own Mr. Rotherwood had opened a door for her to step through! In her surprise, Beatrice froze. Then, late for the back-to-back step, she darted forward, narrowly missing a collision with him.

"Miss Ellsworth!" His hand flew out, either to fend her off or to haul her up if she fell, and though he did not touch her, Beatrice went scarlet all the same as every dancer's head turned their way.

"Pardon me," she uttered. "I was—astonished how quickly you performed that calculation."

To her amazement, his marble features cracked in a grin. "I am a former mathematics tutor, you know. Or perhaps you didn't know. But I must ask, Miss Ellsworth, is this stumbling about a habit of yours?"

For the thousandth time the memory flashed through her brain: her bathing gown pinned; no air to be had; murky waters; hands gripping her to wrench her back to life.

"N-no," she answered, swaying slightly. "At least, I hope not."

He leaned toward her with some concern, and she wished he wouldn't, for she knew by the prickle along her neck that they were still being observed. *Come now! You must shake this off and buckle to, girl!*

Lifting her head, renewed resolve in her eye, she took his hands to go in circle. "If those building the Regent's Park do not do so with an eye to the future, they ought to. Just as the city has grown and grown since the Tower was built, so it will continue to do."

His brows rose at both the unusual topic and the unusually firm grip. "Are you greatly interested in building and planning, Miss Ellsworth?"

"Greatly," she lied stoutly.

"How...curious."

"Are you not?"

"I confess I have not thought about it much. Until recently I lived in two rooms and hadn't the means to build or plan anything."

"Yes, well. But here you are now." But she could see him already retreating into indifference, and panic flooded her. What should she do? Baldly ask for money? If he and his mother were as rich as everyone said they were, were they already dunned on all sides by those wanting to share their wealth?

Beatrice closed her eyes one fleeting moment to gather her courage. What was the worst that could happen? She could ask; he could say no; they could avoid each other ever after.

The tempo of the music slowed. Oh, heavens! The dance was about to end—*was* ending!

Mr. Rotherwood bowed, his lips forming the words to thank her, when Beatrice rushed at him, fingers fluttering. "Please, sir," she hissed from the side of her mouth, "might I have a word with you...apart?"

For a terrible moment she thought he would refuse. Then he gave the barest nod and extended an arm to escort her from the floor. It would not be an exaggeration to say most eyes in the room followed them; nor could Beatrice stop her ears when a wave of murmurs rose, composed of indignant, buzzing voices pitched just loud enough to be overheard. "Who is she?" "Some country girl of medium fortune and connections." "Did you see how clumsily she danced?" "Did you see how she pretended faintness?" "How dare she seek to monopolize him!"

It seemed too much to hope the murmuring escaped Mr. Rotherwood, but he gave no sign either way, merely stopping at the refreshment table to hand her a cup of lemonade.

"Thank you." Gulping down a sip to cool her heated face, she was disappointed to find the beverage lukewarm.

"You had better have your say, Miss Ellsworth," he returned, just audible, his lips scarcely moving. "For I can't spare much time. I'm afraid it's my duty to stand up with as many partners as possible, to keep the wolves at bay."

Then he *had* heard the unfortunate remarks. Beatrice went even redder. Choking down another tasteless sip, she replaced the cup on the table.

"I'm so sorry," she whispered, trying to speak as quietly as he had. "But I promise I'm not trying to marry you."

Her own attempt to thwart eavesdroppers met with less success, the lemonade having made her hoarse, and Mr. Rotherwood politely inclined toward her. "I trust I heard you amiss, Miss Ellsworth. You can't have said you're trying to marry me."

"Marry you!" she squeaked. "No—I said just the opposite! This is not a marriage proposal—even if young ladies could offer such things—it's more of a...commercial proposal. About the development of London."

Whatever he imagined she might say, this was not it, and he looked both puzzled and mildly curious. "Intriguing. Although our man of business tells us he has been inundated with commercial proposals of stunning variety and levels of foolhardiness, I confess this is the first time I have been approached directly with one, and by a young lady, to boot."

"Yes, well..." Beatrice had no fitting response, so she held up her palms appealingly. "Will you hear me out?"

"Miss Ellsworth, I will do you the justice of not hurrying you," he answered. "Why do you not write to me of your proposal and send it around to North Audley Street? I assure you I will consider it, whatever it is, and respond in a timely manner."

"Write to you?" she gasped.

"It's unusual, I daresay," Mr. Rotherwood conceded, "but if you were to send it to our man Pinckney, I have no doubt you would hear nothing for months, if ever, and odds are, when you did, it would be a standard refusal."

"Very well, sir. I will write to you."

A loud throat clearing interrupted their tête-à-tête, causing Beatrice to spring backward guiltily. Mr. Rotherwood, on the other hand, only turned slowly to peer at the interlopers.

"Oh, good evening," said Beatrice, when it seemed her companion was not going to say anything at all. "Mr. Clayton! Miss Kempshott. Marjorie." Finding her voice embarrassingly squeaky, Beatrice gave herself a surreptitious thump on the sternum. She had never seen Mr. Clayton look as he did now: cool and distant, as if he had never met her before in his life and saw no need to curry acquaintance now.

"Yes, and this is Mr. Dodson," supplied Miss Hufton breathlessly, her beady eyes flicking from Beatrice to Mr. Rotherwood and back.

"My cousin Mr. Dodson," added Miss Kempshott. Of them all, she appeared the most at ease. Indeed, to judge by the twitching of her lips, she found it all very amusing.

A silence fell among them.

In such a situation it would have been proper then for the new acquaintances to exchange dance partners, if they were not going to stand around and talk, and Mr. Rotherwood did turn toward Miss Kempshott, but then a cotillion was announced, and he halted, like a deer at the crack of a shot.

"Did they say it was La Strasburgoise?" asked Marjorie.

Mr. Rotherwood was grim. "They did. You must excuse me, but I hope, Miss Kempshott, you might honor me with the following dance and Miss Hufton with the one after that?" They curtseyed their acceptance, and he was gone the next instant. Even if he were not so tall it would have been easy to follow his progress toward Lady Sylvia Stanley by the universal turning of heads to track him.

Miss Kempshott gave a chuckle and nudged Beatrice. "Don't despair, Miss Ellsworth. He might have promised Lady Sylvia that dance, but he didn't look too happy about it."

Her cousin Mr. Dodson gave a snort of his own. "And you needn't look too happy either, Kitty, for dancing with Rotherwood will make *two* of five. I see a cart whip in my future, most definitely, for Rotherwood's mark of approval will bring others in his train."

She shrugged and huffed out a breath. "So it will, Doddy, so you may as well dance the cotillion with me now."

CHAPTER SEVENTEEN

We ought to be very careful not to charge
what we are unable to prove.
— Edmund Burke, Letter (1785)

With Miss Kempshott's and Mr. Dodson's departure, only Beatrice, Marjorie and Mr. Clayton remained. Knowing Mr. Clayton's limited dancing experience, Beatrice did not expect him to ask either of them, even had he been his usual friendly self, but Marjorie fixed inquiring eyes on him.

The awkwardness mounted as more couples formed up for the cotillion, and Beatrice felt anxious for his sake. But just when she was on the point of speaking, Mr. Clayton said, "Miss Hufton, I pray you will pardon me for—"

"For asking Beatrice to dance?" Marjorie broke in. "Say nothing of it, sir, for I know you have a prior acquaintance. I will rejoin my mother."

He colored. "No—I was going to—that is, I do apologize for not asking you to dance, Miss Hufton, but I was not going to ask Miss Ellsworth either."

"Oh?" Marjorie favored Beatrice with wide eyes, as if to say, *There's rudeness for you!*

Hastily, Beatrice intervened. "I know you only began to learn in Bognor, Mr. Clayton."

"Really? But he just danced with Miss Kempshott without mishap," observed Marjorie, as if the man weren't standing right beside them.

"Did you?" Beatrice turned wondering eyes on him. "Well done, for that was a complicated one. Figure eights and heys and such."

"More complicated than La Strasburgoise, at any rate," Marjorie sniffed.

"You will force a full confession from me," Mr. Clayton said. "Priscilla and I have been taking lessons. And while I felt bold enough to attempt a longways dance, we have not yet mastered any cotillions."

Of course such an announcement met with questions—from Miss Hufton, at least. Beatrice was battling a feeling of lowness. Her happy memories of dancing with Mr. Clayton in Number Four, Spencer Terrace, all spoiled—for now lucky Miss Brand was the one dancing and learning and practicing with him!

It is wrong *to feel toward him as you feel,* she reminded herself ruthlessly, taking hold of her own elbows. *It is* wrong *to covet him. And if you cannot help him purely from motives of friendship, you ought not to help him at all.*

She tightened her grasp. *I can help him as a friend. Of course I can. I will. Mr. Rotherwood says I may write to him about my commercial proposal, and I will!*

Clayton was inwardly making his own vows about Rotherwood. What had the blasted man been saying to Miss Ellsworth as he leaned over her? And why should Miss Ellsworth say she would write to him? What need had they for writing to each other? Clayton was no society man, but even he knew an unengaged young lady should not be writing to an unengaged man.

He shot her a furtive glance, hating to suspect ill of her. But if he was not to suspect ill of her, would he rather imagine her correspondence did fall within the bounds of propriety—that she wrote to Rotherwood because they were, or would soon be, engaged?

Impossible.

They could not be.

They had only met the other day at the rout, hadn't they? Even Dodson who minded the betting books at the clubs had not heard whispers of Miss Ellsworth before this evening.

What, then? Could it be something to do with her offer to help him raise funds? But if it was, why did she now avoid his gaze and stand clutching her elbows as if to keep herself from flying apart? She, who had been so open, so eager, when she spoke to him at Lady Aurora's.

He remembered again the way she looked at Rotherwood a few minutes earlier—the little glow, with sparkling eyes lifted. He remembered Rotherwood reaching for her as if, like Clayton did, he just wanted to feel her vivid self under his hand.

Stop it.

This must stop.

"—The master?" asked Miss Hufton.

Clayton had not heard the question. He gave himself a mental shake. "Pardon me, Miss Hufton. Could you repeat that?"

"I asked," she frowned, "the name of the dancing master."

"Saint-Cloud," he replied promptly. "Hubert Saint-Cloud. Though the academy itself belongs to a Mr. Wilson, of whom Priscilla and I have seen neither hide nor hair. At every lesson, it has been Mr. Saint-Cloud instructing us."

"At every lesson"? Beatrice hung on to herself for her life. How many lessons had there already been?

"Well," said Miss Hufton, "I hope this Saint-Cloud teaches you and Miss Brand your cotillions soon."

He bowed. "In the meantime, Miss Hufton, perhaps you might favor me for the next longways dance?"

"Thank you, sir. Except for the one I have promised Mr. Rotherwood, I am unengaged."

They might have stood there meanwhile till world's end, except Mr. Dodson's prophecy proved as true for Beatrice as it would for his cousin Miss Kempshott: Rotherwood's notice drew the notice of other gentlemen, and some young puppy shortly dashed up to beg her to join a new foursome.

"We've missed a few minutes, Miss Ellsworth, but you know how it repeats over and over," he panted.

She did know and went obediently with him. How strange and painful it could be to discover that, much as she had wished herself free of the discomfiture of Mr. Clayton's presence a moment earlier, she no sooner joined the dance than she wished herself still beside him.

As the night wore on and partner after partner followed, Beatrice began to fear they might not have another chance to speak. Why, oh why, did he not ask her to stand up with him? He danced with Marjorie and even older Mrs. Rotherwood and a couple of other young ladies Beatrice didn't know, but then the rest of the time she saw him holding conversation with various gentlemen. Beatrice didn't mind the gentlemen—surely he was talking about the canal with them—but she did mind that he never came near her. Marjorie was right—it was rude! Downright discourteous. He *ought* to ask her to dance. If it had been Aggie here instead of herself, she could not imagine Mr. Clayton failing to do so.

Neither did Mr. Rotherwood speak to her, dance with her, or even come near again, but Beatrice hardly noticed. Mr. Rotherwood was a challenge to be faced later, when she had pen in hand and no Mr. Clayton destroying her peace.

Round followed longways set. Reel followed quadrille. When the puppy came to beg a second dance, Beatrice demurred. "Thank you, but I would like to rest a while." Rest and perhaps covertly watch Mr. Clayton. But once she was seated on a bench beside her step-aunt, she found her view frequently blocked by the other dancers and chaperones and passersby. Lady Hufton herself paced back and forth before her, scrutinizing her daughter's movements.

"She is dancing again with that young man, to whom I have yet to be introduced, the dandyish one with the waving brown hair," she said, tapping her fan against her palm. She glanced down at Beatrice on the bench. "Do you know him, dear?"

Beatrice leaned to peer through a gap in the throng. "It is a Mr. Dodson, madam. The son of the Mrs. Dodson we met at Lady Aurora's rout and thus a cousin of Miss Kempshott."

"Hmm." Lady Hufton frowned as she watched her daughter duck her head and titter at something Mr. Dodson said. "If you would excuse me, Beatrice. You will be just fine waiting here for me, while I step over to have a word with Mrs. Dodson and Miss Kempshott..."

Beatrice suspected it would be the what-manner-of-young-man-is-Mr.-Dodson-and-what-are-his-prospects sort of word, but surely Lady Hufton would deem Mr. Dodson an improvement on the drunken groom Sam Hughes at Stourwood Park.

With her aunt gone, however, the urge to discover the whereabouts of Mr. Clayton proved too strong to resist, and she rose to look about. But scarcely had she hopped up before the buzz of conversation grew louder. Necks craned, and those nearest her crowded together to form a solid wall. Clicking her tongue indignantly, Beatrice bounced on her toes to peep over those in front of her and immediately spied the problem: the Rotherwoods were making their departure. Heavens—it must have been like this along the streets of the capital when the Allied sovereigns visited earlier in the year, for here everyone was, lining the route, standing tiptoe in hopes that a mere pair of rich people would notice them.

The rich person of chief interest to the young ladies somehow detected Beatrice in the press as he passed. No great feat from his height, she supposed, or maybe he had been looking for her. In any event, pausing mid-stride, he nodded his marble jaw half a degree, and then lifted a gloved hand in quick pantomime. Thumb, forefinger and middle finger together and a curving motion. Beatrice interpreted it at once: *write to me*. Heads swiveled to identify the fortunate recipient of this particular communication, and, to hide her confusion, Beatrice swiftly imitated them, looking back and forth, an inquiring expression pinned on her rosy face.

The danger passed and the Rotherwoods moved on, leaving her to sink again onto her bench, too shy now to go hunting for Mr. Clayton.

But there was no need.

"You have been a busy young lady," said the man himself.

She jumped, having no idea how long he had been there or even how he had come to be beside her.

Her mouth worked a moment, but then she managed, "Do you mean dancing?"

He made a gesture—it seemed to be a night for gestures. Mr. Clayton's was a careless ripple of his fingers. "You know. Dancing, enlarging your acquaintance...drinking lemonade."

She looked sharply at him. She had only had the one cup of lemonade all evening, the one given her by Mr. Rotherwood.

But Mr. Clayton's countenance was smooth, unreadable.

"You have been busy yourself," she returned. "Would you say it was a successful evening? Or, at least, a promising one?"

"Do you mean, did I succeed in climbing to new heights?"

Again her head snapped up. Was he trying to quarrel with her?

"I referred to your attempts to find investors," she said carefully.

He took a slow breath, as if trying to master himself. "I did. Make progress. I made some beginnings, that is. Thank you." But then he added in a rush, "What of you? Did you make progress in your own goals?"

"My goals?" She echoed. *Goals, in the plural?* Had they not agreed she was not in London to pursue the typical young lady's goals? Well—perhaps he phrased it thus because it would be too coarse to ask if she had raised any money for him yet. Delightful as it would be to tell him that Mr. Rotherwood gave her permission to write to him, it might all come to nothing, and Beatrice did not want to raise Mr. Clayton's hopes prematurely.

"I *hope* so," she answered therefore.

A little silence fell, and Beatrice cast about for a fresh topic. How easily they had once spoken to each other! But Bognor felt a lifetime ago. They might once have laughed together and challenged each other to swim races, but now— Why, it was difficult even to picture Mr. Clayton in bathing costume, his dark hair wet and his smile easy. The Almack's version of Mr. Clayton, with his formal tailoring and formal manners, was a horse of another color. Beatrice would not presume to call the Almack's Mr. Clayton a friend, he was so cool and forbidding. And people thought Mr. Rotherwood unapproachable! At least Mr. Rotherwood danced with her. Mr. Clayton still had not asked her; nor did it appear he was going to.

"How have you enjoyed your dancing lessons?" she ventured next. "You seem to have fared very well with your partners." The next second she could have bitten off her tongue, for it made it sound as if she had been watching him the entire time. "Your new lessons must not be held in a private drawing room with only a couple or two, if you learned the longways dances."

For the first time, there was a hint of a smile in his voice. "No. Wilson's Academy in Wells Street has many pupils. And the lessons take place three times per week."

"Then I praise Mr. Wilson's efforts. Not that you weren't an apt pupil," said Beatrice, a little downcast at his smile. Three times per week? To tear himself from his desk so often? He must like these lessons better than those received from the Ellsworths. Or else he liked to be with Miss Brand as much as possible. Who knew—maybe he was not tearing himself from his desk but was walking to Wells Street arm in arm with his intended, a whistle on his lips, having already spent the morning with her.

"Thank you. But I remind you it isn't the vaunted Mr. Wilson who deserves your praise," Clayton answered, "for I begin to think he does not exist. Our instructor has always been the Hubert Saint-Cloud fellow, an elegant young man who, in my more fanciful moments, I imagine to be descended from a French *vicomte*."

"A *vicomte*! Wouldn't that be something?" She repressed an urge to sigh. "He must indeed secretly be one though, to give you that idea, for you don't strike me as a fanciful person, Mr. Clayton."

This provoked a wry grimace. "Don't I? I suspect several of the gentlemen I approached this evening would call me precisely that—fanciful. With my talk of canals extending into the heart of London. I daresay they thought me a dreamer. A speculator."

"That's different," Beatrice insisted, defending him. "To build something—anything—one must have the idea for it first and convince others of its rightness. What would the world do, without such men? That is not what I meant by 'fanciful.'" Then the sigh did escape her. "To my mind, a fanciful person is someone with unlikely, sentimental ideas about people, imagining stories for them, as you do for your dancing master. I meant I did not suppose you were *that* sort of fanciful."

"Who is not, on occasion?" he replied tersely, almost coldly. "Do we all not sometimes dwell on what might be, if not for…"

"If not for…?"

"If not for what in fact *is*," he finished. He made an impatient movement. "I have done all I can here. All I should. To stay longer would be—"

But what staying longer would be was left to Beatrice's own fancy, for Mr. Clayton gave an abrupt bow and disappeared into the crowd before she could even think of rising, and she found herself blinking back the sudden threat of tears. "But staying longer would be a *waste of time*," she finished for him under her breath. "That's what you were about to say, was it not? That staying longer would *serve no purpose*."

And was he not right? Beatrice might help him in attracting investors to the Cumberland Arm project, but there was nothing to be gained by continuing to cultivate her friendship. Friendship between an unmarried man and young lady was unconventional and rare in their world. And as for anything beyond unconventional friendship—well, that was altogether impossible.

He would probably be set upon by footpads, Clayton thought as he crossed Jermyn Street. Not in St. James, most likely, nor even in Marylebone after crossing Oxford Street, if he kept to the well-lit Portland Street, but perhaps when he was within shouting distance of his lodgings in darker, narrower, less-frequented Warren Street.

But he could not bring himself to be concerned about it, much less to seek refuge in a hackney coach. Other matters pressed on him, and he must walk in the cold air to clear his mind. At least, he hoped it would clear his mind.

For while Mr. Hubert Saint-Cloud might have the carriage and deportment of a *vicomte*, Clayton himself seemed to be turning into a bear. Only a bear would treat Miss Ellsworth as he just had, not asking her to dance, growling at her, pulling faces, fleeing when he could no longer trust himself to meet even the bare requirements of courtesy.

And why had he disgraced himself thus? Because she danced with Rotherwood? She had danced with others. Because she and Rotherwood were somehow become correspondents?

Two inebriated dandies with their arms about each other's shoulders for support were singing and swaying their way along Piccadilly.

They called to him, hurling mocking curses when he passed without a sign, but Clayton failed to notice, being too intent on turning over the question again of why Miss Ellsworth should write to Rotherwood. Even if he had not overheard Rotherwood's invitation to do so, he had seen the little motion made at her, prior to the man's departure from Almack's. But what on earth did Rotherwood expect Miss Ellsworth to write? If Clayton were a more confident man—or a more conceited one—he might persuade himself that Rotherwood meant, "That four hundred shares you asked me to buy? Consider it done! But be sure to write to me, so I will know where to send my draft." But if that were the case, wouldn't Miss Ellsworth have crowed to him in triumph? Wouldn't she have turned upon him the radiance she turned on Rotherwood, as she announced the solution to his problems?

She had been, on the contrary, reserved and uneasy.

Hope had flickered when she referred to Bognor. Bognor, which was never as far as it should be from his mind. If Miss Ellsworth referred to it and to their happy dancing lessons, did it not mean she too thought, and thought fondly, of those bygone times? And then to hear her spirited defense of builders and their work! He might have kissed her for it.

But the sweetness of those fleeting moments was its own torture, and he had not been able to prevent his bitterness showing. She did not think him a fanciful person? If she but knew the half of it! For he was not only fanciful, he was a fool—for letting fancy run away with him. Indulging in memories which could lead nowhere. Indulging in rose-colored visions of continued friendship between them. An utter fool. Did he think he could hold his hand to the flame and never suffer a burn?

They could not be friends.

Indeed, Clayton hardly knew if he could trust himself in her presence again, if he could not school his features and his words better than he had this evening.

It was the gravest misfortune that his business trials might continue to throw him into her path, and he must wrap up his dealings as soon as humanly possible.

"A hundred shares from Stanley. Ten from Dodson," he muttered, avoiding eye contact with a pair of women calling to him from under the lamp at Mortimer Street. "Skinner showed interest. I must follow up with him." Another grimace. Ten shares here and ten shares there! What he needed to do was to approach the wealthiest first, and the wealthiest by far was Rotherwood.

He saw again in his mind's eye Miss Ellsworth's eager glow as she spoke with the Marble Millionaire. He heard again Dodson saying, "Some at the betting post would be calling that pretty one there an *outside*." He remembered Rotherwood's tiny, telling gesture and Miss Ellsworth's blushing response.

"I can't do it," he declared aloud, his pace quickening. "I won't do it. I won't ask Rotherwood for a penny, not if he intends to rob me of her." He halted abruptly then, his fingers going to his forehead as he could not smother a groan.

What was this, if not being fanciful? Rotherwood could not "rob" him of someone who did not—and never could—belong to him.

St. John Rotherwood had his liberty, as did Miss Ellsworth. And if they chose each other—well, there was nothing Clayton could do about it. If Miss Ellsworth accepted Rotherwood, it would surprise no one in London. The only criticism her choice would provoke would be cries of protest that the season's most eligible bachelor could not then be captured by any of the hundred other young ladies vying for him. And as for Rotherwood choosing to love Miss Ellsworth…

How could Clayton blame him if he began to find Miss Ellsworth endearing? There might not be a more endearing creature alive.

No, it seemed all too obvious that he must brace himself for the realization of his worst fears. He must prepare to hear that she was lost to him forever. More lost than she already was.

Reaching the intersection with the New Road, Regent's Park spread before him, a vast, formless darkness.

Like my future.

But he had never been a man who wallowed overlong in self-pity, and—heaven help him—he had no intention of beginning now. He gave himself a shake. "That's enough of that, old fellow. It's time to set your steps toward home."

He did just that, and if any footpads had been lurking in Warren Street, the rain and cold drove them indoors, so that he arrived without mishap.

But as he took his candle and climbed the cramped staircase to his chamber, only the shadows were yet awake to hear him say, "But I still don't want a penny of his money, all the same."

CHAPTER EIGHTEEN

It is better to dwell in the wilderness,
than with a contentious and an angry woman.
— Proverbs 21:19, *The Authorized Version* (1611)

Finding a private moment to compose a supplicatory letter to Mr. Rotherwood proved easier said than done, for Beatrice awoke to discover her once-sulky stepcousin Marjorie had swung like a pendulum to exultation.

"I've lost my heart!" Marjorie cried, whirling like a madwoman in Beatrice's bedchamber before flinging herself across the counterpane. "And I must be a sad flirt, for who could have imagined I might forget Sam so quickly?"

"If you have, it's glad I am to hear it, miss," spoke up the maid Crook as she unbraided Beatrice's hair to brush it out. "For if anyone's a sad flirt, it's Sam Hughes."

Instantly Marjorie sat up, eyes narrowing and nose wrinkling. "You hold your tongue! I may prefer someone else now, Crook, but I still won't hear a word against Sam. I know everyone from below stairs at Stourwood Park was jealous, as servants will be, if any one of them receives special favor."

"It wasn't the favor, so much as Hughes getting ideas above his station," persisted Crook, undaunted by her mistress's command or show of temper. "Sir John and Lady Hufton were right to take you away, and most of us were of a mind Hughes should be dismissed at once, if not for his mother working for the family since Sir John was in his cradle."

"Wh-whom do you prefer now?" Beatrice interjected hastily, having already felt Crook's brush strokes increase in speed and vigor.

The distraction succeeded, for her cousin left off disputing with the maid to regard her archly. "Not Mr. Rotherwood, as you do, Beatrice, so you needn't fear."

"Mr. Rotherwood! I have no designs on him."

"Pooh. That's all gammon. I saw how you looked at him and tried to get him to yourself," Marjorie said. "But I should say, even though he did glance your way before he left, I don't think he felt any more for you than any other girl there, so it would be better not to pin your hopes to him."

"My hopes aren't the least bit pinned to him!" cried Beatrice, swelling with indignation.

"But you won't be the only one disappointed," continued her cousin, not listening. "—Think if Lady Sylvia fails to attach him! Mr. Dodson was telling me how the 'Rotherwood Wedding Wagers'

are up to a thousand pounds now, in sum, with the odds still favor-
ing the earl's daughter. But I'll grant you, in Mr. Dodson's opinion,
you have at least an even chance."

Beatrice could not believe her ears. "You—you let the man speak
of me, in such a context?" she gasped.

"What? What are you going red about? Yes, he spoke of you, as
did I. We got into quite an amusing little argument about it as we
danced."

Thrusting aside the hairbrush Crook applied to her, Beatrice
sprang to her feet. "For shame, Marjorie Hufton! Bandying my
name about with someone you hardly knew, while he spoke of betting books! I—I take offense at it, when I have only shown kindness
to you."

"Goodness me, how you fire up," observed Marjorie, cocking her
head to one side. "Is it the fact that Mr. Dodson and I discussed you,
or is it *really* that this touches you to the quick? Because I say if you
do like Mr. Rotherwood, it needn't be some great secret, when half
the girls in London are determined to be in love with him."

"I am *not* in love with Mr. Rotherwood!" Beatrice fairly roared.

"You see how candid I am with you," said Marjorie, folding her
hands over her breast with an air of deprecating humility which
made Beatrice want to kick her. "And I believe it always best to be
honest with oneself."

"I *am* being honest with myself, as well as with you," she replied
through gritted teeth. "I have no wish to marry Mr. Rotherwood.
None whatsoever. If I—looked in any particular way at him, it was
not for that reason."

"Oh, please. Then what reason was it, Miss Petulant?"

"It was because I was eager to—to make a business proposal to him."

This prompted derisive snorts from both Marjorie and Crook, but when Beatrice only raised her chin, crossing her arms over her midsection, mirth gave way to incredulity. Marjorie's mouth popped open, and Crook left off shaking out and brushing Beatrice's discarded attire to gawp at her.

"*Business* proposal?" repeated Marjorie. "What on earth can you possibly mean? Have you something to sell to him?"

In truth, Beatrice would have preferred to keep her canvassing of Mr. Rotherwood secret, not only because she might fail, but also because her unconventional conduct would certainly be deemed unladylike. But if Marjorie was going to accuse her of setting her cap for Mr. Rotherwood, there was no alternative but to tell the bald truth.

Taking a steadying breath, she resumed her seat and patted the cushion beside her. "Let me explain. It has to do with Mr. Clayton's work. You know that—that I—consider him a friend, from having known him at Bognor. Well. He is the secretary and chief engineer of an arm to be built off the Regent's Canal, but before work can begin, he needs investors to buy shares of it." She folded her hands in her lap, but her knuckles were white with the tightness of her grip. "So, in an attempt to be of assistance, I—thought Mr. Rotherwood would be a good person to...canvass. Therefore, I told him at Almack's I had something of the sort to say, and he told me I might write to him about it. That is the whole of the matter."

Instead of appearing reassured by this declaration, Marjorie was shaking her head decidedly before the end of it. "See here, Beatrice. I know you are not much used to society and have spent most of your life buried in Winchester, but I am a baronet's daughter, and you ought to be guided by me. No, no—hear me out. I am sorry to tell you, but well-bred young ladies do not intrude themselves in such situations. What would your parents say? Advising Mr. Rotherwood on what he should do with his money! Indeed, he will not thank you for your interference, and nor will Mr. Clayton. Selling shares in a canal? Why, you might as well go and hawk butchered hogs in Smithfield Market!"

Before Marjorie had finished this speech, Beatrice was scarlet with indignation. To be condescended to by a girl two years her junior, who, if not for her parents' interposal, would have pledged herself to a household servant with a reputation for drunkenness and flirtation? What right had Marjorie Hufton to be dispensing advice? A fig for her "baronet's daughter"!

"Mr. Clayton knows of my intention," Beatrice rejoined at last, vexed to find her voice shaking, "and he has made no objection. And if Mr. Rotherwood disapproves of my actions, I daresay he will be gentleman enough to say nothing of it to others."

"Mr. Clayton knows you intended this?" marveled her cousin. "Well. *Well!* Goodness. But I suppose he has not been much in society either, if he saw nothing improper in it. But I assure you, he ought not to have enlisted you. So very, very unseemly! I would not be surprised if Mama asks Papa to have a word with him, to enlighten him and ensure he does not talk of it where he shouldn't."

Beatrice was on her feet again. She could stand Marjorie's criticisms of her—to a point—but undeserved aspersions of Mr. Clayton were not to be borne.

"If you tell Lady Hufton, and she tells Sir John, there is nothing I can do about it, but I will certainly speak up in Mr. Clayton's defense. He is no gossip. *He* was not the one tossing my name about at Almack's and mentioning it in the same sentence as 'bets' and 'odds'! That you would do so, Marjorie Hufton, I consider most uncousinly and reprehensible." In this retort, Beatrice made an unfortunate misstep, but she did it completely unawares. That is, she hardly suspected Marjorie would take a reproach squarely aimed at her and apply it instead to Mr. Dodson.

Thus it was Marjorie's turn to bolt up, arms akimbo and beady eyes flashing. "Mr. Dodson is not a gossip!" she snapped. "It is not gossip for him to speak to me of my own cousin, and I see it as more friendly than otherwise for him to warn me of possible dangers and disappointments. Can he help it if he knows the contents of betting books? Can he help it if he's a member of various exclusive clubs? This is what I mean about you having no understanding of society, Beatrice Ellsworth. Worthy young men of the world like Mr. Dodson are driven by—by chivalry alone!"

"Bother his chivalry, then," Beatrice retorted, "and bother his worthiness!"

Marjorie was as flushed as Beatrice, but she was a great deal more used to fighting than the latter, having spent her childhood opposing her younger sister and, more recently, her parents. Though she had been forced to yield to the latter, giving up her wretched groom to come to London, she had nevertheless succeeded in exacting her pound of flesh through sullenness and sauciness, as Beatrice had witnessed.

"How dare you!" Miss Hufton cried now, swelling up even as Beatrice shrank with chagrin at her own loss of control. "How dare you sneer at the virtues of a man's character?"

Tears starting to her eyes (though they were provoked in equal part by anger and dismay), Beatrice choked, "Pardon me for my outburst, cousin. It's—it's true that I don't know Mr. Dodson and cannot therefore judge his motives. But you must understand that I don't care to hear my—friends—maligned."

Despite what this effort to smooth Marjorie's ruffled feathers cost Beatrice, her cousin did not reward her with any corresponding softening.

"Nor do I care to hear *my* friends maligned," Marjorie said with a scowl. "And Mr. Dodson is now my friend. That is what I came in here to tell you, only you and Crook were so provoking. I was so happy, but you had to spoil my mood."

After such an introduction to Mr. Dodson, Beatrice was not predisposed to love him, but she managed to reply, "That was not my intention. I am...glad for you, Marjorie."

Her cousin merely viewed her with glittering eyes, but the maid thrust herself between them, holding up Beatrice's pink and white poplin. "Don't you mind her, Miss Ellsworth. She's always had a right temper on her."

This perceived confederation between the family maid and up-start stepcousin only added fuel to the flames, however, and Marjorie stood simmering, waiting for Beatrice's head to reappear through the neckline of the dress before she attacked again.

"I don't think you're glad for me one bit," she accused. "I think you just don't want me to go telling tales on you."

That was true enough, and Beatrice's hesitation unfortunately only confirmed the assertion. Before she could muster either the will to deny it or a convincing lie, however, her cousin gave one last irate sniff and flounced from the room with a mighty slam of the door.

"Oh, dear," sighed Beatrice.

Clicking her tongue and wagging her head, Crook began to tuck in Beatrice's chemisette. "Temper, temper. From the time she was a child. You're cooked now, miss, sorry to say. What you've got on your hands now is war."

"War?" Beatrice echoed, her eyes round. "What a word to use, Crook!"

"Some words are just right for the purpose," answered the maid with a shrug. "And when you run afoul of Miss Hufton, it's war, all right, and war to the knife."

24 November 1814

16 Green Street
London

Dear Mr. Rotherwood,
It was an honor to meet you and to dance with you yes-
terday at Almack's. Please forgive both my boldness in

accepting your offer to write to you and the hasty nature of this message. For fear of offending my relations or being forbidden altogether to send this, I do so in haste, without time to beat about the bush or even to make a fair copy.

Despite these apologies, however, what I wished to speak with you about was not a bit scandalous. It was only related to our talk of the wonders of London. Many of those wonders do indeed date from long, long ago, but I hope there are still some yet to be built. I have had the honor of becoming acquainted with Mr. John Clayton, chief engineer and administrative secretary for the planned Cumberland Arm of the new Regent's Canal, and have been captured by the vision he proposes. When his work is complete, goods from everywhere in the world may be brought directly into the heart of London by one of two routes: via the Grand Junction Canal to the Regent's to the Cumberland Arm; or alternately, in the other direction from Limehouse to the Regent's Canal to the Cumberland Arm. You see what an unprecedented reduction in transportation costs and time this will be to the sellers and manufacturers and traders, with corresponding benefits to all London buyers. Mr. Clayton is at present seeking subscribers for this undertaking, and each share may be had for £10. I myself will be purchasing a share.

I suspect you have many demands on your fortune, but I hope you will consider this one. If you find it to your liking, investments may be made through Mr. Clayton's lawyer, Mr. Alan Braham of Cursitor Street.

Your obedient servant,
Beatrice Ellsworth

It was not a composition to rejoice in, surely failing to persuade anyone out of a halfpenny, much less a hundred pounds. To make matters worse, her usually flawless hand was untidy and the page marred by more than one blot, but hunched at her escritoire, fearing every moment Lady Hufton's knock, Beatrice was relieved to have produced anything at all so quickly.

Cracking her door two inches, she hissed and beckoned to the nearest servant. "Take this to the Rotherwoods in North Audley Street. I don't know the number of the house, but it was the third or fourth from the end along the eastern side, as you go toward Grosvenor Square. And for pity's sake, confirm with whoever answers the door that you are delivering it to the correct place."

"Do I wait for an answer?" asked the footman with a disapproving frown. He could foresee the mistress rating him soundly for fulfilling this errand and wished he had not been just then at the head of the stairs.

"No, no. There will be no answer," she assured him, which was true enough. Mr. Rotherwood could hardly be expected to respond instantly; moreover, she had not asked in her letter to be told what he decided in either case. An oversight, perhaps, but she did not want to justify any of Marjorie's denunciations by engaging in a genuine correspondence with the man, and she hadn't time to change the note now. No—she would simply have to wait and hope. And if, by a miracle, Mr. Rotherwood did decide to invest, and if, by a second miracle, Mr. Clayton should see her again and tell her of it, that would be soon enough to celebrate. Oh, how she hoped there would be something to celebrate! Mr. Clayton had been so brusque and cold the previous evening—she would like to believe it was because his business cares weighed on him, and not because of anything she had said or done. With Marjorie's accusations drumming in her head, Beatrice now feared he shared or would come to share her cousin's opinion, thinking that Beatrice behaved in an unfeminine, reprehensible manner.

She heaved a sigh. Well, if he did, it was out of her hands now. Literally.

In the meantime she must endure not knowing. That, and the unpleasantness with Marjorie.

Squaring her shoulders, she descended to join the Huftons in the breakfast room. The meal had been cleared away, but in the armchairs by the window still sat Lady Hufton and Marjorie at their needlework and warming himself at the fire stood Sir John. From the moment of her entrance, Beatrice sensed the strained atmosphere. The baronet made her a short bow, his eyes skating past her to meet his wife's. Clearly Lady Hufton had been taxed with taking charge of the Situation. Marjorie kept her own gaze trained on her tambour frame, but Beatrice saw the corners of her lips curl.

"Ah, good morning, dear girl," began Lady Hufton, laying down the mending of her husband's shirt. "Do come sit down. We missed you at breakfast, but Crook tells me she brought you toast."

Had Beatrice not been fretting over what lay ahead, she might have pitied the older woman, having to contend with these new trials so soon after congratulating herself on Marjorie's improvement.

"Good morning. Yes, she did," said Beatrice. Taking up her own workbasket, she chose the seat farthest from Marjorie, deliberating. Would it be best to open the attack, rather than be forced into a defensive position? Yes, surely. It would show goodwill and perhaps go some way toward appeasing Lady Hufton. Judging by Marjorie's barely hidden smugness, it might already be too late. "I had a note to write."

"Yes, so Marjorie told us."

There was a pause, in which Beatrice stitched while Lady Hufton worried her lip.

Beatrice shut her eyes briefly. Let them have it all out and be done with it. "And I—sent it. My note."

"Oh, my." More lip worrying. But when Beatrice took a breath, determined to begin her explanation, Lady Hufton raised a hand to stop her. "Wait a moment, please. Am I correct in understanding this note was addressed to Mr. St. John Rotherwood? I see. Oh, dear. Oh, my. No—no—please—allow me to speak. My dear girl, I had better say straight off that such things—writing to young men—really ought not to be done, for whatever reasons, unless you are engaged to the person in question, which is not the case here—"

"I know that, madam," Beatrice interrupted. "Truly I do, and I—have no intention of defying such a-a-a rule in general, but this was not me writing to him as a young lady to a gentleman, per se, but rather simply as one *person* to another person. I only wanted to make a-a-a recommendation, you see. A business proposal."

Lady Hufton passed a hand before her eyes. "Yes, yes. Frankly, I don't know if a 'business proposal' isn't worse! Marjorie said it was something to do with Mr. Clayton's canal...?"

"It was," said Beatrice, unhappy to find her aunt shared Marjorie's opinion. "I thought Mr. Rotherwood, having so much money, might like to buy shares in the project."

Beginning to fan herself, Lady Hufton glanced again at her husband, but Sir John only cleared his throat and fiddled with the glass door covering the face of the mantel clock. "Oh, my dear," she said again, "while you are in London, you are under Sir John's and my care. We stand *in loco parentis*, and I believe I may safely say that your parents, my brother Colin and Mrs. Wolfe, would not like you to...write to strange young men, nor to...interfere in such a masculine province as—as raising sums of money, to say nothing of canal-building. Please promise me you will refrain in future."

For a minute, Beatrice only stitched, the handkerchief she was embroidering for her stepmother blurring before her eyes, but she willed no tears to fall. She would *not* cry. She would *not* give Marjorie the satisfaction of seeing her weep. Swallowing, she succeeded in mastering herself so far as to give a clear nod.

Yes.

She would refrain in future.

It pained her to promise, for what if Mr. Clayton did not succeed in raising the necessary funds? And what if he thought she had forgotten her assurances of help?

I will tell him, she decided. *The next time I see him. If I see him. I will tell him that, however much I would like to, I have been forbidden to do so.*

But the worst was not yet over. For after releasing a long, relieved breath and giving Beatrice's forearm a squeeze, Lady Hufton said more cheerily, "Thank you for that. My goodness! Of course you girls cannot know of the dangers lurking under every bush and behind every post—I say this only half in jest. What *is* the world coming to? It used to be one could trust not encountering such folk—'engineers' and builders and their ilk—in Mayfair. I blame Lord Stanley. An earl ought to know better than to be forcing an engineer on folk who are not used to such things. I'm sure Mr. Clayton is harmless in his way, but a gentleman would never think of asking a well-bred young lady to—Oh, heavens! What is it, Beatrice?"

For the latter had gone crimson as a boiled lobster and was now clutching the crumpled ball which had been her sewing. "Mr. Clayton is a gentleman," she declared in a shaking voice. "And he did not ask me to help him. I offered."

"Well, if he had indeed been a well-bred man, he would have known to reject such an offer," spoke up Marjorie, her pointed chin outthrust.

"I was *flattered* that he did not reject my offer," insisted Beatrice. "I thought it showed trust and—and respect for me."

"And why should you care if some ambitious young nobody trusts and respects you?" demanded her stepcousin, almost jeering. "One might almost think you cared for him!"

If possible, Beatrice went even redder, and Lady Hufton, who had been on the point of remonstrating to her daughter, froze mid-up-raised-finger to stare. Any doubt she might have had that Marjorie had struck home was dispelled the next instant when Beatrice burst into furious, humiliated tears.

With a cough, Sir John fled the room, leaving the calamity to his wife, and even Marjorie clapped a horrified hand to her mouth, squeaking, "No! Then it's true? You *do* care for him?"

No answer was needed, even if she had been capable of it, there being such a confession in her looks, and it was all Beatrice could do to cover her face and try to stifle her sobs.

And poor Lady Hufton, a woman not given at all to fainting, began all at once to see the allure of it. The speed of her fanning increased, and she could hardly draw breath. "You have come to care for an engaged man? Oh, merciful heaven! To yearn for an engaged man and seek to make him beholden to you! Oh, Lord. It would have been better after all, had you been writing love notes to Mr. Rotherwood! That, at least, the world would understand, even if it could not be condoned. But—*this*, Beatrice!"

That was all Beatrice could bear. Heedless of Lady Hufton's distress or Marjorie Hufton's horrified triumph—heedless even of the servants who scattered when she burst from the room, she made her blind, stumbling escape.

CHAPTER NINETEEN

It is a madness…to look a gift Horse in the Mouth.
— John Stevens, translation of F. de Quevedo, *Comical*
***Works* (1707)**

A tap at the door roused Clayton from his brown study.

"Enter," he called, haphazardly rearranging the pounce pot and inkstand to feign occupation.

Mrs. Oakes marched in, rag and feather whisk in hand. "I'll come back later if you're busy, sir."

"No, no. Go ahead. I might go for a walk anyway."

"Not a bad idea, though it's wet out," she said, briskly dusting and straightening. "You've been sitting there a week now, it seems to me. Writing and calculating and pacing. If not for those dancing lessons of yours, you would not have left the house."

"Correspondence," he answered vaguely, waving at the desk.

"Oh, yes," Mrs. Oakes said wisely. "So I've seen. Notes flying all over town to 'esquires' and 'Barts,' to say nothing of the occasional 'Sirs' and 'Lords.' And they make reply! You might beat me down with a feather, to have a tenant who mixes with such high comp'ny. I suppose soon you'll be wanting to live somewhere more fashionable than Warren Street."

He would have denied it more plausibly if she were not that moment inspecting an item propped on the mantel, sent by the earl. Absently she drew the whisk across the wall sconce, not even watching what she was doing. "An invitation to a ball," she murmured. "A ball, Lor' love you, given by Sir August and Lady Finlay of Mount Street." Turning the card over, she drew a sharp breath. "Ooh, and Miss Brand and Miss Croy may join you!"

His mouth twisted. Yes, Miss Brand and Miss Croy might join him, if he liked. Though he had seen the two ladies since receiving this card, he had somehow neglected to mention it. A pointless delay, really. He intended to go, and, unlike with Almack's, there was no reason this time to exclude Priscilla and Miss Croy. So why had he hesitated?

Avoiding the question, he said to his landlady, "I'll be needing the parlor shortly, Mrs. Oakes. That was the gist of the note Mr. Braham sent earlier. He's coming to call."

"Bless me, a lawyer," she replied, punching his pillow. "So long as he hasn't any business with me."

Precisely to the minute, his caller was ushered into Mrs. Oakes' neat and mahogany-dark front room, where Clayton sat by the fire, boots on the fender and a leathern portfolio at his elbow.

"What couldn't wait, Braham?" he asked, after rising to make his bow. "I would have called in Cursitor Street to see you next week as usual, and it's a bitter day out. Not that I mind you coming, for I've been eager to show you my progress." This with a tap on the portfolio.

"If it's anything like the receipt I carry, the Cumberland Arm must be altogether in clover," said Braham with an uncharacteristic smile.

"Has another sum come in, then?" he asked eagerly. "If it was from Ferry or Lord Reading, I'll eat my hat. They each hemmed and hawed so, I assumed there was nothing to be gained from either."

Braham held up his palms in a shrug. "No Ferry or Lord Reading, so your hat is safe. But see for yourself." Reaching into his coat, he retrieved a paper to pass to him. "Cursed dark in here, Mr. Clayton. Can't you pay your landlady a little more rent, so she won't be so sparing of the candles?"

Without replying, Clayton carried the paper to the window to peruse, and the lawyer waited for the whoop of joy he knew must greet it. But his client neither whooped nor capered; he only held quite, quite still.

"Can you not make it out, man?" demanded Braham, impatient.

"I can make it out."

"A hundred shares!" Braham declared, as if Clayton needed to hear it aloud to understand. "You're another hundred shares to the good!" He shook his head, giving a dry chuckle. "It didn't even come through his man Pinckney. I suppose, when you're the Marble Millionaire, a thousand pounds is mere pin money. Rotherwood probably turned out a few pockets and sent me whatever he found. Whatever you said to him, Clayton, you did very, very well."

"Said to him? I said nothing," he replied grimly. "We've barely been introduced."

Alan Braham's brows rose. "Indeed? Well! How peculiar. Then he must have heard of it from Stanley or one of the others you have treated with." Even in the shadowy room the lawyer could see Clayton's face darken. What ailed the man? Could he not recognize his good fortune?

"Was there no note with it?" asked Clayton, turning again to gaze into Warren Street.

"Of course there was," Braham replied to the back of his client's head. "'He, St. John Rotherwood, presented this sum with his compliments for the purchase of a hundred shares in the Cumberland Arm Canal, etc. etc.' And he added that there was no need to disturb his man Pinckney. I was requested simply to send the receipt directly to him in North Audley Street, for he considered this a 'private matter.' Don't you see what this means? The man is now an equal investor to Lord Stanley! I grant you, the bit about 'a private matter' is perplexing. Who knows—perhaps his mother Mrs. Rotherwood or Pinckney set strict limits as to how he might spend his allowance, even if that allowance is more than a middle-rate squire might collect on Quarter Day. No matter. You will have to take that up with Rotherwood, because once his name can be attached to the enterprise, I daresay it will make quick work of raising the remainder."

The only response to this speech after a full minute of silence was a wordless grunt, and Braham wanted to throw up his hands. "Is there something wrong, Clayton?"

Another pause followed, in which the room fell so quiet the lawyer could hear the tapping of drops on the pane. Some detached part of his mind noted that, whatever the inconveniences of living on the edge of town, there was certainly a great deal less traffic.

Then, at last, Clayton said heavily: "I don't want Rotherwood's money."

Braham stared. Doubted. Waited. Sputtered. "Wh-whatever can you mean, you don't want his money?"

Clayton hung his head.

"Have you—heard something unsavory about the family?" the lawyer pursued. "Because I assure you, whatever might be said of the baronetcy from which their wealth came, it was no better or worse than any other in the kingdom, and in the brief time since they inherited, the Rotherwoods themselves can hardly have had time to engage in any questionable practices—"

"I have nothing to say against him or his character," Clayton amended. "I—not knowing him personally, I would prefer to continue seeking additional investors on my own."

"But—that's nonsense! Pardon me, Clayton, but why make any distinction? If you found a shilling on the street, would you not stoop to put it in your pocket, without any qualms? You must use the tools you have been given, including windfalls. I suppose you will have to consult Rotherwood before you advertise his involvement—to get to the bottom of that 'private matter' business—though then you risk him changing his mind—but once you have done so, let that be an end to your scruples. To be candid, you need this money for the work to go forward. Unless you've already got promises for the balance in your portfolio there."

"Not quite." Returning the receipt to Braham, Clayton began to move restlessly about the room. "All told, I estimate there's an additional hundred shares accounted for, on my part, from men whose word I consider good."

"Well, there's a vast difference between a shortage of two hundred and one of three hundred," Braham observed, "so I need hardly say you will want Rotherwood's money, even if he forbids you attaching his name to the project."

When his client made no response, the lawyer tucked the paper away again, frowning. Something was not right here. Something bearing further investigation. But with the practice of long years, he succeeded in regaining his impassive expression. "In any case, leaving Rotherwood's money aside for the present, how many other irons have you in the fire?"

Apparently relieved at the change in subject, Clayton gave a fleeting grin. "A handful or more. You may ask my landlady how diligently I have been talking up the canal, answering questions, working to pin people down. My letters have crossed and recrossed town."

"Mm. I commend you, Clayton, but at the risk of becoming repetitious, I must point out once more that importunate letters are easily dodged."

"Of course they are, which is why I intend soon to make another appearance in the flesh." Opening the portfolio, he slipped out the card Mrs. Oakes had admired earlier.

"Ah. The Finlay ball. Very well. That should be well attended, and I wish you luck." With a shrug, the lawyer reached for his hat. "Only, don't waste your time on Sir August himself. Lord Stanley begged off when he had only the one daughter to marry. Poor Finlay has four."

When the lawyer was gone, Clayton gave a fitful sigh and dragged a hand through his dark hair, throwing himself in the nearest armchair.

What did it all mean? Did it mean what he thought it meant?

Why should Rotherwood, a man who did not know him from Adam, send him a thousand pounds, unless he did it for Miss Ellsworth's sake? Rotherwood who danced with her, spoke to her apart, asked her before everyone present at Almack's to write to him. While all London assumed a union with the glorious Lady Sylvia Stanley would crown Rotherwood's rapid ascent, Clayton could not forget what Dodson had called Miss Ellsworth: an "outside horse."

Surely he could learn more at the Finlay ball. Even if Rotherwood and Miss Ellsworth did not attend, there would be whispers, rumors. He might even ply Dodson for more information.

A terrible twisting gripped his insides—gut, lungs, heart. Was this what it felt like for Miss Ellsworth when the heavy wheel of the bathing machine pinned her gown to the sea floor?

But if Clayton had been the one to save her, who was there to save him?

"Forgive me," he murmured to Priscilla as he took his place in the line at Mr. Wilson's Dance Academy.

"I thought you had forgotten," she answered, eyes lowered. "The lesson began nearly an hour ago. You were working, I suppose."

After his unaccompanied attendance at Almack's, Clayton had been deeply in his intended's disfavor (another reason for his holing in Warren Street to work). And it would hardly improve her opinion now to confess the hour had slipped away while he was lost in thought about someone else. Therefore he made no such confession. Instead, wryly calling himself a coward, he chose the surest way out of her black books.

"You will never guess what I have received," he said, the words barely uttered before he winced. Oh, heavens, had he acquired Priscilla's pernicious habit of forcing the listener to prompt her to continue?

She liked it, at any rate, her head lifting eagerly. "What? What did you receive, John? Do tell me!"

The masterful Hubert Saint-Cloud turned his elegant head four degrees in their direction at that moment, however, and Priscilla instantly put a finger to her lips, hissing, "Shh! We are interrupting. But tell me quickly!"

His news had to wait for Mr. Saint-Cloud to deliver his soft, iron-hand-in-a-velvet-glove instructions, however, and for the dance master once again to shunt Clayton from the line, that he might demonstrate with the blushing Priscilla as his partner.

"Goodness, what a pet he's made of you," her intended remarked when the accompanist launched into The Merry, Merry Milkmaids, quite their most advanced dance yet, with its shifting stars and figure eights.

But his partner glowed to see his chagrin, mistaking it for flattering jealousy, and she lowered her lashes in a coy smile. "So Cissy says. But come—tell me your news."

First he had to weave his way through the series of figure eights, however, which was more complicated to his mind than tallying long columns of figures or calculating odds on which investors might be coaxed into giving what amount. But he completed the pattern with a minimum of bumbling and answered, "We have been invited to a ball given by a Sir August and Lady Finlay."

"And—you think we might attend?" she breathed, with a pathetic look of entreaty as if she deemed him the sort of person who would raise a cup to her lips only to dash it away before she could take a sip.

He must do better than this, Clayton thought ruefully. She thought him a beast to her, and perhaps he was.

Aloud he said, "I have a few people I must hunt down. Therefore, yes—we certainly will attend."

Priscilla forgot herself so far as to give a shriek and clap. "Oh! Oh! Truly?"

So unusual was such an outburst in this setting that their fellow pupils stared and gasped, and the masterful dance master was obligated to raise *both* his hands, in addition to one eyebrow, to restore order.

Well, that's one of us happy, Clayton thought, as he musingly watched Priscilla float and beam. When she armed left with him, she smiled from ear to ear, as if the Almack's incident had never been. When she cast around Miss Croy, she giggled and whispered the delightful tidings and her plans for it. And when Mr. Saint-Cloud drifted near, she even braved his potential restrained ire by blurting, "Oh, Mr. Saint-Cloud! At last I am going to a ball!"

The elegant man paused in his measured walk, one finger lifted. Then he nodded and continued along the line, but Clayton swore he saw Saint-Cloud's upper lip twitch, a reaction which in a more demonstrative person might translate to an oath or a swoon. Priscilla appeared gratified by it, at least, for the corners of her own mouth tucked in a pleased, kittenish smile.

Briefly Clayton wondered if he was going to have to say something to her about the dancing master. *Was* she developing an improper and impossible attachment to Saint-Cloud? Begad, if the man only were in truth a *vicomte*, with a tidy little chateau and acceptable income, he would be welcome to her, and how many problems that would solve!

"Excuse me," he muttered to the shipbuilder's daughter when his lapse of attention caused him to miss her hand. She gave a titter, to be addressed by the good-looking young man, but he failed to notice because an unwelcome thought had returned to him. Why, even if

Priscilla conveniently jilted him to elope with another man, and he were set free—free as the air—was Miss Ellsworth now forever out of reach? Did something else equally impossible to overcome now subsist between her and the confounded Rotherwood?

He feared it did.

And whether he had a right to know or no right at all, John Clayton was determined to discover precisely what that something was.

CHAPTER TWENTY

When you do dance, I wish you
A wave o' the sea, that you might ever do
Nothing but that; move still, still so,
And own no other function.
— Shakespeare, *The Winter's Tale,* IV.iv.2013 (c.1611)

After some debate, the Hufton party traveled to the Finlay ball on foot, Mount Street being but a ten-minute walk from their home in Green Street. Though chilly out, the rain had passed and the pavements were dry, allowing the young ladies to don warm list shoes over their slippers for the journey. Lady Hufton had wanted the carriage, but Sir John observed that, with the crush of traffic it would add a half-hour of alternately creeping along or waiting motionless while competing coachmen argued. But it was not her husband's powers of persuasion which carried the day; it was

Beatrice's suggestion that, if they walked, they might choose their moment of arrival and do so without fanfare. Picturing her charge alighting from the carriage between the Scylla and Charybdis of Mr. Rotherwood and Mr. Clayton, Lady Hufton yielded at once.

Beatrice had spent the week not in disgrace, precisely, but encouraged to "lie by for some Time in Silence and Obscurity." It had not been entirely without benefits. Sir John might avoid her eyes, and Lady Hufton might sigh and shake her head whenever her gaze fell upon her, but when the Dodsons invited them to supper, Beatrice was allowed to plead headache. Apart from her stepcousin Marjorie (whom she could hardly avoid), Mr. Dodson was the last person on earth she wished to see again. Even Marjorie's boasts of the elegance of the Dodson home and the excessive amiability of Mrs. Dodson and Miss Kempshott toward her left Beatrice unmoved, though she had sense enough to feign chagrin.

"And Mr. Dodson, who is *such* a gentleman, sang beautifully while I played," Marjorie rejoiced the following day, hugging herself. "How he excels at anything musical! Don't tell my mama, but he asked if he might have two dances at the Finlays' ball. Two! He says there are four Finlay daughters, and he must do his duty by each of them, but if I would partner him before and after he did so, he would consider himself 'well rewarded.' What do you say to that?"

Beatrice mustered the careful reply, "I think it must be pleasant to have two dances safely accounted for," but she must not have sounded downcast enough because Marjorie sniffed, "I suppose you expect to dance with Mr. Rotherwood, but if he hasn't yet answered your note, I wouldn't count on it."

Swelling with annoyance, Beatrice said shortly, "I didn't ask for an answer to my note. And it's all the same to me whether he asks me or not."

But her stepcousin had the last word, giving a shake of her head and an if-you-insist shrug. "Well, I'm sure Mama would rather you stood up with Mr. Rotherwood than with the Other One."

The Finlay home spread along a goodly portion of Mount Street, light streaming from every window on the ground and first floors. Hastily Beatrice and Marjorie removed their list shoes and gave them to Crook before looking about them.

Beatrice picked out "the Other One" almost at once, and she thought ruefully it was an astonishing skill of hers. To light upon him so easily, with only the glimpse just inside the open front doors of a sliver of his fine form. But the sliver was enough to set her pulse flying and the blood rushing to her face. He was here!

Fortunately the Huftons lacked her supernatural power and remained oblivious to his presence, allowing Beatrice time to school her features. *He does not belong to you. He hardly even* likes *you, to judge by his conduct at Almack's!*

It was not as if she were going to hurl herself up the steps to accost him. Even if that were in her nature, Beatrice had made Lady Hufton a solemn promise that never, by word or deed, would she compromise the family through her behavior toward—him—or indeed anyone. There would be no more unauthorized correspondence, no unseemly displays, nothing. She had written the same to her step-mother Mrs. Wolfe as both an act of penance and an attempt to share her side of the story before Lady Hufton did. But all those assurances did not prevent her from wishing with all her heart that she might dance with him or speak with him, or at the very least catch his eye in the course of the evening. She would be watched closely and would have to make every effort to hide her feelings, but she would rather make the attempt than otherwise. There was always the chance Mr. Clayton would seek her out, if Mr. Rotherwood had followed her recommendation and invested money. Mr. Clayton would tell her, wouldn't he?

Her thoughts were recalled by a sharp gasp from Lady Hufton and a jab from Marjorie. "It's the Rotherwoods!"

So it was, the Marble Millionaire and his dark-blue-clad mother, alighting and proceeding up the steps, Mrs. Rotherwood nodding graciously to those saluting her while she clung proudly to her son. Both her gaze and her son's skimmed past the Huftons and Beatrice without pause, leaving Beatrice's companions to turn anxious (Sir John and Lady Hufton) or spiteful (Marjorie) looks on her to see how she bore it.

In comparison to disguising her response to Mr. Clayton's presence, this was child's play, and Beatrice merely gave a rueful shrug. "I suppose it means he won't be investing in the canal, then." That would be disappointing indeed, if it was the case, but not a complete surprise, given her hasty and unconventional appeal. If providence offered an opportunity this evening, she would ask him if he received her note, but did not otherwise think there was anything more she would be allowed to do.

Choosing to err on the side of caution, however, Lady Hufton dallied outside some minutes, exchanging greetings and introducing the girls to anyone they had not yet met, until she deemed the danger of meeting the Rotherwoods in the entry had passed. Beatrice bore this with decent equanimity, but Marjorie whimpered and groaned under her breath, hopping from foot to foot and craning her neck so that she might not miss the Dodsons or Miss Kempshott. "Mama, *please!*"

By the time they entered and were received by Sir August, Lady Finlay, and two of the indistinguishable Misses Finlay, the dancing was well under way, leaving Lady Finlay to indicate with her closed fan her oldest daughter Miss Finlay dancing with a paunchy peer at the top of the room and—with overflowing pride and a flourish—"You see our second there, Miss Flora Finlay, standing up with Mr. Rotherwood."

"They do you credit," said Lady Hufton graciously.

Lady Finlay appeared gratified, but being a mother of four unmarried daughters was not a burden easily carried, and her smile was thinner than pleasure alone could make it. "Thank you. I do hope Flora makes the best of it and does not talk too much of her cats."

Then the Finlays must greet their next guests and the Hufton party passed on to the ballroom.

"Oh, oh!" cried Marjorie. "It's grander than Almack's! And look there! There's Mr. Dodson dancing with his cousin Miss Kempshott."

Sotto voce, her mother bid her temper her enthusiasm. "And don't point, dearest."

"But Lady Finlay pointed at Miss Finlay and Miss Flora," Marjorie frowned.

"Yes, and they were her daughters," replied Lady Hufton. "Perhaps I should have said don't point at the gentlemen."

At this her daughter gave a resentful huff. "Very well, I won't point, Mama. But really, I don't know why you must reprimand me more than Beatrice, simply because I am your daughter."

"Beatrice wasn't pointing," her mother returned, noting with vexation that Sir John chose this moment to flee for the card room.

"Perhaps not, but we both know she has been doing *far worse things*."

In spite of herself, Beatrice could not help regarding her indignantly. Honestly, how long was the girl going to go on and on about Beatrice's sins?

Lady Hufton hushed Marjorie again, even as she nodded and smiled to a nearby matron, but Marjorie hissed, "If either of the you-know-whos ask her to dance, will you permit her to accept?"

"Unless she has sprained her ankle or otherwise incapacitated herself, I would not only permit it, Marjorie—I would prefer it. Your cousin has assured me she will give me no further cause for concern. I wish I might say the same of you!"

While Beatrice appreciated Lady Hufton's sentiment, she nevertheless wished it unsaid when she saw the fire in Marjorie's eye. Fortunately the end of the dance provided a welcome distraction, both young ladies unconsciously shrinking back, lest they look excessively keen to find a partner.

Despite her lowered gaze, Beatrice knew Mr. Clayton and Miss Brand had ended at the bottom of the room, far, far from her, but she was still disappointed when the paunchy peer loomed at Lady Hufton's side and begged to be introduced. The moment it was accomplished, Lord Downes asked for the honor of Beatrice's company, etc. etc., and off she went, her gloved hand in his, left to wonder if this would be a repeat of Almack's, with Mr. Clayton cool and distant.

As Lord Downes was followed by a Mr. Pickford and Mr. Pickford by a Sir Keane, it seemed all too likely. Determined to keep her word to her aunt (and *not* to behave like Marjorie), Beatrice refused to twist and turn and look around for Mr. Clayton, but that did not prevent her mysterious sixth sense from tracking him around the ballroom, whether he was dancing or standing to the side in conversation. Once she felt a prickle on the back of her neck and wondered if *he* was watching *her*, but when she circled to face outward and ventured a peep in his direction, she met only with his profile. His jaw was set, even hard.

It was almost an accident that Beatrice danced with Mr. Rotherwood. She was standing near the Misses Finlay when Mr. Rotherwood returned the eldest Miss Finlay to the flock. The Finlay daughter nearest Beatrice—was it Miss Felicity? Miss Fiona?—then held her breath and almost strained forward in anticipation, and Mr. Rotherwood must have felt it, for when he involuntarily straightened in response he spied Beatrice just beyond her.

"Ah. Miss Ellsworth. There you are. Would you do me the honor...?"

Beatrice's blushes were due entirely to fears of what the Huftons or the tiresome Mr. Dodson might be thinking or saying about this development, but she lay her fingers on his arm and let him lead her out. The dance was an active one, with much looping in and out and interacting with the person on one's diagonal as well as one's partner, leaving little time for private conversation. Moreover she was resolved this time not to stumble or blunder or do anything which might draw the attention (and raise the suspicions) of others. Therefore it was not until the fourth time through the figures that she blurted, "Mr. Rotherwood, pray, did you receive my note?"

He had been absently watching a young lady with bright hair further up the room but returned his attention with a start to his partner. "Note?" Then, "Er—note. Right. Yes, I did. You said through the servant that no reply was necessary, and I thought it might be awkward in any event. The proprieties and such."

Separated again by the figures, Beatrice had to tamp down her impatience until he was leading her up and back a double. But then she was amply rewarded because Mr. Rotherwood said, "I found your enthusiasm persuasive and made a purchase of a hundred shares."

She gasped audibly, turning to stare at him and thus missing her next step with the lady on her right. This earned her a frown and left her out of position for the diagonal cross, and she was obliged to scurry belatedly around the second diagonal to reach her designated spot. Here was bumbling indeed, but she couldn't bring herself to care. He had bought a hundred shares! A hundred shares! Why, that was a thousand pounds! Oh, where was Mr. Clayton?

"Thank you!" she whispered at the next opportunity. "Thank you, thank you, thank you, sir!"

Rotherwood eyed her with some amusement, taking in her beaming features and how her whole person nearly vibrated with joy. Most peculiar interests for a young lady—canals and commerce—but there was no accounting for taste. Nearly every person in London, male and female, might be buzzing around the Rotherwoods' fortune like flies at the honeypot, but at least this one was content and would not press for more. In fact, she seemed robbed of further speech, and he almost thought tears stood in her eyes. Surely that was a trick of the candlelight, however, for *crying* over canals and commerce would have shaded past "peculiar" territory into "downright bizarre."

Rotherwood was not the only witness to Miss Ellsworth's curious behavior, by any means. In fact, it would not be an exaggeration to say that, as so often where the Marble Millionaire was concerned, most of those nearby watched covertly or openly, but Beatrice was too elated to notice. She could hardly wait for the dance to end, for she had decided she would no longer wait for Mr. Clayton to approach her. She would find him! It would not be wrong. It could not be. She merely wanted to impart the good news to him, if he had not yet heard.

When the closing strains sounded, she did not have far to look, for Mr. Clayton was in conversation with Sir August, not five steps from Lady Hufton.

"Ah, my dear," her aunt greeted her, with a blush and a curtsey to Rotherwood. The man nodded and stalked off, but the matron beside Lady Hufton regarded Beatrice measuringly.

"Well! That's twice he's partnered you, is it not, Miss Ellsworth?"

"Mm. Yes. I suppose. Once at Almack's and once here."

"Well, Jenny, I commend you on your luck. I doubt there are more than a handful of girls here who could boast two dances with him. Your Miss Ellsworth, Lady Sylvia Stanley..."

But Beatrice didn't care a straw who Mr. Rotherwood had partnered or for how many times. Daringly she swept open her fan with raised arm and began to wave it, as if to cool her heated face. Then, behind its screen, she turned just far enough to peek at Mr. Clayton.

He was watching her.

Beatrice's breath caught, and she felt the blood rush to her cheeks, but she managed to give a nod and an attempt at a smile. *Come here, sir! Please, please, please come over here.*

Either her silent summons worked or he had wanted to speak with her in the first place, for he excused himself from Sir August to approach.

"Good evening, Miss Ellsworth, Lady Hufton," he said gravely.

Beside her, Beatrice felt Lady Hufton stiffen in apprehension, and she mustered as innocent an expression as she could to counter her aunt's fears. *See? I am not going to throw myself at his feet, making declarations!*

It must have sufficed, for Lady Hufton returned his bow before introducing the matron beside her. Beatrice later could not recall the woman's name, because her blood was roaring in her ears and she had no attention to spare, but Mr. Clayton murmured appropriate responses. Whoever the lady was, Beatrice heartily wished she would take herself off, so she might share her good news with Mr. Clayton. Though her aunt believed the less said to Mr. Clayton the better, surely she would come around when she learned how Beatrice's unconventional efforts had succeeded! Mrs. Whoever stuck to them like a species of barnacle, however, so whatever Beatrice said to Mr. Clayton, it must be before an audience of two. Never mind. Beatrice would not let it thwart her.

"Here you are at another ball, Mr. Clayton," she addressed him brightly, "yet instead of dancing, I find you talking again." (Lady Hufton gave a troubled cough, and Beatrice supposed belatedly that did rather sound like a hint, as if she expected him to ask her next for the honor. She winced.)

He smiled, however. "So I was. Talking. But I have already partnered Priscilla and Miss Croy and one of the Miss Finlays. I have not been altogether remiss in my duties."

"Not *altogether,* then," she agreed, smiling in return. "Though three dances is far from a respectable number, sir. You will give your dancing master a bad name."

Beatrice felt a touch at the back of her arm and understood it as another caution from her aunt. Oh, heavens—she must have sounded too glad. Or flirtatious, even. She couldn't seem to help it. How could she, when she loved nothing more than to talk to a friendly Mr. Clayton. And he was indeed friendly at present. If Lady Hufton had only witnessed his coolness at Almack's, she would have understood Beatrice's current delight.

Unaware of the attempts made to rein in his companion, Mr. Clayton continued in the same vein. "You would have me give up talking, then?"

"I would have you practice both talking and dancing in equal measures. And some people do even talk *while* they dance, I dare-say."

"Ah. That would be the best solution, to be sure. I would be guided by you, Miss Ellsworth—there are few people who would hold greater sway over me—if I were certain I could manage both to talk and to dance at the same time without mishap. Not everyone can, you know."

"You're right about that," she agreed. "I have blundered more than once when trying to do both, but a young lady does not always have the luxury of sitting out a dance. If someone asks her, she must stand up with him."

"Is there someone you danced with whom you would have pre-ferred to refuse?"

"If there were, it would hardly be proper of me to name him!" she laughed. "No, no. I only meant, when I am thinking too hard about something, my dancing does suffer. In which case it would probably be better if I simply stood and *thought*. Better not only for my partner, but also for those around me. During this last dance, for instance, I'm afraid my distraction exasperated the young lady next to me in our foursome."

A pause, and then he rejoined in an altered tone, "Rotherwood must have given you a good deal to think about, it seems."

Then he had seen her dancing with Mr. Rotherwood? That would make introducing the subject easier, though Lady Hufton and Mrs. Thingum continued to listen attentively, and she could almost see them now leaning closer. Could she perhaps speak in a sort of code?

"He *does* give me a good deal to think about," she replied, trying to pick her way, even as her eagerness grew. "A man of such...means and—and prompt decisions."

Here Beatrice waited for either glee or puzzlement to cross Mr. Clayton's features. Glee, if he knew of the large investment, or puzzlement, if she must further enlighten him. Truth be told, she hoped for the latter because what fun it would be to be the bearer of happy tidings! But instead of either expression, a shadow crossed his features.

"Has Rotherwood made a prompt decision, then?" Clayton asked slowly.

Tilting her head, she tried to read him. "He has!" A little bounce escaped her, and she felt again Lady Hufton's touch to her arm. "Oh, Mr. Clayton, if you have not heard—if your man of business has not yet told you—or if Mr. Rotherwood has not yet...done all that it involves or requires, or whatever—and yet I believe he *has*—or thinks he has—"

"Yes?" he interrupted. "What then?"

Abashed at his sudden curtness, her elation faded a little. "Then I believe he intends to buy shares of your canal."

His response could not have been further from what she expected. Nay, his mouth compressed in a hard line, a muscle in his jaw standing out, and she saw his chest rise and fall. Good heavens! What could the matter be?

"Is this common knowledge, Miss Ellsworth, or why would he inform you of it?"

With Mrs. Whatshername over her shoulder, Beatrice knew better than to mention having put the request to Mr. Rotherwood—in writing, no less—so she prevaricated a little. "Oh, well, as I said—talking and dancing...In the course of conversation he—er—mentioned it to me."

"Is Rotherwood in the habit of discussing his investments with you?"

Her mouth worked a moment. "No, indeed. It just—came up! I can't—er—recall why. Maybe we spoke of—of—of traveling on the Thames or something." She gave an uneasy laugh, being rather a wretched liar. "Yes. The Thames. Waterways and such. In any case," she hurried on, "he mentioned buying quite a few shares in—your project. Quite a few. You might...ask him about it. I'm certain you'll be pleased. Aren't you? Pleased, that is?"

But Lady Hufton could bear no more—no more of her charge's embarrassed fumbling and no more of Mrs. Dormer's raised eyebrows and palpable curiosity. "The supper dance!" she cried. "Beatrice, did you not promise it to Mr. Dodson? I see him coming this way with your cousin Marjorie." And then, in her desperation, she shot at a venture, "Good evening, Mr. Dodson. Do remind me—was it my Marjorie or her cousin Miss Ellsworth you asked for the supper dance?"

Having just danced for the second time with Miss Hufton, courtesy did not permit Mr. Dodson to do other than beg now for Beatrice to stand up with him. And, as Beatrice had observed to Mr. Clayton, courtesy did not do other than to force her to accept, though she had never done so with a less willing heart.

CHAPTER TWENTY-ONE

It was a commendable Ambition,
rather to aim high than to look low.
— N. W., *The History of George A Green* (1706)

Lady Hufton's announcement of the supper dance jarred Clayton into awareness. Blast. He had told Priscilla he would find her for it, but he had been too occupied first in keeping an eye on Miss Ellsworth without being too obvious, and then with speaking with her, that he had no idea where his intended bride could now be found. Before he could bow and excuse himself, however, the beady-eyed Miss Hufton wriggled her way to his side, whipping open her fan and erecting it as a barrier between her mother and herself in much the way Beatrice had.

"Good evening, Mr. Clayton."

"Good evening, Miss Hufton. I would ask you for the honor of the supper dance, but—"

"Never mind that," she said quickly, *sotto voce*. "I have a partner who will be here soon enough, I warrant. I merely wanted to thank you for your continued kindness to my poor stepcousin Miss Ellsworth."

She could not have chosen more effective words to arrest him, and he gave her a sharp look. "'Poor'? In what way is she unfortunate?"

"You saw how my mother Lady Hufton must keep a close eye on her. If you were not a friend of the family and of Miss Ellsworth in particular, I should never mention it, but it happens that Beatrice is in hot water." Miss Hufton screwed her features up in what was meant to be concern but resembled instead advanced myopia. "You see," she hissed, "she has by her own confession been writing to Mr. Rotherwood!"

She must have been gratified by the effect of her revelation, for Clayton went alternately white then red. "Been writing to"? *Then she had indeed written to Rotherwood, and possibly multiple times?* The man made the little gesture at Almack's after the two had been in discussion, and Miss Ellsworth had complied, then. Could it mean anything other than that they were secretly engaged?

A secret engagement would explain everything—her clumsiness in mentioning the man, the warmth with which she regarded Rotherwood when they danced—But why, for mercy's sake, should it be kept a secret, and who would have wanted it so? A young lady would hardly insist on it, when the secrecy left her open to gossip. It must have been he who demanded it.

Instinctively Clayton had turned from Miss Hufton, or she would have seen the fire in his eyes. Did that scoundrel have intentions of playing Miss Ellsworth false? If he did, Clayton would throw his money in his teeth and expose him to the world, canal or no canal.

Though this bitter blow was no more than he had feared, the reality of it nearly felled him. Had he been alone in his rooms in Warren Street, he would have given way to his feelings. He would have cursed. Wept. He might even have kicked at some of Mrs. Oakes' flimsy furnishings. But here in the Finlay ballroom he could do none of these things.

He must, must master himself.

Miss Hufton unwittingly assisted him because, when he finally looked her way again, the pleasant effect of her bombshell had brought a gleam to her eye and curve to her lips, and Clayton immediately, contrarily leapt to Miss Ellsworth's defense.

"Yes," he replied, mild as milk. "It does not surprise me at all that such an innocent and well-meaning young lady would not realize the seriousness with which society would view her actions. I'm afraid she had ideas of wanting to assist me. You see, she learned I sought additional investors for the Cumberland Arm project and took it upon herself to broach the matter with Rotherwood. Though I would not recommend such means in general, I cannot help but be glad Miss Ellsworth took pen in hand, for he has indeed—been in conversation with my man of business." Mid-speech Clayton remembered Rotherwood's request that the matter be kept private, leaving him to end his speech in this vague manner, but Miss Hufton did not press him for details. She was too busy biting her lip, like a child whose toy had been snatched away.

Then she gave a shrug. "If that is how you see it, Mr. Clayton. But I do hope you will join us in warning her against such improprieties. I'm sure you would not like your Miss Brand writing to strange gentlemen or conducting business negotiations on your behalf. But here is my partner...if you will pardon me..."

Snapping shut her fan, she marched away, Clayton in his mind's eye helping her along with a mighty shove. Mischievous creature! But perhaps he ought to have blessed her, for his swift anger against her had afforded him a moment's reprieve from wretchedness—wretchedness which now returned full force.

Miss Ellsworth engaged! What, in all that life and the world had to offer, was left for him?

"John. *John!*"

Starting, he looked down to see Priscilla beside him. His betrothed had her arms crossed indignantly. "It's the supper dance. Had you forgotten?"

"I had not forgotten. I do beg your pardon, but Miss Hufton was speaking with me. Where is Miss Croy?"

"Some old person asked to stand up with her." She gave a dismissive jerk of her chin in the direction of the top of the room. Eyeing him reproachfully, she added, "I have been enjoying myself so, meeting so many people and dancing every dance."

"I am glad of it. But perhaps you might welcome a respite, then?" he asked.

"Respite? But we will rest all through the supper, once the dance is ended."

"In truth, there is something I would ask you, Priscilla."

Her protests died on her lips, and she regarded him warily. "What is it? Was it something Miss Hufton said?"

He grimaced. "No."

Extending his arm to her, she smothered a sigh and took hold of it, allowing him to lead her to one of the benches. Then she folded her hands in her lap, her gaze trained wistfully on the more fortunate young ladies setting and circling and passing in hey. After a minute, when he still had not spoken, Priscilla turned to frown at him and was surprised by the bleak look on his face.

"Goodness," she cried. "Are you unwell, John?"

He gave himself a shake. "No. I am well. Perfectly so." Taking a deep breath, he reached to grasp both her hands in one of his own. "Priscilla, we have been engaged over two years, have we not?"

"Yes...since before Papa died." Color flooded her cheeks, but she did not pull away from him.

"And in that time, I have not...*we* have not spoken of when our marriage would finally take place."

"No." She looked back at the dancers. Miss Croy and her partner were working their way down the room.

"You were still in school, of course, when your father died," he went on, "and we did not know each other well. But now—"

"Now I am older and have finished my education," she whispered. However she did not say, *And now we know each other well*, and neither did he.

"Yes." He lowered his eyes to contemplate his gloved hand enclosing hers. "And therefore, what would you say to setting a date?"

There was a long, long silence. That is, Priscilla Brand was silent. All about them music played, dancers hopped and glided, partners and onlookers chatted.

At last she shifted restlessly, and Clayton released her hands, bemused, trying to quash the wild hope which raised its head. Could it be, after all this, that in the end Priscilla would not want to marry him? The words rose to his lips before he could stop them, though he managed a jesting tone: "Unless you have decided you want no more to do with me."

"Of course I want to be married," she cried, extinguishing his bright thoughts instantly. "Of course I do. You caught me off guard is all. To bring it up in this place and so suddenly."

He swallowed, muttering something apologetic and giving a nod. Not that Priscilla was looking at him. "We might be married by license," he suggested, "as we are new to town and practically unknown. No need for the banns to be read aloud to strangers for three weeks."

But Priscilla pouted. "We may, of course, if that is what you wish. Don't you think it's a little...furtive? Because we could be married at St. Anne's, couldn't we? Since Miss Croy and I attend there. Wouldn't you rather have the banns read?"

Then he must yield, naturally, though Clayton could not help but think he would rather she express her opinions straight out, if consulting his own was a mere pretense. "Let the banns be read, then," he answered blandly.

"Yes, that would be better all around," she said, satisfied. "And St. Anne's is a grand church, though the altar is only wood, painted to look like marble. Do you know what Cissy said about it?"

He pinned an expectant look on his face, but when she only waited for further prompting, he succeeded in forcing out one syllable: "What?"

Priscilla frowned at this perfunctory effort. "Cissy said that she could never get married in a church so vast as St. Anne's because it would make her feel insignificant. She would prefer a tiny little chapel or even being married over the blacksmith's anvil!"

Thinking it unlikely poor Miss Croy would be requiring either, he only smiled. "Well, it is fortunate you do not suffer from similar compunctions. So—if we must wait at least three weeks, it will be Christmastime. Do you have enough money to make your purchases and preparations, or shall I give instructions to Braham to give you more?"

"Perhaps a little more," she said coyly. "You would not want me to appear shabby on my wedding day, would you, John?"

"You could never appear shabby," he protested dutifully.

"And—and don't you think it would be best to invite a few people?" she pressed.

"Whom would you suggest? Besides the Prince Regent and Wellington, I mean."

"The Prince Regent and—! Oh, you're joking, aren't you?" She made a sound in her throat to approximate a laugh. Then, picking at the tassel of her fan for some moments, she ventured a peep at him. "Well—I don't suppose Lord Stanley would come, or-or some of your business associates?"

Clayton stared. "Priscilla, inviting the earl or such people—"

There was no need to finish his sentence, for she guessed the rest and turned her head away from him to watch the dancers again. "Very well. I don't see the harm in asking, but if you don't think of them as your friends, or don't think they would be pleased to share in your joy or to see a young bride..."

Briefly he shut his eyes, wishing he could rub his hands over them. Good heavens. Barring illness, catastrophic injury at the building site, or the Second Coming, this would be the rest of his life. The rest of his life spent managing Priscilla's expectations, whether they were reasonable or not. The rest of his life taking up promptly and appropriately the conversational cues she fed him. The rest of his life making the best of a bad bargain.

"...And Miss Ellsworth?"

Clayton stiffened. "Pardon me, Priscilla. What was that?"

She favored him with a long look, and it occurred to him that her manner toward him was changing. Gone was her earlier timidity and eagerness to please. In fact, there was something decidedly waspish in her current regard.

"I *said*, I suppose you would have no objection to inviting our humbler acquaintances, such as the Dodsons and Miss Kempshott, the Huftons, and Miss Ellsworth?"

He repressed a shiver, his glance going involuntarily down the room to where Miss Ellsworth and Dodson performed a Hole in the Wall crossing, facing each other as they passed, and then retreating to their new positions. What objection could he give? She had made her choice and he his. The sooner their decisions were made permanent, the sooner they—he—would heal.

"By all means," he muttered. "When I have arranged matters with the parson, you may make what communications you will."

"But who will give us a wedding breakfast, John? Will it all fall upon Cissy?"

"I suppose we might host something at a hotel."

She gasped, seizing his sleeve. "Might we truly? At Blake's or Durant's or the Grillion?"

Trust Priscilla to suggest exclusive establishments in Mayfair. Well, it was her money, at any rate—at least until the moment she married him. And then, at one fell swoop, by law it would all become his. What injustice! It was a wonder every woman in the kingdom did not rise up in protest.

"Where you like," he replied.

She sighed with satisfaction and went so far as to lean her head an instant on his shoulder, much as a cat would nudge one's hand to encourage a caress. And, one of his foster parents having had a cat, a very long time ago, Clayton's hand lifted in what might have ended as a pat, only she straightened abruptly and said, "What about Mr. Saint-Cloud? May we invite him?"

"The dancing master?" He managed not to roll his eyes, even as his impatience flared anew. How could she in one breath want to invite Earl Stanley and in the next a man who earned his bread a stone's throw from the stalls of Oxford Market?

"He has such an air!" declared Priscilla. "And he is so kind and elegant. Cissy and I are quite enamored of him."

Clayton gave up. He might as well save his breath and leave her to invite the street sweeper and the king, while she was at it.

"As you please," he said. "Now, come. The dance is ending. Shall we to supper?"

As she stepped through the figures with Mr. Dodson, Beatrice decided she must be the most ungrateful girl in the world. Here she was in London, after all, at a lovely ball. Despite her recent actions, the Huftons had forgiven her and made no further reproaches. Even Marjorie, who might never become a friend, was at least no longer openly hostile. And then, added to these blessings, Beatrice had danced with the most popular man in the room and learned her efforts had not been wasted. With such investors as Lord Stanley and Mr. Rotherwood, Mr. Clayton's canal would surely go forward now, and Beatrice could comfort herself for having contributed materially to his success. She had not done it for his thanks, so there was absolutely no reason she should feel so bereft now. If she felt a pang, it should only be because she saw him sitting beside Miss Brand, her hands clasped in his. It should have nothing to do the visible displeasure on his face when their conversation was forced to end. Therefore she must be an ungrateful girl. One who did favors in order to receive thanks, and not for goodness' own sake. One who did favors in hopes of being praised and smiled upon and—perhaps—danced with. Why would he never ask her to dance anymore?

If she had not promised Lady Hufton to be all that was proper and unexceptionable in a young lady, Beatrice would have been tempted to seek Mr. Clayton out again, Miss Brand or no Miss Brand. Not to attempt to steal the affections of an engaged man, but rather to wring one more moment from him of their former easiness.

But she had given her word and must therefore bear Mr. Clayton's inexplicable moods as best she might, though perplexity threatened to eat her up.

Therefore Beatrice smiled and chatted with the languid Mr. Dodson while they danced. She could not understand his appeal, for his greatest interests in the world seemed to be betting of any kind, followed by Mr. Rotherwood. Indeed, he had as many questions about Mr. Rotherwood as Mr. Clayton had, but without the frown and air of disapproval. Beatrice only succeeded in turning the subject at last by saying with a laugh, "I declare, Mr. Dodson, if you are so very curious about Mr. Rotherwood, you might ask him to stand up with you next."

As the Finlays' guests made their way to the supper room, many of the crowd openly jockeyed for seats near Mr. Rotherwood and his partner, a pretty young lady with blonde hair whose name Mr. Dodson diligently asked several people until someone informed him she was a Miss Caroline Sidney, a perfect nobody. Mr. Dodson nevertheless repeated Miss Sidney's name several times under his breath and later, when they were seated, Beatrice saw him extract a tiny notebook and record it.

"Another name for the betting books?" she inquired wryly.

"Ah, Miss Ellsworth," replied he, tapping his forehead sapiently with his pencil before stowing it, "*Nam et ipsa scientia potestas est.* Knowledge is power, you know."

Sadly for Beatrice, Mr. Clayton and Miss Brand found seats at the farther end of the table and on the same side, so she was deprived of the sight of him for the duration of the meal. And then, an hour later, when people began to rise again from their seats and the musicians to tune their instruments, and Beatrice's hopes to lift despite her best intentions, Mr. Clayton came nowhere near. Instead he gathered his intended and Miss Croy and escorted them to Lady Finlay, clearly in order to take their leave. Beatrice's spirits plummeted accordingly.

She found herself doing as she had earlier in the evening: sending him a silent message. *Look at me, Mr. Clayton! Don't go without looking at me! Please!*

And for the second time, it worked.

Far across the room, he raised his head, his dark eyes meeting hers.

He did not smile; he did not wave. But his lips moved.

And even at the distance, Beatrice thought she read the word there.

Good-bye.

Chapter Twenty-Two

Notwithstanding the interior of the kingdom is almost wholly intersected by canals, this is the only one which, for commercial purposes, has yet been extended to the metropolis.

— Publisher Loongman, Hurst, Rees, *The Picture of London for 1813* (1813)

A week passed. Ten days. November passed into December. The Huftons and Beatrice attended a musical evening, a supper, a performance at the opera. Almack's again. They drove in Hyde Park when the weather permitted. They called and received callers. One afternoon they toured Bullock's Egyptian Hall in Piccadilly with the Dodsons and Miss Kempshott, examining stuffed animals on display and paying the additional shilling to venture down a rocky corridor to the Pantherion of tropical plants.

And everywhere they met the same faces, each face a slice of the never-varying whole.

But nowhere in this time did Beatrice see Mr. Clayton. And if he was spoken of by anyone, it was not in her presence. Nor could she bring him up to the Huftons, naturally. And with no sight of him, no sound of him, it was as if he had never existed.

When she could bear it no longer, Beatrice sought relief in pouring out her heart to her stepmother in a letter. She had always been confidential with Mrs. Wolfe, but the time away from home made her dear Mama seem an even safer repository for secrets, far away as she was in Hampshire. But Beatrice's letter must have crossed with Mrs. Wolfe's, for in her own communication Mrs. Wolfe made no mention of the elusive Mr. Clayton, filling the page instead with odds and ends concerning the family. At the very bottom of the page, however, and curving up the margin was appended a sentence: "Darling, Mr. Wolfe says we will come to town with the boys when the short half ends."

With a squeal, Beatrice kissed the sheet and then clutched it to her breast. Her parents and Willsie and Edmund coming? Clattering down the stairs, she found the Huftons in the parlor, Sir John reading, Lady Hufton working, and Marjorie at the pianoforte.

"Lady Hufton," she cried, "did you know my family was coming to London? Not my whole family, to be sure, but Mama and Mr. Wolfe and Willsie and Edmund."

Marjorie left off with a jangle, and Sir John and Lady Hufton exchanged a glance.

"I did know," said Lady Hufton, resuming her stitching. "For my brother Colin wrote to me of their plans."

"Will they stay here?" Beatrice asked eagerly. "And for how long? I know the boys will not need to return for spring term until after Epiphany Day."

"They will stay at Mivart's in Brook Street, not a ten-minute walk from us," replied Lady Hufton, "and as the apartments there are let by the month, I daresay they will be here several weeks."

With difficulty Beatrice stifled an unladylike *hurrah!* and it only occurred to her later—much later—to wonder at the exchanged glance. Had Lady Hufton begged her brother and his wife to come? Had concern over Beatrice prompted the visit? But she could not bring herself to mind. It only mattered that they were coming.

Lady Hufton would not hear of meeting the Wolfes' coach at the Swan with Two Necks on the day they were expected. "Venture into Cheapside in the evening, when they will merely climb down from one coach and climb into another, to be taken to their hotel? Absolutely not."

Therefore Beatrice was made to wait until the following morning, but her family did not disappoint, appearing in Green Street while the Huftons were still at breakfast.

"Mama!" Beatrice flew around the table into her stepmother's arms. "Mr. Wolfe. And dear Willsie and Edmund." Her younger half-brother and stepbrother submitted to her embraces, William good-naturedly shouldering the additional burden of his sister's exclamations about how he had grown, and Edmund maintaining his customary silence. But as soon as all the courtesies had been dispensed with and seats found, William produced *The Picture of London* guidebook to wave at her. "Look here, Bea, Mundo and I spent hours in the coach marking everything we want to see, so we hope you haven't done everything already."

"Unless you happened to place tick marks beside Almack's, Assemblies, and Crushes within Lofty People's Homes, your choices are likely safe," she assured him. "What shall we do first? The Tower? Astley's?"

"Neither, if you please," William answered, skimming through the pages.

"Packet," said Edmund.

"Packet?"

"Voilà!" William declared, thrusting the book at her.

"Passage boat," said Edmund.

With some trepidation, Beatrice took the guidebook, open to a page headed with "The Grand Junction Canal" and read, "'A passage-boat, or packet, sets out from Paddington to Uxbridge, every morning exactly at eight o'clock, and sets out from Uxbridge, on its return, precisely at four o'clock in the afternoon.'"

"You wish to take a boat ride on the Grand Junction Canal?" she asked, blinking.

Mrs. Wolfe intervened hastily. "It seems your brother Tyrone has been reading everything about canals he can lay his hands on and has created something of a canal fever at home."

"You did not mention this in your letters, Mama." Not that Beatrice was surprised at the omission, under the circumstances.

"He and Aggie talk of making a trip to Basingstoke, to take a packet there on the canal as far as Aldershot, or even Woking!" said William, bouncing a little on his chair. "But then Mundo and I saw this ride and thought a passage boat on the Grand Junction would make Ty eat his heart out with jealousy, for what's old Basingstoke in comparison?"

"Is that the object, then?" Beatrice asked faintly. "To make Tyrone envious?"

"Everyone's in a pother," sighed her stepfather, removing from the window seat to join his wife on the sofa. He rubbed at a smudge on his Hessian boot. "For the more Tyrone read, the more decided he was on purchasing shares in—Mr. Clayton's Cumberland Arm project."

"And then Aggie worked on her father Mr. Weeks and even on one of her brothers-in-law," Mrs. Wolfe hurried to add.

"So then what choice had I, but to be swept away by the same furore?" teased her husband with a mock-plaintive air. "Tyrone may end in bankrupting the county, but at least we will all go down together."

"He exaggerates," Mrs. Wolfe said. "It comes to nearly three thousand pounds, taken altogether, and even if the enterprise fails, I daresay everyone will bear his share of the loss."

"Oh," breathed Beatrice, torn between delight at this unexpected influx of riches and alarm, when she remembered how Mr. Clayton asked that she *not* canvass Tyrone for funds. Would she have an opportunity to explain that her brother had done it of his own accord, or would this simply add to the reasons Mr. Clayton grew more and more distant and more and more displeased with her?

"So you see," resumed William, "we *must* go for this ride. It's *research*. The packet trundles from Paddington to Uxbridge and back—"

(Edmund: "Two shillings, six pence.")

"—Or we might only go halfway, if you prefer, say six to ten miles—"

("One shilling, six pence.")

"—If it's raining or wretched out."

"In *any* weather, my dear Colin and Mrs. Wolfe, would this be advisable?" Lady Hufton spoke up. Beatrice guessed precisely what troubled her, even if her parents had not then regarded each other speakingly, and she hid her embarrassment by pretending to peruse *The Picture of London*. But it was Marjorie who put their thoughts into words.

"Ought we to be going anywhere near any canals, when—one never knows what sort of people one might meet there?"

William stared, taken aback by such a ridiculous, just-like-a-girl objection, but a lifted brow from his mother succeeded in making him think twice before he voiced his disgust. Mr. Wolfe, however, said mildly, "Given the proposed size of our party and those who compose it, I don't foresee any danger, but thank you for your caution, my dear Marjorie."

Being no more afraid of her uncle than anyone else, Marjorie persisted. "Sir, I am thinking of Beatrice here, and wanting to spare her distress."

"Are you?" he returned, looking from his niece to his stepdaughter's shrinking discomfiture. Before he could say more, however, Beatrice's chin lifted. Honestly—what point was there in beating about the bush, if everyone (except possibly her younger brothers) knew to what Marjorie referred?

"If you fear we will encounter Mr. Clayton," she said, "I will point out that every time we have seen him in London, it's been in—in some fashionable setting, not—not dockside or anything."

"So far," retorted Marjorie, not at all abashed. "And we haven't seen him anywhere fashionable lately. Nor have we ever been 'dockside,' so who knows what the man does when he isn't hanging from the coattails of the fashionable."

"Marjorie," remonstrated her mother, even as Beatrice gasped with indignation.

Marjorie sprang up, throwing down her tambour frame. "Why am I the one at fault here? *I* have not been dangling hopelessly after an *engaged* man and have been nothing but a model young lady since we came! And yet you and Papa behave as if I must still be watched and warned!" With a last flash from her beady eyes, Miss Hufton growled, "Excuse me, everyone," and stamped from the room.

When the door finished rattling in its frame and Edmund's muted whistle died away, an awkward pause followed. Then Lady Hufton rose. With a quick touch to Beatrice's shoulder, she hurried after her daughter, muttering as she went, "Pardon me. Colin, Miranda—it—is the matter I mentioned in my earlier letter."

Beatrice looked to Mrs. Wolfe when Lady Hufton was gone. Then it was not only worries about Beatrice her aunt had shared in her letters? What concern could Marjorie have caused? But Mrs. Wolfe only clapped her hands, saying briskly, "About this passage boat, boys—does the book say where one meets it in Paddington?"

All the fuss was for nothing, thought Beatrice, when the narrow-beamed packet, operated by crew in smart blue uniforms with yellow capes and yellow buttons, arrived again at the terminus of the Paddington Arm. In hindsight it had been silly to imagine at all that they would see Mr. Clayton. Simply because he worked on canals did not mean he would be found leisurely riding passage boats on an entirely different waterway; nor would Mr. Clayton's proposed project connect directly with the Paddington at all. Indeed, as one of the boatmen pointed out to them, it would be the not-yet-opened Regent's Canal which would eventually complete the connection to Limehouse on the Thames.

"And what of the Cumberland Arm when it is built?" Mr. Wolfe asked him, a listening boy to either side of him.

"That one, when it's built—if it's built—will be a spur off the Regent's Canal, about two-thirds of the way to Camden Town," answered the knowledgeable waterman. "You might have a look yourself where it will branch off, if you were to drive along the

New Road and then north up the Portland Road. But Lor' knows when they'll start work again on the Regent's. No, no, it isn't the weather that's stopped them. It's the fighting with Mr. Agar over the land rights, and Homer the superintendent having made off with a good deal of the funds. They'll be having to go hat in hand to the subscribers again, mark my words. But Morgan—that's the chief engineer, you know—aims to open that first leg to Camden Town by next year, come weal come woe. When he gets the say-so again, he'll have the workers back at it with hammer and tongs."

News of the superintendent's scandalous embezzlement had failed to penetrate to Hampshire, so Mr. Wolfe had many questions, but it was William who asked what Beatrice wanted to know: "If people have to raise more money for the Regent's Canal, won't that harm the backing for the Cumberland Arm?"

"There'll be no mixing them up in the minds of them that know," pronounced the boatman, clearly including himself in this group. "Mr. Clayton as is raising funds for the Cumberland is no more like that wily Homer than chalk is to cheese."

The difficulties impeding the construction of the Regent's Canal made new Cumberland investor Mr. Wolfe anxious to see where activity had left off, as well as whether it would delay work beginning on the Cumberland spur, and he suggested they drive out to see for themselves. Of course William and Edmund were all for it, and having had several hours to talk herself into sense, Beatrice made no objections. But once crammed in the coach between Edmund and her stepmother, with William full of effusions and observations about canals and packets and Paddington, she seized the chance to steal a few minutes' private conversation.

"Mama, why did you not write to me about this enthusiasm which has swept everyone up?"

"I could not find the right moment, my dear, when you were so caught up yourself, but with the added complication of your feelings for—him."

"When I suggested asking Tyrone to buy shares, Mr. Cl—*he*—asked me to refrain, telling me in so many words that he would prefer not to mix friendship with business. I do hope he won't think I defied him, when he learns it has happened all the same."

Mrs. Wolfe squeezed her arm. "Surely he will be so overjoyed he will forgive anything and anybody. You heard the man on the packet—here is the much larger Regent's Canal held up in part for lack of funds! How much more grateful Mr.—*he*—will be, to be funded in full."

"Perhaps, then, it might make him feel kindly toward me again," Beatrice replied wistfully. "Though our paths may no longer cross in person, I hate to think of him somewhere, out in the world, unhappy with me."

Mrs. Wolfe suppressed a sigh, wishing that, whatever Mr. Clayton might think of Beatrice Ellsworth, it would be far better for Beatrice Ellsworth if she ceased altogether to think of John Clayton. While Mr. Wolfe assured her it would happen with time, Mr. Clayton's reappearance in their daughter's life had dismayed them both.

As if guessing her thoughts, Beatrice continued, "I am sorry my conduct distressed Lady Hufton. Be plain with me, Mama—your visit is not entirely due to 'canal fever,' is it? Did Lady Hufton summon you to deal with me?"

"We were not 'summoned,' but I confess I wanted to see you with my own eyes. On the contrary, Beatrice, Lady Hufton said your conduct has been 'everything she might wish' since she spoke to you and was given your promise. If anything, it is Miss Hufton who occupies her thoughts again. You know, do you not, that she received an offer from Mr. Dodson?"

The wideness of Beatrice's eyes answered Mrs. Wolfe's question, even if she had not admitted, "I'm afraid Marjorie and I have not become particularly close."

"Ah—well. You are two very different sorts."

"But why would Marjorie have refused him? She seems fond of him."

Mrs. Wolfe bit her lip. "She did not refuse," she whispered, though there was no danger of her being heard over the others talking or the creak and jumble of the carriage. "But Sir John would not give his blessing because Mr. Dodson reportedly has some tendencies toward excessive gambling."

Beatrice did not doubt it. Well! This would explain Marjorie's continued ill temper. To be denied again the wishes of her heart, first with the drunken groom and now with the gentleman gambler. One would think Marjorie might relent toward her, Beatrice, in the sympathy of disappointed hopes, but perhaps she feared Beatrice might still somehow snatch happiness from thin air.

The coach carrying them was the only one on the road when they turned away from town to travel along the eastern flank of the uncompleted Regent's Park, and in the wintry, smoky afternoon dimness Beatrice was not the only one to shiver with unease. With the work stopped on the canal, would there be anyone abroad at this hour but highwaymen?

Mrs. Wolfe's lips parted to suggest they come another time—one bright morning, perhaps—when the wisps of fog obscuring Edmund's view from the window parted momentarily and the youth said, "Footpads."

"Colin," breathed Mrs. Wolfe, reaching across the space to grasp her husband's knee, even as the coach slowed.

"Fool," muttered Mr. Wolfe under his breath, referring to the coachman, "if the brigands are on foot, why does he not go faster?" He gave a rap on the roof to express just this, but their driver slowed further, calling to the horses. With a roll of his eyes, Mr. Wolfe grimaced. "Well, Miranda, thank God we're in a hackney with two schoolboys, and because of our outing we're hardly dressed as if we'd come from Mayfair. Let's just hope they won't be disappointed with their takings."

To the party's surprise, however, no shouting followed, and the coachman leaped down to open the door.

"Here's service," remarked Mr. Wolfe.

"This is as far as we go," said the driver, touching his cap when he saw the ladies. "Bit of a to-do here."

One of Edmund's footpads stepped around the coachman to pop his head in, causing a chorus of gasps. "Apologies," he said politely, stepping back when the imposing Mr. Wolfe half rose to prevent his ingress. "But we've closed the road temporarily. A little ceremony to break ground."

Beatrice's gasp of alarm was succeeded by another, though this second one had nothing to do with fear.

"Breaking ground!" she exclaimed. "Why, Mr. Clayton, how marvelous!"

CHAPTER
TWENTY-THREE

The end must justifie the means;
He only sins who ill intends.
— Matthew Prior, *Hans Carvel* (1718)

M iss *Ellsworth*?"

A great deal of staring and stammering and stumbling ensued, in which every person present save Edmund and the coachman participated, and during which it would be hard to determine who was more astonished.

At last, however, the Wolfes and Ellsworths clambered from the coach to be introduced to Mr. Clayton by a blushing Beatrice, the other gentlemen whom Edmund had mistaken for footpads hanging back to await the end of the interruption.

"Wolfe," repeated Clayton. "So you are the Colin Wolfe of Winchester who invested in a hundred shares? I did not at the time know your connection to Miss Ellsworth, but I assumed there must be one. The name Tyrone Ellsworth was plain to me, but can anyone identify a Mr. Weeks?"

"He's Aggie's father," said Beatrice quickly. "And—Aggie or Tyrone must have said something to him, for, of course, I am not in Winchester, and even if I had been, I remembered you asking me not to press my family—"

"Indeed, sir," Mrs. Wolfe interposed, seeing her stepdaughter's confusion, "if you preferred to avoid Wintonian investors, you would have done better to place the interdict upon Tyrone, for it was he who whipped up such zeal for your project among our family members."

"Are you really breaking ground for your canal?" blurted Willsie. "May we see?"

Clayton smiled at the youth's eagerness. "We are and you may. It's purely ceremonial, however, so you will likely be disappointed. A mere gathering of a few bigwigs to watch me turn over a spade of soil."

"May we, Mr. Wolfe?" demanded William, even as he and Edmund began backing toward the so-called bigwigs. And as soon as Mr. Wolfe gave his nod, they turned and dashed away.

Gesturing for the others to join him, Clayton followed the boys at a more dignified pace. "Have you been long in London?"

He flushed as soon as the words left his lips, for of course the Wolfes must have come to meet Rotherwood. He did not imagine they would withhold their blessing either, and then how long would it be before Miss Ellsworth became Mrs. Rotherwood? However the Wolfes answered him Clayton was hardly aware, but he said, "Well, whether you came this way to investigate the route or by sheer serendipity, it gratifies me exceedingly to meet you and to have you witness this first step."

A red ribbon enclosed a plot of overgrown ground marked off by stakes. Around the perimeter stood several men whom Clayton introduced as the Lord Stanley, a Mr. Alan Braham, and sundry Parliamentary and city dignitaries, the last of whom exclaimed, "Is this your pretty Miss Brand, Clayton? Miss Brand, I congratulate you. It happens I attend St. Anne's, and I heard the first reading of the banns last Sunday."

"This is not Miss Brand, Mr. Hogwood," Clayton replied instantly. "Allow me to introduce Miss Ellsworth and her family..." His back was to Beatrice, or he would have seen the color flood her face, only to drain away with alarming rapidity. And though Mrs. Wolfe was behind her daughter, she made haste to release her husband's arm, that she might put a hand to Beatrice to steady her.

The first reading of the banns! Mr. Clayton and Miss Brand had finally set a date then! And three weeks hence they would be married. And why should they not? There was no longer any need to wait, now that he had cut the Gordian knot preventing the commencement of his work.

In a daze, she managed to smile feebly at the abashed Mr. Hogwood and to murmur something—who knew what—before retreating to stand on the other side of her brothers. Looping an arm through Willsie's drew a glance from him, but he was too excited to question her, much less throw her off, and she drew comfort from his puppy-like warmth and effervescence. William would have to enjoy the ceremony enough for the both of them, for Beatrice heard not a word.

Clayton was scarcely better, though he mechanically read the speech he had written on a card and mechanically shook hands all around afterward and mechanically answered questions put to him. Then it was over, and all the important men were climbing back in their carriages, not unhappy to escape the damp fog, and he finally dared to glance at her.

She had mastered herself enough by then to meet this look, and she came forward with her hand held out. "Mr. Clayton, I congratulate you. Not only on raising your funds, but also on your impending nuptials."

Through their gloves and the numbness caused by the cold, he felt no more the touch and weight of her fingers than he would have the brush of butterfly wings, and he had to resist the urge to clutch at them. "Thank you, Miss Ellsworth. Yes. I do believe Priscilla intends on inviting you and the Huftons to the wedding breakfast. She and Miss Croy make the arrangements."

A tremulous smile met this, and from the corner of his eye, Clayton saw Mrs. Wolfe whisper something in her husband's ear. A suggestion that they, too, depart and seek warmth, most certainly, but Clayton could not bear yet to see them go—to see *her* go. If the next time he saw her would be at his own wedding—if she herself were not gone by then on her *own* wedding journey—he could not let this chance to speak slip away.

"Would you like to see the planned route?" he asked suddenly, addressing the boys in particular. "I showed it to the others before you arrived. It's a little over a half-mile in length, but we needn't go the entire way."

This suggestion met with delight from William and Edmund and was approved by Mrs. Wolfe after Beatrice gave her the hint of a nod. *Yes, please.* For she shared Clayton's thought. This might be the very last time they met as friends, the very last stolen moment for conversation. She could not resist its pull, even if it hurt her.

Beatrice took William's arm for the walk, but he was constantly dropping her to investigate something Clayton pointed out or to imitate his stepbrother Edmund, who had found a stick to whip through the grasses.

"You had better take my arm, Miss Ellsworth," Clayton said at last. "There's no ditch to tumble into as yet, but some of the ground is uneven. I wouldn't have you twist your ankle, or how would you dance at the next ball?"

Her heart beating faster, she wordlessly took hold of him, and each felt the bittersweet joy of being so near the other. But soon Beatrice began to fear she would have to content herself with his nearness alone, for of course he must describe what they were seeing, and of course her stepfather and Willsie had questions he must answer. Even Mr. Clayton's native kindness worked against her, for when Edmund made one of his monosyllabic utterances, what must Mr. Clayton do but draw him out, coaxing from him a rare sentence?

It was not until they could see the Jew's Harp House and Tea Gardens in the distance across the fields that they turned back and the group naturally began to travel at different paces, the boys rushing ahead to leap and scramble, while Mr. and Mrs. Wolfe strolled unhurriedly behind.

Only then did Beatrice take her courage in her hands and say, "Mr. Clayton, I hope you believed me when I said I did not encourage my brother to purchase shares, even though I wanted to, because you asked me to refrain. But it didn't matter in the end because it was your own merits—that is, your merits and the merits of the project—which carried the day with him."

He was silent a moment but then answered in a low voice, "Miss Ellsworth, if you think I can be so ungrateful to you or to Providence as to complain of my good fortune—No. It was my pride which asked you to forbear. My pride and my unwillingness to...impose upon the friendship you Ellsworths so kindly offered in Bognor."

"Offered!" scoffed Beatrice unhappily. "Sir, you know better than anyone what we owed to you—"

"I am not saying I did not do you a service," he rejoined, "though I thanked God then, and continue to thank Him now, that I was at hand that day—but you and the Tyrone Ellsworths gave me more than your gratitude in return. As I once alluded to—I hope I do not overstep by confessing—I have always been alone, in a way. Without family and, once Donald Brand died, without companionship. I had my work, but I could not say I had ever before experienced the—joy of having friends. That brief time in Bognor—and the memory of it—changed everything." His throat closed on these last words. He would have confessed that it—that *she*—had changed the whole course of his life, only the groove of that life—his outward life, at least—was so deeply scored by that point that there was no escaping.

Nor was an immediate reply possible for Beatrice. The wistfulness of his words, the loneliness of them pained her. Though Beatrice could not have Mr. Clayton for her own, she nevertheless would always have as a source of comfort her vast, enveloping, merry, loving family. But he—?

He would have Miss Brand. But was Miss Brand not a companion to him?

Something shifted in Beatrice's heart, and she thought, *So this is what love is. For Mr. Clayton's sake, I would have him love Miss Brand and love her dearly, and she him, so that he would never feel alone again.*

Having to release him from her heart and her wishes, even in the privacy of her own mind, caused a pang as if she were uprooting something within, inch by inch, but she struggled against it to muster a reply. "Mr. Clayton, we too have...treasured the memory of that time." Heat washed over her for what felt like the baldness of her declaration. The transparency of it. But this would be the last time.

She went on. "If you had not already guessed from Tyrone and Aggie's keenness to support your efforts—and—my own avidity, you may...rely always upon the firmness of our friendship.

We—we—we wish you every success in your work and every joy in your union with Miss Brand."

"Thank you." His voice was barely audible. Clayton knew he ought to return in kind her generous sentiments. He ought to wish her prosperity and wedded bliss with Rotherwood, but he could not. For the life of him, he could not.

"In terms of the money, I find myself steering a course between the frying pan and the fire," he said, his gazed fixed ahead on where Edmund and William were now bowling clumps of sod to imaginary batters. "That is, I must accept both your family's contributions and Rotherwood's to make up the required sum, though doing so might wreck me."

Her step hitching momentarily, she regarded him in puzzlement. "Mr. Clayton, we have already settled the matter of my family choosing to purchase shares, and I daresay you will survive a little friendship being mixed with business, but what earthly problem can you have with Mr. Rotherwood's money? Heaven knows he has enough of it and likely forgot all about sending it to Mr. Braham the moment it left his hands."

Clayton winced at this reminder of the man's riches. "Yes. Perhaps neither the amount nor the gesture itself caused him any inconvenience..." He trailed off, perceiving the dangerous verge he approached.

"But it is harder to receive sometimes, than to give?" she prompted. When she saw his jaw tighten, she gave his forearm the merest pressure. "I understand that. Gratitude can be a ticklish thing." Trying to make him smile she added, "I would have been very sorry if it had been Bonaparte, say, who rescued me from drowning that day in Bognor, but it has been a pleasure to be beholden to *you*, Mr. Clayton. So if Mr. Rotherwood chose to invest in your enterprise after I—told him of it, if you don't like being grateful to him, cannot you skip right over him and be grateful to me? Then I would have repaid you, in a manner of speaking, and we might be quits!" She delivered this with a delighted laugh, only to break off with some embarrassment when he did not join her.

"Miss Ellsworth. I am grateful to you—again, for applying to Rotherwood. That is, I honor your intention, even if—"

"Even if...?" She waited, but when he did not resume, she said with her heart in her throat, "Even if you did not approve of my methods?" Was that what he had been on the point of saying? Had he somehow learned of her writing to Mr. Rotherwood? When he did not answer, Beatrice felt panic flutter in her. They were nearly back to the starting point of their walk, and anything which must be said must be said now.

"Sir, do you refer to me writing to Mr. Rotherwood?" she blurted. "Because I confess I did do that. There wasn't time to discuss it all with him at Almack's, and he told me I might—write to him—so I did. I was determined not to lose the opportunity out of fear of offending the proprieties."

"Of course, if you are engaged, there is no impropriety to speak of." His dark eyes met hers and held, and Beatrice prayed he could not feel her pulse hammering through the fabric of her glove and his sleeve. On the pretense of adjusting that glove, she dropped his arm.

"There is no engagement," she answered, her chin lifting though her voice was not quite steady.

"You are not engaged to Mr. Rotherwood?"

She wanted to say, *Of course not! Why would I be engaged to him? All female London pursues him! You must think very highly of me, sir.* But, as Lady Hufton and Marjorie had observed, her action in writing to Mr. Rotherwood implied that very conclusion.

"I am not," she said therefore, inspecting the cuff of her wool redingote. When he said nothing, she threw him an almost defiant glance. "I suppose you disapprove of my writing to him, as the Huftons do."

His lips parted and then shut again, and Beatrice felt indignation sweep her. After all this, after all his talk of supposed friendship, was he just another Marjorie Hufton? Believing the worst of her and condemning her actions from the heights of his own supposed faultlessness? *This* was ingratitude! Her normally mild eyes sparking, her strides grew quicker, so that he was forced to increase his own pace. "I do not ordinarily do such things, sir," she hissed. "Write to young men, I mean. And if I did so in this instance—which I do not deny—it was for your benefit! Not that I try to place any blame on you for my—misconduct—but I do deplore your—your—" (She could not think which word to hurl at him, needing one which encompassed "your ability to think poorly of me when I love you with my whole heart, you horrible man.") "Is this why you don't want his money?" she demanded. "You think it's—sullied—by the manner in which it came to you?"

"Beatrice."

"Throw it back at him, then! Though I daresay he won't even recall having sent it. And you may go whistle for my help in the future."

He threw up his palms. "I will take the money. I *have* taken the money. Braham's already tossed it in the bucket with all the rest so that we might begin to engage laborers. I only wanted to know the circumstances by which it came to me."

"And now you do."

"Wait a moment, Miss Ellsworth." His hand reached for her, falling again to his side when she halted. "I have been very clumsy about this. Unforgivably clumsy. Let me say again that I appreciate the efforts you have made. I did not, by questioning their...manner, mean to detract from that. Only, let me say one final thing—as your friend."

The anger which had lit her eyes faded, to be replaced by wariness. She gave one nod.

"Did you...write to Rotherwood in the *hopes* of engaging yourself to him?"

"Are you asking if I hoped to entrap him?" Beatrice gaped. "Entrap him by any means fair or foul?"

He shook his head. "I do not judge your means. If anything I judge him, for misleading you if *he* has no intention of—of—"

Of doing what I would give anything to do.

He swallowed. "Please. Only do me the courtesy of answering the question. Do you have such hopes?"

A rueful smile curved her lips, and the look she bestowed on him was almost pitying. Ah, how blind he was. Though she should thank

God for that blindness. For there was only one man she loved in all the world, and he was the one man she could never tell.

She said only: "No, Mr. Clayton. I have no such hopes."

And then she turned to join her brothers.

CHAPTER TWENTY-FOUR

**If that which is commonly spoken be true,
that to have companions in misery is a lightner of it,
you may comfort me.**
— Thomas Shelton, *Translation of Don Quixote* (1612)

S o that is that," said Beatrice to Mrs. Wolfe, when they climbed back into their waiting coach. "I wonder if I will ever see him again, apart from the morning of his wedding."

Her stepmother regarded her sorrowfully. It would do no good to say she had liked the man very well, so she took her daughter's hand, lacing their fingers together. Nor could she promise that Beatrice would one day love again—Beatrice with her steadfast heart and her aversion to change.

Mr. Wolfe, aware of her feelings, refrained from praising Clayton as well, but the same could not be said for her younger brothers.

William and Edmund (well, mostly William) had much to say, their admiration plain. "Mama—must I go up to Oxford after Winchester?" Willsie complained. "I would rather be a canal engineer! You heard Mr. Clayton: as the speed and cost of transportation shrink, so will our world. What a shame it would be, to moulder in New College and miss such goings-on! The first thing Mundo and Peter and I will do when we return to Hampshire is to dig a canal between Beaumond and Hollowgate."

Edmund nodded his approbation, but Mr. Wolfe said, "If you boys can manage such a feat before your spring term begins, Clayton will hire you himself."

Even her return to Green Street did not spare her, for Lady Hufton quickly took her aside to say, "My dear girl, we have this very morning received an invitation from Miss Brand, inviting us to attend her wedding to Mr. Clayton, followed by breakfast at the Grillion. I do not see how you can avoid it, unless we were to claim you were ill, but if we do, that excuse must wait for the eleventh hour or you would have had time to recover."

"Lady Hufton, do not fret yourself," Beatrice answered calmly. "I will be perfectly able to attend."

In the days which followed, Beatrice divided her time between two circles. With her younger brothers she visited the Tower and Bullock's museum; with both the Huftons and the Wolfes there was Shakespeare at Drury Lane and a night at the opera; and with the Huftons alone she attended a musical evening on one occasion and a supper on another. But in none of these places did she glimpse Mr.

Clayton again. Only at the supper did she once catch his name. Two gentlemen unknown to her discussed the stalled Regent's Canal, the first saying to the other, "Good thing Clayton can be trusted not to abscond with the funds. Wouldn't surprise me if he gets his branch dug before Morgan's Irish pick up their spades again." A thorough analysis of the Regent's Canal embezzlement followed, but while Beatrice listened with all her ears (to the point that the gentleman on her own right had to repeat himself several times), this was the only hint of him in her world.

The night of the supper she lay in her bed, hair braided neatly and a brick wrapped in flannel at her feet. Sleep eluded her, however, and she had spent an hour or two watching the flickering shadows on the ceiling and thinking of Mr. Clayton, when a muffled thump and squeak made her rise up on one elbow, listening.

A scratching. Another thump. A muttered complaint.

Throwing off the coverlet and snatching up her dressing gown, Beatrice stole into the passage. She hadn't far to go however, for Marjorie's room adjoined hers. Without knocking, she burst in to discover her cousin wrestling the casement open.

"Marjorie! What are you doing?"

Her cousin shrieked in surprise, turning her back on the window as if she might prevent Beatrice seeing it.

"Why are you dressed?" Beatrice demanded. "Are you sneaking away? Eloping?" Pushing past her, she rubbed the glass and peered down into the little garden.

"There's nobody there," snapped Marjorie, tugging on her dressing gown to pull her back. "Go back to bed. Why don't you mind your own business?"

"But Marjorie—" said Beatrice helplessly, "how can I? Could *you*, in my place?"

Her stepcousin scowled at her in the moonlight, her dark eyes bottomless pits and her pointy nose wrinkling. But as Beatrice watched, those distinctive features began to change. The eyes blinked. Once, twice, and then rapidly. The nose wrinkled further. And then Marjorie clapped both hands to her mouth to stop a wail and fell against Beatrice, much as she had at the rout weeks earlier.

"My parents are so cruel!" she burst out. "So heartless! I wasn't eloping—Doddy doesn't know about it—but I was going to run away to him and beg him to marry me!"

"Marjorie!" gasped Beatrice, almost awestruck by the magnitude of her cousin's recklessness. It quite eclipsed her own ill-starred *tendre* for Mr. Clayton, much less the writing of an unauthorized letter to Mr. Rotherwood.

"Why shouldn't I?" Marjorie sobbed into Beatrice's neck. "He *wants* to marry me, and I him, and only my parents' stubbornness prevents us!"

"Oh, Marjorie, you didn't say anything to me of it." While it did not surprise Beatrice that Marjorie had not confided in her, she was glad this now made it possible for her to pose questions, even ones she knew the answer to. "Why do they object to the match?"

Digging a handkerchief from the pocket of her cloak, Marjorie blew her nose at length. "They said—they said his expectations were not what they would have been, had he been less fond of the races and the clubs. But—oh, Beatrice—what can they expect? A gentleman must live like a gentleman, and gamblers will have their lucky runs as well as their unlucky. *My* fortune would see Doddy over the unlucky patches, but Papa and Mama are so unbending!" More tears flowed, and she resorted to the handkerchief again. "Twice I have loved and been loved in return, and twice I have been denied! I can't account for it! You would think *I* was the one who pined for an engaged man or who wrote clandestine letters to someone who didn't want me—you needn't look at me like that, Beatrice Ellsworth, when you know it's true."

"But it isn't altogether true," insisted Beatrice, afraid she and Marjorie were going to have another towering quarrel. "It's true I shouldn't pine for Mr. Clayton, and I am determined to overcome it, but as for Mr. Rotherwood, as I have said more than once, it was only the one letter, and I wasn't asking him to love me but to invest in Mr. Clayton's canal!"

Waving these over-nice distinctions away, Marjorie threw herself across her bed and buried her face in the pillow.

Beatrice gave a silent chuckle. Well, indeed. Suppose the situation had been reversed: suppose Mr. Clayton were free and her parents had forbidden her to marry him—would she then have any patience for Marjorie's explanations and justifications about Mr. Dodson?

Sitting beside her prostrate cousin, she gave her a tentative pat. "I'm sorry," she murmured. "How hard things are."

It was the right note to strike. Abruptly Marjorie rolled over and seized the folds of Beatrice's dressing gown. "You needn't stand guard over me now," she sniffled. "I couldn't let Doddy see me like this. I suspect my eyes and nose are red."

"Honestly, Marjorie, what would you have done? Gone and knocked on the door of the Dodsons' townhouse?"

"I don't know. Most likely my courage would have failed, and I would have skulked home without seeing him."

"Or been taken up by the night watchman!"

This elicited a groaning sigh. "I had to do *something*, Beatrice. Something rebellious. Something in protest. If only for my own sake. Because you saw how I gave up Sam. If I am to give up Doddy as well, I wanted to mark my displeasure."

Beatrice thought Marjorie had proven her ability to mark her displeasure in other ways, but she wisely kept this opinion to herself.

"I will never marry now," Marjorie vowed, picking at the embroidery on the coverlet. "If I can't have Doddy, I won't have anyone. It will be my revenge on Mama and Papa."

"But don't you think that would be cutting off your nose to be revenged of your face?" Beatrice asked. "Suppose someone else came along whom you liked?"

"Is this what you say to yourself?" accused Marjorie. "That you'll like someone else soon enough?"

"No," she admitted.

"I didn't think so," said Marjorie. Pushing herself up, she tossed aside her sodden handkerchief and began to unbutton her cloak, and Beatrice was surprised to see her tears now dried and her face calm. But she was even more surprised when Marjorie leaned to kiss her cheek.

"You have comforted me, cousin," she said. "Or your own unhappiness has. Shall we make a pact that we will not try to talk each other out of our broken hearts? Let the rest of the world marry as they will—you and I will allow each other to be as miserable as we please."

As it happened, the first person of the rest of the world who chose to marry was none other than Mr. St. John Rotherwood.

"Rotherwood engaged?"

The news swept Mayfair with the force of a hurricane and an equal lack of preciseness. First it was said his mother Mrs. Rotherwood had eloped with a servant. Then it was amended to Rotherwood himself absconding with the lowest scullery maid, which report soon yielded to one of Rotherwood and Lady Sylvia Stanley, not eloping at all but setting a date at St. George's, Hanover Square. Rotherwood and Lady Sylvia—what was the least bit interesting about something which had been predicted from the first? Society sighed to be robbed of its scandal, but no sooner was the innocuous match bruited than Lady Stanley rose to rebut it, with admirable vigor and venom.

"I consider Sylvia well out of danger," the countess proclaimed to any who would hear her. "Imagine Rotherwood allying himself not only with a nobody, but a scandalous nobody! His mother is beside herself."

Even when they heard the name of the scandalous nobody who won the catch of the season, Beatrice and the Huftons did not know if they could have picked her out of a crowd, though in a crowd was exactly where they would have met her, for the scandalous nobody Miss Harriet Hapgood had reportedly attended both Lady Aurora Robillard's rout and the Finlays' ball.

"She has reddish hair!" proclaimed Marjorie, as if this were a fault which should have disqualified her at once. "Reddish hair like Miss Brand. But when I rack my brain to think who this Miss Hapgood might be, I can only picture Miss Brand."

The girls were sitting and sewing together. Indeed, ever since Marjorie had made her "pact" with Beatrice, she stuck to the latter like a burr to wool, as if determined to make up for lost time. And while Beatrice preferred this unrelenting fellowship to the hostility it replaced, her puzzled brothers grew impatient with it.

"What's that to do with anything?" demanded William. "Reddish hair?"

Marjorie tittered. "Young man, you will understand if you ever aspire to fashion. Reddish hair is decidedly not fashionable."

Beatrice could not stifle a laugh at William and Edmund's appalled expressions. It was a trying afternoon for them, Mr. Wolfe having some business in the City to transact, leaving them in Green Street with the Huftons.

"Not only does she have unfashionable coloring," Marjorie continued, "but my maid Crook tells me that there has been all manner of gossip about her recently. Something about a scurrilous print and a masked ball in the Argyll Rooms! Why do you suppose he would choose such a person? He, who might have had an earl's daughter! Why, Beatrice, your escapades are nothing compared to this Miss Hapgood's."

"Thank you," said Beatrice dryly.

Marjorie scooted closer to snake an arm about her waist. "*Not* that I wish he had chosen you, even for his own sake. Because if he had, who would *I* have had to sympathize with?"

This was too much for the boys.

"Shall we go out, Bea?" demanded William. "For a walk or back to the British Museum?"

"Tattersall's," Edmund suggested.

"But it's so dreadful out," protested Marjorie. "I'm sure Beatrice would rather stay home with me."

"No, no," Beatrice demurred quickly, "my family won't be here much longer. I would far rather the boys see what they would like. I'll get my cloak and the umbrellas."

With a huff and reproachful look, Marjorie reluctantly put aside her needlework. "All right, then, if you insist—"

Beatrice was shaking her head. "Of course I don't mean you need to come out, Marjorie! As you said, it's not very pleasant, and Willsie and Edmund are my responsibility, after all."

"But I have to come!" she insisted, though behind her William made a pleading face and Edmund drew a finger across his neck. "Suppose I should have a fit of melancholy by myself, without you near to condole with me?"

However trying Beatrice might have found her career as Marjorie Hufton's sole Source of Consolation, it was mercifully short-lived. For upon their return from the British Museum at Montagu House, Lady Hufton hastened to meet them in the entry.

"The Dodsons are here," she hissed, scrambling Marjorie out of her cloak. "Both Mr. Dodson and his mother in the drawing room with your father. William, Edmund—you two go to the kitchen for a cup of tea. Now quickly, girls!"

Marjorie dug her fingers into Beatrice's arm. "What can be happening? Help me, Beatrice—I will faint. I know I will."

"Nonsense. If you were going to faint, you wouldn't be on the point of snapping my arm in two. Courage, dear Marjorie."

They entered the drawing room decorously to find Sir John and Mr. Dodson flanking the mantel, the baronet's hand on the young man's shoulder, while Mrs. Dodson beamed, rising from her armchair.

"You will wonder what brings us here," began Mr. Dodson, when bows had been exchanged and the ladies had each found seats, Marjorie collapsing onto the sofa beside Beatrice like the morning's load of coal dumped in the basement bin. In answer to this address Marjorie could only move her lips and issue a squeak, but her eyes never left his face.

"Ah, I see you are speechless, Miss Hufton, and I have not even shared my news," he chuckled. "My very, very good news."

Helplessly, she shook her head, her mouth still working silently, and Beatrice was put in mind of the fish which the Lord instructed Peter to catch, to pay the temple tax. Their vicar Mr. Spence said the shekel in the fish's mouth was perhaps the size of a crown—too large for Marjorie—but she might have fit a farthing.

"I have been the recipient of a stroke of good fortune, Miss Hufton," he announced. "That is, I am fortunate in that your father tells me it will be enough to marry on. And while I was not close with my great uncle—"

Marjorie gasped and swayed, guessing at once that a sentence which begins with a great uncle must end, as the night follows the day, in an inheritance. And so it was, though her fainting fit delayed the full story for some minutes. But at last all was revealed: the great uncle had parted in anger from his son, Dodson's uncle, a mere fortnight before dying of apoplexy, and while he could not alienate the son from inheriting the property, he worked like a fiend to distribute elsewhere as many assets as he could. And Dodson, being his oldest nephew, came in for a great deal.

"Therefore, charming Miss Hufton, if you will still have me, in a matter of months I may boast of being a man of considerable means."

"Oh, Doddy!" Marjorie cried, trying not to burst into tears, lest her appearance suffer. "I am so happy!" But the urge to weep proved unstoppable after her mother embraced her, eyes welling, and Mrs. Dodson joined in. Embarrassed to be the only female with dry eyes, Beatrice screwed up her features and dabbed at them with her handkerchief, while the satisfied husband-to-be accepted the outpouring of feminine emotion as his due.

The rest of the evening continued in the same vein, as the Dodsons stayed for supper, and Beatrice soon wished she could have escaped back to Mivart's hotel with her brothers. As it was, she too must smile vacantly at the lovers, who mostly murmured to each other, unless Mrs. Dodson called down the table to tell Marjorie of a brooch she must wear on her wedding day, or to ask that Miss Kempshott might attend her on that all-important occasion.

It appeared Mr. Dodson had instantly and thoroughly superseded Beatrice as Marjorie's Source of Consolation, but would he be a good one? When his suit had been denied by the Huftons, Beatrice had of course refrained from reminding the mourning Marjorie of his flaws—what would be the use? But now that Marjorie would soon be joined to him for life, ought she to point them out?

Fate decided for Beatrice, she concluded afterward. For that night, just as she was about to snuff her candle, Marjorie stole into her room.

"Thank heavens, you're still awake. I must tell somebody, or I will surely explode. Make room for me, Beatrice." Climbing atop her bed, she snatched up one of the pillows to hug to herself, while Beatrice braced herself for another hour enduring the praises of Mr. Dodson.

"You mustn't tell Mama this," whispered Marjorie, "but Mr. Dodson's inheritance was not the only windfall."

"No? Has he turned highwayman as well?"

Her cousin giggled and crept closer. "Wouldn't that be dashing? But, no. I told you his luck would turn, and it did."

Beatrice pulled a face. "He had a good run at the clubs, you mean? Oh, Marjorie, you mustn't depend on such things. *He* mustn't depend on such things. I hope he will not risk his inheritance—or your fortune—thus."

That did it. Marjorie's brows flew together, and she gave Beatrice's leg a push through all the quilts and coverings. "What a spoil-sport you are! You just don't want to hear me say I was right. Because I was. He did win at the clubs, but it wasn't all luck. It was his own powers of observation, as well."

"What are you talking about? Do you mean he cheated?"

This earned Beatrice a blow with the pillow Marjorie held. "Certainly not! I only mean Doddy is more clever than the other bettors, for they all wagered Mr. Rotherwood would choose Lady Sylvia, and Doddy was the only one who took all his money off of her (and eventually off of you and Miss Kempshott, I'm sorry to say, if it hurts your feelings), and entered a new wager in the books: 'Rotherwood will marry none of the above-named.' Well! Everyone thought he was mad to rule out the three top candidates, so they all bet against him, and now he has won! Doddy says there was such an uproar about it—he thought Lord Brinmore would call him out because the marquess had wagered five hundred guineas! And then Doddy thought *he* would have to call out a few of them because they were saying he must be in league with Rotherwood to rob them all—why, Beatrice, whatever is the matter?"

For Beatrice had groaned and covered her face with her remaining pillow.

Marjorie tugged it away. "—But Doddy reminded them that Rotherwood need not resort to such measures when he was already rich as Croesus, and that turned the tide, and now Doddy is owed four thousand pounds! And being debts of honor they must be paid over as soon as the wedding has taken place."

Debts of honor, fiddlestick! thought Beatrice. What had honor to do with such things?

"What is it?" Marjorie asked again, thunderclouds gathering in her eyes. She sat up on her knees as if to prepare for battle.

Knowing her cousin's temper, Beatrice herself struggled up to lean against the headboard. She could hardly risk telling the truth while lying down. Why was it easier to say whatever she pleased to her sisters and brother, when they were just as likely to retaliate? *For one thing, not one of them is as impossible as Marjorie. And for another, not one of them would have to be told why I don't like my name to be entered in betting books!*

"I have already told you what troubles me," she said cautiously. "That I think it...ungentlemanlike to gamble upon young ladies as if they were horses or dogs, and—and—and nor do I think it gallant for Mr. Dodson to discuss me, or indeed Lady Sylvia or Miss Kempshott (his own cousin!), in such a light manner."

Steeling herself for the wallop of the pillow which must follow, Beatrice was alarmed to see Marjorie's rage surpassed such easy release. The girl was visibly vibrating, even to the ends of her hair and fingertips, and she suddenly thrust herself off the bed, nearly falling to the carpet in her haste.

"You're just jealous!" she shrilled. "Jealous of me because I got what I want and you never will!"

Scrambling from beneath the bedclothes, Beatrice hissed, "Hush! Do you want your parents to hear you?"

"Jealous!" accused Marjorie, stamping her foot. "Jealous jealous jealous! Because I am happy, and you wanted me to stay miserable with you!"

"Why you wretch!" Beatrice cried, goaded. "I wasn't delighted when I thought you got your heart broken!"

But her cousin was now stamping in a circle, as if she would wake not only her parents and the household, but all of Green Street. "Jealous jealous jealous!"

Beatrice had enough.

With a bellow which might even have caused her younger brothers to quail, she flew at her, whether to clap a hand to her mouth or to wrestle her into submission they would never be certain, for Marjorie took to her heels. A chase ensued, around the bedroom, over the bed, through the window curtains. The shriek Marjorie sustained throughout would have done credit to a screech-owl, only breaking off when Beatrice caught hold of her nightgown, and Marjorie had to gasp for breath to tear herself free before taking flight again. The pretty oval-backed Hepplewhite chair was knocked over and water from the basin slopped, which, on their next circuit Marjorie slipped in, skating across the polished floorboards to collide with the Chippendale writing table. Ink bottles, pens, pen knife, books, candlesticks—all tumbled down, raising a racket worthy of the end of the world.

And then the door opened.

Lady Hufton stood, eyes agog and candle upraised, Sir John behind her. "Girls! What on earth?"

Before Beatrice could formulate a possible response, much less catch her breath to deliver it, Marjorie sprang to block her view, her narrowed eyes expressing once more what the maid Crook had so eloquently called "war to the knife."

"It's nothing, Mama, Papa," Marjorie threw over her shoulder at her parents. "I was only hurt because Beatrice said she wanted to return to Winchester with her family, even if it meant missing my wedding."

"Heavens! Was such...violence necessary?" asked Lady Hufton. "Is—this so, Beatrice?"

For a moment as she panted she thought of gainsaying it. But what difference would it make? The Huftons already knew Mr. Dodson gambled to excess at times—it had been the cause of their original refusal. If they now hoped his current circumstances would last, or that the steadiness brought by marriage would prevail, there was nothing more to be said. And to add her own complaints about his lack of gallantry...Marjorie was right. Likely they would deem her opinion sour grapes and not look very kindly on her for trying to mar her cousin's joy.

She met Marjorie's unwavering glower with resignation. Well—she had spoken her mind to her cousin, at least, and one thing was certain: if Marjorie ever did decide she wanted her Mr. Dodson to give up betting and gambling, Beatrice almost thought she could carry her point.

Therefore, smoothing her rumpled nightgown, she took a slow breath and replied calmly, "Yes, Lady Hufton. I—I'm sorry to disappoint Marjorie, but seeing my family has reminded me how much

I miss Winchester. While I am so grateful for these weeks with you all and for your generosity in hosting me, and while I am sorry to miss Marjorie's wedding, I think when my family goes next week, it will be a good time for me to accompany them. I think I had better go home."

CHAPTER TWENTY-FIVE

And ye shall know the truth,
and the truth shall make you free.
— **John 8:23,** *The Authorized Version* **(1611)**

H e was the last to know.

Which was his own fault, really, because he withdrew almost entirely into his work. In his defense, now that ground on the canal had been ceremonially broken, Clayton was plunged head over ears into a hundred preliminary tasks: meetings with potential resident engineers and undersecretaries; surveys; negotiations with every wharf- and warehouse-owner in the Cumberland Basin; the hiring of overseers, diggers, masons, bricklayers, smiths, carpenters, horses, and equipment.

And if his intended bride suffered neglect, Clayton could at least tell himself Priscilla would prefer sharing him with the Cumberland Arm than with daydreams and painful musings about Miss Ellsworth. These, thank heaven, he managed to push to a far corner of his mind by keeping so breathlessly busy. Only when he staggered to bed, exhausted, in the few minutes before sleep overtook him, did she come to him. She came dressed for a ball, or in the redingote in which he had last seen her, or sometimes even drenched, her bathing gown outlining her limbs. She came laughing or dancing or swimming. She came delighted or indignant. And Clayton's last conscious thought was always the same: *She will marry and forget me. If only God would be so merciful to me.*

It was a terse note from Priscilla which summoned him at last, one without greeting or signature: "Cissy and I have continued with the dance lessons. If you would be so good as to show your face in Marlboro Street, I would speak with you."

Feeling like a schoolboy called in to the headmaster's office, Clayton bent his steps toward Soho. The day was drizzly and dank, smoke and shadows obscuring all, but he paused in crossing Oxford Street, his gaze sweeping up and down. There was nothing to see, of course. Nothing and no one.

Priscilla's butler Keezer opened the door to his knock. "Mr. Clayton. It has been too long."

Clayton might have known Keezer since he was fourteen, but in his current mood even the butler's greeting sounded reproachful. He nodded shortly, allowing the man to take his hat and coat. "I'll show myself in. They're expecting me, I daresay."

The parlor of 12 Marlboro Street had undergone a transformation since Priscilla became its mistress. Gone were the framed maps and engineer's drawings, as well as Donald Brand's worn padded armchairs, to be replaced by satinwood Hepplewhite and gilded mirrors. Priscilla's harp occupied one corner and an open spinet another, but she was at neither instrument when he entered. Instead she stood at the window, arms crossed beneath her bosom.

"Mr. Clayton," murmured Miss Croy feebly. With a quick duck of a curtsey the companion retreated to a chair by the fireplace, her apologetic face seeming to say she would flee the room altogether if she could. *Was* it his imagination, or was he further down the page in Priscilla's black books than even he had suspected?

"Where has Keezer gone?" she asked. "We should have tea. It's dreadful out, and I suppose you walked."

She spoke of walking as if it were some shameful activity, and he paused in removing his gloves. "I am entirely to blame for Keezer's absence because I told him I would find my own way. Shall I call him? I need no tea for my own sake because the walk—and I did walk, I'm afraid—warmed me, but if you and Miss Croy would like some...?"

"Never mind, then." A frown fleeting across her young features, she made a restless movement. "Well? You may sit if you like."

"I don't mind standing, if you prefer to stand."

She did, apparently, her head turning toward the window again. For a minute nothing was heard but the muted crackle of the coal fire in the stove and Miss Croy's (also apologetic) throat-clearings.

With a grimace, Clayton resolved to take the bull by the horns. "Priscilla, I suspect you are not pleased with me."

A shrug.

"I know I have been very busy."

This met with a short laugh. "Have you? I would never have guessed."

Sarcasm? This was new.

Looking about him, Clayton chose a seat after all. Gracious—look what he had done to the poor girl, that now she should have acquired these traits. Poor Priscilla, who had always been cheerful and desirous of pleasing was now snappish and sarcastic? He must do better, he told himself for the thousandth time. He must accept his fate and do better. It was not fair to her. Because none of this was her fault. Not any of it.

His chest rose and fell in a silent sigh. "And I confess," he continued, feeling his way, "that once the money for the work was raised, I no longer gave priority to our dance lessons, seeing no further need to fetch and carry and curry favor with the great and good. Or, at least, with the wealthy."

She made no response but began to tap her fingernails on the casement. Tap-tap-tap, in rhythm with the raindrops.

So much for my excuses, he thought wryly. *Shall I try buttering her up next, craven that I am?*

Clearing his throat, he pinned a bland smile on his face. "I'm surprised you yourself saw the need to continue with lessons, Priscilla, considering how often Saint-Cloud has said that you excel at dancing."

At this she whipped around to say through tightened lips, "I continued because otherwise who knew when I might have another occasion to dance? You clearly only did so to meet your own ends, with no thought to how I might feel about it."

He stared at her, not in resentment, but rather in surprise. Surprise that turned him thoughtful. This direct young lady who spoke her mind was new to him. He had provoked her with his neglect, yes, but altogether he thought he preferred this version of Priscilla to the coy one who hinted and prompted and danced around subjects to try to make him say what she would like to hear.

Perhaps I have *helped her after all*.

"You're absolutely right," he agreed willingly. "I did not take into account your feelings on the matter but selfishly thought only of my ends."

"Why—yes. That's exactly what I mean, John." Some of the stiffness left her, though her lower lip trembled until she bit it, and she crossed her arms once more.

"Priscilla, won't you sit down, so we may discuss this?"

After a hesitation, she complied, taking the seat opposite. Miss Croy glanced up from her sewing, peeping from one to the other.

"And it is not only in regard to the dance lessons where I have vexed you," he went on, determined to have it all out. "I have left you alone to plan the wedding breakfast."

When this met only with an ambiguous "hmm," he knew there were still more wrongs charged to him.

Very well, then.

"But it has gone on longer than that, Priscilla," Clayton resumed, putting his shoulder to the wheel. "I have been an indifferent lover, making little to no effort to woo you, and thus jeopardizing our future happiness."

Still she regarded him with creased brow and flared nostrils, and he felt the first flicker of annoyance. His own eyebrow arched. "Have you anything else you would like to add to my account before I attempt to discharge it?"

Giving one short, sharp shake of the head, she blurted, "What do you mean, 'discharge it'?"

He shifted his chair nearer hers, turning his back to Miss Croy's ever-present presence. "I mean, Priscilla, shall we try again?" he murmured. "Wipe the slate clean and try—in earnest—to make our match a happy one?"

Truthfully, he expected her to unbend and for a smile to bloom on her features. He even steeled himself to receive a clutch of his arm and to smile and clutch in return.

But she did neither.

Instead she took a deep, deep breath and met his gaze squarely. "John. I am willing to pardon you. I do, in fact pardon you, though everything you say is true, and it has hurt me a great deal." Ignoring his conciliatory nod, she rose again to pace the distance to the window and back. Seeing him get to his own feet, she waved him down. "Don't bother standing, John. No—sit back down. I would prefer you to be seated because of what I have to say."

"What you have to say?" he echoed warily. But he obeyed her command and resumed his seat.

"Yes. What I have to say." Another deep breath followed, though it was an uneven one. "Which is—I mean to say—I no longer want to marry you."

"Wh-what?" And indeed, had he still been standing, he might well have collapsed.

Behind him, a fearful whimper leaked from Cecelia Croy.

"You heard me, John. I no longer want to marry you."

"But—you just said you pardoned me!"

"And so I do, pardon you. But it's too late to think about making our match a happy one."

Clayton put his hands to his face and rubbed it, half to rouse himself from what must be delirium, and half to hide the hope shooting up inside him. He had no idea if it was working, but thankfully Priscilla continued her pacing, her hands stretching and balling into fists repeatedly.

"I know Papa loved you like a son, and I know he was afraid of what might happen to me when he was gone, but there is no need to kill two birds with one stone. Especially if neither one of us wants it particularly. That is, I thought I wanted to marry you," she continued, as Clayton now had his elbows on his knees and his head in his hands, fingers twisting through his dark hair. "Because it was exciting to be engaged and because you're handsome and because you know or have met important people. But John—it isn't enough. It wasn't enough. All those things might be true, but it's also true that your mind is always on your work, and you're not very—good—about making conversation, and you can be so—remote—and intimidating! You never say nice things to me, and you just admitted that the dancing lessons were all for the stupid canal and not at all for my sake—"

"Priscilla—"

But she would not be interrupted. "Yes, I said the 'stupid' canal!" she fired up. "I hate your canal! Your—your—*ditch*! I hate every canal which was ever dug! They always kept Papa from me, and now they keep you away. The only thing I like about them is the money they bring. That's right. Papa left me a tidy fortune, I know, and it is mine, though Mr. Braham manages it for now. And I say your salary will be paid out of it for the duration of the work, as Papa intended, but I don't see why I should hand the rest to you, so that you might go on and on, grubbing in the dirt and dragging me to and fro across the kingdom!"

Good heavens! If Clayton had ever wished Priscilla Brand simply speak her mind without beating about the bush, here it was with a vengeance!

Her outburst proved too much for her in the end, for the next instant she broke out in a storm of tears which brought Miss Croy scurrying across the room, only to be pushed away with a mortified "Leave me be, Cissy!"

"Oh, Mr. Clayton," dithered Miss Croy, "you mustn't pay any attention to what she says today. She's been in a perfect *state*—"

"Of *course* he must pay attention to what I say!" roared Priscilla with a stamp of her foot. "Isn't that just the trouble—that he never pays any attention to what I say or what I do or what I think or feel or—or *anything!*"

Her companion fluttered distraught hands, retreating, but by this time Clayton had mastered his expression, despite the unexpected urge to laugh now adding to the welter of emotions assailing him.

"Priscilla," he said again, his voice steadier than he would have thought possible. "Priscilla, you do not have to marry me if you don't want to."

She stopped suddenly. Stopped with the pacing and the waving fists and flying tears. "I—don't?"

"Of course not. I'm no ogre." His lips curved derisively. "Or if I am, I'm just the neglectful, remote, grubbing, dull sort of ogre. Not the lock-you-in-a-room-until-you-marry-me variety."

"But—" she was breathing now as if she had been running up a hill, and she quickly resumed her seat opposite him, her color coming and going. "But John—really? You won't make me, even though you promised Papa?"

"No." He was trying to stay in the conversation with her, while his mind leapt far, far ahead. He saw himself going straight from Marlboro Street to call on the Huftons. To call on Miss Ellsworth. He would have to keep himself on a tight rein. She had thought of him as Miss Brand's intended almost as long as she had known him; he could not therefore, that very afternoon, throw himself at her feet—

"But what about my fortune?" demanded Priscilla.

He blinked at her, unwittingly provoking her yet again (could the man not even pay attention when he was being jilted?). "Your fortune?" he said bemused. "It will remain yours."

"That's precisely what I mean!" she declared. "Didn't you want to marry me because I am an heiress?"

"Frankly, Priscilla, I think you will derive more enjoyment from your money than I would have," answered Clayton. "Though I do thank you for honoring the terms of my contracted salary." His brow furrowed thoughtfully, however. While *he* didn't mind losing Priscilla's fortune, would Miss Ellsworth's family object to his resultingly modest means? "Modest"? Impoverished, more like.

"...Then I am my own person, and I may marry whom I please," she was saying, and he shook the clouds from his head again.

"I beg your pardon. Did you—have another person in mind?"

Her chin came up and she flushed a deep rose. "Possibly. Only Cissy knows because, of course, I was engaged, so there was no use in thinking or saying or wishing anything."

"Good heavens. Is it Saint-Cloud?"

Priscilla's mouth dropped open and behind him Miss Croy screeched. "How—how did you know?" gasped his former betrothed.

"It's hardly an unfathomable mystery," Clayton couldn't help laughing. "In fact, I can't think of another person it could be. But I'm afraid it won't do, Priscilla."

"What do you mean, it won't do?"

"I mean that it is one thing to break our engagement because we are not inclined to marry, but another entirely for me to approve a match which your father would most certainly have forbidden. If I am not your husband or intended husband, the fact remains that I am your guardian. And in that role I certainly must fulfill my obligation to Mr. Brand."

Priscilla sputtered, firing up again, but Clayton held up his palms to forestall her. "I'm sorry, but it is so. You are my ward until you come of age, and as your guardian I cannot allow it."

"You monster!" she cried. "I suppose because he is poor and humble and works for his bread? So are you, you force me to point out."

He made a motion, as if touching the brim of a hat. "Too right. But listen to me, Priscilla. If you and I had married, I would have continued with my work. I would not have retired to live off of your fortune. Do you think the same could be said for Saint-Cloud?"

"I—don't know. I suppose not," she admitted. "Although he has once or twice expressed his resentment of Mr. Wilson who owns the academy—"

"Then there *is* a Mr. Wilson?"

"Of course there is. He even appeared once when you weren't there. Quite a perfumed, wigged, puffed-up old fellow who didn't help Hub—Mr. Saint-Cloud one bit! He only observed for a minute and then glided away. Mr. Saint-Cloud said to me on that occasion that he dreamed of opening his own school for dance." Her eyes lit up suddenly. "Oh, John! What if I were to invest in Mr. Saint-Cloud, so that he could open just such an academy? I would buy—shares—in it. It would be an investment. And then he would earn his own money and more of it, and—and—we could see what sort of person he is."

Clayton regarded her, one corner of his mouth lifting. What a day for surprises! This forthright, enterprising Priscilla—! It really was so, then—he and she had been a bad match. Instead of bringing out each other's best qualities, they had only succeeded in frustrating each other.

"It's not a bad plan," he said. "Though we had better sound Braham for his opinion before you go making suggestions to the dance master. And it wouldn't hurt to remind you that, if you were to elope with Saint-Cloud, he would likely never see a penny. I think your father then divides your fortune between you, me, and a trust for a future canal, or some such."

"I won't elope, then," she assured him calmly. "Because if I don't want you to marry me for my money, nor do I want anyone else to. And I certainly, certainly don't want my fortune going to any more tiresome old canals."

Then he did laugh, and the two unsuccessful lovers regarded each other with the first easy goodwill they had ever experienced together.

But Clayton was too energetic a fellow to loll about when he had more pressing matters to attend to. Rising, he retrieved his gloves from the table and began to tug them back on. "I will write to Braham to call here tomorrow or the day after, and we will share our news with him. Hmm—I suppose I'd better speak to the vicar of St. Anne's as well, before he reads the banns for the third time."

"Please do, or Cissie and I will have an awkward time of it this Sunday," agreed Priscilla.

"And I suppose I may ask you to cancel the arrangements for our wedding breakfast?"

She favored him with a wry look. "You had better leave it to me, for I would lay odds you don't even remember which hotel it was going to be at."

His guilty grin was answer enough.

"Exactly." She shook her head in amused exasperation. "It's just as well, since I don't know if anyone would have attended after all. They have a wedding of their own to plan, you know, over there in Green Street."

Clayton was very still. "A wedding in Green Street? Is—Rotherwood—finally engaged, then?"

"Of course he is! And has been for days," Priscilla said incredulously, marveling anew at this evidence of his obliviousness. "Everyone in London has been talking of little else. Even the pupils at the dance academy knew of it. But Mr. Rotherwood doesn't live in Green Street, I don't think. Of course I was referring to the Huftons."

He shook his head, perplexed. "Huftons? You can't mean Miss Hufton. You must mean Miss Ellsworth."

"What? No! I mean Miss Hufton."

"Is engaged to Rotherwood?"

Before Clayton or Priscilla could throttle each other in their impatience to be understood, Miss Croy made haste to interpose. "Miss Hufton is engaged to Mr. Dodson. Mr. Rotherwood is engaged to one Miss Hapgood."

Clayton stared at her, and she gave a little gasp at his paleness. "Say that again, Miss Croy."

Carefully, she repeated her words.

He released a long breath. Sagging visibly in relief, he took hold of the back of the sofa to steady himself. "Not Miss Ellsworth, then."

"Good gracious," said Priscilla, who had not taken her eyes from him. "Good...gracious, John. This news affects you mightily."

He pressed his lips together. Because what was there to say, in any case?

"You care for her," she murmured, pondering.

It was not a question.

"You care for Miss Ellsworth."

Denial was impossible, even to spare her feelings. "I...did not mean to."

She gave a mirthless chuckle. "I'm sure you didn't."

"I'm sorry, Priscilla."

"Was it in Bognor that you began to like her?"

"Yes."

She was silent a minute. However willingly she had jilted him, and however relieved she might be for the way matters ended, it would be unreasonable to expect any young lady to welcome such a blow to her vanity. And he, though he felt a great weight lifted off to have the truth known, did not want to add insult to injury by dashing off to see his beloved.

But while Priscilla might have been young and possessed of an ordinary amount of self-love, their meeting had done its work. If her betrothed had not loved her, it had nevertheless been she who sued for liberty from him, sued and prevailed. Nor had she been positively denied Mr. Saint-Cloud at some future date, if he could only prove himself.

Slowly she regained her composure, and he felt a new admiration for her, to see her gather her dignity about her. He need not worry for Priscilla, it seemed. She was learning her own strength.

"I will see you out, John," she said. "Cissy, wait here for me."

In the entryway she handed him his hat. "Does Miss Ellsworth know of your feelings, John?"

"Of course not."

That provoked an arch smile. "But she will, I imagine. And something tells me you will not be so desultory in your courtship of her as you were when your heart was not concerned."

But this was too tender a subject for him to banter about, and Priscilla relented, wondering wistfully if Mr. Saint-Cloud ever thought of her with such a mixture of fierceness and doubt in his eyes. Holding out her hand, Clayton took it and carried it to his lips.

Then he was gone.

Chapter Twenty-Six

And I will come again, My Love,
Tho 'twere ten thousand mile.
— Robert Burns, "Red, Red Rose" (1794)

S he was the last to know.

Beatrice had spent the morning helping the vicar's wife Mrs. Spence hang and tie and tuck greenery around the pulpit and pews of St. Anastasius'. That is, Mrs. Spence had pointed and directed, while Beatrice and the sexton were the ones climbing the ladder and being pricked by the holly.

"Thank you, dear Miss Ellsworth," Mrs. Spence said in her quiet, firm voice when the task was done. "How very pleasant to have you back from your travels, and we will see if our good Hampshire air and some peace and quiet cannot restore the roses to your cheeks."

Beatrice bore the kindly comment with what equanimity she could. She flattered herself that she had been her usual cheerful self since her return from London, but she could not help her complexion.

"Will all your family gather at Beaumond for a joint of beef and some roast goose?"

"I believe my oldest sister Mrs. Fairchild would like to host us at Hollowgate."

"And why should she not? All the former Ellsworth children gathered again under their childhood roof—what a pleasant occasion that will be. I remember Mrs. Fairchild's mother when she was Miss Baldric. Such an heiress, with every gentleman in pursuit of her for miles around! But it was your handsome father who won her hand, and look where we are now." The elderly lady smiled over her reminiscences, and Beatrice was glad the infamy of her father's four marriages and six assorted children had mellowed with time into a nostalgic neighborhood fairy tale.

When the adornment of the little church was complete and Mrs. Spence had pressed some surplus mistletoe and holly upon her, Beatrice made her slow way along the wooded footpath back to Beaumond.

"Who would have thought it possible?" she said to the bare-limbed trees and sodden leaves underfoot. "That I would miss the racket of London? That dear Winchester could seem so tiny and sedate? It won't be like this at the next Assizes, of course, much less during the races, but the Assizes and the races seem so very far away." At home there was peace and quiet of a different nature, of course.

Despite the rumpus of her younger brothers (frequently joined by their cousin Peter from Hollowgate), at home Beatrice was spared the temper and changeableness of Marjorie Hufton. She was spared being clung to one day and attacked the next.

But not even to the sleeping trees would Beatrice say a whisper of Mr. Clayton. It was foolish, really, to miss him more because a day's journey now lay between them. In that last fortnight, how often had she seen him, though only a half-hour walk through Marylebone separated them? But in London there had always been the *chance* of seeing him, she realized now, and that chance had fed her hopes.

Mrs. Wolfe was in the kitchen, overseeing the mince pies. "Back so soon, Bea? How is Mrs. Spence today?"

"The same as ever. Did you wish me gone longer?" Beatrice asked, reaching for an apron.

Her stepmother blushed. "Of course not. Here. Would you rather chop the ginger or grate the nutmeg?"

"I'll do both."

She had reduced the ginger to a tidy heap when her stepfather entered. "Oh! Beatrice—back so soon?"

Beatrice frowned. "It wasn't that soon, and why did everyone wish me to stay away?"

"What nonsense," chided Mr. Wolfe, stealing a few of the dried currants to pop in his mouth. "Do you not think, Miranda, that one unfortunate consequence of our Beatrice's time with the Huftons is that she has become suspicious, imagining evil where there is none? A shame, and probably due to her cousin's influence. But if I might have a word with you, my dear wife, to discuss what may be done with her..."

"He's a hopeless one for teasing, miss," the cook Mortimer said bracingly when the Wolfes were gone, as she continued to shred the suet. "You mustn't mind him."

Beatrice knew this well enough and could have dismissed it from her thoughts, were there not other mysterious signs in the days which followed. Visits to her sisters, where conversation would come to an awkward halt when she entered. Her aunt Jeanne flitting from house to house and presenting her with various little trifles and adornments: a length of pleating lace, a sprig of silk flowers for her bonnet, a pot of lotion to restore those cursed roses missing from her cheeks.

On Christmas Eve, when Beatrice proposed walking into town to look in the shop windows, her stepmother replied, "What a splendid idea," only to have Mr. Wolfe clear his throat violently. When his wife jumped, he said, "Good heavens, Miranda—look at the time. How it *flies*."

"Oh, yes," his wife rejoined, with a glance at the clock. "Er—Beatrice, how can we possibly? We must deliver the Christmas boxes today."

"But I thought you said we would do that in the afternoon."

"Well, one of the boxes is for old Mrs. Jerome, and wouldn't you rather get done with such a task so that nothing remains but enjoyment? We can walk into town later."

Beatrice yielded, of course, but by the time the boxes were ready, it already was afternoon, and then Mrs. Wolfe said, "Dear me, Florence has asked if Mortimer and I might make up a dressing for the goose. It seems Wilcomb at Hollowgate turned her back, and the dogs made off with the entire chain of sausages. Could you possibly take the cart and deliver the boxes yourself?"

"Go alone, Mama?"

"Never mind about that. No one will think a thing of it because it will be obvious what your errand is. And now you might save old Mrs. Jerome for last and plead encroaching darkness to excuse the brevity of your visit."

"Back from gadding about in London, are you?" old Mrs. Jerome barked when young Mrs. Jerome admitted her and received the Christmas box with a curtsey and thanks.

"Yes, madam," said Beatrice, following young Mrs. Jerome on the pretense of helping her unpack the hamper. Several young children of varying ages and states of cleanliness crowded about to see what treasures would appear, and it would have been a merry occasion if not for their curmudgeonly grandmother who soon snapped, "Leave all that to Ann! Come and be seated. What is it—talking to an old woman not worth the time of day, Miss Hoity-Toity?"

What could Beatrice do then but surrender to her fate? Young Mrs. Jerome made an apologetic face and gestured to her empty chair, beside which was arranged all the materials for her spinning, but Beatrice demurred, stifling her sigh and picking up the settle to place beside the old woman.

"How have you been, Mrs. Jerome? We wish you a happy Christmas."

The old woman grunted. "As you see me. And you? I see you've come back without a sweetheart. Here you turned up your nose at the best of Winchester, only to find those London swells not so easy to catch, eh?"

Longing for the earth to open and swallow her up, she only managed an uneasy laugh. "I am not engaged, at any rate. Though my stepcousin Miss Hufton is."

Old Mrs. Jerome clicked her tongue, wagging her head like a billy goat. "That's right. You've come home again to be a worry and a burden on your parents."

The younger Mrs. Jerome interrupted here, calling her mother-in-law's attention to the mince pies and pears, a plate of which the older woman accepted after a show of reluctance. "I'll warrant Mrs. Wolfe has put too much spice in, and it'll wreak havoc on my insides." But she munched down two, heedless of her grandchildren's longing eyes. "Where is Mrs. Wolfe, anyway? It's been an age since she troubled herself to call. Ever since she remarried..." And so on and so forth.

Only after a full twenty minutes and two hints about the short winter days was Beatrice allowed to escape, stumbling outside gratefully and giving one of the Jerome boys a penny for having held the horse. Dreadful old woman! How could she complain of infrequent visits when she was so cross? And when she loved to find a person's most tender spot and to pick at it mercilessly?

Climbing into the now-empty cart, Beatrice left the horse to find its own way back to Beaumond in the grey dusk, the familiar landmarks of the Weeke Road blurring in her vision. She would not cry. She would not let old Mrs. Jerome put her out, though Beatrice suspected she already had.

It was the appearance of a figure coming along the road which made her hastily wipe her eyes.

And then wipe them again.

For there was something familiar about the man's stride.

"Whoa," Beatrice croaked to Pilgrim, giving a tug on the reins. Her heart seemed to be occupying the whole space in her throat where air usually passed.

The man removed his hat, revealing a head of dark hair, and raised a hand. "How fortunate to encounter you, Miss Ellsworth, for I am quite lost."

"Mr.—Clayton!" she yelped. "Whatever are you doing here?"

He studied her, and Beatrice feared the lost roses in her cheeks were again in full bloom.

"I had unfinished business," he replied at last.

"I see," she said. Or tried to say, for little sound escaped her.

"I only arrived this morning, but I have already seen your brother Mr. Ellsworth and have just now come from Beaumond, where I spoke with Mr. Wolfe."

She nodded idiotically throughout this speech until she made the effort to stop. "Oh. I see. Were you—wanting to call upon Aggie's father Mr. Weeks at The Acres now? Or perhaps you are returning to town?"

"Neither, I'm afraid. I was heading back to Hollowgate. Ellsworth—your brother—drove me to Beaumond and assured me it was easy enough to return on foot, but I had not counted on speaking with Mr. Wolfe for as long as I did."

Pilgrim whickered here, annoyed to stand in the road when he had already been made to stand at every hovel and cottage surrounding Beaumond, and Beatrice remembered herself. "I can drive you to Hollowgate. I am surprised my stepfather did not offer to do so."

"He did, but I—preferred to walk, after my hours in the Flyer. Are you certain, Miss Ellsworth? Surely you were returning to Beaumond, and it grows darker."

"It's such a short drive between Hollowgate and Beaumond, and Pilgrim could accomplish it blindfolded," she replied, notwithstanding what she had told Mrs. Jerome about not liking to drive in the dark. "Will you climb up?"

After a hesitation, he took hold of the side of the cart and complied. The elegant little cabriolet had been a wedding gift from Mr. Wolfe to his bride, and it was not especially large. In fact, when the Wolfes went for a drive together, they used the gig, that the giant Mr. Wolfe might fit more comfortably. Clayton was not built to the same proportions as Mr. Wolfe (few people were), but he was by no means a small man, and Beatrice found herself in contact with him from hip to knee, the most she had touched him since he fished her from the Channel and carried her in his arms. Flustered and burning still rosier, she tried to shrink against the far side, even as he half stood again to shift himself off her skirts. The vehicle rocked with the change in balance, causing Pilgrim to snort and take a step forward and sending Clayton tumbling back against Beatrice.

"Ooh!"

"Pardon me, Miss Ellsworth—have I injured you?" Their arms interlaced in the mutual scramble to untangle themselves, several of Clayton's fingers somehow running up the sleeve of her redingote. He whipped them out at once, awkward though the angle was, muttering further apologies, and Beatrice prayed he had not felt the jump in her pulse.

Pilgrim protested the continued jouncing and swaying of the cabriolet by taking additional steps before Beatrice could retrieve the reins, leading to further bumbling and confusion, but at last they were both seated, exactly as close as they had been before their attempted adjustments, only this time out of breath and red in the face.

Clayton began another round of apologies, but his eye caught the twitch of her lips and the irrepressible glint of merriment which accompanied it. Breaking off mid-sentence he favored her with a rueful smile. Beatrice made a small coughing sound, her shoulders hunching, but she could not contain it any longer, and the next moment the smallest laugh escaped her. Hunching further, she pressed her lips together, but it was all in vain. Soon peal after peal rang out, her amusement so infectious that he had to join her. Had ever a man done a more awkward job of climbing into a carriage? Thank heaven for her sense of humor.

His gaze drifted to her inviting mouth.

Speaking of carriages, mustn't get the cart before the horse.

But he fully intended to wring every ounce of pleasure from the situation. To be in her company again was a source of deep joy, to which the thrill of her limb pressed along the length of his was mere incidental benefit. But it was indeed a benefit, for Miss Ellsworth made no more efforts to shrink from him.

She did, however, recover from the surprise of seeing him again enough to remember the circumstances in which they parted. Clicking her tongue to Pilgrim to set him in motion, she pulled on one of the leads to steer the horse in the direction of Hollowgate.

"You drive well, Miss Ellsworth," he murmured as they trotted along the Weeke Road. "Did you ever display your skills in Hyde Park?"

"Never."

"What a missed opportunity."

"Speaking of missed opportunities, sir, I confess I am amazed you can tear yourself from London right now, what with the work on the canal beginning and your—wedding to Miss Brand." Just saying Miss Brand's name made Beatrice feel guilty for letting any part of her person press against his, but to draw away now would only draw attention to her discomfiture. And what a lovely leg he had—well-shaped and firm.

"The weather has been inclement, so though I found a resident engineer and hired several teams of workers, I told them to begin on the 27th—the soonest I thought I could return." Seeing questions rising to her lips, he added quickly, "I plan to be in Winchester through Christmas."

"But—" she could not imagine why he would choose to spend the festive day apart from Miss Brand, and so near their wedding day!

"Your brother—or perhaps I should say the *Fairchilds*—but surely it was Ellsworth who arranged it—have invited me to stay at Hollowgate until—until I need to be back in London."

"But—surely Miss Brand and Miss Croy—"

They had reached the Cock Lane Gate, however, and Beatrice must leave off while they passed the tollbooth, the man within nodding at them and touching his cap.

"Not much farther to Hollowgate," she said. But then her brow knit, and she glanced behind them in the direction of Winchester's West Gate. "But you know that, do you not, if you walked from the George Inn earlier today?"

"Oh—er—Ellsworth—your brother—picked me up in town."

"Ah," she absorbed this a moment. Then she turned slightly in the seat to regard him, "Which clearly means that...my brother, and likely my stepfather as well, already knew to expect you."

"...They did. Naturally I wrote to them to propose the—meetings."

Biting her lip she turned away again. Her whole family in league against her! Inviting Mr. Clayton to Winchester and to stay(!) without her knowledge? What did they hope to accomplish? She thought again of the walk into town her parents talked her out of—why should they try to hide his coming, if the man would be at Hollowgate through Christmas? Could Tyrone have invited him on impulse, without telling the Wolfes? *How impulsively could he have done it, if he must ask Flossie and Robert for their permission first?*

"Is it...usual to trouble yourself thus?" she ventured. "Could the business not have been conducted through your usual method of writing countless letters?"

Running a finger under his neckcloth he replied, "Not this business."

When she did not speak, he steeled himself for the plunge. "Miss Ellsworth," he began again, "you were going to ask me about Miss Brand and Miss Croy. I am sure you were wondering why I should leave London at this time, business or no."

"I did think it...curious," she admitted softly. "I spoke from surprise, though, and of course it is no concern of mine. Here is the gate."

"Wait a moment. Could we stop briefly here? There is something I would say."

Poor Pilgrim was made to stand once more (with some difficulty, as he was used to treats and coddling from the Hollowgate grooms and resented being checked in his anticipation).

"Yes?"

She raised those hazel-and-brown eyes to his, sweet but guarded, and Clayton reminded himself not to act precipitously. Not to seize her in his arms and crush his mouth to hers, for instance.

"It may be 'no concern of yours,'" he smiled, "but my leaving London was hardly a concern of Priscilla's either. Because before I went she—she asked to end our engagement."

Beatrice's hand flew to her lips. "Oh, Mr. Clayton. I didn't know. I—am sorry for you."

"Are you?"

"Of course! That is, I don't imagine anyone—that is to say—of *course* I am." He was no longer engaged? To prevent additional babbling—nay, to prevent herself from singing or smiling from ear to ear—she folded her hands in her lap and clutched them till her knuckles whitened beneath her gloves.

He let it rest. There would be time enough to say everything which need be said of Priscilla, though none of it would matter if Miss Ellsworth did not care for him. If she cared for another. Therefore he said, "But I daresay no one in London will notice if my wedding fails to take place. Not when there is another of greater prominence to occupy the world's attention."

"You mean my cousin Marjorie and Mr. Dodson?"

"No, indeed. I—confess I forgot all about them. I meant Rotherwood and that Miss Hapgood person." He regarded her steadily, alert to every change in her expression.

"Mr. Rotherwood and Miss Hapgood?" echoed Beatrice. "Have they set a date, then? My cousin will be sorry to be eclipsed, if they should pick the same day."

"What about you? Would *you* not be sorry?" he asked.

"Why should I? If all London chose to marry on the same day, what would that be to me, here in Winchester?"

Rubbing a finger back and forth on the seat cushion he said carefully, "I meant, will you be sorry when Rotherwood marries, on whatever day it takes place."

Even at this late date she felt a surge of vexation. For goodness' sake—was he still harping on her supposed designs on Mr. Rotherwood?

"No," she said with heat in her voice. "No, I will not be sorry. I do not care a straw for the man. He might marry Miss Hapgood or whomever he pleases or no one at all, and it would all be one to me. Moreover, I would be grateful if you would never mention Mr. Rotherwood again, Mr. Clayton, at least in connection to me. Now shall I drive you to the house, or would you prefer to alight here?"

To her complete perplexity, instead of being affronted by her brusque response, the very ear-to-ear grin Beatrice had suppressed in herself bloomed on him. Taking hold of the seat with one hand and the polished side of the cabriolet with the other, he sprang lightly from the vehicle.

"I will walk, thank you, Miss Ellsworth. Even if the horse knows his way, I would prefer you not to have to drive in the dark. Good evening to you." With a bow and a touch of his hat, still grinning like a madman, Mr. Clayton strolled away up the Hollowgate drive.

CHAPTER
TWENTY-SEVEN

Christmas commeth but once a yeare.
— William Camden, *Remaines* (1614)

Only at the Fairchilds' Hollowgate or the Wolfes' Beaumond could the entire family gather comfortably, so of course the Fairchilds hosted the feast. And shortly after breakfast and church, the hamper of Beaumond contributions at their feet, the Wolfe coach retraced Beatrice's journey of the day before along the Weeke Road.

"Flossie and Robert and Peter and Robbie are four," William began to count on his fingers. "Lily and Mr. Kenner and Edward and Katy and Henrietta make nine. Then Minta and Carlisle and Dotty is twelve. Plus Tyrone, Aggie, Joanie, and Margaret for sixteen. And we are four, for a total of twenty."

"Twenty-one," said Edmund. "Canal man."

William snapped his fingers. "That's right. The canal man. Clayborne."

"Clayton," corrected Mr. Wolfe.

"Clayton," Willsie agreed. "Twenty-one people!"

"It would have been more," Mrs. Wolfe observed, "if your uncle Charles and aunt Jeanne and cousin Austin weren't in Oxfordshire with Benjamin and his Maria."

"Still," said her son. "Twenty-one! What a hullabaloo this will be."

William was not wrong. The drawing room buzzed with nieces and nephews ranging in age from two months (Henrietta Kenner) to Peter and William and Edmund's thirteen years. The doctor Mr. Carlisle bent to inspect the forehead of a wailing child who had collided with the chimneypiece; Minta pounded on the pianoforte keys to be heard over the din, while Tyrone accompanied her with his fiddle, Aggie dancing with little Joan in her arms. Florence and Lily immediately descended on Mrs. Wolfe to consult her about the meal, and several servants threaded their way through, dispersing after the final instructions for the feast were given. Yet somehow, amidst all this, Beatrice's eyes flew at once to Mr. Clayton, standing quietly beside her brothers-in-law Mr. Kenner and Mr. Fairchild.

As if he belonged there, she thought, detaching little Margaret from about her knees to lift her up for a kiss.

Her stepfather Mr. Wolfe went at once to join them, and Beatrice's younger brothers convened with their cousin and schoolmate Peter as they always did, younger Edward trailing after, upon the older boys' sufferance.

Tearing her eyes from the object of her affections, Beatrice crossed the room to the instruments, sitting beside (or hiding behind) Minta on the bench, but Aggie soon seized her hand. "Help me roll up the carpet! How can we have this great crowd gathered and not dance?"

Seeing their aunts' intentions, the host of children eagerly joined in the efforts. In a twinkling not only the carpet, but every piece of furniture without a person disposed upon it was cleared away, and Beatrice found herself partnered by her nephew Peter when Minta struck into The Merry Merry Milkmaids. Around they whirled and wound and wove, laughing at how Edmund towered over tiny Katy and how Robert swooped Flossie up before she could finish consulting Wilcomb about the puddings. Little Joan and Margaret and the Carlisles' Dotty watched with round eyes, Joan clapping and Dotty sucking her fingers and Margaret hopping up and down as if she yearned to join them.

As she circled, beaming, Beatrice could not but be aware of Mr. Clayton's gaze following her. Unmarried, unengaged Mr. Clayton! Surely he would dance with everyone before the evening was over. Everyone, including her. Surely.

Minta concluded on a thundering chord, to be shooed from her seat by Mrs. Wolfe. "Dance, dance! Everyone—not just the children."

Husbands and wives made their way to each other, Beatrice standing hesitantly by, wondering if her stepfather or Willsie would partner her, but Mr. Wolfe went to turn the music for his wife, and before William could reach Beatrice—

"Miss Ellsworth, if I might have the honor."

She curtseyed, shivering despite the warmth of her exercise when Mr. Clayton took her hand. She had thrown aside her gloves in order to roll the carpet, and he—he must have removed his as well, seeing the informality of the intimate gathering.

When the set was formed, Mrs. Wolfe chose Hole in the Wall, played at a decorous pace and calling out the steps for the sake of the children. Beatrice was sorry the dance did not afford many opportunities for private conversation (if that were even possible when every couple before and behind and beside was composed of her family members), but they managed a little whenever they took hands to lead up the center back to their place.

"I need not wish you a happy Christmas, Miss Ellsworth. This gathering is joy itself."

"My brother William called it a 'hullabaloo.'"

"Miss Ellsworth—when we reach the bottom of the set—"

"Yes?"

She waited, pulse fluttering, through the corner crosses and the circling with Lily and Simon—

"Might we have a word apart?"

Gladness flooded her. Then their conversation the day before was not all he wished to communicate? He had more to say? If not for her open, glowing look, her reply would have sounded downright flirtatious: "Again? What was yesterday's talk, then?"

More crossing and circling, but the bottom of the room drew nearer.

"Mere preliminaries." As mild as his answer was, the hooded look which accompanied it made Beatrice's breath catch.

Cross, circle, cast, take hands. Cross, circle, cast, take hands. Beatrice's mind worked feverishly. Where could they go? The long gallery would give them privacy, but likely it was chilly in there and servants would be coming and going. The terrace? At least they could not be overheard outside, but they could be seen, and it would be even colder than the gallery. The dining room was out of the question. That left the small parlor. But would Mr. Clayton think such a closeted setting an affront to propriety? After the rumpus of her unauthorized correspondence with Mr. Rotherwood, she hardly wanted to give Mr. Clayton more reason to think her wanting in decorum.

No, no. Better to err on the side of caution.

When they had cast below the Carlisles, Beatrice blurted, "Minta, excuse us. I have to—show Mr. Clayton something—that Mama and I brought in the hamper."

Her sister laughed, "*Now?*" But she waved them off, and, with a timid glance at Mr. Clayton, Beatrice led him from the room.

Hurrying down the passage, she opened the door to the dining room where the table was beautifully set for the meal to come, silver and glass and porcelain dishes gleaming, garlands winding between the candlesticks. As yet only the wall sconces were lit, shedding a pleasant dim glow which she hoped would hide any awkward blush-es.

When Mr. Clayton preceded her into the room, she hung back beside the door, leaving it well ajar.

"We brought the holly and mistletoe and ivy from Beaumond," she said, pointing. "In the hamper. As I told my sister I would show you."

A corner of his mouth curled. "Very nice. I would go so far as to say *extremely* nice. But then, I am inclined to think well of everything in my present mood."

"Oh?" she asked primly. She did not want to keep hovering by the door but had no idea what to do next.

"Miss Ellsworth, I have a confession to make."

He found his confidence flagging when she neither moved further into the room nor shut the door. Was she hoping—praying—some-one would rescue her from what was to come? Having never actually proposed to anyone—his engagement with Priscilla took place by Donald Brand's deathbed, when the father placed the daughter's hand in his—Clayton felt his inexperience. If only he had made a clean breast of it all the day before! But he had not wanted her driving back to Beaumond in darkness.

"Oh?" said Beatrice again over the tightness in her throat. No other word seemed to remain in her head.

Absently he twiddled a sprig of the holly on the table until it caught on his skin and had to be plucked out. *Confound it, man, out with it! If worse comes to worst, you will be out of here tomorrow, never to show your face in Hampshire again.*

"Yes," he tried again. "A confession. Miss Ellsworth—"

Whistling a carol, Bobbins the footman elbowed the door wide, starting with surprise when he saw Beatrice and nearly dropping the dish of hothouse fruits. "A few minutes yet, miss."

"Of course, Bobbin."

His gaze slid from her to Clayton. "Did you—require anything?"

"No, nothing. I was just—showing Mr. Clayton how lovely Mrs. Fairchild made everything." Beatrice flapped a hand at the table.

The footman nodded, a wrinkle in his brow perfectly expressing his skepticism of this explanation. Pressing a tuft in the carpet under his shoe, he then said to no one in particular, "That being done, I should say there will be a great deal of going in and out of here now, and perhaps the gentleman might be shown next Mrs. Fairchild's new jasperware sconces in the parlor."

"Of course," she said, both embarrassed and inwardly grateful for this suggestion. The parlor! And Mr. Clayton could not blame her for taking him there, when it was Bobbins who proposed it.

Holding the door for them, the servant gestured them out, and Beatrice hastened to obey, leading her companion to the next door along the passage. Florence Fairchild's new ormolu sconces, inset with blue and white jasperware were indeed very pretty, but neither Beatrice nor Clayton bothered to inspect them. In fact, Clayton noticed nothing of his surroundings, his nerves stretched to their limit. But the little parlor had been familiar to Beatrice from earliest memory. Her mother had died when she was only six, leaving no very distinct impressions, but Beatrice could remember early years spent cuddling beside her eldest sister Florence on the sofa. She could remember Tyrone lounging in the armchair, reading, a leg slung over one side. Lily sewing, Minta and Aggie playing draughts, her father beaming upon them all as he sat beside his last wife, the current Mrs. Wolfe. But now—oh now Beatrice feared the little parlor would bear witness to the most fateful scene of her life.

Somehow they were standing beside the mantel, a fireplace-width apart, Beatrice trying to pin a vague, pleasant expression on her face, while Clayton thought how much easier it was to beg money from a dozen earls than to bare his heart to this lovely creature who held his every chance of happiness. But for fear of another servant bursting in to tend the fire or—equally unwelcome—a family member coming to call them to supper, he metaphorically held his breath and dived in.

"Miss Ellsworth, the business which brought me to Winchester was not the canal alone."

Her vague, pleasant expression wavered but held. She blinked rapidly, taking hold of one of the stone scrolls ornamenting the jamb and following the curve with her fingertip.

"I wanted to—explain to you how I came to be engaged to Miss Brand. You see, when I met you and the Tyrone Ellsworths in Bognor, Priscilla and I had already been engaged two years. Since the time of her father's—my mentor's—death. Because he cared for us both, it was Donald Brand's dearest wish that she and I could then—care for each other in turn when he was gone. A neat idea, you see. I would be provided for financially, and Priscilla, though still in the schoolroom—"

"Would one day have a husband," Beatrice finished, nodding. "A husband he approved of. I understand."

Some of the tension in his nerves loosened at that, and he unconsciously drew a step closer. "I did not mean to deceive anyone in Bognor," he continued. "I suppose wherever there are single young men and young ladies involved, questions as to eligibility arise. But at first I thought it would not pertain—you come from—a genteel family of means and education and land, but I—" He gave a shrug. "Who was I? Nobody. No money or family to speak of. No public school or university formed my mind. I had not even spent many consecutive years in any one place and had been, through no deliberate plan, a rolling stone. It did not occur to me to...warn anyone against me."

"Please, Mr. Clayton. You did nothing wrong."

"Ah, but I did. I accepted your family's friendship. Nay—I *sought* it. Enjoyed it. And only too late realized I might have given the wrong impression and made you think I was a single man."

Beatrice's head hung lower, and she murmured, "You can only have felt culpable if you imagined I—that we—had designs on you."

"No. That, I did not think. I attributed no sinister motives to any of you," he said with a rueful grin. "I mean only that I *might* have endangered you—your feelings—without meaning to. And for that I apologize. But my conduct at Bognor had other certain, absolute, undeniable victims."

Her eyes came up then, searching and sweet. "Do you mean Miss Brand? Did your friendship with—us—make her unhappy? Is that why she ended your engagement? If so, I am very, very sorry."

He took a steadying breath. Now for it.

"Priscilla was indeed one of the victims I referred to, in that, after I met you Ellsworths, I could no longer imagine learning to love her as a wife would wish to be loved. We were not people who would naturally have been drawn together, if not for the circumstance that we already *were* inextricably tied. My realization changed nothing—could change nothing, except to make me...regretful for what could not be changed. Still, if I could not love her, I could do my duty, I told myself."

Beatrice hung on his words, even as she was so flustered and running ahead that she could scarcely comprehend him. What precisely had doomed poor Miss Brand in Mr. Clayton's eyes? Did her humbler background no longer please him after he had befriended the Ellsworths? Or was it the obvious marital complacency between Tyrone and Aggie which made him despair of finding the same with Miss Brand? Had meeting her, Beatrice, had no effect on his situation, then?

"But my idea of doing my duty and Priscilla's notion of it was yet another place where the two of us did not see eye to eye," he went on. "It was not unhappiness with our friendship which led to her ending our engagement. Not directly. Rather, she accused me of neglect. Perfunctoriness, you might call it. I might be the husband her father chose for her, but that was when she was a schoolgirl, and now that she was older, I would not be the one she chose. I was too wedded to my work. Too indifferent to the things she most enjoyed: dancing, society, excitement."

"I am sorry for it," said Beatrice again. "That must be very difficult for both of you."

The space between them shrank another step. He was shaking his head slowly. "I daresay both Priscilla and I have emerged astonishingly unscathed. She will see me nearly as often as before because I am still her guardian until she marries or comes of age, and Priscilla would likely add that my demeanor toward her won't change in the slightest, considering what an indifferent lover she thought me. She wasn't wrong, either. If I were as poor a canal-builder as I was a lover to her, I would shortly have to find a new profession."

"Then, if you are both none the worse for ending your engagement, why should you call Miss Brand a victim?"

Another step.

"Because my duty was not enough," he answered softly. "Priscilla fell a victim because *I* fell a victim. You see, one morning in Bognor, finally feeling more the thing after a recent illness, I decided to try the bathing so many recommended. It was cold and bracing, with the novelty of being pushed about by something more powerful than myself. But I did not yet know the meaning of helplessness. For then I heard a cry from the neighboring dipper. Without an inkling for how my life was about to change, I went to her aid and pulled from beneath the waves—a...parting of the ways with everything which had come before. With the solitude I had known since Donald Brand's death, where I had no intimates among the people all about me. But more shockingly, a parting with my own heart."

She drew a sharp breath, and then he was beside her, not touching her and yet every atom of her thrilled to his nearness.

"By rights I should have had no heart to give," he whispered, "having promised it away two years earlier. But on this occasion I did not give it intentionally. It was taken from me entirely without my permission. By you, Miss Ellsworth."

She was trembling now, waging a war on two fronts: against the tears of joy which threatened and against a swirling lightheadedness. Clayton could do nothing for the former, but he saw her sway and caught her by her arms.

"Breathe, Beatrice," he urged. "Take a deep breath and tell me my fate."

"Oh, John!"

It was invitation enough.

He lowered his lips gently to hers, groaning a little at their warmth and softness, and soon they were wrapped in each other's arms, the tightness of his hold doing nothing to help her breathing and much to impair his own. Her caressing hands stole up his back, exploring the solid weight of muscle and bone, while his gripped her waist and the nape of her neck, his fingers winding in the tendrils there. *Closer.*

It was only some minutes later, when her kisses took on a distinct flavor of salt, that he drew back, short of breath and grinning, to regard the wetness of her eyes and beloved face. "Good heavens, it's Bognor all over again. Are you once more in danger of drowning?"

"If I am," she laughed, "do save me, John."

His prompt rescue cost Beatrice a comb and several pins from her hair, as well as the previously immaculate appearance of his neckcloth, and then they must both repair themselves before the narrow mirror over a side table.

"Stop, stop!" cried Beatrice, when he ducked to graze the base of her neck with his lips. "We will be called to supper any second, and what will everyone say?"

"Everyone will say 'hurrah'," he murmured, taking hold of her again. "For I told Mr. Wolfe and your brother of my intentions yesterday, expecting it to be a much harder bargain to strike than the sale of a few canal shares."

Against his lips, Beatrice asked, "Did you really? But why should it be a harder bargain to sell?"

He lifted his head. "Isn't it obvious, my love? Because without Priscilla's fortune, I am well-nigh penniless. Add to that, I must work for my living, and add to *that*, I would steal you away to London and then to wherever my work would take me in the future."

"London is not terribly far," said the selfsame Beatrice who to this juncture had never wanted to roam much beyond the walls of home. "Several coaches make the journey every day. And as for working for your bread, I suspect every male in my family already thinks your work splendid and forward-looking. In fact, if you are not careful, Mr. Wolfe and Tyrone—and Willsie and Edmund, for that matter—will likely beg to be on your board of directors, or to form one, if one does not yet exist. But what did you tell them about the penniless part?"

"I told them...I—will—rise." He punctuated each word of his vow with a kiss, one to her collarbone, one to her ear, and the last to her lips. "But until that happens, would they be so kind as to hand over your sizeable marriage portion for me to fritter away? I suppose the first expense will be to find us a home, unless you wish to share my Spartan little room in Warren Street."

"As long as you were there, John, I wouldn't mind," she declared with charming, if naïve, conviction.

"Well, *I* would, to think of you in such a setting when I am away overseeing the work."

"Couldn't I come with you? I wouldn't bother you a bit, I promise!"

He pressed the tip of his nose to the dimple in her cheek fondly. "The men can be rough and the conditions uncomfortable, but if you choose to walk or drive beside the Regent's Park on a beautiful day, I will not prevent you. After all, without your efforts with Rotherwood and the zeal of your family members, who knows when work on the Cumberland Arm would ever have begun?"

"Yes," agreed Beatrice with a toss of her chin. "*Now* you thank me for persuading Mr. Rotherwood! Before, my only reward was your coldness and disapproval!"

"And my jealousy. Let's not forget that."

"Was it really, John? Jealousy! How silly of you, when it was obvious you were everything to me."

"'Obvious,' stuff! I don't know about 'obvious'."

"Obvious to me, at any rate." She blushed. "And to the Huftons, I suppose. When there was that fuss about me writing to Mr. Rotherwood, I was forced to confess to them that, not only was I not trying to entrap the man, but I didn't care a button for him—and then they guessed the rest."

He studied her. "Is that why you left town so suddenly? Imagine my surprise when I dashed over to Green Street, eager to announce my jilting, only to find you gone!"

Resting her cheek against his shoulder, she said, "No—I left because I'm afraid Marjorie and I had another quarrel. If you talk of frittering away a girl's fortune, I fear Mr. Dodson will do so with hers because he cannot resist gambling in all forms. At least—that was one of the reasons I went."

"And the other?"

"I was too great a coward to attend your wedding to Miss Brand!" she confessed. "I loved you enough to wish you well—sincerely well—but it would be easier to do and think and feel what was right if I did not have to *see* the moment I would lose you forever."

It was so near an escape that they both shuddered in remembrance, and Clayton bent to embrace her again.

"Thank God, then, I was so poor a lover Priscilla cast me off."

Beatrice favored him with a teasing smile. "I hope you will never neglect me, sir, nor treat me in a perfunctory manner."

"My dear girl, if you ever hope to know a moment's peace from my attentions, I would advise you to remain behind in Winchester." Clayton would gladly have followed this assertion with many supportive proofs, but the long-expected steps in the passage were heard at last, and they were obliged to release each other.

An announcement of what their absence had accomplished hardly proved necessary, for the joy and understanding which flashed between them spoke volumes. Nevertheless, Clayton uttered a word in Mr. Wolfe's ear, which the man communicated instantly to his watching wife by a wink and a nod, and she to everyone else by going at once to take Beatrice in her arms and kiss her. Mrs. Wolfe was followed by a swarm of siblings and their spouses, Beatrice being hugged and kissed and screamed over, while the gentlemen pumped Clayton's arm and clapped him by the shoulder.

"What is it? What has happened?" Katy Kenner asked, plucking at her papa's sleeve.

"Your aunt Beatrice is going to marry that fellow there, and you will have a new uncle," Simon Kenner replied.

"All that kissing," Katy's brother Edward said with a grimace, after Clayton gave his bride-to-be a decorous peck on the cheek, and then another. "And everyone has forgotten all about supper."

But young Edward was mistaken, and when the merry family was ranged about the bounteous table and he had had as much as he could hold of goose and oysters and sausage and pudding and mince pies and apples and hot chestnuts, then even he didn't mind, and even he thought it wouldn't be a bad thing, if one day a girl smiled upon him the way his aunt Beatrice did upon her Mr. Clayton.

New adventures begin with *By His Grace and Favor*, the first book in my next series Lord Dere's Dependents.

THE HAPGOODS OF BRAMLEIGH

The Naturalist
A Very Plain Young Man
School for Love
Matchless Margaret
The Purloined Portrait
A Fickle Fortune

THE ELLSWORTH ASSORTMENT

Tempted by Folly
The Belle of Winchester
Minta in Spite of Herself
A Scholarly Pursuit
Miranda at Heart
A Capital Arrangement

PRIDE AND PRESTON LIN

www.christinadudley.com